Books by Patricia Paris

A Murderous Game
Run Rachael Run

THE GLEBE POINT SERIES
This Time Forever
Letters To Gabriella
Return To Glebe Point
The Cottage

THE BONAVERAS
Lucia
Caterina
Eliana

Caterina

A BONAVERA NOVEL

PATRICIA PARIS

Windswept

Livonia, Michigan

Edited by S.M. Ray
Proofread by Shannon Dolley

CATERINA

Published by BHC Press
under the Windswept imprint

Library of Congress Control Number:
2018936813

ISBN Numbers
Trade Softcover: 978-1-947727-62-5
Ebook: 978-1-948540-14-8

Visit the publisher:
www.bhcpress.com

Acknowledgments

To my readers, I appreciate every one of you. Thank you for spending the time to read my stories, they are for you.

To Annette, Ali, Diana, Kyrah, Nadine, and Tracy, I am so grateful to each of you for taking the time to read the earliest drafts of *Caterina* and provide such wonderful feedback. You, ladies, are the best!

To Ali and Tracy, for helping me flush out thoughts on *Caterina* during our writers' retreat, and for always being inspiring, supportive, and ready to share ideas over a glass of wine. Cheers!

As always, to my amazing editor, Sandra Ray. Woman, you are *la crème de la crème*. Thank you for caring so much about my work and wanting my readers to have the best possible experience when they journey through one of my stories.

To my publisher, BHC Press, for believing in me, encouraging me, and turning my books into such a beautiful product. It is a joy to work with you.

And last, but always foremost, to my husband John. Words are never enough!

Caterina

One

*"One cannot think well, love well, sleep well,
if one has not dined well."*

Virginia Woolf

The newly erected wooden frame stood in stark relief, a skeleton in the diminished light of a low-hanging moon. The Blue Ridge marched behind it, cloaked in misty twilight, a familiar sentinel that grounded everything in its shadows: the skeleton, the valley, the vineyards—her.

A breeze kicked up, laced with the scent of fresh sawdust—the scent of progress—a scent that pleased her. Caterina slid her hands into the pockets of her favorite bomber jacket: red leather, well-worn, familiar as an old friend. The familiar gave her comfort, and she welcomed both it and the extra bit of warmth the jacket lent against the descending chill of an early November evening. A shiver raced through her. She hugged the bomber tighter and stood, staring silently at the framework Liam Dougherty and his crew had finished putting up that afternoon.

If everything went per plan, she and Lucia would be opening the doors of Serendipity to the public by late summer next year. Lucia would get the boutique hotel she wanted. Their architect, Antonio DeLuca, who also happened to be Lucia's new fiancé, had created an amazing design. Caterina knew that with her sister's decorating flare, and the special attention she gave to their guests' comfort, the hotel would be truly special.

My restaurant will be no less special.

There were times, in moments like this, when her vision of what it would be was so clear she feared she'd wake from a deep sleep only to discover her dream of opening a restaurant was merely that...still a dream. But the concrete foundation in front of her stood solid; the wooden skeleton rising above it in the shadow of the mountains was as tangible as she was, and Serendipity was less than a year from becoming a reality.

So much had changed in five short years. Things she hadn't, couldn't have planned for. Big life things that altered people. Five years ago, she'd been living in New York, working at one of the city's top restaurants. Moving back to Virginia to help run the family winery where she'd grown up had been nowhere on her radar.

She'd scored a great position at a three-star Michelin restaurant right out of culinary school. At twenty-two, she'd been promoted to sous chef, the youngest ever to work there, and her plan had been to keep moving right up the line until she ran the place or one of her own. They'd been high aspirations for one so young at the time, but she'd always dreamed big, and she believed that with the right strategy, and a willingness to go the extra distance, anything was possible.

She'd had the willingness, and her creative flair in the kitchen had been encouraged and appreciated. The work never felt like a job. Her goals, however, hadn't allowed much time for socializing. Not that she didn't have friends. She did. They were just few, and she kept them casual. She'd decided early on that she needed to advance her career first. Once she secured her future, she'd focus on developing personal relationships.

A fox ran in front of the foundation, not twenty feet from where Caterina stood. She'd been so still, she wondered if it knew she was there. She watched it trot into the woods beyond the apple orchard, off to hunt under the veil of night. Yes, a lot had changed, and those changes had led her far from New York City's bright lights and skyscrapers.

When Marcella, her twin, implored Caterina and their sisters, Lucia and Eliana, to try to make a go of the winery they'd inherited after their parents' death, Cat hadn't felt that she had a choice.

The winery was Marcella's lifeblood, the only thing she'd ever known. If they'd let it go, it would have destroyed her. They'd already lost Mom and Dad, and although she knew her other sisters wouldn't have held it against her if she didn't agree to go in with them, they'd probably have lost the winery—the home where they'd all grown up. How could she have refused just because it didn't fit her five-year plan? They were hers, all she held most dear...family. Family stood with family.

So, she left what she'd thought would be her future in a puddle in the middle of Greenwich Street, just down the block from Robert De Niro's Tribeca Grill—one of Manhattan's most famous restaurants in the triangle below Canal Street—and moved back to Virginia, securing a job as head chef at Caulfield's, a restaurant in Ashburn, working for Mitch Gregory.

In some ways, she'd probably be reaching her goal sooner than if she'd stayed in New York. And, in retrospect, she'd missed her sisters more than she had allowed herself to admit.

With Serendipity she had a focus again, a purpose, a new and better plan—something she desperately needed. Her life had been one big, jumbled mess the last six months. In large part, thanks to Mitch. Lying, cheating Mitch.

She wasn't stupid, but she'd been stupid where he'd been concerned. He'd charmed her. He knew how to turn it on. He'd made her head chef at Caulfield's, giving her all the autonomy she craved. They'd become lovers. She'd been blindly happy with him and the job at first, and blindly summed it up almost too accurately.

She'd taken on increasingly more responsibility, worked extra shifts whenever asked, no questions why. When he'd call at the last minute, needing her to cover for him at the restaurant, she'd change any personal plans and go in.

Her sisters had questions, though: Why was she working so many extra shifts? Why did Mitch need to be away from the restaurant so frequently?

At first Cat had defended him. She hadn't wanted to consider he might be taking advantage of her. She hadn't wanted to believe she'd misjudged him. She wanted to think she'd gotten better at judging a man's character over the years. She hadn't.

If not for a concerned coworker, she still might not know that while she was working all those extra shifts so he could *pursue more business opportunities*, he'd been sleeping around with other women.

She'd been stunned. Yes, she'd begun having doubts about their relationship, how he seemed to have less and less time for her, but she'd never suspected he'd been cheating.

When she learned the truth, she felt foolish, humiliated. She should have seen it coming, would have if she'd paid more attention to the signs, not been so singularly focused on the job.

She hadn't though, and now a big, rusted-out hole existed in the bottom of her trust bucket where men were concerned. What she'd salvaged after her high school sweetheart broke her heart a mere week after giving him her virginity, Mitch had drained dry.

She ended their relationship the night she learned of his infidelity—a Thursday, told him to find a new chef because she quit, effective immediately. The restaurant had had four private parties booked that weekend, with no open reservations Friday or Saturday evening, and she'd been scheduled to run the show.

An employee she'd stayed in contact with told her the weekend had been disastrous. Apparently, Mitch had been unapproachable, reduced to numerous cursing rants to which her name was central, overheard by the staff and, in some cases, customers.

Cat smiled. She loved poetic justice.

She needed to put that all behind her now, move forward... and she would. Her life would undergo another major change with Serendipity. A good one, one that would get her back on track.

She pulled out of her pocket the flashlight she'd brought along, clicked it on, and then picked her way across the construction site toward the structure.

Over the next few weeks, the plywood cladding would go up, windows and doors would be framed, the roof would go on. She'd told Liam Dougherty she wanted a schedule every two weeks, in writing, outlining exactly what would happen next.

She didn't care if their surly contractor thought she was a pain in the ass. It was her project. She had a right to know what to expect. If he didn't like it, too bad. He could scowl, grumble under his breath, and roll his eyes all he wanted whenever she dropped by the site. She wanted to ensure things happened as planned. And no matter how great Lucia, Eliana, or Marcella thought Dougherty was, Caterina believed *someone* needed to hold the man accountable.

That left her.

When she reached the foundation, she took hold of one of the framing boards, hoisting herself up onto the plywood covering that had been laid down on top of the floor joists. She trolled the light over the sheets of wood to make sure there were no gaping holes or obstructions to avoid.

At this stage it was merely a shell, outlining her dream. Soon though, the outlines would be filled in, rooms would begin to take shape with the addition of internal walls, floors, lighting, paint, appliances, furniture—and with each step, her vision moved closer to reality.

Seeing no obvious hazards to prevent her exploration, Caterina circled the perimeter. She stopped at every third or fourth framing board, compelled to give them a random jiggle.

She moved to the middle of the expansive space, looked up. The night sky was clear. A million stars were the only roof over her head at this point. A bug buzzed nearby. She felt it land on her ear, slapped it away.

The finished building would have three floors. The restaurant and kitchen would be on the back half of the first level, running the full length of the building. Stacking doors would open from the restaurant to a large terrace for alfresco dining. Antonio's design included three large fire pits built into the flagstones, for ambiance, and to extend the outdoor dining season.

With nothing other than the new framing to inspect since her last visit, Caterina walked back to the perimeter. The soles of her leather boots resounded against the plywood sheeting, a muffled echo in the darkening night, a reminder she was here alone, just as she'd planned.

She crouched, placed one hand down—flat against the top of the foundation wall—, and dropped to the ground. A moment later, she ducked under the yellow caution tape surrounding the perimeter, glanced back at it, and smirked.

Liam didn't want her or Lucia poking around the site unless he, or someone from his crew, was on-site. Safety reasons, he'd said. Well, she'd been careful, and she didn't want to wait three days to see what they'd done. No one need know she'd been there, and this way, she'd satisfied her curiosity without him shooting daggers at her through cool, disapproving eyes—shards of aquamarine ice that bore into her, found her lacking, even though he knew nothing about her.

Intolerable man.

She brushed her hands against the sides of her jeans and, having accomplished what she'd come for, tramped up to the side of the road where she'd parked her Jeep.

THE FOLLOWING MORNING, instead of the scones or muffins she usually baked fresh for guests at the winery's bed-and-breakfast, Caterina made country sausage and blueberry pancakes to accompany the usual fruit, bagels, and assorted cold cereals.

She'd had a taste for pancakes and sausage, so Lucia's charges had been the benefactors of her desire. After clearing away the morning setup, Caterina drove to the Whole Foods in Ashburn. It was her fallback in the off-season when the local farmers' markets weren't operating. She preferred knowing where the food she used came from, wanted the freshest she could get and to support local farmers, fishermen, and other suppliers whenever she could, but that wasn't always possible.

She'd already begun experimenting with Serendipity's menu. Today she needed to get some specific ingredients for recipes to test this week. Their grand opening might still be almost a year away, but it was never too early to plan.

An award-winning dish didn't just happen. Like most things excellent, it resulted from practice—making it over and over until you mastered every nuance, until it became a symphony for the palate. She didn't care what it was; if it came out of her kitchen, it would sing to her customers.

The store was always bustling on Saturdays. Cat didn't mind. She liked being around people—in theatres, at concerts, in the grocery store—you could be around them without being *with* them. If you wanted to interact, you could strike up a conversation. Generally, she found most people felt safe enough telling you what they planned to make with the leeks and shitake mushrooms in their cart. Fruits and vegetables tended to be nonthreatening topics, even among strangers.

After checking that the wheels on her cart all went in the same direction, she strolled over to the floral section near the front of the store. Various mixed bouquets mingled with bunches of daisies, roses, alstroemeria, and the exotic-looking orange and purple-blue bird-of-paradise. Charmed by their simple beauty, she chose a bouquet of pale, blushing-pink and white roses for her nightstand. She despised clutter, wasn't keen on knickknacks, but what woman could resist the romance of roses?

Next, she meandered through the produce section, stopping here, there, inspecting, sniffing, and gently squeezing various fruits and vegetables as she made her selections.

Spying a bin piled high with bright-orange, baby pumpkins, Caterina maneuvered around a couple of other shoppers and stopped next to it. Antonio was in Italy, visiting his grandfather, and wouldn't return until Monday. She and her sisters had invited friends over this evening for a long-overdue girls' night. She planned to make a hearty hors d'oeuvre with the tiny squash and see how it went over.

She chose eight with evenly flat bottoms. She would hollow them out, stuff them with the rich, savory filling she used in her chicken pie, top them with fontina cheese, and serve them right in their beautiful rusty-orange skins. If they were as good as she imagined, she'd include them on Serendipity's fall and winter menus.

Moving on, she took time picking over the heirloom tomatoes, getting a few beautiful Romas that she'd seed for the guacamole she intended to make, three young red onions, a bunch of bright green, fresh cilantro, and three nice, firm bulbs of lovely, purple-skinned Marino garlic.

She worked her way around to the avocados. Looking them over with a critical eye, she selected a dark green one with no indentations. Holding it in her palm, she gave it a firm but gentle squeeze to test for ripeness. Perfect.

Spotting a nice-looking one toward the back of the bin, she leaned forward and reached for it. Someone stepped up beside her, on her right, and began indiscriminately picking up pieces of the fruit and dropping them into a bag. A man, and based on her observation, clueless about his selections.

Cat glanced up. Her breath caught in her throat. She took a step back.

"Liam." The name tripped off her tongue, which was unaccustomed to speaking it.

He swung his head toward her, a question in his eyes that dissolved into recognition, and with it, his gaze narrowed as it settled on her with the familiar coolness she'd become accustomed to from him. He gave a curt nod, grunted, looked away, then dumped the avocado he was holding into the bag.

A grunt? Seriously?

He couldn't open his mouth to say *hey*, or *hi*, or *what's up*? Couldn't expend the meager amount of energy it took to form a word? What had she done that he couldn't extend her the most basic courtesy?

She couldn't delude herself that whatever his problem, it wasn't about her, that he was just miserable by nature. He didn't treat her sisters this way. He knew how to use whole words around them. She'd observed him with other people enough to know he could be pleasant when he chose. It seemed he reserved the grunts and scowls solely for her, and she was getting damn tired of it.

He couldn't just single her out for his surliness and expect her to accept it. If he didn't like her, fine, but she refused to let him treat her so dismissively without a pushback, not when it was so unwarranted.

Caterina picked up another avocado. "I never would have expected to run into *you* shopping at Whole Foods."

"Man's gotta eat."

Words...progress. "What are you going to do with those avocados?"

He tied a knot in the bag and dropped it into his basket. "What do you think I'm going to do with them?"

Cat shrugged. "I don't know, hide behind something outside and throw them at me when I'm walking back to my car? They've got to be as hard as rocks, except for that last one. It's overripe and would probably splatter like a water balloon on contact."

He rolled his jaw. *Prickly man.*

"Just a guess. You know, considering our brief history." She gave a smarmy smile. He'd earned it. "But anyway," she said with a dismissive wave, "you can't be planning to eat them, unless you wait several days—five, six maybe."

Liam cocked his hip, assuming a look that smacked of condescension. "And why's that?" he asked, all smug, acting like he really didn't care why either way. She felt tempted to give him a concrete reason to dislike her, like ramming him up against the produce bin with her shopping cart. She never would, of course, but...

"They're not ripe." She reached into his basket and pulled out the bag he'd just dropped into it.

"What are you doing?" He grabbed for it. She held it out to her side.

"Doing you a favor. One you don't deserve given the way you treat me, and which I'm sure you won't appreciate. But I won't stand by and allow these little fruits to be blamed for a tasteless meal, when the fault would be entirely yours for expecting more from them than they're able to give yet."

"They're avocados," he said with a smirk, and absolutely no clue. He reached for the bag again. Again, she held it out of his grasp.

"Are you intending to eat them tonight?"

"For Christ's— " Liam put his hands on his hips, glowering. "They're for my sister-in-law. She needs them for dinner tonight and asked if I'd pick some up on my way over."

"Wow. That's a lot of words." Caterina tore open the plastic bag, dumping the avocados back into the bin. Liam gaped at her. She picked out four perfectly ripe ones, put them in a new bag, tied it off, and handed it to him.

"You can tell your sister-in-law I said *you're welcome*." She smiled tightly, spun on her heels, and gripped the handle of her cart.

She had more shopping to do and was quite positive the temperature would feel a lot less frosty in some other aisle.

CATERINA AND HER sisters sat around a large, round table in the solarium with three of their girlfriends. This was the first girls' night they'd had in a while because they'd all been so busy, and before quitting her job at Caulfield's, Cat rarely had a night off.

Most of the guests were out for the evening. If anyone came back early and needed something, all they needed to do was follow the sounds of laughter and easy conversation drifting from the solarium.

"You need to include these on the fall and winter menus, Cat. They're wonderful." Lucia scraped her spoon around the inside of a miniature pumpkin shell to get out the last bit of filling.

"And they're so adorable." Jenna, who managed Twining Vines, a favorite local restaurant, and someone they'd all known since their school days, leaned forward, and picked up a bottle of sauvignon blanc from the center of the table. "You could do a whole *Harvest Sides* selection served in baby pumpkins."

"Since I was using you gals as a test group, I'm glad you like them. I've already got plans along those lines, Jenna, including some desserts: pumpkin mousse, pumpkin cheesecake, pumpkin brulee."

"Customers will love that." Jenna filled her wineglass, passed the bottle to Marcella who sat to her right, and then flashed a toothy smile at Caterina. "If you need someone to test the brulee, or any of the other desserts, I'm willing to make the sacrifice. What are a couple of pounds for friends?"

"I'll keep that in mind," Cat promised.

"I can't wait to see Serendipity when it's done," said Anna. She and her twin, Reese, who rounded out the group, had been in the same class with Cat and Marcella every year since junior high. They'd bonded early on, sharing their experiences as twins, and had been friends ever since.

Anna raised her glass. "I think we should toast your future husband, Luch, for designing you and Cat the boutique hotel and restaurant of your dreams."

"I'll drink to Antonio anytime." Lucia's eyes sparkled, dark glistening sable, as she tipped the rim of her glass, and took a sip.

"I finally figured out who he reminds me of. David Gandy," Jenna said, and then panted for Lucia's benefit.

Marcella furrowed her brow. "David who?"

"Oh, poor little sister." Eliana, who sat on Marcella's other side, patted her arm. "David Gandy, the model. Not that I'd expect you to know who he is, since clearly, you couldn't care less about fashion or updating your wardrobe."

"I've got better things to do than waste my time looking through fashion magazines."

"That's okay, honey, the rest of us have your back. If you ever find someone you're interested in enough to want to get his attention, we'll dress you." Eliana winked at Marcella.

"Okay, thanks." Marcella refilled her glass. "I should be able to sleep nights now."

Eliana chuckled. "So how about it, Luch? You think Antonio looks like Gandy Candy?"

Lucia angled her head, looking thoughtful. "I can see the resemblance, but I think Antonio's better-looking."

"Gee, that's a surprise," Cat said with a laugh. "I have to admit, I'm as clueless as Marcella who David Gandy is, but he must not be too shabby if he looks like Antonio."

"Yeah, the scenery's been improving a lot around here lately. First Antonio, then Liam." Eliana blew on her fingers, giving them a shake. "We're surrounded by hotties here at the Bonavera Winery."

"Who's Liam?" Anna asked.

"He's our hunky contractor." Marcella dipped her head in Eliana's direction. "El's lusting after him."

"I seem to recall your jaw dropping the night we met him, too," Lucia said teasingly, pinning their youngest sister with an amused air.

"My jaw didn't drop. I'll admit I had a *wow* moment, but that was just the initial shock of seeing him for the first time. The difference is, I can appreciate beautiful things without slobbering all over myself, unlike some people."

Eliana balled up one of the paper napkins that said, *What's a nice girl like me doing without a drink*, and pitched it across the table at Marcella. "I didn't slobber. I just happen to have dewy lips."

Marcella sniggered as she ducked the wadded ball.

"What do you say, Cat?" Anna, who sat on her immediate right, nudged Caterina with an elbow. "Are they exaggerating, or is this guy really as good-looking as they say?"

Cat shrugged. "I guess you might find him attractive if you can get past his surly attitude, but good luck with that. I've never seen him when he wasn't scowling, and I don't find angry or sullen men particularly attractive."

"Okay, time to change the subject," Lucia said, interjecting. "For whatever reason, Cat and Liam both seem to dissolve into foul moods at little more than the mention of the other's name, and this evening is for catching up with friends and having fun. So, subject closed."

"Agreed." Eliana lifted her wineglass. "To fun, and good times with friends."

Fine by me, Caterina silently approved. Lucia was right. Liam Dougherty could turn her mood sour quicker than the smell of rotten eggs could turn her stomach. She cringed. She couldn't think of a more offensive odor.

"Does everyone have plans for Thanksgiving?" Cat asked. "I'll be cooking dinner here since I'm not working at the restaurant anymore. If you aren't already committed, there'll be plenty of food if anyone wants to join us."

"If I can bring crazy Flora and Russ with me, I'd love to come," Jenna said. "I planned to make dinner for the three of us, but I'd much rather be with a larger group. I think Russ might be a keeper." She lifted her hand and crossed her fingers in the air. "But exposing him to my peculiar aunt for several hours with no one else for her to focus on could send him packing before he realizes what a great catch I am."

"Trust me, he already knows what a great catch you are," Lucia said. "I saw the way he looked at you when Antonio and I doubled with you guys."

Jenna caught her bottom lip between her teeth to contain the grin threatening to swallow up her face.

"So." Cat looked at Anna and Reese. "A couple of lovebirds and one eccentric aunt. What about you two?"

"Jeff's coming home from school, and Mom's planning the traditional family feast, so Anna and I will be expected there. If we even suggested we might be thinking of going someplace else for dinner, we'd never hear the end of it." Reese exchanged a knowing smile with her twin.

The rest of the evening sped by. Caterina hadn't laughed so much in a long time, and it made her realize just how much she'd given up for her career—and for Mitch. Friends were important. She wouldn't fool herself. She knew she'd obsess over Serendipity, but she would make a conscious effort to ensure her life didn't become so unbalanced again.

MOONLIGHT WASHED OVER the vineyard, a hushed glow bathing row upon row of the gnarly vines that had sustained her family for two generations.

Caterina wrapped the quilt her mother made for her when she went off to college around her shoulders to ward off the night's chill. Her sisters had all received one when they left the nest for the first time, too. Cat's had graced her bed at school, her apartment in New York, and now remained back in the room that had been hers since childhood.

She loved the soft pastels of the interlocking circles, how delicate they looked against the white background—double-wedding-ring—that's what Mom had called it. The pattern was predictable, yet pretty. It appealed to her sense of definition and order.

Definition and order. Cat sighed. Her life was about as well-defined right now as an amoeba. Since leaving Caulfield's, she'd done little more than drift from day to day, filling in for Lucia when needed, helping El with tastings, and, between the few catering jobs she'd picked up, doing whatever busywork she could invent to avoid the dogged restlessness constantly nipping at her very soul.

She breathed in the night's crisp, late-autumn air—cold enough she felt the bite of it against her nostrils—and looked out over the vineyard. The Blue Ridge loomed in the distance, low and long, a snaking shadow in the night beneath a clear, star-filled sky. Solid, grounded...what she wouldn't give for a little solid ground right now.

She needed to find something interesting to do until Serendipity opened—something other than handling the continental breakfasts and afternoon setups when guests were in residence and the occasional catering job or picking up the slack when Luch and El needed backup. She wasn't sure what that could be yet, but she couldn't take much more of this rudderless coasting.

A sudden, deeper chill made her shiver. Clutching the quilt tighter around her shoulders, Cat turned and went back inside, pulling the balcony doors shut behind her. She folded the quilt and laid it on the bed, smoothing it out over the thick white down comforter that enticed her to remain nestled under its warmth longer than she should most mornings, now that the mornings had turned cool. With so little going on in her life, she could be easily seduced to burrow in for a few extra hours of blissful sleep, if it wouldn't make her feel even less purposeful.

It was late, almost midnight. She'd usually be sleeping by now, but didn't feel tired. Probably still wound up from their girls' night. Cat smiled lightly. It had been fun. They needed to make it a more regular event.

A rustling sound drew her attention toward the balcony doors. They stood slightly ajar. The white, floor-length, voile curtains wafted against the glass panes. Frowning, Caterina walked over and closed them, latching them this time. She thought she'd shut them when she'd come in, but apparently not all the way.

She looked around the room, not sure what to do with herself. It felt downright cold. Maybe because she'd left the French doors open for the last twenty minutes while she'd been out on the balcony contemplating how to jump-start her life before she got too punchy.

She retrieved the quilt she'd just arranged so neatly across the bottom of the bed, and wrapped it around herself like a cocoon. When she turned around, she froze mid-step. She stared at the balcony doors, then shook her head.

"Okay...no. I latched you. I'm sure this time. There's no way you could have just drifted open again."

She marched to the doors, latched them again, gave them a rattle, and then turned and faced the room.

Silence greeted her, but she suspected she might not be alone. When unexplainable things happened around the Bonavera home, there was a good chance the family ghost had something to do with it.

Unlike Marcella and Eliana, who'd always been open to the possibility, Caterina and Lucia had been reluctant to believe their great-aunt Rosa haunted the place. After everything that had happened over the last six months, though, they no longer doubted their ancestor's presence.

"Hello?" Caterina's voice sounded tentative, barely above a whisper.

She shifted her eyes from side to side. Rosa had never singled her out before, and it kind of creeped Cat out. They agreed that their deceased aunt seemed benevolent. Aside from locking Lucia in the attic once, and another occasion in the kitchen with Antonio, she usually didn't mess with them too much.

That could change though, if one of them did something to upset her. And since they had no idea why she haunted the place, that could be just about anything.

So, yeah...she was a little creeped out, and not really in the mood to stay in her room to deal with a ghost on her own right now.

Caterina went downstairs to the kitchen with the intention of sidestepping her ancestor and getting a late-night snack. When she entered the room, Marcella sat at the old family table they'd grown up sharing meals around, sipping a cup of coffee.

"You're up late," Cat said.

Her twin eyed her. "You too."

"Need to decompress before you can sleep?" Cat knew that even though Marcella had seemed to enjoy their girls' night, having to be extroverted for an entire evening would have drained her.

"Yeah, I guess."

"I'm going to make myself a snack." Cat walked over to the refrigerator, opened the door, and then looked over her shoulder. "You want something?"

"Is there any apple pie left?"

Cat looked inside. "Yep." She pulled the pie out and set it on the countertop. "I think I'll have the same. Want some whipped cream on yours?"

"Pffft. You don't think I want to eat it naked, do you?"

Cat grinned, grabbed the can off the door, fixed them each a plate, and took them and the whipped cream to the table.

"So, what's got you up roaming the halls this late?" Marcella asked as she shook the can. She sprayed a dollop onto the back of her hand, licked it off, and then lathered her pie with a thick coating of fluffy white cream.

"Just restless. I couldn't sleep, and I didn't know what to do with myself."

"You could read. That usually helps me if I'm having trouble falling asleep."

"Yeah, but I didn't feel like it." Cat took the can from Marcella when she held it out. She outlined her wedge of pie, then filled in the center with neat evenly piped rows. Picking up her fork, she cut the tip off the slice and put it in her mouth. "Mmmmm, so good."

"And then," she said after swallowing, "Rosa dropped in for a visit. I wasn't up for dealing with her on my own, so I bolted and came down here for a midnight snack."

Marcella propped her chin on her hand, eyeing Cat a moment. "I'm probably not going to be able to go up and fall right to sleep after that revelation, so tell me, what did Rosa want?"

"Your guess is as good as mine. I'm not positive she was there, but the room got downright frigid, and the balcony doors kept opening on their own, even after I'd latched them."

"Sounds like Rosa's M.O.," Marcella agreed. "She has a thing for messing with doors and windows."

"Yeah, what's with that?"

"Don't have a clue. It's weird. She barely made her presence known to anyone but Mom while we were growing up, but now she seems to have taken an interest in us. It's odd that she focused so intently on Lucia for a while, who didn't believe in her." Marcella looked thoughtful. "You two had that in common."

"If she's trying to convince me she exists, she doesn't have to. After everything that happened with Luch, I'm a believer." Caterina mused over another bite of pie, then looked up at the ceiling. "Did you hear that Rosa? I believe in you. So, you don't need to visit me to prove you're real."

"Maybe there's more to it than that." Marcella pondered, biting her lower lip. "Maybe it's not about her, or wanting you to believe. Maybe she's decided to focus on you because of something...I don't know, something in your life right now."

"Well, if that's the case she'll be disappointed. There's nothing interesting enough in my life right now that anyone, alive or dead, would want to waste their time focusing on it."

"Could be that's exactly why."

Caterina frowned. "Like what? She thinks I need a little excitement, so she's planning to haunt me to jazz up my life a bit, or something?"

Marcella shrugged. "Or something."

Two

"I am out with lanterns, looking for myself."
Emily Dickinson

*M*onday morning, Liam pulled off the road that led to his latest project, and onto the construction site. He maneuvered his truck over the frost-hardened ruts left behind by the flatbeds that had delivered the framing materials the prior week.

Three other pickups were already there, parked in a row in front of the yellow safety tape perimeter. He pulled up next to his brother Burke's—big, bad, and bright red. It was a beast, and Liam gave up a little jealous drool every time he saw it.

He grabbed the coffee thermos off the passenger seat and got out. He was a stickler for punctuality, from his employees and himself, but some things were more important than the clock. Riley was one of them.

He saw Burke standing next to the foundation, reviewing the construction docs with Elliot, one of their regular crew members. His brother's last project had ended a couple of weeks ago, and the permits hadn't come through yet for the next one, so he'd been putting in a few days a week on the Bonavera job to fill the gap. He looked up as Liam approached, and then tapped his watch.

"It's a shade past eight, bro." Burke rolled up the drawings and slid them between two of the frame's studs. "We're ready to start giving this baby some skin."

"Yeah, I know. Couldn't be helped. It was Riley's first day at the new preschool."

Burke nodded. "I forgot that was today. How'd it go?"

"Fine, I guess. By the way, I need to cut out early one day this week to take her to the doctor. She needs to get a physical, and I need to pick up her shot records. The daycare owner told me they need a copy by next week, or Riley won't be able to return until I provide one."

"I can stay late on Thursday if you want to shoot for then."

"Thanks, I'll see if I can get an appointment in the afternoon." Liam raked his fingers through his hair. "I wanted to stick around a bit, make sure she was okay. You know, strange place and all. None of the other kids cried or anything when they got dropped off. I figured that was a good sign."

"Yeah, probably means the staff's not smacking them around too much after their parents leave."

"Bite me." Liam scowled. "It's her first time in daycare. It might take some getting used to."

"I'm sure it will—for you." Burke slapped him on the back. "Relax, Liam, Riley will be fine. You know how much she loves being around other kids. I'll bet she hasn't thought of you once since you left."

Liam shrugged. He'd been torn about what to do after Mrs. Trent had told him she was moving to Florida to be closer to her daughter and grandchildren. She'd been Riley's nanny since Sylvie's death. He trusted her, Riley adored her, and since the woman had lived next door, the arrangement couldn't have been more convenient.

Becca, his brother Shawn's wife, had convinced him it might be better for Riley if he enrolled her in a preschool program rather than hiring another nanny. She'd said Riley would enjoy having other kids to play with, and it would help her make the transition into kindergarten the following year, where most of the children would already be used to a more structured environment.

Instead of being nervous or upset, his daughter had been excited about, in her words, getting to go to school like the big kids. Burke was probably right; the transition would be harder on him than his little girl.

He knew he overthought things when it came to Riley, but she was the most important thing in his life. As a single dad, he wanted to make sure whatever decisions he made that impacted her were good ones. Yeah, he'd screw up from time to time, but hopefully not with the big stuff.

Telling himself Riley would be fine, Liam turned his focus to the job. It didn't take long to fall into the rhythm of the morning as familiar sounds surrounded him—the hum of the generator, saws buzzing, nail guns popping, and Daryl's radio pumping out a steady stream of classic rock.

The crew broke for lunch at noon. Liam sat down on the plywood subfloor, stretched out his legs, and took one of the ham sandwiches he'd made that morning out of the dented, green metal lunch pail that had seen him through every construction job since he and his two brothers had stepped into their father's shoes and gone into business together.

He leaned back against a framing stud and looked around as he ate, mentally envisioning how things would come together. He had to hand it to Antonio; it was one hell of a beautiful design. Aside from the annoyance of having to work with a certain someone he'd rather not ruin his lunch break thinking about, he was excited to have landed this job. The finished product would be something else and would look good in the company's portfolio.

Sun streamed down through the open rafters, forming geometrically balanced grid patterns over the plywood subfloor. Something glinted in the sun several feet from where he sat, drawing his attention. Liam angled his head, squinted, but couldn't make it out. After finishing his sandwich, he poured some more coffee from the thermos, stood up, and walked over to see what had caught his eye.

Frowning, he stooped down, picked it up, and turned it over in his palm.

"That meddling little—"

He should have known he wouldn't be able to make it through a week without having a run-in with Caterina Bonavera. Talk about a control freak. She dropped by the site whenever it suited her fancy, poked her nose where it didn't need to be poked, and questioned him why they were doing this or that, wasting his time with things she had no understanding of.

She was a disruption he didn't need, sashaying around in those ridiculously high heels she wore, distracting his crew, and darkening his mood.

Liam rolled his jaw. He'd met her demand for a work outline every two weeks, even though he considered it unnecessary since he and Antonio gave her and Lucia status updates on a regular basis. That wasn't good enough for the woman, though. And now, it appeared she'd taken to snooping around on her own after he and his crew left for the day—something they'd all agreed she and her sisters wouldn't do at this point, for obvious safety reasons.

He dropped the evidence into the pocket of his flannel shirt. Client be damned. Like it or not, this was one area where she'd have to do things his way.

"Where are you going?" Burke asked when Liam stomped past him on the way to his truck a few minutes later.

"I've got a bone to pick with a certain Bonavera sister."

"What did she do now that's got you spittin' nails?"

Liam got into the truck and slammed the door, not bothering to respond. As he backed out, he looked in the rearview and saw his brother, standing with his hands on his hips, shaking his head.

Burke and Shawn thought he needed to lighten up when it came to Caterina, but they weren't the ones who had to put up with her interference or the unreasonable expectations on a weekly basis. They also didn't know some of the things he did about the woman, things that didn't speak well about her character.

He couldn't disagree with them that she was a knockout in the looks department. He'd be lying if he did. But strip the pretty wrapping, and you would expose another shallow, self-absorbed princess who thought she could do whatever she damn well pleased, and tough shit if someone else had to pay the price for it.

"FINE! TELL HIM I'll be down in a few minutes."

Caterina dropped her head backward and groaned. "Just what I need to set the tone for the rest of my day. Mr. Macho himself. Man of a million moods. None of them good." She placed her index finger against her temple. "Ptshoo," she said, mimicking a gun going off.

She got up from the chair where she'd been flipping through a restaurant supply catalog and went into the bathroom to brush her hair before going down to reception where *himself* waited... expecting her, no doubt, to stop whatever, to rush down at his beck and call.

"Humph."

She applied some lip gloss and a little mascara and then changed out of the black leggings and oversized, long-sleeve T-shirt she'd slept in, into a pair of dark chocolate skinny jeans and a white, blousy tunic. She pulled on a pair of brown suede over-the-knee boots, then secured a wide leather belt low around her hips, so the tunic draped softly around it.

She didn't care if she looked good when he saw her. Changing clothes and putting on a bit of makeup had nothing to do with his unexpected arrival. She'd been planning to get dressed and run some errands when Lucia called up to tell her Liam was in reception. Now, she could just leave after he got off his chest whatever had his boxers in a bind.

Liam showing up without a scheduled meeting forecast an unpleasant encounter. He never came to the winery to talk to her unless they had an appointment, or he had a problem with something. Since they didn't have anything scheduled, then—

Caterina rounded the corner into reception more than ten, but less than fifteen, minutes after Lucia's call. A perfectly acceptable time frame, to Cat's way of thinking, when someone dropped in without notice. She stopped just inside the wide doorway from the hall.

Liam stood across the room, leaning against the antique mahogany break bar. He was flipping through one of the brochures from the spinner rack that they stocked for guests. He wore a gray and white plaid flannel shirt and a pair of well-worn jeans. His floppy, dark blond hair hung down across one side of his forehead. He looked reckless and a touch dangerous.

Eliana thought he was gorgeous, in that raw, purely sexual way some women found attractive. Fortunately, her sister had decided after their first meeting that he wasn't her type, and she was content to just ogle him covertly. A wise choice, Cat thought, to avoid a man like him—a man who expected you to accept whatever he said as gospel, got annoyed if you dared to question him about anything, and treated you like little more than an annoyance that had to be tolerated.

She digressed. Mitch had done that, and it still stung when she thought about what a horrible judge of character she'd been.

It probably wasn't fair to attribute all her ex-boyfriend's failings to Liam, but in some ways, he treated her as if she was just as unreasonable and bothersome as Mitch had.

Liam's behavior baffled her. She'd given him no reason to dislike her, at least not in the beginning, when they'd first met. After three months of his sneers and condescension, she'd given up trying to play nice. Why should she?

She noticed he'd taken his boots off and left them by the front door, so as not to track dirt over the floor. Apparently, his mother had instilled *some* good manners.

He had on thick, navy socks. The one on his right foot had a hole on the side of the big toe. Did he know?

She looked up. He hadn't noticed her come in, but now he had, and he stood watching her. His eyes traveled down the length of her body, skimmed back up, and settled on hers. Caterina swallowed, hiking her chin.

Liam frowned. "I thought we had an agreement about you and your sisters not being at the work site when neither my crew nor I am there."

"Hello to you, too, Liam." She walked over to the front desk, glancing down at her sister Lucia, who regarded her with a look of caution. Cat leaned her hip against the edge of the desk and gave Liam a false smile. "Can I take it from your tone that you're not here to thank me for the chocolate chip cookies I dropped off for your crew last week?"

Lucia—the proverbial peacemaker and soother in the family—cleared her throat in what Caterina took as a gentle warning. Cat didn't like conflict either, but Liam had set the tone for their relationship.

His green-changeling-blue eyes narrowed frostily. Cat tasted his dislike, raining over her from that sea-glass glare. She wished she could say it didn't bother her—it did—but she was done trying to please men in the hope that they'd treat her better.

Lucia stood up and came around the desk. "I haven't had anything to eat yet. Since you're here, I'm going to go grab something from the kitchen. I won't be long." She leaned close to Caterina's ear and whispered, "Behave. And be nice."

"I'll try," Cat said.

When they were alone, Liam put the brochure back in the spinner rack and crossed his arms over his chest. "You were at the construction site snooping around sometime this weekend after my crew and I left Friday."

"I'm not sure what you're talking about. Did someone *tell* you they saw me snooping around the site?"

"No one had to tell me anything. I know you were there."

"Really? What makes you so sure? Do you have some magical power that can pick up traces of a person's presence?"

He reached into his shirt pocket and pulled something out. "This look familiar?" He extended an open hand.

The diamond stud earring she thought she'd lost winked at her from his palm. Cat strolled over and plucked it up. "I wondered what happened to this."

"So you admit it's yours."

"It's mine, but it doesn't prove anything. Maybe I lost it when I dropped by Thursday afternoon with the cookies." She put the stud in her ear, making a mental note to go back upstairs for the other one before she went out, and returned to stand by the desk, putting some desired distance between them again. "You weren't there. Daryl said you had to run an errand. I might have lost it then."

"We didn't put the subfloor down until Friday morning. And I swept it clean before I left for the day, like always. That little rock you just stuck in your ear wasn't there then."

Cat realized he had her. She rolled her eyes. "Okay, so I stopped by Friday night to look at the progress. I don't know what the big deal is. It's not like I sabotaged anything."

"The big deal is that it's an active work zone. And aside from there being OSHA standards I've got to try to comply with, as I've explained before, it's not safe for you to be poking around on your own. What if you'd gotten hurt?"

"I didn't," she countered and saw the muscle in his jaw twitch.

"You could have. I don't want to get slapped with a lawsuit because my client's too—" He snapped his mouth shut, jerking his glance away.

Cat stiffened. "Too what? Foolish?"

"You said it, not me."

"It's what you were thinking, though. I'm not a fool. I don't consider wanting to stay on top of what you and your crew are doing foolish. I think it's smart. Maybe you're used to getting carte blanche from your other clients, but that's not how I operate. I want to know what's happening, and I think I have a right, since I'm paying the bill. Don't you?"

His expression hardened, and she wouldn't have been surprised to hear a low growl. In his current mood, he looked almost feral. *Angry much?*

Well, too bad, she didn't like being called foolish. Maybe he hadn't said the word, but it had been on the tip of his tongue.

Liam started toward her, his eyes boring into hers. If they were swords, she'd be bleeding all over her beautiful white tunic. He stopped less than a foot in front of her.

Cat tensed. He was big, strong. He could probably hurt her with minimal effort.

Maybe she should move around to the other side of the desk, put a barrier between them. Her feet remained rooted where she stood.

Liam reached up, cupping her jaw. Caterina felt a moment of fear, but surprisingly, his touch remained light. His fingers didn't grip. She could easily bat his hand away if she chose. His eyes locked on hers. She held her breath, trapped between indecision and fascination. The wiser woman in her head urged her to retreat, to step away, but Cat ignored her, giving in to the curious one intrigued about what would happen next.

"You're right; you're signing the checks. You have every right to see what you're paying for." He spoke softly, but she sensed a hardness just below the surface of his words. "You want to check out the site? *Ask*. We had an agreement. I told you and your sister that anytime you wanted to tour the site, I'd arrange for myself or one of the crew to show you. I've held up my end. I expect you to do the same. It's called trust, Caterina. I hope I can count on you to honor it going forward."

He dropped his hand and stepped back. Before she could respond, he turned and walked to the door.

Caterina shivered. What had just happened?

She felt stunned, like he'd immobilized her with the simple touch of a hand. And what he said made her feel guilty, but why should she? It was her project. She had a right to expect certain things. She had a right to know what they were doing. She had a right to inspect the site and...and he'd given her that, hadn't he?

She wrapped her arms around her waist. She felt unsteady and unbalanced as she watched him tug on his boots. When he finished, he straightened back up and faced the door.

"What did I ever do to make you dislike me so much?" Caterina asked, putting forth the question she'd asked herself so many times in her head.

Liam glanced back at her. He reached up, rubbed the back of his neck, and then walked out without answering.

CHRIST! WHAT THE hell had he been trying to prove in there? Getting in her face like that—her space—and putting his hands on her. He should have known better. Should have known, when his fingers started to twitch, that he'd entered dangerous waters.

Liam got into his truck and stared out across the vineyard. He rubbed his hands over his mouth, blew into them, pushed them up through his hair, and held them there a few moments before slamming them down against the top of the steering wheel.

"You idiot!"

He smacked the wheel again.

He could've just gone in there, returned her earring, and explained to her, *again*, that it wasn't safe for her to poke around an active work site by herself. That there were laws about that kind of thing, and he had an obligation to adhere to them. He could have told her, *again*, that he would give her, and any of her sisters, a walk-through if they requested one. They need only ask. He could have done it without turning it into a confrontation, without baiting her.

He could have done it without giving in to the temptation that had lured him to touch her.

He hadn't been prepared for the surge of lust. If he had been, he'd have been better able to resist the urge. It caught him off guard—a sucker punch.

Liam dropped his head back against the seat's headrest. He'd been a breath away from kissing her, from shoving his fingers into all that rich chestnut hair and devouring that belligerent mouth of hers. *Jesus!* What if he'd given in?

It was physical, purely physical. He was human. Only human, and probably hornier than normal because he hadn't slept with a woman in over a year. Kind of hard to arrange when you were a single parent with a four-year-old daughter.

He needed to remember who she was. She may have looked vulnerable when he stood over her, staring down into those big doe eyes, and when she asked him what she'd ever done to earn his dislike. But Caterina Bonavera was no innocent.

She was one of Mitch Gregory's women. The same bastard who'd been screwing Sylvie behind his back and gotten her hooked on the pills she eventually OD'd on.

From what Antonio told him, Caterina had dated the guy for almost a year and had been pretty broken up when it ended. If she'd been mixed-up with a guy like Gregory, it didn't speak well for her character. The man was scum.

No, she was no innocent. She might come off as smart and confident, but for all he knew, she was just as screwed up, just as irresponsible, as his wife had been. He didn't care how hot she looked, or how tempted he'd been to find out what those lips tasted like. Acting on the desire would have been a huge mistake.

If it happened again, he just needed to think about Riley because no woman would ever be worth putting his daughter's happiness at risk the way Sylvie had.

"WE SHOULD REALLY try to find out more about Rosa," Marcella said the following week after Caterina and her sisters finished their Tuesday update meeting.

She glanced at her twin. "In case Cat failed to mention it to either of you, Rosa paid her a midnight visit after our girls' get-together last week."

In response to Lucia and Eliana's inquiring looks, Cat filled them in.

"All we know about Rosa is what Mom told us." Marcella picked up where Cat left off. "And that's not much. If we knew more, it might help us figure out why she's here and why she's showing more interest in us, when she never did before."

"You mean become more meddling," Lucia said.

Eliana, who sat next to Cat on one of the library's sofas, leaned forward and poured herself a cup of coffee from the silver carafe that had been their mother's. She took a sip and glanced at Lucia. "And if Rosa hadn't meddled and locked you and Antonio in the kitchen the night you got engaged, who knows how long the two of you would have danced around each other instead of kissing and making up? You should be grateful she forced you to deal with each other."

Lucia conceded. "You're right, and I am. And I agree that we should try to find out what her story is, so count me in. I'm sure Antonio would be game too."

"Game for what?" Lucia's fiancé strolled into the room from the hallway.

"Oh, hey," Lucia said. "We were discussing Rosa. Marcella suggested we make a more concerted effort to find out more about her. I said we'd be on board to help."

Caterina brought her knees up and tucked her feet under the throw she and Eliana were sharing. "I know I used to be a skeptic, but it's hard to ignore her presence or that she's taken a stronger interest in our lives. It would be nice to know why."

Antonio stopped behind the couch where Lucia sat and rested his hands on her shoulders. "I've been curious about your aunt since I first heard she might be haunting the place. I know she was murdered here, but there's got to be more to it than that."

"I think you're right," Marcella said. She stood up and set her cup down on the coffee table. "Sorry, but I've got to get over to the barrel room. I'm not sure where to start with Rosa, but since we all agree we should try to find out more, I guess the next step is to think about how we do that."

"Why don't you let me spearhead this," Caterina said, volunteering. "I've got more time than the rest of you right now. I'll come up with a plan to get us started, and if any of you have ideas, let me know."

"That'd be great since planning and organizing are right up your alley," Marcella said. "You don't mind?"

"No. Like I said, I've got the time, and I'll enjoy having something to do that I might be able to sink my teeth into."

"Okay, I'll catch up with you guys later." Marcella grabbed one of the cranberry scones Cat had baked for their meeting from the platter on the coffee table and headed out.

Antonio patted Lucia's shoulder. "We should get going too. I need to stop at the site and talk to Liam about something before we go spend another exciting hour looking through wedding invitation books."

"I'll make it up to you later," Lucia said with a promising, suggestive smile.

Caterina rolled her eyes, and when they walked off, she turned toward Eliana. "Any chance you don't have something pressing like everyone else?"

"I've got a phone meeting at four but nothing before then. Why?"

"I'm feeling restless, like I need to get out. Want to get some lunch with me at Twining Vines?"

Eliana studied her a moment, then rubbed a hand over Cat's knee. "Sure, sounds like a great idea. Your car or mine?"

IT WAS ONE of those beautiful November afternoons that flirts with seventy degrees, making one forget winter lies in wait around the corner. Caterina and Eliana decided to take advantage of the temperate weather and eat outdoors. There were several space heaters set around the patio, unnecessary that day, and with no breeze to speak of, the day begged for dining alfresco.

A few roses still bloomed on the arbor stretching over the length of the patio. A curious squirrel ducked in and out from behind them and the knotty wisteria vines twined around the structure's frame, checking out Caterina and Eliana from above.

Lucia's best friend, Jenna, who managed the restaurant, saw them as she made her rounds and waved. She stopped by to chat for a few minutes but excused herself when their orders arrived. "It was great to see you both. We need to do another girls' night, and I'll host next time. Enjoy your meals," she said, "and thanks for coming. Tell Luch I said hey."

After Jenna left, Cat zeroed in on Eliana. "So, what's the story with this Drew guy? Marcella said you went out with him again Saturday night. What's that, like the fifth time?"

"Third."

"Okay, third. That's twice more than most of the guys you go out with. Any chance this one's a keeper?"

"I don't know." El crossed her legs, kicking her foot back and forth. She looked around the patio, smiled at one of the waitresses who passed by carrying a tray of food, and then picked up her spoon and began tapping it against the table. "He's very sweet. And he's got these beautiful blue eyes that if you did nothing but gaze into them could easily make you lose your train of thought."

"But?" Cat lifted a brow. There was always a *but* with Eliana.

Her sister sighed. "I don't know if it's going anywhere. I hoped it would. I keep telling myself, he's such a nice guy, give it a little more time, but...there's just no zing. I want the zing. I want to meet someone and fall in love, without even thinking about it, without having to talk myself into it."

"Ah, the zing." Cat nodded knowingly. "I wish I could tell you it's not important. If you just wanted a friend, it wouldn't be, but a friend and lover—you need some zing."

"Right, and I'm not faulting *him*, but the chemistry just isn't there. Maybe it's unrealistic to think the man of my dreams is out there somewhere, but I don't want to settle for just liking someone. I want love—a deep, heartwarming, satisfying love."

"Have you thought about what this dream guy needs to be like?"

Eliana nodded. "He'll probably be a blond-haired, blue-eyed hunk. Smart, great sense of humor, kind. He'll love how I love him, think I'm the sugar in his chocolate, and whenever we look into each other's eyes—" A slow grin lifted the corners of her mouth. She looked across the table at Cat. "Zzzing!"

Cat laughed. "Okay, well, good luck with all that."

Eliana's smile faded. "You think I'm being too picky?"

"No." Caterina shook her head. "I think you have every right to want what you want. And I'd never suggest that you continue in a relationship if you're not feeling it. But you may need to be a little more flexible with your criteria. Like not crossing someone off the list if he's got brown eyes instead of blue, for example."

"Yeah." El's grin returned. "I could do that. Seriously, you know looks aren't the most important thing to me. That's what he'd be like if I could special order him. But if all I wanted was a blond, blue-eyed hunk, I could walk down the road from the winery and cozy up to the one who's building you a restaurant."

Caterina stiffened. "He's the last man I'd want you getting involved with."

El flicked a hand through the air. "Don't worry. He's a pretty one. That's a fact. And he seems nice enough, if a little on the quiet side, but the chemistry's off. It's like with Drew. I enjoy looking at him, but that's not enough. So really, no worries." She shooed away a bee that seemed to have a taste for chardonnay. "I've got no interest in Liam, sis, if that's why you've been holding back."

Cat furrowed her brow. "Holding back from what?"

Eliana picked up her fork and speared one of the pear wedges from the autumn salad she'd ordered, held it in the air as she spoke. "From making a move on him. I like him as a person, but that's the extent of it. So, if you want him, go for it. He's all yours, Cat, with my blessing."

"What?" Caterina couldn't believe Eliana thought she was interested in Liam Dougherty. "You're joking, right?"

"Why would I be joking?" El popped the fruit into her mouth, chewed and swallowed it, then said, "It's obvious you two flip each other's energy switch."

"Oh, we flip each other's switch all right! But not the way you're suggesting. All that *energy*...it's got nothing to do with attraction. We're more like two opposing magnets, forced into proximity, but wanting nothing to do with the other."

"That's not what I've observed."

Cat snorted in disbelief. "Really? Have you ever *seen* the way that man looks at me?"

Eliana caught the tip of her tongue between her front teeth and grinned. "Oh, I've seen it. Heat, honey. There's a whole lot of heat burning in those smoldering, aquamarine eyes when they're set on you."

"Humph. That's not heat, not the kind you're implying. The man doesn't like me. And I can't believe you don't see it."

"Well..." El took a sip of wine. "I've only seen the two of you together a few times. There might have been a little negative tension, but I'm pretty good at recognizing when a man is attracted to a woman."

Eliana leaned in toward the table. "And believe me, honey, whether he likes it or not, Liam Dougherty wants to do more with you than review appliance dimensions for Serendipity."

Caterina shook her head. "I'm not doubting your talents, but as good as you might be, in this instance, you are so off base that you're not even on the playing field."

Eliana started to object, but Cat raised a hand to cut her off.

"No. Trust me on this. Liam doesn't want anything to do with me. But even if he did, it wouldn't matter because I don't want anything to do with him."

Her sister didn't look convinced, but it didn't matter what El or anyone else thought because Caterina knew Liam would probably rather eat a bucket of nails than spend a minute more than he had to in her presence.

"So, now that we've cleared up that misunderstanding, let's talk about something more pleasant." Cat clutched her fingers around the stem of her wineglass. "What ideas have you come up with for Lucia and Antonio's wedding?"

Three

"All sorrows are less with bread."
Miguel de Cervantes, *Don Quixote*

Caterina pulled a white silk cami out of her lingerie drawer, put it on, and tucked it into the waistband of her jeans. She then sat down on the edge of her bed and pulled on the blue suede UGGs she'd bought the prior fall. She didn't know how long she'd be out today or where her research might take her if she stumbled upon anything interesting, so she'd dress for all-day comfort.

She went to the closet to select a sweater. Her clothes were organized by item first, then by color—lightest to darkest—tops and pants on one side, skirts, dresses, and overcoats on the other; purses on the top two shelves against the back wall, shoes on the middle four, and boots lined up on the floor just below.

Her sisters teased her about being obsessively organized, but a good system just made sense. She knew exactly where everything was, could put her hands on whatever she needed within minutes. Having a place for everything, and everything in its place, wasn't just a way to simplify one's life, her line of work demanded it. What if she needed to whip egg whites and couldn't find her ball whisk? They'd be flat, not airy. What if she advertised butter-poached lobster tails with Dijon mustard sauce as one of the evening's specials, only to find she had no Dijon mustard? She would disappoint her customers.

She chose a sweater with a front zipper, almost the exact slate-blue color as her boots, slipped it on, and zipped it up half-way. If she ended up spending several hours holed up in a stuffy, third-floor room of the library, scouring through old newspapers, and got too warm, she could pare down.

She didn't think she'd need a jacket since she'd be back before evening, and they'd been enjoying a smattering of warmer days. She got a navy down vest anyway and tucked it under her arm to bring it along. If the day decided to turn cool, she'd have it. If she didn't need it, she could roll it up and put it into her backpack.

Exiting the closet, she went into the bathroom, put on a little makeup, brushed out her shoulder-length bob, and then, after checking the list she'd made the night before to ensure she hadn't forgotten anything, grabbed her purse and her backpack, and went downstairs.

Marcella, Lucia, and Antonio were in reception.

"Where are you off to?" Lucia asked when Cat strode into the room.

"Starbucks for a cup to go, and then to the library in Purcell-ville to scour over old newspapers and anything else I can dig up that might shed some light on Aunt Rosa or Uncle Gino's lives." Caterina hiked her backpack up on her shoulder. "Not sure how long I'll be gone. It'll depend on whether I find anything or not."

"I admit I'm kind of jealous," Marcella said. "I'd love to spend the day bumping about in a library, surrounded by books and all that glorious quiet."

"You should have all the quiet you crave holed up in the barrel room," Cat said. "I'll admit, though, even though it wouldn't typically be my kind of thing, I think I'm going to enjoy delving into this project."

"I'll be too busy this week, but I'm looking forward to helping out when I have some spare time," Antonio said. "After all, if it weren't for Rosa, my future bride here might never have given me the chance to persuade her to marry me."

Lucia bumped her hip into his, and he grinned down at her. "Speaking of busy," he said, "I've got to run. I have a meeting with Shawn in half an hour, and I promised Liam I'd drop off these revisions this morning."

Antonio glanced at his watch, then shook his head. "Probably should text Shawn to let him know I'm going to be late."

"I can drop those off if you want," Caterina offered. "I'll be driving by the site, and the library doesn't open until ten, so even with a Starbucks run, I'd probably still be standing outside waiting for them to open."

"If you don't mind, I'd appreciate it."

"Don't mind. As long as I don't have to explain anything about them."

"No. If Liam's got any questions, I can go over them with him later." Antonio handed her a rolled-up drawing.

"Thanks." He swooped down and gave Lucia a quick kiss that, for its brevity, sizzled.

Some girls had all the luck, Caterina mused. Maybe someday she'd be fortunate enough to meet a man who would fall as crazy in love with her as Antonio had with Lucia.

HE'D BEEN PUNCHY all week—out of sorts—and he had a good guess why. Liam poured a steaming cup of coffee from his thermos and took a sip, scorched his tongue, cursed.

The sound of gravel crunching under tires made him glance over his shoulder to see a shiny red Jeep Grand Cherokee pull up beside his truck.

Liam frowned. Think of trouble, and *she* appears. What did she want now? Last week he'd given her the stupid schedule she insisted on getting every two weeks, so she shouldn't be bugging him for another one yet.

He set the thermos down on the foundation's ledge, stuffed his free hand in his pocket, then turned around and watched her get out of the Jeep. For once she'd had the sense to wear a pair of shoes to the site that didn't make him worry she'd fall and break something he'd have to file a claim for.

Caterina opened the back door and leaned inside. Liam had an unobstructed view from where he stood. He swore under his breath and glanced away. Trouble and temptation—a bad combination—one that, despite certain body parts that lacked a brain were trying to convince him otherwise, he wanted no part of.

He heard the door shut and watched her again, blew on his coffee, took another sip. She glanced around, saw him, and hiked her nose in the air. She looked down it at him, the way she always did, as if he didn't meet her standards. He didn't really give a shit. He wasn't trying.

Liam narrowed his eyes, met hers. She narrowed hers back. Oil and water. *Let's see which one of us looks away first, sweetheart.*

Neither did. Tough—he had to give her that—and damn sexy. He wouldn't lie to himself. Too bad it wasn't enough. He imagined he could find a whole lot of pleasure between those mile-long legs.

She stopped about three feet in front of him. "This is from Antonio." She held out a rolled-up drawing, probably the one Antonio said he'd drop off that morning.

Liam reached out and took it from her.

"He was running late for a meeting," she said, "so I told him I'd drop it off since I was passing this way. He said if you have any questions to call him later."

He set his cup down next to the thermos and began to unroll the drawing. In his peripheral vision, he saw her arms go around her middle. After a few seconds he heard her mumble "Unbelievable." Then she said quite plainly, and with an air of clear sarcasm, "You're welcome."

"Yeah, thanks." His conscience nudged him. He usually had better manners. The fact that she rubbed him the wrong way was no excuse to be rude. His mother would be disappointed in him.

"Right." She shook her head, spun around with a snort, and went back to her car. She slammed the door after getting in. Meant for him, he supposed, and he probably deserved it.

"WHAT DO YOU say we go out for pizza tonight?" Liam asked Riley when he picked her up from preschool later that afternoon.

He hadn't done a grocery run in a couple of weeks, and anything he managed to throw together from whatever they had at home probably wouldn't appeal to either of them.

"Yes!" Riley pumped her fist. "Can we get the circle meats on it?"

"Pepperoni? Sure."

Fortunately, his daughter wasn't a fussy eater. He didn't know many people who didn't like pizza, but she would have been just as happy if he'd suggested sushi. He'd lucked out when it came to Riley. She was a happy kid. He'd been scared as hell when faced with the prospect of raising her on his own, but he'd managed to stumble through the last two years without screwing things up.

When they got to the truck, Liam opened the back door, and Riley scrambled up into her car seat. He strapped her in, then leaned down and kissed the top of her head. She looked up and gave him a big, dimpled grin, and there went his heart, the same way it always did. Here was one female who'd always have him wrapped around her finger.

Fifteen minutes later they walked into Bartelleti's, the Italian restaurant they liked to go to for pizza, and found an empty table in the center section. Riley liked to sit there because the tables were situated around a fountain. Water spurted out of the mouth of a fish, and Liam always gave her whatever change he had in his pocket to throw in for wishes.

"Do you want me to make a wish for you, Daddy?" she asked as he handed her several coins.

"The wishes are for you, princess. I've got you, so I already have everything I need to make me happy."

Riley beamed at him, then skipped over to the fountain. She clutched her hands in front of her, and when she glanced over at him, he could see her mouth wiggling as she contemplated what she should wish for.

Liam winked, and she scrunched her eye in return. When she turned back to face the fountain, he chuckled.

"Hey, Liam, I thought maybe you'd gone into the Witness Protection Program the way you disappeared after the last time I saw you."

He glanced over his right shoulder. "Hey, Krista. Yeah, I guess it's been a while."

The woman sat down in the seat where Riley had been sitting, and Liam glanced over at his daughter. He'd never introduced her to any of the women he'd gone out with after Sylvie's death, not that there'd been many, or one he'd dated for long.

He'd gone out with Krista three or four times. The last time he'd gotten the sense she wanted a more serious relationship. He thought she should have what she wanted; it would just have to be with someone other than him.

"You don't mind the company, do you?" She leaned her elbows on the table and smiled at him.

"Actually, I'm here with someone."

She looked around. "Oh. I thought maybe—"

"Daddy, Daddy." Riley called as she hurried over to the table. She stopped and looked at Krista and then sat in the chair next to him. Leaning sideward, she put a hand to his ear. "I made the best wish for you. Even though you said you didn't need nothing."

"What'd you wish for?"

She shook her head and put a finger to her lips. "I can't tell. If I do it won't come true."

"Well, hello, pretty girl," Krista said from the other side of the table.

Riley leaned into him, looking somewhat unsure.

"It's okay, honey," Krista said, her smile wide as she regarded his daughter. "I'm a friend of your dad's."

"Oh," Riley said. "I'm Riley." She nibbled on her lip. "I don't remember you."

"Well, that's because we've never met, but now that we have, maybe you and I can become friends too." She reached her hand across the table. "I'm Krista."

Liam narrowed his eyes in silent warning, but Krista didn't see it. Riley took Krista's hand, shook it, then looked up at him. Liam smiled for her sake.

The waiter delivered their pizza, setting it in the center of the table. "Will there be anything else?"

"That's it, thanks." Liam nodded at the waiter, then glanced back at Krista.

"If you'll excuse us, Riley and I are going to eat this while it's still hot."

"Oh. Sure." Krista cleared her throat and stood up. She took a few steps forward, then turned back. "Give me a call sometime, Liam." She leaned toward his ear and lowered her voice so only he could hear. "It doesn't have to mean anything."

After she left, Liam lifted a piece of pizza and put it on Riley's plate, then got one for himself. Riley folded hers in half and took a bite. She tilted her head as she chewed, a crease marking her brow. He could tell she was thinking hard about something. Hopefully not his relationship with Krista.

"What are you thinking, honey?"

"Do you think I'll be pretty like your friend when I get big?"

"My friend? You mean Krista?"

Riley nodded. "She has pretty hair. I never see'd anyone with red hair, except, like Ariel, but she's a mermaid. Do you think she's pretty?"

"Do I think Ariel's pretty?"

"No, silly. The lady who's your friend."

"Yes, I'd say she's pretty, but there are a lot of things more important than being pretty, Riley."

"I know, like always tell the truth, and don't be mean to anyone, and put all your toys away before you go to bed so your room doesn't get so messy your dad can't find you in the morning."

"Right." Liam chuckled and took a bite of pizza. "And," he chewed around his words, "don't be worrying about growing up too fast. I'd like to enjoy you being a kid for a few more minutes."

Riley giggled. "Daddy, don't you know I have to get ten before I'm not a kid? That's two numbers." She raised a hand and counted off on her fingers. "I got six more numbers to go."

"So you do. I guess I can relax then." He lifted the slice for another bite. "Now eat your pizza, pumpkin."

He had no intention of calling Krista. He'd gotten the message but didn't enjoy meaningless sex. He didn't need to be in love with the person, but a mutual attraction and respect would be nice.

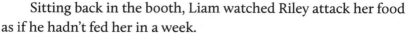
Sitting back in the booth, Liam watched Riley attack her food as if he hadn't fed her in a week.

No...don't grow up too fast, little one.

CATERINA STOOD AT the counter in the kitchen later that day after returning from the library. She selected three nice-sized potatoes from the wire basket hanging over the kitchen counter and scrubbed them under running water. She sliced them and dropped them into the pot of water boiling on the range to parboil them. Lyonnaise potatoes were on the menu—her mother's recipe and still the best of any other she'd tried.

Her first foray into the mysteries of Rosa's past hadn't been as mind-blowingly revealing as Caterina had hoped. She'd found bits of information on her great-aunt and uncle, but nothing out of the ordinary.

Anne, one of the librarians she'd spoken with, had given her some good ideas on how to get started, including telling her about several resources that she hadn't known about before that day that might prove fruitful.

Anne had suggested doing a family tree. Cat planned to begin making one that evening. She'd start with her and her sisters and trace that branch backwards on her father's side to their *nonno* and Uncle Gino and their parents. The other branch would trace Rosa's ancestors. Who knew, maybe she'd uncover another ghost or two poking around in the limbs.

Today had been fun...well, interesting anyway. It felt good to have something to do. It was a task she'd do well with and something she could really delve into, if she wanted to, until they got closer to opening Serendipity.

In the months before they opened, she'd have a plethora of things to do to get ready: purchasing everything for the restaurant, from serviceware to linens and chairs; finalizing the menus; hiring staff; contracting with vendors. It was a monumental list—and it thrilled her to no end.

But that was months away still. Serendipity wouldn't open for almost a year, possibly longer if they ran into problems during construction. She didn't plan to let that happen, not if she had anything to do with it, which was why she insisted on staying on top of the progress at the construction site. Like it or not, *Liam Rude McDude*.

Cat snorted. Just the thought of the man set her blood simmering like the water boiling for her potatoes. He was the big, bad thorn on her rose bush—sharp, pointed, and pricklier than a porcupine. She'd read somewhere that, in fact, porcupines had very soft fur and their quills lay flat, hidden beneath it—painful barbs that could be hard to remove if you were unfortunate enough to get one under your skin.

"Humph." Didn't that just describe their contractor to a T? All pretty boy with his tousled, surfer-boy blond hair, and cyan eyes, which she couldn't decide were more green or blue. And he had those cocky hips, and all that hard, lean muscle, and that tight ass that made a woman itch to curl her hands around both cheeks and give them a good squeeze, and...*Whoa!*

Wasn't that just the point? He was exactly like the porcupine, luring you in with all its soft fur, then piercing you with its hidden spikes as soon as you touched. And no, she didn't want to feel up his ass—well, maybe a little just to see if it was as hard as it looked—but if she ever succumbed to that temptation, she'd make sure she gave him a world-class wedgie he wouldn't soon forget before she walked away.

Maybe a good wedgie would jar loose that cocksure attitude of his.

Caterina breathed in and then released a slow, exasperated sigh. Why did she let him get to her this way? Dragging her into this unproductive, festering battle with him, when she didn't even understand its root? So, he had a problem with her. Did she have to make it her problem too?

Couldn't she choose to take the high road, to be the bigger person? The mature one? She could, except that she couldn't avoid dealing with him. If she could, turning the other cheek wouldn't be so difficult. But to allow him to continually use her as a pincushion, while she stood on higher ground rubbing salve over the constant pricks, well...that appealed to her about as much as eating raw liver. She'd never even liked it cooked. Besides, letting him get to her gave him power over her emotions.

She could, however, not let him see how he affected her, threw her off her stride, or let him know how much time she wasted stewing over his attitude about her. What she should do is find a way to prick his surly hide right back, tit-for-tat, see how he liked it.

Maybe whenever he talked to her about the project she should just grunt, or narrow her eyes, or refuse to answer him until he called her out for having poor manners, the way she'd had to prod him into thanking her for dropping off the drawings from Antonio that morning. Maybe she should be as blatantly surly as he was with her, so he knew she didn't like him much either. Let him chew on that instead of those mint-flavored toothpicks he liked to gnaw.

How could Eliana have thought Liam was attracted to her?

"Ungh!" Cat practiced one of the grunts she might use the next time she saw him. Her sister had to be delusional if she thought she'd seen something other than distaste simmering in the man's eyes.

What about when he found your earring and confronted you about going over to the work site when you weren't supposed to be there?

The thought drifted into her head out of nowhere. What about it? He was angry, so what? She shredded the cheese for the casserole with a little more effort than required.

Yeah, but when he wrapped his fingers around your chin, you felt something.

Oh no, I did not!

You did. Don't deny it. You felt a tingle in your tingly place.

I thought he might hit me. That was trepidation.

It was lust. And maybe, just maybe, Eliana's right. Maybe he felt it too.

Caterina shoved aside the parchment paper she'd been grating the cheese on and picked up a Vidalia onion. She cut it in half, peeled off the skin, and attacked it as if she were racing to beat the clock on *The Next Great Chef.*

"Oh, voice in my head," Cat said with a skeptical laugh, "you are wrong. Just as wrong as Eliana. Wrong, wrong, wrong!"

"What's Eliana wrong about?"

Cat started, then half-turned to see Marcella standing just inside the kitchen doorway.

"I was thinking aloud. I didn't know anyone was there."

"Clearly. I just came in for a bottle of water. Didn't mean to interrupt your internal argument." Marcella walked over to the refrigerator and pulled one out. "Curious though, what's El so wrong about?"

Cat gave the knife she'd been dicing the onion with a dismissive spin in the air. "Just this ridiculous notion she has."

"About what?"

She snorted. "She thinks our contractor...she thinks he wants to...she says he's attracted to me."

Marcella unscrewed the bottle cap. "Yeah, and?"

"What do you mean, yeah, and?"

"Well, that's obvious." Marcella raised the water bottle to her lips, took a sip. "But what's the thing she and your little head voice have all wrong?"

Cat stared at her twin as if she and the rest of the world were wearing blinders, and only Cat saw things clearly. She shook her head, incredulous.

"Marcella! That *is* the thing. Liam is no more attracted to me than I am to him."

Her sister arched a brow, gave her the *really?* look, and grinned in response.

"What? Are you kidding me? You too! Cel, the man barely tolerates me. Have you not noticed the way he scowls at me, that his mood turns sour the moment I show up, or that he can't manage more than a few monosyllabic words and grunts when he has to speak to me, even though he has no problem with sentence structure when he's talking to anyone else?"

Cel shrugged and took another sip of water. "I've noticed."

"Then how can you think he likes me?"

"I didn't say I thought he liked you. Maybe he doesn't, or maybe he doesn't want to. That doesn't mean he can't still be attracted to you. They can be mutually exclusive."

"Well, I'm telling you he's not. He doesn't like me. He's not attracted to me. And it would probably take an act of God to thaw the ice between Liam and me whenever we have to deal with each other."

"If you say so." Marcella screwed the cap back on the water bottle. "I've got to get back to work."

Her sister made for the door.

"I do say so!"

"Yeah, okay." Marcella raised her bottle in the air, gave it a tilt of acknowledgment. "It's possible El and I, and the voice in your head, are all wrong." She stopped, glanced back when she got to the door, and gave Cat a wink. "But it's also possible we're not."

After Cel left, Cat drained the potatoes and started putting together the layers for the casserole.

Could one be attracted to someone they didn't like? She frowned. Well, she didn't like Liam. He made it easy not to. She didn't hate him, want scorpions to climb up inside his pant legs, or wish some other kind of physical harm on him, although she *would* like to give him a taste of his own medicine. And still, if she was honest with herself, maybe some lust was mixed in with the anger juices he whipped up in her. And if it was possible with her...

What if Marcella and El really had noticed something she'd missed because she hadn't been able to see past the churl?

If they were right, and she did in fact spark some heat in his blood, it probably pissed him off more than anything she could say to him. The corners of her lips twitched, and Caterina grinned over the possibility. No, Liam Dougherty would not want to want her.

Maybe she'd just found the needle she'd been looking for to do a little pricking of her own.

Four

"*Men are like wine—some turn to vinegar,*
but some improve with age."
Pope John XXIII

The change we wanted to talk about will mostly impact the restaurant layout." Antonio looked between Caterina and Lucia. He unrolled a sheet of drafting paper that had a rough pencil sketch on it. They usually met on Thursdays, but he'd said he and Liam wanted to meet with them Monday morning to discuss some layout changes and get their input.

Cat stole a glance at Liam. He watched her from beneath hooded eyes. She had a childish urge to stick out her tongue. It perched on her upper lip, ready to demonstrate what she thought of him, but she quashed the impulse. The gratification would be fleeting, and she knew she'd regret him knowing he could reduce her to behaving like a twelve-year-old.

Liam's eyes drifted down to her mouth, and it went dry. She licked her lips. Something flickered in their icy depths, right before he jerked them away. He shifted on the couch. She saw the muscle in his jaw flinch, then it hardened.

Interesting. Her lip licking hadn't been planned. It had been an uncalculated response, she realized, to him looking at her mouth. She'd experienced that brief tingle, but...he'd felt something too. She knew to the tips of her toes that he didn't like it any more than she did, but whatever electrical current she felt, it had been traveling in two directions.

She looked back to Antonio and cleared her throat. "Please don't tell me you need to take space from the restaurant."

"No, nothing like that. The changes have to do with design and flow, and they don't impact the kitchen area at all." He leaned forward and tapped his pencil against the sketch. "The idea is to create an atmosphere that capitalizes on one of the area's biggest draws. You're in the middle of northern Virginia wine country. Bonavera Winery is a popular stop for tastings. If you think about most of your customers, they typically plan a day of tastings, stopping somewhere for lunch at some point in between or for dinner afterward."

He looked at Lucia. "The same as you and I did on one of our first dates. We did a couple of tastings, went to lunch at your friend's restaurant, then continued on our way."

"Yes, it's a popular way to spend a day, or weekend, in the area," Lucia agreed, "but how does that play into the restaurant's design?"

"Okay, so here's what we were thinking. We design parts of the restaurant to emulate the look and feel of a barrel room, like the one at the winery, minus the vast number of barrels filled with wine, of course. There would be a larger, more open area with access to the veranda, but with several half walls skirting it. These would be clad with shaved barrels, about five inches deep with the metal rings left intact. Just enough depth to give the impression of stacked barrels. These half walls would create several smaller, more intimate dining areas within the larger one."

He outlined the rest of the idea and then leaned back, crossed his ankle over his knee. "It's entirely up to the two of you—mostly you, Cat—whether you want to stay with the original design or incorporate the changes. We're early enough in the process that, if you like the idea, we can make the changes without impacting anything else. The area wineries are a huge draw, not only for tourists, but locals as well. We can capitalize on their appeal by creating an environment that makes patrons feel like it's part of the whole winery experience."

"I think it's brilliant," Lucia said and then looked at Cat. "The decision's totally up to you, though. It's your restaurant, but in case you wanted to know."

"Of course you think it's brilliant." Cat angled her head toward Antonio. "She's dazzled by everything you do."

"Not true," Lucia said with a laugh. "I do think he's pretty amazing." She slid Antonio a look that should have carried an "R" rating with it. "But I can still be objective when I need to be."

Liam sat with his arms crossed over his chest, watching the interaction silently. Cat couldn't imagine him ever being playful with a woman the way Antonio was with Lucia. He didn't impress her as a man who owned a fun, or a softer, side.

"What about you, Cat?" Antonio asked.

She really didn't have to think about it but gave herself a moment in case anything popped into her head that she should consider. Nothing did. She loved the idea.

"I think it's brilliant too." She chuckled when Lucia leaned over from where she sat in the chair and punched her lightly on the shoulder.

"Really," she said, addressing Antonio, "it's wonderful. I like the concept of having a large central dining area, but then having some more intimate areas customers can request if they're celebrating a special occasion, or just want more privacy. And the barrel room idea is great! I do still want it to have an elegant feel, but we can accomplish that with tablecloths, candles, crystal, fresh flowers..." She paused in her thinking and then waved a dismissive hand. "We can talk about that later, though."

She leaned forward and rested her forearms on her knees. "Let's do it. I think patrons will love it."

"Okay, if you're both in agreement then, I'll go ahead and redo the dining room drawings. There's plenty of time for all of us to review them together before we get to that stage." Antonio reached out and shook Liam's hand. "Nice work, Liam. Congratulations."

"What's Antonio congratulating you for, Liam?" Lucia asked. "Are you celebrating something?"

Liam shrugged. "It's nothing."

"The idea to tweak the restaurant design was Liam's." Antonio stood up and tucked the paper under his arm. "And as you both think it's brilliant, I want to give credit where it's due."

"It really is a fabulous idea, Liam," Lucia said. "And it only confirms for me that we made the right decision when we chose you, knowing you've got our best interests in mind rather than just looking at our project as a construction job."

"If the customer's happy, then I'm happy."

"Well, I am happy, and since my sister loves the idea, I know she is too. Right, Cat?"

"It works." Cat picked at the hem of her skirt. It did more than work. It made wonderful sense. It added depth to an already good design, created mood, inspired romance. How had a man with the personality of a stone come up with such a creative vision? Why would he spend time thinking about ways to enhance her customers' experience, when all he'd been hired to do was put up a structure, attach a roof, and build out some walls?

Liam stood up from the other end of the couch where they'd both been sitting. Because they didn't get along, she was being small and letting his indifference influence her reaction. She could be petty, which wouldn't make her feel very good, or she could refuse to let his contrary attitude get the best of her and be the bigger person. They may not get along, but she couldn't honestly deny he was an exceptional craftsman. She'd seen his work, looked for flaws, but had never found any. He clearly took pride in his work; that was something she understood.

Clearing her throat, Cat stood too. "Thank you, Liam. The changes you proposed are..." She smoothed her skirt, her fingers brushing away invisible lint. "They're...good."

When she got to her room about ten minutes later, Cat flopped down on the bed and stared up at the ceiling. She could have told him they were *brilliant*. She'd told Antonio they were. But thinking his idea was brilliant would have meant something to Antonio. Liam probably didn't care what she thought of him or his ideas.

She threw an arm over her eyes and sighed. Here she was, again wasting time thinking about a man she didn't enjoy thinking about, but who always seemed to be creeping around her thoughts, anyway. She'd let him get to her, with his grunts, narrowed glances, and shrugging indifference. She knew not everyone she crossed paths with in life would like her, and if they didn't, she had to let that be their problem, not hers. Well, she needed to be done with it. Stewing over him was wearing her out.

Caterina rolled over and grabbed the other bed pillow, hugged it against her chest, and closed her eyes. It wasn't even noon, but she thought she could easily fall asleep and take a nap. This afternoon she would log into the library's website and...

A long-forgotten melody drifted through her head, something she'd heard her mother humming from time to time. She smiled and hugged the pillow closer.

THERE WERE NO guests in residence at the moment, not unusual for a Wednesday this time of year. Lucia and Antonio had driven to D.C. and wouldn't be back until late afternoon. Eliana had a meeting with a woman in Leesburg for a possible freelance job, and Marcella was out in the vineyard, worrying over her vines.

Caterina dragged the fourth of the hefty boxes she intended to go through out of Antonio's attic office and into the hallway. The boxes had been overpacked and were too heavy to carry. With a little ingenuity, she thought she could maneuver them down the stairwell and to her room.

She'd have to resign herself to waiting for help with the two old trunks she most wanted to delve into. They had belonged to Rosa or her parents and were more likely to hold insights into her ancestor's life but were too heavy to manage on her own.

Antonio had said he'd bring the boxes and trunks down to her room when he got back, so she could search through them for anything that might help in their research. She didn't wait well, though. Not once she decided on a course of action. Those boxes should be enough to keep her busy for a few hours.

Her future brother-in-law could lecture her later for not waiting for him. She'd rather listen to a *you could have hurt yourself* sermon than waste the entire morning when she could be doing something productive.

Cat stared at the boxes sitting against the hallway wall. If the contents turned out to be nothing more than old books and stuff no one had any use for, going through them still served a useful purpose. She saw no value in clinging to someone else's junk. She didn't hang on to her own things once she'd outgrown them, or they'd lost their usefulness, so why clutter up the attic with her dead relatives' stuff when the space could be put to better use?

Straightening up, she took a couple of moments to catch her breath as she pondered the best way to get the boxes down the stairwell with the least amount of effort.

"Okay, I can do this."

She shook out her arms, then sat down on the floor. Putting her feet against the side of one of the boxes, she pushed with her legs. It moved a couple of feet toward the landing. She scooted forward and repeated the process four more times, until she reached the attic stairwell. She gave the box one more short push, so it balanced over the top step by several inches without being at risk of toppling forward.

Sidling around the box, she sat on the first step down. Reaching behind her back, she gripped the bottom sides. It took a couple of attempts, but she managed to wiggle it forward and angle it downward just enough to rest against her back.

She sat there a moment, taking stock of the weight before making her next move. If she braced her feet against the risers as she moved down from step to step, she thought it would give her more support, and she'd be less likely to lose control. She just needed to keep the box centered so the weight was distributed evenly.

"Just what are you trying to do?"

Cat looked down the stairwell. Liam stood at the bottom, scowling up at her. He shook his head, then jogged up the steps. Stopping directly in front of her, he reached over her head and pushed the box back until it lay flat on the landing again.

"Why did you do that?" Caterina asked in frustration. "It took me three tries to get that box into the right position!"

"To do what, kill yourself? That's got to weigh close to eighty pounds. What's in it, bricks?"

"I don't know what's in it! Which is why I was taking it to my room to unpack, before you got in my way. So, if you don't mind—" She turned to take hold of the box again, but he nudged her aside and, with seemingly little effort, slid it backward.

Cat stood up and braced her hands on her hips. "And now what do you think *you're* doing?"

"Making sure you live long enough to write me a check when I finish your project." He bent his knees, crouched down, then took hold of the bottom of the box and hefted it against his chest as he stood back up again. "Where do you want this?"

"I don't need your help."

"Fine, you're getting it anyway. Now do us both a favor and show me where to put this instead of wasting time deciding how stubborn you want to be about it."

Okay, she could be reasonable. He was big and strong. He lifted heavy stuff all day long. He could probably lift two of those boxes at once without breaking a sweat. The logical thing would be to take him up on his offer. It would save her time, effort, and, if her plan didn't work, prevent her from getting hurt or losing the box to a free fall.

She spun around and started down the stairs. "For your information, I'm not stubborn."

Cat heard him grunt behind her.

"There's a difference between being stubborn and being determined," she said.

"Whatever definition makes you feel better."

She ground her back teeth. "I don't have to try to make myself feel better. Just because you don't like me doesn't mean I don't like myself. I like myself just fine."

He didn't respond. She envisioned him rolling his eyes. So what? She didn't need his approval. She didn't care if he thought she was stubborn, or wound too tight, or interfering, or whatever the hell else he thought about her.

She reached the bottom of the stairs, rounded the landing, and continued down the hallway toward her room. She could hear his footsteps close behind. She couldn't hear him breathing—she would have been panting by now, if she'd even managed to get the box down from the attic.

When she reached the door to her bedroom, she opened it and stood aside for him to enter, then followed him in.

"Just put it down by the bed." She watched from just inside the doorway as he carried it over and crouched to set it on the floor. The faded jeans he wore tightened over the muscles in his legs and hugged his backside. He didn't have an ounce of fat on him. Just hard, lean muscle that made her mouth go dry in unguarded admiration. He stood back up, her eyes following the fluid power and grace of his movement.

Cat swallowed. When she refocused, she saw him scrutinizing her, his gaze a blue-green mask that revealed nothing. Had he caught her ogling him? Well, not ogling. She'd just been looking, and it hadn't been intentional. Her eyes had just sort of drifted over him on their own before she realized she was...unintentionally checking out his form.

Glancing away, she cleared her throat. "What were you doing roaming around up here, anyway?"

"Looking for Antonio. I couldn't reach him on his cell."

"He and Lucia left about an hour ago to drive into D.C. They won't be back until later this afternoon."

Cat tried to avoid looking at him. Her feelings for Liam were complicated. She didn't like him, but at the same time, she felt a craving whenever he was around. Those little electrical currents would start zipping around, make her tingle, break her focus.

She turned around, away from him, and walked out of the room. Liam followed. She continued down the hallway until she got to the attic stairway.

"Thanks," she said, because it was the right thing to do, even though she hadn't asked for his help, and he hadn't given her a choice about accepting it. "I'll tell Antonio to give you a call when he gets back."

She started up the stairs and heard him curse.

"What?" she asked, when she looked around and saw him shaking his head.

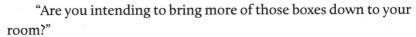

"Are you intending to bring more of those boxes down to your room?"

Cat screwed up her mouth. "A couple."

Liam came up the stairs behind her. He passed her on her right, glanced down at her as he did. "Like I said, stubborn."

When Cat reached the landing, he asked which boxes she wanted. She pointed to the three in the hallway. "Those, but you don't have to carry them down. Antonio told me he'd do it when he got back this afternoon, so seriously, there's no reason to put yourself out."

He smirked. "His offer didn't stop you from trying to piggy-back them down the stairs on your own, anyway. Excuse me for being a skeptic, but why should I believe that the minute I leave you won't try to pull another stunt like the one you were attempting when I got here?"

"I could have managed."

"You could have gotten seriously hurt."

"I don't think I would have. I have strong legs."

He looked at her legs, as if to judge for himself. His eyes lingered there a moment, and she saw him swallow. "Look, I'm not going to argue with you about it," he said, hoisting one of the boxes up into his arms to prove the point. "Just go back downstairs. I'll bring the rest of these down and put them with the other one."

She didn't want to argue with him either. It wouldn't get them anywhere. He seemed insistent, and she knew he could get the job done a lot easier than she.

Cat gave a slight nod. Now she felt she owed him one. Not a position she liked.

LIAM CARRIED THE last of the boxes down the second-floor hallway and into Caterina's room.

He'd had no choice but to bring the rest of them down. When he saw her attempting to brace that box on her back, he couldn't believe she'd intended to try to get it down the stairs using her body as a strut. One slip, and the weight could have propelled her forward. She could have been seriously injured.

He'd learned one thing in his dealings with her, though: Caterina did what she wanted, regardless of the potential consequences. Like snooping around an active work site at night when no one else was around, despite the danger. She hadn't cared about that. She'd wanted to snoop, so she snooped.

Stubborn—he'd been right on that count, and if he hadn't brought down the rest of the boxes, he didn't trust that she'd have waited for Antonio. She was accountable for her own actions, but still, if she'd gotten hurt when he could have prevented it, but he did nothing, he'd have felt responsible.

He set the box down beside the others and glanced around as he stood back up. Her room surprised him. There were feminine touches here and there, some overstuffed white throw pillows propped against the headboard, and a vase of flowers on the dresser, but the walls were a no-nonsense blue—pale and serene. The color appealed to him.

The bed had a simple down comforter, crisp and white, like the curtains covering the two tall windows and French doors. A handmade quilt, in soft pastels, lay neatly folded across the foot of the bed. The room looked clean, uncluttered, and the things he did see sitting out were neat and organized. He'd expected something more...frou-frou. Something more...indulgent.

"Thank you," Caterina said from where she stood in front of the French doors that he assumed led out to a balcony.

"No problem." Liam turned to leave and saw that she'd closed the bedroom door after he carried in the final box.

He frowned. No, that couldn't be. She'd been standing just where she was now when he'd come in. He must have bumped it with the box and accidentally pushed it shut.

He glanced over at her and she shuffled, appearing uncomfortable. He wasn't sure what to make of it. She usually came across as being self-assured, to the point of being haughty.

She clasped her hands in front of her, rubbing one of her thumbs over the opposing hand. "I feel like I should repay you somehow."

"Forget it. It was just a few boxes."

"I'll bake some cookies and drop them off at the site tomorrow. If you don't want them, you can give them to your crew."

"Suit yourself." Liam made for the door. He reached out and turned the knob. The door stuck. He gave it a gentle tug, but it held firm. "Is there a trick to this door?"

"What do you mean?"

"It won't open."

"Did you accidentally turn the lock?"

"How would I have locked it with a box in my hands?"

Cat marched over and tried the door. When it didn't open, she frowned and pulled harder on the knob. "This has never happened before. I can't imagine what could be making it—"

She stepped back, a strange expression coming over her face, and her lips parted slightly. Her eyes drifted shut a moment, and when she opened them again, she shook her head and started glancing around the room, turning slowly, as if looking for something.

"No," she intoned quietly, as if to herself. Her eyes roamed up to the ceiling, darted back around the room. "No."

"No, what?" Liam didn't know why the door wouldn't open or why Caterina had started acting strange, but he had things to do. His sense of responsibility had already cost him enough time.

She gave him a vague look—one that confused him even more. He got the distinct impression she knew exactly what was going on with the door. And why did she keep looking around the room as if she expected something to materialize out of nowhere?

Shit. Maybe she had a handful of loose coins jangling around in that pretty head of hers. Just his luck, do a good deed, and get stuck locked in a room with an unpredictable nut job. Maybe there was a trick to the door. A fault that caused it to lock when it shut, something she knew about but, for some reason, pretended to know nothing about. If that were the case, she also had to know the trick for getting it open; otherwise, she'd be getting stuck in here all the time. But what could she hope to accomplish by playing a trick on him that kept them locked in her room together? It wasn't as if she enjoyed his company, so why would she delay his leaving?

Caterina walked over to the French doors and pulled on them. They didn't open. Were they really stuck, too, or was she putting on a show for his benefit? Liam strode across the room and tried them for himself. Secured by some hidden lock, just like the other door.

What the hell? Had the woman booby-trapped her bedroom doors for some bizarre reason?

He didn't know her game, but he didn't have time to play, and seriously, if she was unhinged and this was all her doing, he didn't want to hang around to find out what she might be planning next.

Before he could confront her, she put her hands on her hips and narrowed her eyes, then said, "All right, Rosa, if you're responsible for this, just cut it out. Do you hear me?"

"What?" Liam scrunched his eyes and stared hard at her. Who the hell was Rosa? An invisible friend? Another personality? Fabulous! He was locked in a room with a deranged woman.

"I don't know what's going on here, Caterina," he said, keeping his tone even. If the woman wasn't quite right in the head, he should probably be careful about setting her off. She might have one of her chef's knives hidden in a dresser drawer. "Why don't you take a deep breath and relax? Then open the door, so I can go back to the site and work on your restaurant. Can you do that? You're anxious for me to make more progress on the job, aren't you?"

"If I could open the door, don't you think I'd have done it? And why are you talking to me like, I don't know...like you think—" She gaped at him. "You think I'm responsible for this? That I somehow made the doors seal shut so we'd be trapped in my room?"

He scratched the back of his neck. "The thought crossed my mind."

"What? You think I can lock doors without touching them?" She laughed. "Do you think I can perform magic? Or maybe you think I'm a witch or something?"

"Or something."

"Yeah, well, I'll just leave that alone for now." She sighed, pushing her hands through her shoulder-length hair and then slipping them into the pockets of her black jeans. She wasn't acting like a crazy woman now, just a dejected one, who looked as frustrated about their situation as he felt.

"Okay," she said, darting him a glance. "You might have trouble believing what I'm going to tell you, but it's the truth. I didn't lock the doors, but I'm pretty sure I know who did."

"Care to enlighten me?"

"Rosa. She's done this before."

"Okay, so where is she, and how do we get her to let us out? Is she a guest here?"

Caterina smirked. "I'm not sure guest is the right word. More like an uninvited visitor with an interfering nature. She pops in and out when she feels like it. I'm sure she's responsible and that she's someplace close by."

"In the hallway?" Liam walked over to the bedroom door, rapped on it. "Hey, Rosa, are you out there? Listen, I can appreciate a joke as much as the next guy, but I've got a lot of stuff I need to get done, so could you be a sport and unlock the door, please?"

He waited a moment but got no indication anyone was in the hall listening. He looked at Caterina. "I don't think she heard me. Maybe she's not out there." He frowned. "This Rosa, does she have all her faculties?"

"She's not crazy, if that's what you mean. And I'm sure she heard you. She's just being a brat."

"How can she hear me if she's not here?"

"Because she is here, you just can't see her."

"But you do?"

"No, I don't see her! Do you think she's able to show herself to only one person in a room and remain invisible to the other?" She stopped and seemed to ponder what she'd just said. "Well, maybe she can. I don't really know...but no, I don't see her."

Caterina was either messing with him, or she really did have some missing screws. The lucidity in her steadfast gaze made him think it was the former. He just couldn't figure out what would motivate her to play him this way, though.

Liam held up a hand. "Okay, I get it. Rosa's a ghost."

"Yes, a very meddlesome one." She gave him a slight smile. "I have to say, I'm surprised you considered anything paranormal. You're more open-minded than I was. I refused to believe in the possibility that we had a ghost living here until I was practically forced to accept her existence."

NOPE. NOT OPEN-MINDED at all, Caterina realized as she took in his expression. Bullheaded. Bullheaded with a side of getting angrier by the minute.

"Enough with the games, Caterina. I don't know why you're doing this or what you're getting out of it, but I'm not amused. Now open the damn door."

"I told you. I can't! Only Rosa can, and she won't until she gets what she wants."

"Then why don't you clue me in to what it is that your invisible, ghosty friend wants so we can end this farce?"

"First of all, she's not my invisible, ghosty friend. She's my great-aunt."

Liam glowered at her. She didn't like it, but really, could she blame him? He'd been trapped in a room with her by her dead ancestor, whom he wasn't buying, and she hadn't even told him her worst suspicion.

"Fine. I'm going to play along for a minute, but only because if I don't get out of here in the next five, I might have to break the door down. I'd prefer not to have to do that." Liam stalked toward her, stopped about a foot in front of her, and locked his sea-blues on her.

"Now, tell me, what has to happen for *Rosa* to open the door?" Sarcasm coated his words, thick as her béchamel, without any of the sauce's lovely subtlety.

Caterina caught her bottom lip between her teeth. "You have to kiss me."

Silence loomed, like a blanket of fog descending upon the Blue Ridge. It closed around her as if it would suffocate her. Pulsed. Condensed. Held her breath captive as his gaze narrowed to a tiny slit that stabbed her.

And then he laughed. Not a happy, you're a hoot, we're having a great time, kind of laugh. No, more like a *you're freaking playing with me and I don't like it,* kind of one.

"You want me to kiss you?" From his expression, you would have thought she'd asked him to trim her toenails with his teeth.

"Not particularly, no. Rosa wants it. I don't understand why. I just know she's got this weird thing about doors and…and people kissing. She pulled the same stunt with Lucia and Antonio." She started pacing, walked over to the door, and however futile, gave it another try.

"And look," she threw out, in case he had some misguided notion that any of this had been her idea, "I'm no more thrilled about it than you are, but if you want her to open that door, then... then I think that's what she's waiting for."

Liam snorted. "This is ridiculous."

Caterina crossed her arms under her breasts and stared at the floor. If her aunt weren't already dead, she'd be tempted to kill her. She'd put Cat in an intolerable position. Liam had never liked her. After this debacle, he'd be adding crazy to the list of things he held against her.

"Okay, you know what? Fine!" He threw his arms in the air, as if in defeat, and crossed the room.

Cat angled him a glance. Was he going to do it?

Liam scowled down at her, clearly unhappy about the prospect. Did he think she relished the idea? No, she didn't, but she wasn't getting all surly about it.

"Just so we're clear." He glared at her, as if to drive home the point. "I will be extremely unhappy if that door remains locked after this."

He put his hands on her shoulders and bent forward. Random electrical currents began pinging off her nerves. He brushed his mouth across hers as if it were a tabletop he was flicking a dustrag over, then straightened and reached behind her to try the door. It remained locked.

Liam's expression hardened. He rolled his jaw. "It didn't work."

The temperature in the room took a sharp dive. Cat rolled her eyes toward the ceiling. "Apparently, Rosa wasn't impressed."

"You're kidding, right?"

"No. She's not going to open the door for...for that. Did you notice the room just got much cooler? That's Rosa's doing, another one of her little tricks. I think in this case it's her way of letting us know that didn't qualify. She wanted a kiss, and that was—"

He rolled his jaw. "Was what, Caterina?"

"As kisses go, pathetic, actually. I've been kissed enough to know a good kiss from a bad kiss, and believe me, that was bad. It might have been the worst kiss I've ever gotten. I'm not surprised Rosa's disappointed. If that's the best you can do, I'm afraid we could be locked in here for—"

Liam grasped her by the shoulders and pulled her hard against his chest. "Then I guess we need to change Rosa's opinion," he said harshly.

Before she could take another breath, his mouth covered hers with a heat that came out of nowhere, burning off the chill that had permeated the room quicker than her electric skillet could melt a pat of butter.

Lightning quick, a bolt of desire caught Cat off guard and ignited a flame in her blood that roared to life. She moaned. Liam increased the pressure, moved her up against the door, worked some kind of delicious magic on her with his lips. She wrapped her arms around his back, opened her mouth to his. A hunger gnawed at her, made her feel as if she'd been starving for this—his kiss—the only thing that could satisfy her craving.

His hands glided down her rib cage and back up again. His thumbs brushed the sides of her breasts, sparking flames of desire that burned along her nerves. He moved against her, his hips pressing into hers, and dropped his mouth to her neck.

Cat let her head fall back. The pleasure of his mouth traveling over her skin—kissing, taking little nips—drove her crazy, made her want. Oh, but he was tempting. She never would have imagined Liam could make her feel so sublime, fill her with such need, or make her melt so easily for him.

Liam...Oh God! She was grinding against the bedroom door with Liam.

She laid her hands on his chest, held him away. He stepped back, short breaths coming hard, like her own, and stared at her. He'd shaken her to her core, but she didn't want him to know how devastating that kiss had been.

She sidled away from him, her mind a confused blur. As she moved aside, the door drifted open. Liam's eyes darted to hers, locked. She couldn't name the emotion she saw swirling in them, read his thoughts or feelings. And she didn't know if she wanted to.

He fisted his hands at his sides but said nothing, then turned abruptly and stormed out of the room.

CATERINA STARED AT the open doorway Liam had just escaped through. She ran her hands over her hair, brought one down, clasped it across her mouth. A tremor rippled down the length of her body. She stood there, frozen, and closed her eyes.

Hot. Reckless. And she'd liked it. Liked it as she'd never liked a man's mouth and hands on her before. Not good...not even in the same galaxy as good.

She shouldn't have baited him, telling him his first attempt was pathetic. She'd provoked him. Maybe part of her had wanted to, had wanted a taste of the raw sexuality she'd told herself she didn't like, but which tempted her nonetheless.

Her breath came fast and harshly. She tried to regulate it by taking deeper breaths. She was young and healthy, with the same needs and desires as most young, healthy women. Why, though, of all the men to cross her path, had she developed an itch for this one? She didn't particularly like him. He clearly didn't like her.

Cat snorted. Talk about understatements. He'd be furious with himself. And he probably blamed her for goading him into proving he did, in fact, know his way around a woman's lips. Her body sighed. Did he ever!

She walked to the door, closed it and then stood with her back against it. It had happened. It didn't matter that he'd stirred a craving that would go unfulfilled. Mind over matter, or in this case, over lust. She wasn't immune, but she wouldn't give in to it. She could control a misguided case of the hots.

She'd lusted after other things in life: that second helping of chocolate lava cake; a third glass of Bordeaux when two were more than enough; the dusty cocoa UGGs she wanted when she already had them in powder blue. She'd resisted them all. Just because she might want something didn't mean she was foolish enough, or indulgent enough, to give in to every little desire. She knew how to exercise self-control over things she didn't need to be happy or that weren't good for her. Like Liam Dougherty.

She pushed away from the door and walked toward the boxes sitting at the foot of the bed.

Was there any chance he hadn't been aware that she'd started grinding against him, just before she realized it herself and pushed away? Caterina grimaced. There was probably about as much chance that she hadn't been aware of his hands traveling over her body or how much she'd wanted to feel them against her bare skin.

Five

"*Do you think because you are virtuous,*
that there shall be no more cakes and ale?"
William Shakespeare, *Othello*

*L*iam got out of his truck and closed the door. He scrutinized the building as he walked across the gravel. They'd finished getting all the sheathing up and the wrap on last week. The roofers would finish tomorrow. The windows and doors were supposed to have been delivered over a week ago but still hadn't arrived. He'd scheduled far enough in advance, so they'd have them here and ready to install as soon as the roof went on, and everything could be sealed up before December hit.

He pulled his cell from his pocket and called the window company, got their voice mail.

He rolled his jaw in frustration and then left a message. "This is Liam Dougherty. I've already left two messages and haven't heard back from anyone, so I'd appreciate it if someone called me today to let me know what's going on with our order. If we don't get it soon, it's going to put us behind. If that happens, you're going to have a very unhappy customer on your hands."

He disconnected, jammed the phone back into his pocket with a mumbled curse.

"What bit your ass, bro?" Burke asked, as Liam ducked under the yellow perimeter tape.

"This is the second time this year that I've had a problem with windows not being delivered when they were promised. We were supposed to have them ten days ago. I've left three messages to find out what the delay is, and if someone doesn't get back to me today with a good reason and a guarantee that we'll have them by the end of this week, they're done."

"Shawn had a problem with them a couple of months ago. He told me that when he called to find out what was going on, the owner told him he and his wife were going through a divorce, and she'd left him with a mess to try to straighten out in the office."

Liam pulled a frown. "Everybody's got shit to deal with. If they weren't going to be able to fill the order on time, they shouldn't have taken it. Now I'm locked in. If I tried to get them from another company at this point, it'd take at least six weeks. I don't have that kind of time."

"See if you can move some of the subs up a few days, and deal with the windows when they get here."

"Yeah, you try getting a sub to change their schedule with only one or two days' notice. And forget next week with the holiday."

Burke held up his hands. "Only trying to be helpful. You don't have to get pissy about it."

"I'm not getting pissy! If those windows don't get delivered soon, and I can't switch things around, it's going to push us back another week. With Thanksgiving next week, make that two, since we're not working Thursday or Friday."

"We've all had to deal with delays before, Liam. Yeah, it sucks, but something always comes up to throw a schedule off. You know that. So, whatever's been going on with you the last few days, get over it. If you're not slamming things around, you're nitpicking over something trivial. Yesterday you reamed Elliot out because you didn't like the way he tucked the wrap near the foundation wall. In case you haven't noticed, people are starting to avoid you."

"There's nothing going on with me. And you're the last one to point a finger at someone for wanting things done right, Burke."

Liam started to push past his brother and felt his cell vibrate in his pocket. He pulled it out and looked at the screen. "You better be calling to tell me my windows are on the way," he said when he saw the number.

He swiped the screen to accept the call. "Liam Dougherty," he said in a firm tone and cast a glance at his brother.

Burke shook his head and walked away. Liam frowned after him. He wasn't the one who had Caterina, the control freak, breathing down his neck for an account of every minute of every day. And after what happened in her room the day before yesterday, he didn't particularly want to deal with her any more than he absolutely had to.

After getting a guarantee from the owner of the window company that his windows would be there on Monday, Liam ended the call, then joined his crew inside the building. If the windows arrived as promised, they could get everything sealed in before they halted work for the holiday.

He'd still need to play some catch up, but he could probably shift some of the subs, as Burke had suggested, and manage to get back on schedule. Then he wouldn't have to tell Caterina they were behind and have her trying to micromanage him.

She needed to get another job until they were done with the construction. Something to keep her busy so she'd stop trying to do his. What did she do all day, anyway?

Liam conjured an image of her sitting at the top of the attic stairs. What was in those boxes that was so damn important she couldn't wait for Antonio to take them down to her room? He'd considered turning around and leaving when he'd first seen her, before she knew he was there. But when he realized what she was attempting, he couldn't let her endanger herself that way.

Yeah, and look where that got you. Locked in her room, supposedly by some crazy ancestral ghost, with a kiss as ransom.

He didn't know what to believe about the story she'd fed him. A ghost aunt who held people hostage until they did what she wanted? It was a big pill to swallow, but he hadn't been able to figure out how Caterina could have locked the door or how it had just drifted open after Rosa supposedly got what she wanted.

And why would Caterina try to trick him into kissing her? He doubted she'd wanted to lock lips with him any more than he had with her. Not that he hadn't wondered what she'd taste like. That didn't mean he'd intended to find out. He'd just been curious.

He wasn't curious anymore. He was furious. Furious because she'd made him burn in a way he hadn't imagined possible. Not with her. Maybe not with any woman. And now, no matter how hard he tried, he couldn't wipe the taste of her from his mind. Worse, he had a dangerous craving for more.

THERE WOULD BE eleven for dinner tomorrow. Caterina would be cooking for a crowd and was glad for it.

She would make all the traditional fare because that's what everyone looked forward to, expected, and because it was tradition. But she would put her own touch on things: a twist on the stuffing for the turkey; the sweet potato casserole; add a bit of lemon and lime zest to the cranberry sauce. Just a few little tweaks to infuse some surprise to tease the palate.

Thanksgiving had always been Caterina's favorite holiday. She used to love helping her mom with the meal, breaking up bread to dress the turkey, and grinding fresh cranberries in the old, metal hand grinder that they would bolt to the side of the table and then manually turn the handle to crush the berries. Cat still used it, not because it was convenient—it wasn't—but because it was a link to her mom, a connection. It was during those times, spent with her mother in the kitchen, that her love of cooking took root.

As she headed for the kitchen to start prepping things, the front door swung open, and Burke, Liam's brother, walked into reception with a little girl in tow.

"Good morning, Burke."

No one else was in reception, so Cat stopped to see if she could help him with anything. "This is the first time I've seen you over here. Are you looking for your brother?"

"Hey, Caterina. No, for Antonio. I've got a remodeling job starting up next month that I brought him in on. I thought if he was around I could grab a few minutes to talk to him about it."

"He's not here. He and Lucia volunteered to pick up some of the stuff I need for tomorrow's meal, so I could do the baking and some of the prep work. They probably won't be back for at least another hour. Do you want me to have him call you later?"

He shook his head. "That's okay. I'll catch up with him next week."

"So, who's this?" Cat asked, smiling down at the adorable girl holding Burke's hand. She had his eyes, the same blue-green that his brother had as well, but dark hair, inherited from her mother no doubt, as Burke's was blond, like Liam's. It made for a stunning combination. Burke would probably have his hands full fending off the boys when she got older. She was going to be a beauty.

"This is Riley. She's—"

His cell phone rang, and he glanced down at the screen. "Sorry. It's one of our clients. Do you mind?"

Caterina shook her head. "Take it," she said, waving a hand in the air.

84

Burke listened a moment, frowned. "I'm sorry he's giving you a hard time, Mrs. Fey. Let me see what I can do. I think the county offices close at one today because of the holiday, but I'll shoot over there now to see what I can do, okay?"

He listened again. Cat could hear a woman's voice on the other end. She couldn't make out the words, but from her tone she sounded quite distressed.

"I know it's upsetting," Burke said soothingly, "but I'll get it straightened out. The stairway is supposed to be grandfathered, so he shouldn't be able to do that. Just hang tight, and I'll call you as soon as I know something."

He disconnected a moment later and shook his head.

"Problem?" Cat asked.

"County inspector put a stop work order on one of our jobs. Shawn's the lead on it, but he took the day off, so he could go with his wife to her obstetrics appointment, which is why the client called me. Now I'm going to have to go talk to the chief inspector to see what I can do."

Burke looked down at Riley and sighed. "I'm really sorry, honey, but we're not going to be able to go to Chuck E. Cheese's for lunch. I've got to take care of a problem for work, and unfortunately, you're going to have to come with me. But I'll make it up to you, okay? I promise I'll take you another time."

Riley looked down at her feet. "It's okay," she said with an accepting but disappointed sigh. "Am I going to be bored out of my gourd?"

Caterina bit back a chuckle. She didn't want to make light of the girl's feelings, despite finding her question amusing. How many times had Burke had to drag her on an appointment and used that expression as a warning, she wondered, only to try to make it up to his daughter later?

"I'm afraid you might be, but I don't have any other option. Aunt Becca and Uncle Shawn had to go to the baby doctor, and I don't know anyone else I could leave you with for a couple of hours on such short notice."

Riley sighed again. Cat's heart went out to the girl. She could envision her sitting in a stuffy office, full of adults, with nothing to do while her dad tried to deal with work problems. No *might* about it, she'd absolutely be bored out of her gourd.

"If you'd like," she offered without giving it any more thought, "you could leave her here with me and pick her up after you deal with the problem. I'm going to be here all day making cookies and doing some other baking for the holiday, and I'd love having a helper in the kitchen."

"Seriously?" Burke asked. "You wouldn't mind?"

"No, of course not. I love kids, and if she'd rather stay here, I'd be happy for the company."

Riley was looking up at him like she wasn't sure but thought maybe she'd just been granted a reprieve much more to her liking.

Burke got down on his haunches, on her level. "Would you like to stay here and bake cookies with Miss Caterina, Riley, or do you want to come with me? It's your choice."

"Oh, I'd much rather bake cookies," she blurted without hesitation. "I like being with you and everything, but, well…"

"It's okay, pumpkin." Burke leaned forward and kissed her forehead. "It doesn't hurt my feelings if you'd rather stay here than go to some boring office with me. To tell you the truth, I'd much rather stay here and make cookies, too, but I have to take care of this problem."

"'Cause you're an adult and sometimes adults have 'sponsibilities they gots to take care of."

"Right." He tapped her on the end of the nose and then stood back up and faced Cat again.

"I shouldn't be more than two hours, three at the most if they give me a problem."

"Don't worry about it. Like I said, I don't have any other plans for the day, so we'll just be here making magic in the kitchen."

"Do you know magic?" Riley asked, her eyes going wide.

"Cooking is like magic," Cat said, smiling broadly at Riley's expression. "Would you like me to show you how?" She held out a hand.

Riley nodded enthusiastically and, giving a wave to Burke, skipped across the reception area and wove her fingers through Cat's.

"Okay then. I guess I'm old news when there's magic brewing." Burke winked at Cat. In looks, anyone seeing him and Liam together would easily guess they were brothers, but Cat thought the similarity ended there. She'd never met their brother Shawn but guessed there'd be a strong resemblance there as well.

Burke seemed easygoing, friendly, approachable. From her limited exposure to him, she liked him. She could say none of those things about Liam and wondered what had happened in his life that made him the way he was.

"WOULD YOU LIKE to do the other one by yourself?" They were putting together pumpkin rolls that would go on tomorrow's dessert table. Her mother had always made them for the holidays, so she kept up the tradition. Caterina had made the sponge cakes the day before, but she and Riley had made the cream cheese filling together and were now finishing them off.

"Sure." Riley unrolled the cake log the way Cat had shown her and peeled off the wax paper that kept it from sticking to itself. Scooping up a large dollop of the filling, she slathered it on the cake, glancing up at Caterina every few seconds for confirmation that she was doing it correctly.

"You're doing a great job, Riley. Are you sure you've never made these before?"

"I never did. I never even baked anything else either." She held the tip of her tongue against her upper lip, concentrating intently on the job at hand, scooping up more filling, and spreading until she'd managed to cover the entire cake.

"Can I roll it up like the other one too?"

"Go for it. When you're done, we'll wrap them in plastic wrap and put them in the refrigerator. Tomorrow, when it's time to set out desserts, I'll sprinkle them with confectioners' sugar to make them pretty."

When the second roll was complete, Riley ran her finger around the empty mixing bowl to scrape up the remnants of cream. "My dad lets me make waffles in the toaster, but this is more fun." She licked the filling off her finger and then looked up at Cat with an impish grin.

"I'm a big fan of toaster waffles myself." Cat pulled a box of plastic wrap out of the long drawer on the work island and tore off two pieces. "I like to cover mine with fruit and whipped cream. What about you?"

"I only had them plain, but I like whipped cream. Maybe my dad will buy some and I can try that."

"You only put syrup on them?" Cat asked, as she wrapped the pumpkin rolls in plastic.

"No." Riley shook her head. "Just toasted."

Who ate toaster waffles plain? Were her parents trying to limit her sugar intake?

After putting the pumpkin rolls in the refrigerator, Cat returned to the island and pulled the two trays of macaroons forward that had been cooling there after she and Riley made them. Cat had let Riley form the cookies before putting them into the oven. If she'd done it herself, they'd all be the exact same size, measured out and leveled off, in perfect rows, precise.

As it was, no two looked the same. Some were the size of grapes, some of golf balls, and a few were big enough to share. A few others were flattened like pancakes and had turned out to be macaroon crisps instead of the soft, chewy cookies most people were used to.

Cat had caught herself about to reshape Riley's cookies as she made them, pretty them up, even them out, when she'd been struck with a memory of one of her own first baking experiences. Mom had let her make a cake for a Fourth of July party. She'd only been a couple of years older than Riley was now. She didn't remember if it had come out lopsided or tasted any good, but she did remember how proud she'd felt that she'd done it on her own.

"Do we get to put chocolate on these now like you said?" Riley asked.

"Yep. We're going to dip some of them in chocolate, and we'll leave some plain. That's what this is for." Cat reached for the chocolate she'd had warming in a small melting pot on the side of the island. "I'll do the first one to show you how, and then you're on your own, kid."

She took one of the cookies, turned it upside down, dipped the top into the chocolate, and gave it a slight swirl to prevent drips as she lifted it out. She put it on a piece of parchment and then slid the pot of chocolate closer to Riley.

"Your turn, sweetie."

Riley took a cookie and plunged the top into the chocolate, getting as much on her fingers as she did the macaroon. She put it on the paper, dripping chocolate on the island as she transferred it, and then scratched her nose with the back of her hand, leaving a trail of the chocolate on her cheek and upper lip. What remained on her fingers she licked off.

"How's that?" Riley, a chocolate-faced munchkin, beamed up at Cat with pure delight shining from her beautiful, aquamarine eyes.

"I couldn't have done it any better." Cat ran a hand over Riley's hair. "It's perfect."

Riley's face lit up, and she reached for another cookie to dip.

"Thanks for helping me today, Riley. I hope you're having a good time because you've certainly made it more fun for me."

"Yes." Riley's head bobbed up and down emphatically. "I'm having a great time. Daddy lets me help make stuff sometimes too. I'm not allowed to use the sharp knives yet or cook on the stove, but he lets me do toast and make sandwiches and stuff like that. But this is way funner."

"I'm glad you're having fun. I used to love spending time in the kitchen with my mother when I was growing up: cooking, baking, learning the names of all the different spices and what they tasted like, how different ingredients could completely change the taste of something. When I say cooking is a kind of magic, it's true."

Cat picked up one of the macaroons, gave it a quick swirl in the melted chocolate, and instead of putting it on the parchment to let the chocolate firm up, bit into it with a moan of delight. "You take a few unrelated ingredients, some that don't taste good alone, but you mix them together, bake them, and then—"

She leaned lower, close to Riley. "Magic," she whispered with reverence and a wink for the girl. "Sweet, chewy, delicious, golden-brown mounds of magic."

Riley giggled. "Can I have one?"

Cat straightened and slung a hand on her hip. "Well, of *course* you can! You were the chef, after all."

Riley followed Cat's example, although her swirl was more of a dunking that included most of her fingers again. She took a bite, chewed, and looked up with a dimpled grin that pierced Cat's heart and filled it with longing. She wanted a child of her own someday, and if she could place an order, one like this would suit her fine.

"These are yummy!" Riley finished her cookie, then stuck her fingers in her mouth and proceeded to suck off the chocolate that hadn't found its way to her upper lip, her chin, or the tip of her nose.

"We'll pack some in a tin for you to take home to share with your mom and dad since, like I said, you were the chef, after all. I'll bet they'll be super proud of what a great job you did making them. You can take some of the pumpkin roll, too, since you did all the filling and rolling. And I'll give you a bag of the sugar you need to sprinkle on top to make it look prettier."

Cat reached into one of the cabinets under the island, where she kept an assortment of containers, and pulled out a tin large enough to hold a dozen cookies and half of a pumpkin roll. She got a sandwich baggie out of the drawer, put about a half cup of confectioners' sugar in it, and set it beside the container.

"I don't gots a mom," Riley said matter-of-factly, as she continued dipping and lining up cookies on the parchment. "She had to go to heaven when I was little, but Daddy's not going to believe I did these by myself. He'll be as proud as Peter. He's a peacock! Daddy read me about them in *Peter the Peacock*, and Peter's the proudest of all the animals."

Riley licked more chocolate from her fingers, errantly wiped a little more down the side of her chin. "He likes to strut. Sometimes when I do something good my dad says he's proud as Peter Peacock, and he does this—"

She slid off the stool Cat had pulled over to the island, so Riley would be high enough to work there, put her hands on her hips, puffed up her chest, stuck her nose in the air, and, taking sweeping steps, pranced to the end of the island and back. "That's how you strut. I didn't know how, but Daddy showed me. He's funny when he does it."

Cat stared down at Riley, still absorbing that this adorable child had just told her she didn't have a mother. "Wow," she said, buying herself a moment to collect her thoughts. "That's some good strutting."

"Thanks. l can teach you if you want me to."

"Well...I...yeah, that would be great!" How else, Caterina thought, does one respond to a motherless little girl, who's just offered to show you how to strut your stuff, with all the sincerity of an angel?

LIAM STOOD JUST outside the opening to the kitchen, gaping at the sight in front of him. He couldn't remember ever having been so confused about what he was feeling, and his muddled brain was the reason his feet were still rooted to the floor. His mouth hung wordlessly open as he watched Caterina Bonavera follow his daughter around a large center island in the middle of the Bonaveras' cavernous kitchen.

They started around the far end, and Riley looked back over her shoulder, watching Caterina. "You're doing great!" she said with a giggle, as if she were cheering her on.

"Well, that's because I've got such a great teacher. Maybe you should—" Caterina looked up at that moment and saw him standing in the doorway. She came to a sudden stop and inhaled sharply, clearly surprised and, he guessed, not happy that he'd caught her with her hair down, so to speak. No, not the meticulous, always-in-control, Caterina Bonavera. She did still have her nose in the air—at least some things remained consistent.

"If you're looking for Antonio, he isn't here," she said, and Riley turned to see who Caterina had spoken to.

"Daddy!"

Riley dashed toward him. Liam bent low, caught her, and then scooped her up. She wrapped her arms around his neck and hugged him.

"Hi, pumpkin." He ruffled her hair, told himself to stay calm and hold what he had to say to Caterina until Riley wasn't there to hear it. He didn't want to upset her, and it wasn't his daughter's fault his brother had left her with one of the last people Liam would trust to look after her.

He glanced back at Caterina. She was the one standing with her mouth open now, looking at him as if he'd just sprouted a few more heads.

"You're...Riley's...father?" She shook her head as if trying to clear it. "I thought...I thought Burke..."

So, she hadn't known, had assumed for some reason that Burke was Riley's dad. Would she have offered to let Riley stay with her while his brother dealt with the Fey's problem if she'd known the truth?

"Daddy, I teached Miss Caterina how to strut like a peacock. And we made rolled-up pumpkin cakes, and I made cookies all by myself. They have chocolate tops, and we get to take some home 'cause she said I was the chef after all."

"Really? I'll bet you did a great job, chocolate face." He wet his thumb and rubbed it across the tip of her nose, over her chin, but only managed to wipe off a thin layer.

Liam wasn't happy that Riley had spent the last several hours here, but clearly, she felt proud and excited about what she'd done. He didn't want to take away from that. And, from what he could tell, no harm had come to her.

"I did. Miss Caterina said she couldn't have done a better job. She's a chef, and she knows how to do magic, and I got to do some."

"Magic, huh?" Caterina Bonavera doing card tricks and playing at disappearing coins didn't quite jive with his image of her.

Riley nodded fervently. "We're going to make pies too." She looked at Caterina. "Maybe my dad can help us and see about the magic."

"Well, I..." Caterina looked at a loss for words. He guessed she was as anxious for him to leave as he was to take Riley and get the hell out of there.

"We need to get going, Riley." Liam lifted her down to the floor. "I'm sure Miss Caterina has a lot to do to get ready for Thanksgiving. And you and I need to go to the grocery store on our way home to pick up something to take to Aunt Becca and Uncle Shawn's house tomorrow."

"Can't we make a pie first? I never maked one, ever!"

"Not today, Riley. It's getting late, and we have errands to run."

Caterina walked to the end of the island and angled her head toward his daughter. "It sounds like you need to get going, Riley, but thanks for all your help today. I think your cookies are going to be a big hit with my guests tomorrow."

"Are you going to tell them I made them?"

"Absolutely!"

Riley smiled lightly. "They probably aren't going to believe it 'cause I'm only four."

"They might have a hard time, but I'll make sure they know you were the chef."

"Well, sorry I gotta go, so I can't help you make the pies."

Caterina waved a hand in the air. "That's okay. You were already a huge help."

"Maybe I can come here again sometime, and we can make some pies then."

Caterina stared at his daughter a moment. "Maybe, honey," she said softly. Liam's gut clenched. He didn't know what he would have preferred her to say, but he didn't want Riley thinking of this woman as her new friend.

He leaned down. "Go on out to the porch and wait for me, sweetie. I need to talk to Miss Caterina for a minute, and then I'll be right out."

Riley looked at him, and he thought for a minute she might question him, but to his relief she only nodded.

She started to go but turned back and waved to Caterina. "Bye."

Caterina lifted a hand. "Bye, Riley."

Liam watched Riley walk across the lobby and out the front door. When it clicked shut, he turned back around. It was unlikely that his daughter would see Caterina again. He didn't take her to work with him except on those rare cases when there was no one to look after her, and he absolutely had to be on site that day. The only reason she'd been with Burke that day was because the day-care had closed for the holiday, and Liam had a meeting with a lawyer that he needed to go to.

The crew was only scheduled to work a half day today, and neither he nor Burke needed to be there. His brother had offered to watch Riley, so Liam could keep his appointment.

He'd scheduled the meeting after getting a letter from a lawyer Sylvie's parents had hired, notifying him that they intended to file for custody of Riley. He'd been stunned and thought they were crazy, but after he got over the shock, he'd decided to talk to his own lawyer rather than take any chances that they might pull something over on him that could hurt his daughter.

Caterina looked uncomfortable. They hadn't seen each other since the day they'd been locked in her room. The day the taste of her lips had been seared into his memory, as if someone had burned it there with a hot branding iron. He wished he could shake it, wished he could block the itch that kiss had stirred—the one he'd be crazy to give in to.

Especially now, with Sylvie's parents threatening to try to take Riley from him. Not that they stood any chance of getting her. His lawyer had basically assured him that without good cause, they didn't have a case. They'd never liked him and even blamed him for Sylvie's death. But to try to take Riley away from him...he still couldn't believe they'd go so far.

He'd think about that later, when his thoughts weren't clouded with the image of Caterina Bonavera strutting around her kitchen counter with his daughter, and Riley laughing and cheering her on, as if she were having the time of her life.

Liam shifted. "My brother shouldn't have left Riley with you. It was an imposition and won't happen again."

"She was no bother. I enjoyed her company."

"If I'd known he had to leave her with someone, I'd have made other arrangements. I never would have agreed if he'd called to tell me he was going to—" Liam frowned, considering his words.

"To leave her with me?" Caterina said, finishing what he'd been going to say before he realized how ungrateful it sounded.

"Riley was Burke's responsibility this morning, not yours. I only leave her with family or people I trust enough to—" That hadn't come out any better. "Look, let's just forget it. My brother shouldn't have left her with someone else without talking to me first, but he did, so thanks for keeping an eye on her."

The look in her eyes sliced into him, and he hated it. She wasn't supposed to have feelings he could hurt. She was supposed to be an insensitive, self-absorbed control freak, who only cared about herself.

He turned away from her, walked through the reception area to leave, anxious to be anywhere else but there. When he got to the door, he saw Caterina had followed him out and was walking across the room after him. She carried one of those round metal tins people usually put cookies or candy in.

"These are Riley's. I told her she could have them since she made them. She forgot to take them when she went out to the porch." She held the container out for him to take, and he hesitated, torn between an overwhelming desire to haul her into his arms and kiss her and an equally strong one to get the hell out of there before he did.

Caterina closed her eyes a moment, and he saw her lashes flutter. When she looked at him again, she said, "They're not poison, Liam."

The vulnerability he heard in her voice did him in. He reached for the container with one hand and pulled her toward him with the other. He didn't think—just acted—kissing her because he needed to, and any thoughts that he was making a mistake were trampled to dust beneath his desire.

He had to taste her one more time. Needed to feel her body against his, her mouth opening for him, no refusal. He felt it soften, and something roared to life inside him—a need he couldn't seem to control, pagan and demanding, just like the last time he'd kissed her.

Caterina whimpered, and he slanted his mouth again, and again, and again, unable to satisfy the desire raging through his blood like a warrior with a need to conquer. To make her his.

"Oh...well..."

They broke apart.

"I didn't mean to interrupt." Marcella stood in the opening that led from the reception area to the hallway. "I'm just..." She pointed toward the solarium. "Going in there."

Liam glanced at Caterina, then away. He should probably have said something but couldn't think straight enough to risk what might come out of his mouth. She'd confused him. Again.

She could have said something, but she looked as confounded as he did. No wonder. He'd basically said he didn't trust her, and then kissed her as if she were a filet mignon and he a starving carnivore who wanted to devour her. Talk about mixed signals.

"Riley's waiting for me," he managed to get out somewhat coherently, latching onto his best excuse to bolt and then doing just that.

CATERINA STOOD WITH her mouth hanging open, the same way she had after they'd locked lips in her room, and he'd walked out on her in a similar fashion. Her heart felt like it raced at a million and some odd beats a minute. Who was that man who had just kissed her so passionately? Kissed her as if he'd wanted to, needed to, and hadn't—wouldn't have stopped if his life were being threatened...except that her sister had walked into the lobby to find them consumed by a mutual insanity. An insanity that had taken possession, with God only knew what consequences she'd be dealing with because of it.

She puffed out a gush of air to kick-start her breathing again and headed back to the kitchen.

"I didn't know you and Liam were a thing." Marcella called after her as she went through the solarium, and Cat saw her sister angling to follow in her direction.

"We're not." She kept walking. "And don't ask, because I have no idea what that was about, and I don't want to talk about it."

"Okay. What do you want to talk about?"

"Nothing. My brain stopped working a few minutes ago, and I don't think I'm capable of conversation right now."

Marcella followed Cat into the kitchen.

"I came down to see if you needed help getting anything ready for tomorrow," she said. "We don't have to talk if you don't feel like it. Just tell me what still needs to be done, and I'll pretend I never saw anything. Unless you're in a state of shock or something and really do want to talk, but just don't know it yet."

Caterina pushed her fingers through her hair and groaned. "Oh, Cel, I have no idea what just happened. I'm so confused. I'm just so, so confused when it comes to that man! He doesn't like me. I don't know why, but he doesn't. He doesn't even try to hide it. And then he turns around and kisses me out of nowhere and it's... it's craziness!"

Marcella walked over and wrapped an arm around her in a half hug. "Good crazy or bad crazy?"

"Bad! Of course, it's bad! I mean...why would he do that? He doesn't try to hide that he thinks I'm lacking somehow, and he practically warned me away from his daughter...as if he thought he couldn't trust me around her."

"Liam has a daughter?"

"Yes. I didn't know either, until about fifteen minutes ago. She spent the morning baking with me, and she's the most adorable little girl ever. I can't believe she's his daughter. I thought she was Burke's, but that's a whole other story. The point is, when he found out his brother left her with me, he got all upset because...I guess because he just doesn't like me. And maybe he thought I'd take his surliness toward me out on his daughter." She huffed. "Like I'd ever do anything to hurt a child."

"I doubt he thought you'd hurt her."

"I don't know, Cel, and that's not even the point."

"I get the point, Cat. I think you're overlooking the obvious, though. I don't think Liam can help himself. He's attracted to you. We've all seen it—me, El, Luch. Even Antonio made a comment the other night about the two of you dancing around each other. You two are the only ones who don't want to recognize what's going on."

Cat put her hands on the island to steady her racing thoughts. "That wasn't the first time."

"What wasn't?"

"That he kissed me. It wasn't the first time."

Marcella raised her brows, and Caterina told her about Liam bringing the boxes down from the attic, and how afterward, Rosa locked them in Cat's bedroom together and held them ransom there until Liam kissed her.

"So now, in addition to not liking me, he thinks I'm a flake. A flake who forced him to kiss me by somehow locking the bedroom door with, I don't know…with trickery of some kind and then blamed it on a ghost."

Cat looked at her twin. "And you know what, when you think about it from his perspective, no wonder he was worried about Riley being left alone with me."

"Maybe, but that doesn't explain why he kissed you again today. You did indicate he initiated it, right?"

"Oh, he initiated it! And I guess that's why I'm having such a hard time understanding his motivation. That, and because it was different from the first time."

"In what way?"

"I don't know how to describe it, but I felt something I've never felt with another man. I didn't want him to stop, Cel. It was passionate and full of need, in a sexually needy way, which I've felt to some degree when other men kissed me. But it went beyond that. I felt connected to him, a connection I never would have expected and can't explain. It caught me so off guard, because—"

Caterina let out a shaky breath. "Because this time…this time it was as if I could taste my future in it."

"And that," Marcella said softly, "scared you."

Cat closed her eyes, swallowed the truth in her sister's words. "To death."

Six

"Pull up a chair. Take a taste. Come join us.
Life is so endlessly delicious."

Ruth Reichl

*N*ovember gave way to December and the first snow of the season, a couple of inches that coated the grounds of the winery just in time for *Tastes of the Season*. Bonavera Winery had participated in the annual holiday open house tour since its inception over a decade ago. It was a fun, festive event, and the winery was always a popular stop on the tour.

Cat and her sisters had spent the last two days decorating the guest house inside and out. In keeping with their mother's tradition, evergreen garland, strung with white lights, graced the wide front doors and porch rails. It was attached to the posts with bright red bows that added a cheerful splash of color where it draped gracefully from one stately white column to the next.

Their mom had always decorated two trees inside—one for the entrance and one for the library. She would search and search for the two largest trees she could find and then would have to have them delivered because she couldn't get them home on top of her car.

Caterina looked from the massive evergreen standing to the left of the library's stone fireplace to the equally giant one next to the front entrance. She smiled lightly. Lucia was following right in Mom's footsteps.

The open house was one of the most popular events of the year, with a week of tours and celebrations taking place at a different venue each night. This year's schedule would commence on Monday, with the Bonavera Winery and Guest House to host Thursday night.

She and her sisters agreed that they should get the trees decorated this weekend. They would all be too busy next week to find a big enough block of time when they'd all be available to get it done.

Cat eyed the huge library tree again. They might need Saturday *and* Sunday to get them done, even with Antonio helping this year.

She would make most of the hors d'oeuvres and finger desserts for the event the day before and prep whatever would need heated up just before the festivities. She'd reserve Thursday for any last-minute prep, and to take care of any finishing touches.

She lifted the top flap on one of the boxes stacked in front of the tree that she knew was filled with an assortment of ornaments and peered inside. They were going to need some tall ladders to hang anything on the upper third of the branches. And if Lucia had something creative planned to decorate the tops, Cat wondered how she intended to accomplish it without the aid of a forklift.

"I decided we're having a tree-decorating party tonight," Eliana pronounced, as she whisked into the lobby from the hallway and into the library like a high-end Ferrari with its engine still purring. "When I saw those two hunks from the tree farm delivering these behemoths this morning, I thought, what a perfect excuse for a party."

"I didn't realize you needed an excuse," Marcella, who sat on one of the library couches, glanced up and said, then continued arranging silver and gold ornamental balls in a large, sparkling glass bowl on the coffee table.

Cat chuckled. It was true. El never needed much of a reason to organize a get-together, and in this case, Caterina liked the idea. It would make the job of decorating go much quicker, and it would be a chance to get together with some friends she hadn't seen in a while at a festive time of year.

"I missed the hunks," Cat said. "Maybe you can invite them back for the party. We're probably going to need some strong arms to steady the trees when Lucia tries to scale the trunks to get up to the tops, so she can decorate them."

Eliana gave a shout of laughter. "Like Lucia would ever attempt anything like that. She'll send Marcella up. She's the nature child." She turned toward their sister. "Didn't you win some tree-climbing thing at that summer camp we went to for a couple of years when we were kids, Cel? The monkey challenge or something?"

"Yeah," Marcella said drolly. "The same year you won the award for the most prepubescent eyelash batting when in the presence of boys."

Eliana fluttered her lashes. "Practice, darling. You might want to try it sometime. You might be surprised how many men will start opening doors for you with just a glance."

"I'll keep that in mind in case my arms suddenly become useless and I can't open them for myself, thanks." Marcella rolled her eyes at El, but they both laughed.

"Okay, seriously," Eliana said, "I'm going to start texting people. Should I tell them to come over around five or six?"

"Say six." Caterina pulled her phone out of her back pocket and clicked on her contact list. "I'll make some hearty appetizers, enough that people can make a meal of them, and I've got some desserts leftover from Thanksgiving in the freezer that I can thaw. There are a few people in my contacts who'd probably come on short notice if they don't already have plans."

She turned to Marcella. "Do you have anyone to add to the list?"

Marcella gave her a look.

"Okay, silly question," Cat said, "but don't think you're going to sneak off to your room and read. It's a family tradition to decorate the trees together."

"It's not like anyone would notice if I ducked out after things got going."

"We'd notice," Eliana said.

"Okay fine, I'll be there. I'll even take care of the wine if you tell me what you're going to make, Cat."

"What's going on?" Lucia asked as she strode into the library.

"We're planning a tree-decorating party for tonight," Caterina said. "El's idea."

"Sounds like fun. If we're able to get the trees decorated tonight, that would free up the rest of the weekend for other stuff we need to take care of. I'll see if Jenna and Rus can come, and if it's okay, I'll see if there's anyone Antonio wants to invite."

"We can use all the help we can get," Eliana said. "And if he knows any big, strong men, tell him to call them and bribe them with beer or something."

Lucia and Eliana agreed that they'd give Caterina a head count no later than three, so she could plan how much food to make. They all knew there'd be extra for late responders or the unexpected tagalong. No one would care, and if they ended up having too much, they could eat the leftovers over the weekend.

"Hey, Cat," Lucia asked as the four of them sat on the library floor unpacking the boxes of decorations, "how's your research going? Have you learned anything interesting about Rosa?"

"No, not a lot. I found birth and death records for her and her parents and a record of Rosa and Gino's marriage. That's all public record stuff, so nothing significant. I also found a couple of newspaper stories about the murder. And I started a family tree. Anne, one of the librarians at the Purcellville branch, has been helping me out. She suggested doing one to see where it might lead."

Eliana dug into a box and pulled out a square red tin decorated with poinsettias. "Did you tell her you're researching a ghost?"

"No. I just told her I wanted to find out more about our ancestors since they built the original house where we live. She's been very helpful so far. I don't want to give her a reason to start avoiding me."

"You never know. She might find it interesting. Oh! Look!" Eliana held up a frosted white glass angel with glittering wings. "I've always loved these. I think they're my favorites."

Marcella shifted beside Cat, then said, "Rosa paid Cat another visit a few weeks ago."

Caterina elbowed her twin. She hadn't told Lucia or Eliana about being locked in her bedroom with Liam. They didn't know anything about the kiss he had to give her, so Rosa would set him free. And they knew nothing of the one Marcella had walked in on that had Cat's mind locked in a continuous loop of torment over her increasingly confused feelings about him.

"I seriously believe when she started messing with me it was because she wanted to get me and Antonio together. I don't know why, but looking back, it sure seems that way. But why do you think she's been singling you out lately?" Lucia asked.

"I have no idea," Cat said, "but if she's trying to play matchmaker between me and Liam, she's set herself an impossible task!"

"Why would you think Liam has anything to do with it?" Lucia asked.

"Because she locked the two of them in Cat's bedroom together," Marcella said.

Caterina rolled her eyes. You never handed her sisters a bone. They'd chew it, and chew it, until they got to the marrow, every time.

"Well, that sounds familiar." Lucia scrutinized her a moment. "When she locked Antonio and me in the kitchen, she wouldn't let us out until I agreed to hear him out..." Her mouth curved dreamily. "And you all know where that led."

"So, why'd Rosa lock you and Liam in your room?" Eliana asked. "And more importantly, what did you have to do to get her to let you out?"

There was no hope for it, Cat knew. They weren't going to drop it until they got all the details, so she told them.

"Oh my God, that hunk of gorgeous man kissed you!" Eliana stared at Caterina in expectation.

"Twice," her traitorous twin said from beside her. "I found them locking lips in the lobby the day before Thanksgiving."

Cat scowled at Marcella. "Thanks, Benedict Arnold. If I'd wanted the world to know, I would have posted it on Facebook."

"We're not the world, Cat. We're your sisters, and it's only right that we should know when you're getting involved with someone." Lucia pulled a pretty, floral box out of the cardboard one she'd been going through. "What if we didn't approve of him? I do, by the way, in case you were wondering, and it appears Rosa does too."

Caterina shook her head forcefully. "Just stop right there, before any of you blow this out of proportion. Liam and I are not involved! He doesn't even like me!" She pushed her fingers through her hair and sighed. "The kiss meant nothing."

"Kisses," Marcella said.

Cat groaned and threw her twin a scowl. "Kisses. The kisses meant nothing. The first was because Rosa held the man hostage. He had no choice. And the second...that was...I don't know, a mistake. One he's probably been beating himself up over since it happened."

Her sisters regarded her with varying degrees of humor. Obviously, they didn't believe her. They were wrong. Even if her feelings toward Liam had softened after meeting Riley and learning he was a single father, Cat doubted he'd ever change his opinion of her enough that they could even be friends—forget anything more. And nothing she, her sisters, or the dead might want would make a difference.

Eliana tossed the ornament she'd been holding from one hand to the other. "I've got a feeling that things around here are going to get much more interesting." She grinned broadly. "And I can't wait to see how they unfold."

"MISS CAT!"

Caterina spun around. She froze when she saw Riley standing on the other side of the library. Beside her, holding the girl's hand, stood Liam.

She felt a rush of excitement. *Desire.* She couldn't deny it, so she silently cursed it. Would she never learn? Was it her curse to be attracted to men who were all wrong for her?

Liam had begun to monopolize her thoughts. She tried not to think about him, but it did no good. Wonderings about him always crept back in—a burglar, stealing into her dreams, picking the lock to the secret stash of her desires, revealing what she'd sought to keep hidden from him.

He stirred up every longing she'd tried to suffocate in her treacherous body. Sparked a restless craving that begged for the satisfaction of his touch. Insanity, yes, but she didn't seem to have any control over it—and by the way, why the hell was *he* here?

Riley smiled and waved, as if she was excited to see her, and Cat's heart melted. How could it not? The child was adorable and sweet, and during the short amount of time they'd spent together, she and Riley had formed an affectionate bond.

This was supposed to have been a fun night, but Liam's presence put her on edge. That was no excuse to ignore Riley, though. She was just a kid, and Cat had an especially soft spot for children.

She walked across the room. She could put her feelings about Liam aside long enough to say hello to his daughter. She would even, for Riley's sake, try to play nice with him.

"Hi, Riley. What a nice surprise to see you again." Cat gave the girl an affectionate smile, one that required no forcing. "Did you come to help decorate our trees?"

Riley nodded. "We never went to a tree party before. Daddy said I might be able to help put things on the tree."

"Absolutely. In fact, I need someone to be in charge of hanging the candy canes. They can't be hung too high because next Thursday there will be a lot of kids coming here for an open house, and they all get to take a candy cane home. Some of the kids will be little, like one or two, and they won't be able to get one if they're too high."

Cat rubbed a finger over her chin while looking at Riley. "It's a big job. We have two trees and over a hundred candy canes to hang, but if you think you could handle it, it would be a huge help."

"I can do it," Riley assured her with a confident nod. "And I promise I won't hang them too high."

"Super!" Cat reached out and gave Riley's shoulder a light squeeze. "There are a couple of other children around your age here tonight, and I'll bet some of them would have fun helping you."

Riley gave her father a big-toothed grin. "I'm going to be in charge of the candy canes, Daddy. It's kind of important, so maybe you can take a picture on your phone, so we can look at it later."

"I think I'll do that." Liam winked at her, a playful gesture that didn't fit the image Caterina had cast him in.

Who was this doting, loving father? This man with a teasing side, who read his daughter bedtime stories and strutted like a peacock to amuse her. Caterina wondered.

Realizing her mouth had drifted open, she snapped it shut. Liam looked at her. For a moment, she just stared at him and then acknowledged him for the first time that evening with a head nod. "Liam," she said.

He glanced at Riley again then back to Cat. "Antonio called me this afternoon and asked if I could come over to help out tonight. He said there'd be a shortage of men, and if I could make it, he'd appreciate an extra pair of hands."

"To do what?"

"I don't know. He asked for help, so I came."

Cat wondered if there was more to Antonio's invite, especially given her conversation with her sisters earlier that day. She'd find out later, but Liam was here with his daughter, and it was supposed to be a festive event.

"Well, thanks for coming then," she said, trying to be a cordial hostess. "I hope you both enjoy yourselves. There's food and drinks in the solarium if you and Riley want to get something before we start on the trees." She focused back on his daughter. "I think that's where the other kids are too, Riley. Maybe you can introduce yourself and ask if they want to be on candy cane duty with you."

Riley agreed happily. "Okay. Daddy said there would probably be dessert, and if there was, I could have some."

Cat laughed. "There's plenty of dessert, sweetheart." She slid Liam a glance, unable to hold back a grin or hide her delight with this endearing girl. "Since your dad allows, go help yourself, and I'll see you a little later."

When it came time to begin decorating the trees, Lucia suggested splitting up into two groups, one to decorate the lobby tree, the other, the one in the library. She delegated Antonio to the library group and Liam to the lobby group, saying each group needed to have at least one tall, strong man on it. Then she had everyone else count off by twos.

"One," Caterina said, when it was her turn, and narrowed her eyes at her sister when the counting concluded, and Lucia assigned all the *ones* to work on the lobby tree.

She sidled up to Lucia when they all went into the library to retrieve their boxes of ornaments. "That was not a coincidence," she said under her breath. "You intentionally put me with Liam's group."

"There are only two groups, sis. It was a fifty-fifty chance. Don't be such a conspiracy theorist."

"I'm not. I know you, Luch. And I suspect you put Antonio up to calling Liam and telling him he needed his help tonight."

"Why would I do that? Antonio doesn't have a lot of male friends in the States yet. Is it so hard to believe he might have called Liam because he's one of the few guys he knows well enough to invite?"

"And said he needed his help? Yes. If Antonio had just wanted to invite a friend, he'd be more likely to say something like, 'Hey, we're having some friends over. Why don't you come on by?' Telling Liam he could use another man's help sounds more like an arm-twisting tactic to ensure he'd come. Something one of my sisters might come up with."

"You're so suspicious."

Caterina smirked. "With good reason, I think."

It didn't turn out to be as bad as she'd anticipated. Liam and two of the other men put up the lights. Cat had to admit that his height was an advantage. They still needed an eight-foot ladder, but Liam easily attached the first strand to the very top and, with some steadying hands below to hold the ladder still, wove the lights through the upper branches without incident.

Once the lights were strung, the decorating began in earnest, with Lucia popping back and forth between the library and the lobby, giving instructions on what should go where.

With the upper third of the tree done, Liam and the two other men in their group let the women and kids take over. Caterina gave the kids a box that had unbreakable ornaments, so they could be involved in the decorating until it was time to hang the candy canes. Those that got hung right over top of another one could be moved tomorrow, when they weren't around.

There was only one box of ornaments still to go on the lobby tree, then the kids would hang the candy canes. The last item would be the topper, which Lucia still hadn't revealed, and which would require Liam's help again to put on.

Cat was attaching a beautiful blue glass ornament to the tree when she heard the jingle of bells, like the ones they'd hung with a big red bow in the swag on the front door. She glanced up as the door cracked open, and a man peered inside.

She inhaled sharply and almost dropped the glass ball. There was no way anyone had invited him. No, he wasn't welcome here, and he knew it. If she allowed Mitch to crash the party, it could only end badly.

Cat put the ornament back in its box and, hoping no one would notice, hurried toward the door. She had to stop him before he came inside. She narrowed her eyes in warning. Mitch backed up onto the porch, apparently satisfied he'd gotten her attention and succeeded in getting her to come outside.

She wouldn't let him ruin this night for everyone. Whatever his reason for coming here, she'd deal with him and then send him on his way with the threat of a restraining order if she had to.

LIAM STOOD OFF to the side of the lobby, talking to Rus, a man about his own age, who told him he was dating one of Lucia's friends, and another guy named Derrick, who said he was a friend of Eliana's. He half listened to the conversation, keeping an eye on Riley, and, because he couldn't seem to help himself, on Caterina as well.

She was so damn gorgeous. Tonight, in the company of her friends, she seemed more relaxed. She laughed a lot. He couldn't remember ever seeing her laugh before, at least not so freely. When she did, her face could light up a room.

She'd been good with Riley. Not that he wanted to encourage a relationship between them, but Caterina seemed to genuinely like his daughter. She treated her kindly, despite how she might feel about him.

He watched as she started to hang another ornament on the tree. She looked up toward the front door and seemed to freeze a moment, then clutched the ornament as if she'd been about to drop it. She put it back in the box without hanging it and then just walked away from the tree.

Liam frowned. He cocked his head to look past her. Someone stood just beyond the door on the porch. A late arrival?

When Caterina got to the door, she slipped outside, closing it behind her. If she knew the latecomer, wouldn't she have invited him to come in and join the party?

His curiosity getting the best of him, he strolled across the room, past the door, and stopped on the other side of the front window. He could hear voices, but they were muffled. He couldn't make out what they said, but it sounded like they were arguing.

Trying to be casual, he looked out the window and saw Caterina and a man standing at the foot of the front steps. The man grabbed her arm and she flung it off. The guy spun toward her, and Liam got a look at his face. Mitch Gregory.

Gregory took a step toward her, and she held up her hands, as if fending him off. Without thinking about why, Liam made for the door.

He slid out as quietly as she had, not wanting to cause a scene if his gut was steering him wrong. He saw Gregory grab Caterina by the wrist and yank her forward.

"I told you to keep your hands off me, Mitch!" She tried to break his hold again but failed this time.

He got right in her face, sneering. "You owe me, Caterina. You left me high and dry at Caulfield's. It's your fault business is down and that two of my best servers quit. You can't try to ruin me and walk away as if that's the end of it."

"I didn't try to ruin you. If Caulfield's is suffering, it's your own fault. Maybe you should try spending more time there managing the place, instead of pursuing *other* interests," Caterina said.

Gregory bristled. "No one double-crosses me and gets away with it, Caterina. I found out about your big plans to open a restaurant. Would be a real shame, putting a lot of money into it just to fail. Restaurant business is a tough industry to survive in. It's extremely competitive."

"I'm not worried about the competition. Now let me go, Mitch."

Liam didn't know the situation or whether Caterina would be upset if he got involved, but he knew he didn't approve of the way Gregory was manhandling her.

He walked across the porch, stopping at the edge. "You heard the lady, Gregory. Take your hands off her."

The two turned sharply to look up at Liam, Gregory letting go of Caterina as they did.

"Liam." She gasped, her surprise evident.

"Well, well, well. Liam Dougherty. Fancy seeing you here. Don't tell me we have something else in common," Mitch said.

Liam flexed his fingers. "You and I have nothing in common."

Gregory was here. It didn't appear to Liam that Caterina had invited him, but if by chance they were in an on-again, off-again relationship, in which the guy thought he could just show up, the smart thing would be to stay out of it.

Liam's relationship with Caterina was already strained. He darted her a glance. The way she looked back made his decision.

"Do you want him to leave?"

Caterina nodded. "Yes, I told him to go. I don't want a scene. I didn't want anyone else to have to get involved this time."

"Really, Cat?" Gregory asked, dripping sarcasm. "You don't want to call your sisters out here to insult me the way they did the last time I tried to talk to you?"

Liam descended the steps. He walked up next to Caterina and crossed his arms. "She said she wants you to go."

Gregory stared back at him, and Liam rolled his jaw. Let the bastard come at him. He'd love the chance to plow a fist or two into the guy's gut, but he wouldn't make the first punch. He never had, and if it was within his power, he never would, no matter how much he might want to.

Liam narrowed his eyes. Gregory took a step back, then another. "You've been warned, Caterina," he said, as he continued backward. When he got to the end of the walkway, he sneered at Liam.

"Too bad about Sylvie. We had some good times before she went off the deep end."

It took everything Liam had not to go after him. He had no proof, but he knew Gregory had been the one to give Sylvie the OxyContin she'd OD'd on, and his comment almost snapped his control. Liam hadn't loved his wife, although he'd tried to make things work at first for his daughter's sake, but if he'd found Sylvie in time, he would have done everything in his power to save her.

"Get the hell out of here," Liam said through gritted teeth.

"Yeah, yeah, I'm going. I should have known someone would come running out to fight for her if I came here. Never expected you, though, Dougherty." He droned on as he turned and then made for the parking lot.

Liam faced Caterina, his expression still hard. "Antonio told me you were mixed up with that bastard a while back, but that you'd broken things off." It wasn't any of his business, and he should leave it alone, but he asked, anyway. "Have you been seeing him again?"

"No. He just...he just showed up. He's..." She stopped, shook her head as if it wasn't worth explaining, then looked at him again and swallowed. "What did Mitch mean about you two having something else in common, and when he said you used to have good times together?"

She hadn't understood what her old boyfriend had been referring to, but Liam wasn't in a mood to enlighten her. She'd just said she wasn't involved with Gregory anymore, and he believed her. He shouldn't care, but he did. He'd fought the pull that drew him toward her with little success, and now, he didn't know if he had the will to keep fighting.

"I have to get back inside. If Riley noticed me missing, she'll be wondering where I am." He took a few steps toward the porch, then looked back over his shoulder. "Are you coming?"

"Yes," she said, although it was barely a whisper, and started after him.

LIAM PULLED INTO his driveway and turned off the car. The clock on the dash read 10:18, long past Riley's bedtime. He glanced into the backseat. She hadn't lasted ten minutes after they left the party before passing out. She'd had a ball—his little organizer.

He grinned at the mental image of her passing out candy canes to the other kids and telling them, almost verbatim, Caterina's story about the children who wouldn't be able to reach them if they were hung too high. She'd even come up with the idea that they should get on their knees to hang some, because a one- or two-year-old was very short. Spoken like a true four-year-old, he supposed, amused.

After getting out of the car, Liam opened the back door and unstrapped Riley from her car seat. She stirred when he lifted her out.

"I've got you, princess." He hiked her up against his chest and rested her head on his shoulder. "Close your eyes and go back to sleep." He brushed the dark, silken curls away from her face and tucked them behind her ear, curving his hand over the top of her head.

He bumped the car door shut with his hip, then pressed the lock button on the key fob.

As he turned toward the walkway, a dark-colored Jeep he didn't recognize from the neighborhood cruised past his drive—black or navy, he couldn't be sure. It pulled over and parked on the street a few houses down from his. Someone getting a late-night visitor. He watched a moment, but no one got out...probably texting or talking on their phone. People were so damned tied to their devices. He shook his head, readjusted Riley, and continued into the house and up the stairs to her bedroom.

After getting her settled, Liam went back downstairs. He got a beer from the refrigerator, then stopped next to the kitchen table on his way out to the living room. Setting the beer down, he picked up the stack of mail that had piled up over the last few days and shuffled through it. He saw nothing that needed attention; no bills, no payments, and much to his relief, no more letters from Sylvie's parents or their lawyer threatening to try to take Riley away from him.

Liam tossed the mail back on the table and snorted. How they thought they stood a chance of getting custody blew his mind. If they truly loved Riley, they'd put her best interests first, instead of pursuing some vengeful suit that would land her smack in the middle of a custody battle.

They'd never been able to reconcile with Sylvie's death. How does one come to terms with their only child committing suicide? He could understand how difficult it had to be for them. Any parent would be devastated by the loss of their child, no matter the circumstance. He could even understand them blaming him, so they didn't have to accept the truth about Sylvie's true character.

Liam closed his eyes and swallowed. It didn't matter what he understood because no one would ever take Riley from him. He might not have been the perfect husband, but he was a good dad. Riley was happy, and he wouldn't let anyone threaten that happiness. It wouldn't matter how much money they spent, how many lawyers they hired, or how hard they fought—he'd fight harder.

They have no case, not without just cause. His lawyer had assured him Sylvie's parents wouldn't be able to gain custody. They could still file a suit and try, but Liam hoped they'd received the same counsel he had and realized they stood no chance. The only thing moving forward with the suit would do, would be to create more animosity between him and Sylvie's parents.

Liam rolled the tension from his shoulders. He hoped this was a case of no news being good news, but even if it wasn't, there was nothing to be done unless they went through with their threat. Getting worked up about it at this point served no purpose.

Taking his beer into the living room, he turned the TV on, scrolled through the channels until he found a documentary about string theory that looked interesting, and stretched out on the couch.

Was Caterina still up? Would she be hanging out with her sisters and a few close friends who'd stuck around to admire the trees and share a bottle or two of wine? Or was she in her room, maybe reading a book, stretched out on top of the thick white comforter and all those pillows she had arranged against the headboard that he saw when he'd carried those boxes down from the attic?

He shifted on the couch. Maybe she was asleep, swept up in a dream, her chest rising softly with each breath, lips parted slightly, full, and soft...

Liam sat up and pushed a hand through his hair. Here he was, once again, his subconscious maneuvering him into another fantasy of Caterina Bonavera before he realized it. He took a pull on the beer, silently cursed his body for being an all-too-willing participant in adding to his discomfort whenever thoughts of her invaded his peace of mind.

He was horny as hell. Unfortunately, his horniness centered on exploring and satisfying itself with one very specific, maddening, control freak of a woman. He'd tried to fight the attraction. But the truth was, he wanted her so badly he could taste her.

He cricked his neck. She wanted him too. Oh, she might not want to, would probably deny it to his face if confronted with it, but he'd seen the desire. It had lurked in the depths of those dark sable eyes as he'd stared down into them, tempting him, stroking him, luring him to take what he'd been wanting for weeks.

It had been there in their kiss—heat simmering below the surface, the steam washing over him, dizzy with it—an unquenchable need that drove him, made him want. He wanted her heat. He *lusted* for her heat. He wanted to feel her burn, to watch her lose control, and to know he fueled the firestorm.

Muttering a curse, he pushed up from the couch. He was fighting a losing battle. He needed to get her out of his system before she became an even bigger distraction. He could only think of one way to do that.

The trick would be getting Caterina to cross over the barrier that stood between them—one he'd heaped enough brick and mortar on to know it might require a lot of chiseling to break it down.

Seven

*"When you came, you were like red wine and honey,
and the taste of you burnt my mouth with its sweetness."*

Amy Lowell, poet

e're usually booked a couple of months in advance for this upcoming week, but 1 had a late cancellation this afternoon, so you're in luck," Caterina heard Lucia tell the man who'd come in a few minutes earlier, inquiring about a room.

She elbowed Eliana, who sat beside her on one of the library couches working on her laptop. El glanced up from the screen, and Cat hitched her head toward reception. "Hunk alert," she whispered.

Her sister turned to look and then swung her gaze back to Cat. "Oh—My—God," she mouthed, the corners of her lips curling up sharply, and her eyes going wide as she sucked in a breath.

She set her computer down and started to get up. Caterina grabbed her wrist, held her back. "Where do you think you're going?"

"I've been meaning to ask Lucia if she needs help with anything for the open house. She's been so busy the last few days, and with the guesthouse booked solid this week, I'm sure she could use a hand getting things ready."

"Umm hmm. I thought you preferred blue-eyed blonds."

"This may be one of those times when I'm willing to make an exception." Eliana's dark eyes glistened with animated interest, and Caterina wondered amusedly how good their handsome new check-in would be at handling the whirlwind that was about to sweep him up.

She relinquished her hold on El's wrist, tucked her legs up on the couch, and leaned against the armrest to watch the show unfold.

El strode across the reception lobby, her gait confident. "Hey, Luch," she said, her tone resonating with a casual drift and sisterly affection. "I've been meaning to check if you need help getting ready for the open house." She smiled at the man—a genuine, charming smile that radiated the typical, open nature that was Eliana—and added, "But I don't want to interrupt, so I'll just wait right here until you're through." She stepped to the side of the reception desk.

The man returned El's smile, must have caught his eyes drifting downward, and checked himself from giving her a full-body scan. Smooth, Cat thought as she observed his eye-stutter. The guy had some self-awareness and, apparently, some measure of discretion.

Eliana smiled again, the picture of patience as she waited for Lucia to finish checking in their guest and, Caterina guessed, tried to get the scoop on him without being too obvious.

"You're all set, Mr. Roth," Lucia said a couple of minutes later. "I have you down for five nights, starting tonight, and checking out Sunday morning. You'll be staying in Seyval Blanc. When you bring your bags in, I'll take you upstairs to show you where it is."

"Thank you. Very appropriate." It was a toss-up which was more devastating, Cat thought, his smile or his eyes, dark as ebony and deep as any ocean. "Naming your rooms after wines," Roth said. "I'm sure your guests like it."

"Most do," Lucia said. "My sister Eliana suggested it." She extended a hand to indicate El, standing on her right. "Eliana handles marketing for the winery and guesthouse. She also conducts most of the tastings, if you think you'd like to do one while you're staying with us."

Roth looked at Eliana again. "I think I'd enjoy that very much. Is it possible to get a schedule of when they're held?"

"There's a card in your room with tasting days and times," Eliana informed him, "but we usually do one at four and six on Wednesday and Thursday. Friday, Saturday, and Sunday we run one every two hours between noon and six."

He looked at his watch. "Then I should be able to make the four o'clock tasting this afternoon, unless it's full and I need to make a reservation."

"I think we can squeeze you in, Mr. Roth," Eliana assured him with one of her own, most charming smiles.

"Great. A wine tasting sounds like the perfect way to relax and settle in." He extended a hand toward Eliana. "And call me Damien. Mr. Roth makes me feel like an old man, and I don't think I'm that much older than you."

"Okay then, Damien. I'll add you to the list and include an extra setup. The more the merrier, as they say."

"Unless of course it's Marcella doing the saying," Lucia commented, "in which case more and merry are oxymorons."

"Who's Marcella?" Damien asked.

"Another sister. There are four of us. Marcella oversees the vineyards and the winemaking. She's an amazing vintner, but she'd rather be out in the field or in the barrel room mixing wines than mixing with people."

Damien Roth looked between Lucia and Eliana, his expression seeming thoughtful from Caterina's vantage point, as if he pondered something about her sisters or what they'd said. It struck her as peculiar, because for a brief flash his demeanor seemed to turn more serious. Then, as if she'd imagined it, he appeared amiable and charming again.

"Well, I'm looking forward to it." He reached into his trousers pocket and pulled out a set of keys. "I'll grab my bags, and then if you can show me where my room is, I won't take up any more of your time right now."

Roth went out and came back in within a few minutes, carrying a small suitcase and a duffel bag. When Lucia showed him upstairs, Eliana practically danced back into the library and sat down. She looked like she'd just been given a wonderfully wrapped present that she couldn't wait to open.

Lucia returned a few minutes later. She joined them in the library, her eyes trained on Eliana. "Don't think I don't know what you're up to, sister mine. Just remember, he's a guest, so behave yourself."

Eliana gave a delighted laugh. "It's not like I drooled on him."

"Your eyes drooled, trust me."

"Don't worry, Luch. I'll be good, but nothing ever broke from looking." She leaned forward, her foot moving up and down like a yo-yo on a short string. "So, did you find out why he's staying here? Work? Pleasure?"

"He said he's a photojournalist and that he's working on an assignment to capture holiday celebrations in Loudoun County. This week he's going to be covering *Tastes of the Season*. Since we're one of the hosts, he thought he'd see if he could get a room here as his base of operations."

"I've never met a photojournalist," Cat said. "Do either of you know what one does?"

"They use pictures to tell a story," Eliana said. "Have you ever heard of Steve McCurry? He's a good example, and probably one of the best known. *Afghan Girl* is one of his photos. I know you've seen it; it's iconic. You look at that image and you can't help but wonder about who she is, what's her story. You know the saying; a picture speaks louder than words? That's what photojournalism's about: capturing a story without words."

"I think I know the picture you mean." Caterina stood up with the intention of going up to her room. Antonio had finally gotten around to bringing the two old trunks down from the attic to her room the day before. She'd gone through most of the boxes but hadn't found anything that shed new light on Rosa or Gino. Since she didn't have any plans for the evening, she thought she'd start looking through the trunks. Maybe she'd have more luck finding something important in them.

"It must take an especially talented person to be able to see beyond the surface of something and capture the essence of it in a way that speaks to people," Caterina said, thinking more about what her sister had said. "Maybe there's more to Damien Roth than a pretty face and hunky body, El."

Eliana tilted her head and, looking thoughtful, said, "Maybe there is." She picked up the laptop she'd left on the couch and clicked it shut and then shot up in one motion as if she had places to go and things to do that wouldn't wait. "I've got to make some calls and then get cleaned up before the four o'clock tasting. Later, sisters."

As she breezed through the lobby and disappeared into the hallway, Lucia angled Cat a glance and arched a brow. "Do you think one of us needs to keep an eye on her around our newest guest?"

"I wouldn't worry about it, Luch." Caterina walked with her toward the lobby. "You know El; she's all about the possibilities of the fantasy, not pursuing it. She might indulge in a little flirtation with Roth, but she'll keep it light and fun. I'm guessing they'd both enjoy it. She'll swear he's the most gorgeous man she's ever seen

and that she's madly in love with him. Come Sunday, he'll check out, and life here will go back to normal."

"Hmmm. What's normal for here?"

Cat gave a light snort. "Good point."

"YOU HAVE TO be Caterina."

Cat straightened up from where she was bent over the reception desk, making a note to herself to pick up smoked salmon tomorrow morning for the canapés she'd be making for the holiday open house.

She turned and eyed the six-foot-something of dark good looks, flashing in her direction enviable straight, white teeth, outlined by full lips that had probably stolen many young women's hearts with a kiss. If her own wasn't currently struggling to understand the ambiguity overwhelming it for Liam Dougherty, she might be more susceptible to its effect.

"I am. Damien Roth, right? I was in the library when you checked in and overheard you give your name."

"That's right. I didn't see you, but Lucia told me there were four of you, and since I've already met Eliana and Marcella, I guessed you had to be the fourth. The family resemblance is striking."

"So we're told." She offered a friendly smile, one she'd give any other guest. "Is there something I can help you with? There's not usually anyone working in reception after six, unless we know there'll be guests arriving late. There's always someone on call, but if there's anything you need, I can—"

"No, I don't need anything. I saw you and thought I'd introduce myself. I'm supposed to be meeting your sisters for a drink in the library."

"All three of them?" Caterina raised a brow.

Damien chuckled lightly. "Yes, but I'm not at all as bad as that might make me sound. Marcella stopped in while I was doing a wine tasting this afternoon. I complimented her on the wines, and she asked which was my favorite. When I told her, she said she could recommend another that I might appreciate. She offered to let me sample it at some point during my stay. Eliana suggested we all get together this evening in the library."

"And Lucia?"

"Eliana mentioned it to her after the tasting, and she said she was in. Before I knew what had happened, I had a date with three women for a private wine tasting."

Caterina chuckled. "That's the way things happen around here. We sort of sweep people along with us in whatever direction the water's tumbling over the rocks."

He angled his head, his eyes taking in her face as if he were appraising it. She wondered if he studied her from a photojournalist's perspective, trying to see beyond the surface to who lived beneath the skin over her bones.

She glanced away, not used to, or comfortable with, such open perusal from someone she didn't know. She usually kept her innermost thoughts and feelings to herself. She wasn't as internal as Marcella but was more guarded than Lucia, and with Eliana, if you didn't know El's thoughts or feelings, you weren't paying attention. She wore them all on the outside.

No, revealing her secrets didn't come easy for Cat—especially to strangers—and she felt unsure about someone trying to peer beyond what she chose to reveal.

Damien cleared his throat. "I hope I didn't just make you uncomfortable," he said, as if he'd read her mind. "I have a bad habit of studying people a little closer than I should sometimes. A side effect of the job, I suppose. I'm sure you're all very different, but you and your sisters have so many physical similarities; I find the idea of trying to capture the differences intriguing. Perhaps you'll all agree to let me photograph you for a future story about siblings."

"Lucia and Eliana would probably agree to it, and if they did then I'd go along, but good luck convincing Marcella. She's not much for having her picture taken."

As if saying their names had summoned them, Lucia and Eliana rounded the doorway from the hallway into reception together. Lucia's movements were fluid and graceful, as always, like the steps of a waltz. Eliana's were quick and self-assured, ready to take on the world, spirited and flirty, like a tango.

"Hey Cat," Lucia said, "we're going to break open some wine that Marcella recommended to Mr. Roth. Want to join us?"

Cat glanced up at Damien. He gave her a crooked grin, the kind that lends boyish charm to grown men, even those like the one looking at her, sporting that sexy stubble on his face. "Want to make it me plus four?"

"Why not? I was just going to spend the evening going through a musty old trunk." She regarded her sisters. "Do you think our guest realizes what he's getting himself into, spending an evening alone with all four Bonavera sisters?"

"Oh, it'll be okay," Lucia said. "Antonio's going to join us too. He called about fifteen minutes ago to say he was almost home." She smiled warmly at Roth. "You'll be glad to have another man around. We can be a bit overwhelming if you're not used to us."

Marcella arrived about five minutes later, toting a padded canvas bag from which she pulled three bottles of red and put them in the middle of the large square coffee table nestled between the library's couches.

"Okay, now that I know we're drinking red, I'll go make up a quick tray before Antonio gets here," Cat volunteered. "What kind of cheese do you want me to put out, Cel?"

"It's a cab-merlot blend, so Asiago and Brie if you have it, with bread, not crackers."

"I've got a baguette I can cut up. Do you want any fruit?"

"If you've got dark cherries or red grapes, then yes. And some dark chocolate would complement it nicely."

Cat headed for the kitchen. "I'm on the food. Someone else want to get the glasses and plates?"

"On it." Eliana jumped in and, as Caterina went through the solarium doorway toward the kitchen, she heard her sister add, "I just love an impromptu party."

CATERINA EASED HER foot off the gas pedal as she drove by the construction site on her way back from the store Tuesday morning. What had been done since her last visit? Were they on schedule with the update she'd gotten last week?

She snorted. Last week's? She hadn't followed up on the prior one...not like her at all.

Curiosity nagged her. If she didn't stay on top of things, who would? Her sisters trusted Antonio and Liam without question. Cat trusted them, too, but miscommunications and misunderstandings happened: changes someone thought were for the better but forgot to mention and went ahead with before you could stop them from being implemented; changes you don't like and didn't want but now you're stuck with because you trusted them too completely.

Blind faith—she didn't believe in it. If you relinquished all involvement in something that impacted you and then weren't happy with the results, you had no one to blame but yourself. No, she didn't believe in blind faith, so why hadn't she stayed on top of things with Serendipity as she should have been doing the last couple of weeks?

Cat swallowed back the sour bile of truth. She'd lost her backbone. Liam confused her. Not just confused…worried. He immobilized her to the point that she didn't know what she wanted or what to do about him. It was no excuse.

She couldn't let her apparent inability to manage the jumble of emotions he stirred in her get in the way of her dream. Serendipity was too important. She needed to get back on schedule, regain control. She'd find a way to deal with this unwelcome infatuation for their builder later, when she had more time to think about it and come up with a sound plan.

She coasted to the side of the road and drifted to a stop. On the passenger seat next to her sat a white cardboard box with a dozen mixed doughnuts that she'd picked up as a peace offering. She'd discovered during previous site visits that Liam had a weakness for doughnuts. Sweets to sweeten his disposition if he was in a foul mood. Cat rolled her eyes as she leaned over and picked up the box. Could she get any lamer?

After getting out, she set the box on the hood of the Jeep and then got her red leather bomber from the backseat.

As she picked her way across the gravel a couple of minutes later, she took in the lines of the structure, still dressed in house wrap, and tried to envision what it would look like with the stone exterior and wide front porches, juxtaposed against the Blue Ridge marching behind it in the distance.

Lucia would surround it with gardens: an abundance of roses, night-blooming jasmine, clematis, and wisteria, wherever they could ramble. There would be benches and Adirondack chairs nestled among hydrangea, impatiens planted with abandon, lush, broad-leafed hosta, and Solomon's seal inviting guests to sit in a shady reprieve on warm summer afternoons.

How different it all might be if fate hadn't delivered them Antonio. He'd done such an amazing job with the design, and although she'd never told him, Liam had surpassed her expectations with the construction. She might not believe in blind faith, but it wouldn't hurt to let him know that she was pleased with the work he and his team were doing. After all, they still had a long way to go, and when they started fitting out the kitchen, she had very specific wants. Having a better working relationship with their contractor could only help her cause if she insisted on one thing or another that may not have been what they planned.

After entering the building, Cat followed the *pop-pop* of a nail gun. She found Liam framing a doorway in what would be one of the upstairs guest rooms. His back was to her as he worked his way down a two-by-four that formed one of the sides. When he got toward the bottom, he crouched, holding the stud firm with one hand and running the nail gun down with the other.

He wore a faded black tee shirt and a pair of well-worn jeans that pulled tighter over his muscular legs as he balanced on his haunches. Saliva pooled in the back of her mouth. When she realized that she stood in an unfinished hallway with a box of pastries, salivating over a man, she almost groaned aloud. She was as bad as Eliana.

Cat cleared her throat. Liam glanced over his shoulder. He stood up when he saw her, his movements fluid for his size. He turned around, took her in.

Instead of the narrowed appraisal she'd become accustomed to, his eyes drifted over her, moving down from her face, resting a moment on the box of doughnuts and then continuing their exploration until she felt as if they'd left no inch of her body untouched. He might as well have run his hands up and down that path, the effect was just as devastating to her peace of mind. And damn her, she half-wished he would have. She was *worse* than Eliana!

"I had to go to the store this morning to pick up some things for the open house this week," she said, trying to steer her mind away from thoughts of the two of them getting hot and sweaty together. She held out the box. "I picked these up for you and the crew."

Liam angled his head and watched her but didn't say anything. He probably wondered what she wanted and how quickly he'd be able to get rid of her.

"I know you all like them and...I don't know why you're looking at me like that. I don't have an ulterior motive. It's just—look, I don't say thank you often, for what a good job you're doing. I appreciate it."

The corner of his mouth twitched, slowly rose, turned into a grin. Not a sneer—an actual grin that skimmed the margin of friendly. Made him look downright charming, a word she'd never have used to describe him. This was something new.

"Always good to hear that the customer's satisfied with your work." His gaze didn't waver. It sparkled—crystal-blue seduction with a hint of amusement. If she didn't know better, she'd think Liam was flirting with her. *Was he flirting with her?*

The possibility took her so aback, she didn't know how to respond. She thrust the box forward.

"Would you just stop staring at me and take the damn doughnuts?"

He set the nail gun down on the plywood floorboards and walked toward her. Sauntered, really. With him taking his time, an eternity seemed to pass before he stood in front of her. Her breathing faltered—the air that usually flowed in and out without her having to think about it felt suddenly heavy in her chest. She didn't know what to make of the gleam in his eyes. And it made her nervous.

Liam reached for the box, his fingers brushing hers. Caterina's heart stuttered from one clutching beat to the next, like an engine that wasn't getting enough fuel and threatened to stall out with the next pause in her breath.

"Thanks." The same corner of his mouth curved up again, teasing a shiver that ran up her calf and kept going until it buried itself at the juncture between her legs—the last place she wanted to think about at that moment. Lord help her, if she started drooling, she'd have to slap herself, because none of her sisters were here to do it for her.

"You haven't been here for a while. I suppose you want to see what's been happening," he said without any noticeable contempt. His unusually affable nature threw her even more off guard than her traitorous hormones. She jumped on the offer. Anything to avoid letting the wanton woman that wanted his hands all over her from escaping and possibly jumping him. A danger she feared would increase the longer they remained standing there with him looking at her like he wanted to devour *her* instead of the doughnuts she'd just given him.

"When will you start putting up wallboard?" Cat asked after they'd gone through several of the rooms on the second level, and she'd regained some equilibrium.

"Not for a few months. Once we finish all the interior framing and get that past inspections, we'll move on to the rough plumbing and have all the ductwork done for the HVAC. Then we need to bring in the electricians to run all the wiring through the interior walls, floors, and ceilings. We have to go through another round of inspections for each of those steps before we can put in the insulation and close things in."

"Hmm. It's hard waiting to see it come together, but it's a real process, isn't it?"

"Yeah. Things would move a lot quicker if we didn't have to bring the county in at every turn before moving on to the next step. I agree it's important that they ensure work's being done to the proper standards, but they work on their own timeframe, and yours doesn't matter much to them. And if you get an inspector with a chip on his shoulder for some reason, they can kill your schedule. Most of them are pretty decent, and if they issue a stop work order it's for a legitimate reason, but I've run into a couple

I've had to walk away from and go punch a wall because they put a hold on a job just to show they could."

Cat gawked at him and exclaimed, "Are you serious? They can do that?"

"It's happened. That's what happened the day Burke left Riley with you when he had to go over to the county offices. It usually doesn't stick if it's simply a power play, but you're still hit with delays until you can get it straightened out. We've had a couple of situations when we had to go over an inspector's head and talk to the chief inspector. My brothers and I avoid doing that if we can. You never know if you'll have to deal with that inspector again, and things run a little smoother if you don't ruffle their feathers too much."

"I didn't realize construction could be so political."

"I think it's more about egos than politics. Some people get off on that kind of power. Like I said, most of the people I deal with are straight up, but occasionally you run into some prick who—"

Liam threw her a glance. "Sorry, I probably could have stated that more delicately."

Cat laughed. "If someone put a stop work order on our job just because they got off on pulling a power play, you better believe I'd have something to say about it, and in choicer words than that to describe them."

"If I had to put my last hundred dollars on who'd come out on the top in a battle between you and them, my money would be on you."

She stopped and glanced up at him. "Is that an actual compliment, Liam?" she asked, still unsure if his attitude toward her had changed for some reason, or if she'd just caught him in an exceptionally good mood that even she couldn't dampen.

He shrugged. "You stand your ground for what you want, and you don't give in, or up, easily. At least that's been my experience." He slanted her a glance, his expression turning more serious. "I haven't always enjoyed dealing with you because of it, but I respect you for it."

In the several months she'd known him, they'd knocked heads often enough to give each other a few mental bruises. He could just as easily have been calling her inflexible and stubborn as complimenting her. And in some of their encounters...well...perhaps she had been.

She liked having a plan, keeping things organized and wanting things done to a certain standard. Maybe that came off as controlling, but it was only because she cared—because she knew how horribly things could go wrong when you let the details slip through the cracks.

The sound of a saw blade whirred from someplace on the lower level. Cat shifted where she stood. At some point, she realized, she'd begun to care what Liam thought of her. She didn't want to be Caterina, the bitch, whom he had no choice but to deal with because she'd hired him to build her a restaurant.

You had to respect someone to like them, and he'd just said he respected her—or at least that aspect about her. She might never understand what about her had turned him off from the beginning, but if he'd suddenly decided to put their differences behind them, she'd happily do the same.

Improving her relationship with Liam would make things more pleasant for everyone, and it would make accomplishing her goals for Serendipity easier if she didn't have to battle him every step of the way.

HE'D ALWAYS THOUGHT her so self-assured—an unflappable, untouchable, prima donna whose depth was thinner than air. He'd come to realize over the last few weeks that he'd been wrong.

When he heard Caterina had been involved with Gregory, Liam had cast her in the same mold as Sylvie before he'd even met her. She was one of Gregory's women, so she must be self-absorbed and as lacking in character as he was. Why else would she be involved with that scum?

Liam still didn't understand that story, but there was more to her than he'd given her credit for. If she let him, he thought he'd enjoy getting to know the real Caterina instead of the one he'd unfairly pegged her to be.

"Listen," he said, combing his hair off his forehead with his fingers. "You and me, we sort of got off to a bad start."

She gave a delicate snort.

"Yeah, I know." He grinned at her expression. "An understatement. And although I'm not going to get into the reasons right now, I'll own most of the blame."

"I've always known you didn't like me, and honestly, I've never been able to understand why. So, I won't argue; you set the tone, but I did get snarky in return. I'm usually a lot nicer to people."

"I like to think I am too." Liam gave her a self-deprecating smile. "So, I've been thinking, maybe we should try to start over. This project still has a good eight or nine months left in it. That's a long time to keep trying to come up with new and insulting names to call each other."

She laughed, rich and spontaneous, giving him a glimpse of her humor, a small peek through the shell he grew ever more curious to crack.

"Okay," she said, her lips playing with a smile, "but I never actually heard you call me an insulting name. At least not to my face."

"If you could have read my mind, I probably would have felt the sting of your hand connecting with my cheek once or twice."

"Oh, really?"

"Totally uncalled for. You in no way resemble Cruella de Vil. She's taller, and, you know, she's got that skunk thing going on with her hair."

"You're right, my hand's starting to itch. And how do you know Cruella de Vil? You're a...a builder guy. You're all about driving a pickup, and power tools, and looking all hunky in your worn-out jeans and work boots."

"I do like my power tools. But don't forget, I've got a four-year-old daughter, and she's forced me to watch every Disney movie ever made at least three hundred times."

Liam hooked a thumb through one of the belt loops on his jeans. "As far as my work clothes, I've never considered them date attire, but if you think they make me look hunky, I'll wear them when we go to dinner Saturday night."

"Dinner? Saturday night?" Caterina drew her brows together. "What's Saturday night?"

"Dinner. You're a chef. Surely you've heard of it. Usually involves food being served, and we eat it. Maybe we have some wine with it, and if the portions are small, some dessert."

She reached out and pushed him on the shoulder. "I know what dinner is, Liam." She huffed the words. "I'm just not sure what this is about."

"It's about you and me going to dinner on Saturday."

"Why?" She studied him through eyes that looked unsure, cautious.

"You've got to eat, I've got to eat, so I thought we might try eating together."

"Are you asking me on a date?"

"I'm trying, but I must be doing a poor job of it."

"You're not doing a poor job. I'm just...surprised, and I don't really understand—"

"Hey, Liam," Burke hollered up from below, "could you come down here? I need your opinion on something."

"Be right there," Liam yelled back. He held up the box of doughnuts. "Thanks again for these. I'll let the guys know you brought them." He turned to leave. "Oh yeah." He looked down at her shoes. "I told you not to wear those spiky heels on the construction site. It's not safe."

Caterina put her hands on her hips, gave him a look. Like most things about her, he was ready to admit, it turned him on. It seemed he couldn't help himself. He tucked the doughnut box against his side and cupped the back of her head with his free hand, swooped in and stole a kiss, hard and hot, and ended it too soon for his liking.

She backed up and blinked, looked shaken.

Liam grinned. "But if you want to wear them Saturday night, I won't object. You look sexy as hell in them." He winked and then made for the stairs, knowing the taste of her full lips would remain in his thoughts to distract him for the rest of the day.

"I didn't say yes," she called after him.

"I'll pick you up at six. And tell your sisters not to wait up for you. Riley's having a sleepover with her cousin, so I get to stay out past her bedtime." And, he thought without saying, hopefully get to explore more than those lips in private, without the risk of someone interrupting them at any moment.

Eight

"Hope is the thing with feathers that perches
in the soul—and sings the tunes without
the words—and never stops at all."

Emily Dickinson

What was that tune? Caterina wondered. She heard the soft humming of it in her dream, something she remembered from her childhood. She turned over in her sleep, onto her side. No, her eyes were still closed, but she'd awoken. The humming must be a lingering remembrance from a dream, still fresh in her conscious even though the rest of it had flitted away, as dreams often do.

Rolling to her back, she stretched her arms up into the air until she felt the pull and sighed aloud. It had taken forever to fall asleep the night before. After tossing and turning for hours, her restless mind debating—would she or wouldn't she go out with Liam Saturday night—she'd finally drifted off. She didn't know when, but the last time she'd looked, the bedside clock read 3:33.

And oddly, she'd lost sleep for nothing. Apparently, without consciously deciding, it seemed she'd decided. At some point her mind must have put the question to rest, either because arguing with herself over the whys or why nots had become tedious, or because, deep down, it was what she wanted, and she had only obsessed over it because it was her nature to do so.

Cat sensed that it was still very early, well before her normal waking time. Maybe she should pull the comforter over her head and try to steal a few more hours of shut-eye. Her mind argued, *you've a two-page list of things you need to do.*

The holiday open house was tomorrow night. She had hors d'oeuvres to make, cookies and pastry shells to bake, setups to organize, and a tour schedule to coordinate with her sisters. She needed to get as much done today as she could, so tomorrow all she'd need to do was make the canapés and the fillings for the pastries that couldn't be done in advance and finalize the setup.

She knew exactly how she would dress the buffet tables, how the food would be arranged, and that it would be not only unique, but top-notch. This year, more so than in past years, everything had to be perfect because word was already out that she and Lucia would be opening Serendipity next fall. In addition to a larger boutique hotel, they would have a full-service restaurant. Although they'd only be offering appetizers and desserts at the open house, guests would be able to get an idea of the quality they could expect when the restaurant opened for business.

Caterina intended to make sure anyone sampling from her buffet would not be disappointed with what they had to look forward to.

That humming. She still heard it, in the background, behind her thoughts. She opened her eyes to the dim light of a still-young dawn and flung back the comforter. Swinging her legs out over the side of the bed, she sat up. Then she blinked. Blinked again. She reached up to rub her eyes, and the woman standing next to the bed vanished, the humming evaporating with her.

Cat stared at the empty space, barely breathing. *Did I just see a ghost? Did I just freaking see a ghost?*

Bolting off the bed, she dashed out into the hallway. She flicked on the light and yelled out, "Hey, sisters! Anyone!" She knocked on all their doors. "Marcella! Luch! El! Get out here!"

Marcella appeared first, poking her head out of her door. "Is something wrong?" She pushed back the veil of hair covering half her face, looking only half-awake. "It's like...not even six o'clock."

Caterina darted to Marcella's doorway, grabbed her hand, and tugged her out into the hall.

"What's going on?" Lucia padded out in her nightgown, rubbing her eyes. Eliana opened her door and leaned against the frame. She yawned and then squinted in the light. "Did something happen?"

"Yes! Something happened!" Cat was still hanging on to Marcella as if she needed the physical contact to convince herself she wasn't asleep, hadn't dreamt or imagined her dead aunt standing next to her bed.

"I saw her!"

"Saw who?" Lucia asked, still adjusting to the brightness.

"Her! Rosa! I just saw her. At least I'm guessing it was her, unless we've got more than one ghost roaming around the place. She stood right next to my bed, just looking at me with...with this smile and humming."

"Well, that's kind of creepy," Eliana said with a grimace. "Was it like a crazy, I-might-have-a-knife-behind-my-back kind of smile that's going to make us all have nightmares now?"

"No, nothing like that. It was...I don't know, affectionate...sort of like the look Mom used to get sometimes when she looked at one of us." Cat let go of her sister's hand and hugged herself. She'd been surprised—more like shocked—but she hadn't felt threat-

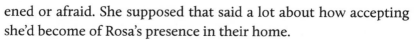

ened or afraid. She supposed that said a lot about how accepting she'd become of Rosa's presence in their home.

"So, she wasn't trying to murder you?"

"Of course not! I think we've already concluded that she doesn't mean us any harm."

"Well, I'm glad there's no emergency." El stretched her arms over her head and yawned. "So why did we all get this early morning wake-up call then?"

"Sorry." Caterina sighed, feeling bad now that she'd woken them all for no good reason. "I didn't realize it was so early. I was just so startled. I guess I wasn't thinking clearly."

"It's okay." Moving to her side, Lucia wrapped an arm around Cat's shoulder and gave her a brief hug. "Any one of us would probably have reacted the same."

Eliana pushed away from her door and walked over to Cat, embraced her for a moment. "Sorry if I sounded insensitive. I've still got my morning grump on. Luch is right. Waking up to find a ghost standing over you would be enough to freak anyone out."

"So now that we're all up," Marcella threw out, "could anyone else go for a cup of coffee?"

"I was just thinking how good that would be." Eliana winked at their sister.

"I'll make it," Lucia offered. "With everything that needs to get done, it'll be good to get a jump on the day."

"I'll cut up some melon and heat up some scones from the freezer." Caterina smiled around at her sisters. "Thanks. There's no way I'd have been able to get back to sleep."

The door to the attic stairwell creaked open to reveal Antonio, standing there in a pair of boxers and a plain, white tee shirt. "Is everything okay? I woke up to the sound of voices, but it's still dark out. I thought maybe something was wrong."

"Everything's fine. We're just having a sisters' meeting," Lucia assured him.

He looked them over with raised brows. "Before sunrise, in the middle of the hallway?"

Lucia walked over and kissed him on the cheek. "Go back to bed, Antonio. I'll explain later." She turned him around and gave him a pat on the rear. "Off with you, now."

He glanced back, scratched his forehead, squinted around at the lot of them curiously, but took himself up the stairs as instructed, to the makeshift bedroom they'd put on the other side of the attic from his office after he and Lucia had gotten engaged. It was little more than a bed and a clothing bureau behind a half wall, which was fine since he spent a fair number of nights in Lucia's room. But it gave him a space of his own when he wanted, without tying up one of the six guest rooms until they got married.

"Doesn't it seem unfair that a man can look that gorgeous after just stumbling out of bed at an ungodly hour in the morning?" Eliana mused when Lucia rejoined them.

Lucia's mouth curled. "Not to me it doesn't."

"I HAVE A theory that Rosa is playing matchmaker," Marcella told her sisters as they gathered around the kitchen table a short while later, sipping fresh-brewed coffee and noshing on orange-raspberry scones that Caterina had pulled from the freezer and heated in the oven.

"When she focused on Lucia, it was like she'd decided she and Antonio belonged together. Like they were soul mates or something. So, she kept doing things to make sure they ended up that way. It wasn't that hard, since they had the hots for each other from the get-go. But when they hit that rough patch where Lucia wouldn't give him the time of day, Rosa locked them in the kitchen until she agreed to hear him out."

El broke a corner off one of the scones and took a nibble. "These are so good, Cat." She took a sip of coffee and then reached for the rest of the scone. "I don't disagree," she said, "but why would she care about our love lives, and why now?"

"I don't know," Marcella said. "Why would she lock them in a room until they dealt with each other, unless she wanted them to work things out? It was like she knew they belonged together and wasn't going to let them screw it up. And now it looks like she's doing the same thing with Cat and Liam."

"Wait a minute." Caterina interrupted, seeing the flaw in her twin's theory. "You can't compare me and Liam to Lucia and Antonio. They were clearly gaga over each other, and if you're one of those people who believes in destiny—which I don't, but that's beside the point—then Rosa's interference might be understandable. But me and Liam? We're the antithesis of the perfect match. He disliked me from the moment we met. He's got to be the most difficult man I've ever had to deal with. If it weren't for my superior self-control, I'd probably be doing time for murder right now, and Serendipity would just have been a nice dream, never to be realized because I killed our contractor."

"Didn't look like you wanted to kill him when I walked in on the two of you trying to eat each other's face in the lobby a few days ago," Marcella said, tilting her head and grinning at Cat.

"That was an aberration." One Caterina had enjoyed more than she wanted to admit. And now, one she wouldn't mind exploring further. Which she may be getting the chance to do if they managed to get through their date Saturday night.

"*This above all: to thine own self be true.*" Eliana waxed poetic.

"Thanks, Shakespeare," Cat said, scowling. Truthfully, she'd much rather spend some time getting to know Liam better now than plotting ways to torture him. Not that she believed for a moment they'd end up falling in love and planning a happily ever after like Lucia and Antonio. But if their date went well, she might consider the possibility of a mutually satisfying, no-strings arrangement. She was a grown woman. She had needs and desires and just knew he could satisfy them.

"Cat," Lucia said and reached out to touch her hand, as if to cushion her next words. "It hasn't escaped any of us that there's been some tension between you and Liam."

Caterina barked out a laugh.

"Okay." Lucia patted her hand. "Clear and obvious tension, mistrust, scowls, and visual daggers. Better?"

Cat nodded. "More like it."

"Nonetheless, neither has it escaped any of us that the two of you have been fighting an attraction that's clearly been consuming you both. And I think, and I'm only saying this because I love you, if you stopped fighting it so much and let nature take its course, you might be a lot happier about it."

"What she means," Eliana said, "is have some hot sex with him, get it out of your system, and you won't feel so bitchy about him anymore. Denial is not a healthy thing, sister."

"I don't know if that's exactly what I meant," Lucia qualified, "but it does seem that you've both got some pent-up passion looking for an outlet."

"Maybe we should rent a boxing ring," Cat suggested, only half-joking.

Lucia removed her hand and picked up her coffee mug, took a sip. "Or maybe you could talk to him about your feeling that he never liked you, and you don't know why. He must have a reason. Despite your differences, Liam's a good guy. The rest of us all like him."

Cat sighed. Her sisters were right. She wasn't sure about the hot sex yet. Not that she'd be opposed to a good romp with a man who knew how to satisfy a woman who needed satisfying, but she'd have to think through the pros and cons of doing the big deed with Liam before jumping into bed with him.

She did want to know why they'd gotten off to such a rocky start, though. And why, specifically, he seemed to go cold with her, when he didn't react the same way with her sisters. He'd defrosted, though, done a turnaround she didn't understand but much preferred. She was just as curious to know what had brought about his change of attitude toward her. Did it have anything to do with Riley? she wondered.

"We're going out Saturday night," she said without any other preamble.

Marcella warmed her hands against the sides of her coffee mug. "About time." She sipped some coffee. "You have my approval by the way."

"Mine too," El and Lucia chimed in unison, then pointed at each other and grinned.

The kitchen lights flickered off and back on again. Cat glanced up.

"It appears Rosa sanctions the date also." Marcella set her cup back down on the table.

"We're just going to dinner, so don't romanticize it too much." Caterina slid her eyes back up toward the kitchen ceiling. "Hear that, Aunt Rosa? If you really are trying to play matchmaker, I'll make my own choices, thank you. There's every chance our date will be a failure that turns out to be the first, last, only. I'd prefer not to get haunted over it if that happens."

The kitchen door blew shut with a bang, and all four sisters jumped.

After a moment, Caterina helped herself to one of the scones and took a bite. "She really needs to work on tempering her rejoinders."

"WHERE DO YOU want these tables?" Antonio asked Caterina the next morning. He stood near the entrance to the kitchen where he'd leaned the three ten-foot round tables against the wall. She'd asked him to get them from the storage pantry after stealing him away from Lucia at breakfast, because she could use, as she'd told them, some muscle to make the job go quicker.

She studied him a moment from where she knelt in front of what had been her mother's favorite antique hutch, where they stored the event linens. What a beautiful man. In a pair of black jeans and a simple gray sweater, he managed to look both elegant and devastatingly masculine at the same time. It seemed they were surrounded by beautiful men here lately. Antonio, Liam, and this week, they'd had the deliciously gorgeous, if a little dangerous-looking, Damien Roth staying at the inn. Yes, there was certainly a lot of eye candy to feast on at the Bonaveras.

"I want them in the center of the room, but more toward the entrance from reception." Caterina pulled out a storage bag that held tablecloths and set it on the hutch, then walked over to where she wanted Antonio to set the tables.

"Here's good," she said, drawing an imaginary triangle for him. "The two tasting stations are going to be more toward the back. That will give us two distinct areas—one set aside for eating and the other for wine tastings."

"Are you doing free tastings?"

"Yes, but they'll be small pours, two ounces. Samples, really, as opposed to what we'd do for a tasting. Marcella's going to be featuring six wines, three red and three white. Visitors can choose to sample any three of the six."

"I'm assuming they'll also be able to purchase bottles."

"Of course, we're a winery. We sell wine. Last year, El suggested offering a ten percent discount on single-bottle purchases, fifteen on six or more. We almost never discount our wines because we're not a large volume producer, but we get a fair number of locals doing the tour who don't otherwise visit the wineries. She thought if we offered a discount, some of them might be encouraged to buy a couple of bottles and give us a try."

"Good idea," Antonio said as he rolled one of the tables across the floor. "I find it interesting that people will travel miles, even across the country, to visit a place like this, or to see something they've read or heard about, and if you ask a group of locals if they've been there or done that, a surprising number will say no."

"I'm guilty of that on some counts. People come to D.C. from all over the world to visit the Smithsonian museums, and I've only been to the Museum of Natural History and the National Gallery of Art. I've never even been to the National Zoo, and I love animals."

Cat held the table while Antonio pulled open the legs. "I've always intended to visit the others. I guess it's because they're so close, I figure I can do it whenever, but whenever always seems to get shoved to the back burner." She glanced up at him and smiled. "Guess I need to find someone to play tourist with and knock out a few more, before I'm an old woman and realize I never appreciated what was in my own backyard when I had the chance."

"Do you need any more help setting things up over here?" Caterina's pulse leaped at the sound of Liam's voice. She turned and watched him walk toward them, all long legs and sinewy muscle wrapped in a pair of well-worn jeans and a long-sleeved navy Henley that hugged his chest and broad shoulders the way she'd imagined doing.

Yes, she wanted to get her hands on him. And with the shift that had been taking place between them over the last couple of weeks, the possibility of that fantasy coming to fruition seemed more likely every day.

"Shouldn't you be nailing something over at Serendipity?" she asked, adding a tongue-in-cheek smile, in case he thought she was being her old snippy self, and not the new, I'm-kind-of getting-into-you self.

"We're waiting on some inspections, so we're in a temporary lull. I thought I'd stop by to see if anyone here needed help with lifting or moving things around for your big event. You know, guy stuff." He looked at her feet and grinned. "It might be easier for me to help Antonio with those tables, than it is for you in those stilettos."

"You'd be amazed what I can do in stilettos, mister." She gave her ankle a turn, and his gorgeous blues sparkled. He held her gaze a moment—a grin that told her, *I'm kind of getting into you, too*, resting comfortably on his gorgeous mouth.

Antonio cleared his throat. "Well, I wouldn't mind the help," he said, his expression one of amusement, and pointed across the room toward the kitchen entrance. "Those two tables need to be set up, and we need to move two of the bars along the sidewall out for the tasting stations."

"I'm also going to need four long tables for the food," Cat added. "And if you could set up eight chairs at each of the round tables, that should suffice. We're probably not going to need all the seating, but I want to have it just in case. There were over two thousand tickets sold for the event. I know all those people won't show up here, or at the same time, but we should still have a good-size crowd coming and going throughout the evening."

Antonio and Liam exchanged a look that they both seemed to understand without the need for words. Some guy code, she guessed. Caterina arched her brows.

Liam chuckled. "Just point us in the right direction."

She had too much to do to try to decipher the male psyche right now. "The other tables should be in the pantry where you got these, Antonio. And we'll need four, not two, of the six bars. Two for each station. I want—" She walked to the rear third of the room. "One station here." She stood on the spot and looked at them to make sure they were paying attention.

"And the other—" She paced off roughly twenty feet toward the opposite side, her heels clicking briskly against the hardwood floor. "Right here. Set each station up in a V-shape pointing into the room."

Liam frowned. "If we do that they won't come to a point. There'll be a wide gap where the inner edges of the two bars meet. Why not butt the ends together and do an *L*?"

Caterina shook her head. "No. Imagine it's an open-ended *V*. I've got plans for those gaps. You just set them up the way I told you and let me worry about the rest."

Antonio nudged Liam with his elbow. "Help me get the other two tables by the door. If she says she has a plan, believe me, she has a plan. And I guarantee it's been written down, revised at least three times, edited, and printed out in duplicate."

"You're preaching to the choir, my friend," Liam said as he walked away with Antonio. "She'll probably be giving us each a blueprint to make sure we put everything exactly where she wants it."

"I heard that," Cat said, swallowing back the drool pooling in the back of her throat as she watched them saunter across the floor. Good Lord, those were two gorgeous butts.

"You think I'm anal," she accused them and tried to refocus her thoughts. "I'm not anal," she said in self-defense. "There are going to be a lot of people here tonight. It's important that there's a logical flow between the eating area, the food tables, and the tasting stations. If we just set things up without a plan, it would be confusing. There would be no logical flow. People would be milling around helter-skelter, getting in each other's way all night, spilling things on one another. It could get ugly."

"I've got an idea," Liam told her. "Why don't you get some masking tape and put X's on the floor where you want us to put things? That way we won't screw it up."

"Shut up, Liam."

He looked over his shoulder, giving her a sexy grin—one far too playful for Cat to get annoyed with him. She stuck her tongue out anyway, which only made him laugh.

Looking away to hide her grin, she marched to the hutch for the bag of linens she'd taken out earlier and took it over to the table she and Antonio had been setting up when Liam arrived.

She pulled out a large, round tablecloth and snapped it open. Spreading it over the table, she smoothed it here and there and then circled the table to make sure it hung evenly all the way around. Next, she went into the kitchen to get everything she needed to assemble the centerpieces Lucia had designed the day before and shown Cat how to arrange.

When she returned to the solarium, Liam and Antonio had the other two round tables in place. She made three more trips to the kitchen for supplies. Once she had everything, she covered the two remaining tables and got to work putting together the centerpieces.

Lucia had such a design flair, Caterina thought, as she put one of the three large, round, cut glass mirrors in the middle of each of the tables. She placed a small Christmas tree in the center of each one. Using boxwood cuttings that she'd collected from around the property, Lucia had made the trees by sticking several cuttings into foam that she'd secured inside white ceramic containers and then clipping them into the shape of a perfect little tree. Silver glass balls, no bigger than kumquats, decorated each tree, with green moss hiding the foam inside the containers.

Around the base of each container, Cat placed snips of box-wood and cedar the way Luch had shown her. Next, she laid on their sides two frosted wineglasses that her sister had embellished with strands of silver stars twining up the stems, overlapping one on top of the other, so they crisscrossed. She did this on three sides of the tree, and between each set of glasses, she arranged three of the large pinecones Luch had decorated with spray snow and silver glitter. Around the wineglasses and pinecones, Cat interspersed votive candles in clear, cut glass crystal holders that, when lit, would make everything sparkle and glow as it all reflected in the mirrors.

Taking her cell from the waistband of her skirt, she pulled up the picture of the arrangement Lucia had put together the day before to use as a sample for the design. Looking between the picture and the arrangement she'd just put together, Caterina nodded with satisfaction that she'd replicated it correctly.

"Wow," she heard Liam say from somewhere behind her. He stood about ten feet away, balancing two folding tables against his legs. "How did you turn a rough wooden table into *that* so quickly?"

"Do you think it looks okay?" She nibbled the corner of her thumbnail. "I'm going to drape evergreen garlands on the front of the food tables, but I think it would be too much for these. And they would get in the way when people are eating. Lucia had a great idea for the backs of the chair covers—simple but pretty—and that should be enough."

Liam looked impressed. "It looks amazing. Like a picture in one of those elegant decorating magazines."

Cat caught her lip between her teeth, then smiled. "It does look elegant, doesn't it? And tonight, with the lights just dimmed and the candles lit, everything will sparkle."

"It's obvious that you and your sisters have put a lot of work into this. Everything looks festive, both inside and out." He carried the folding tables over and leaned them against the side of one of the round tables, then came to stand next to her, admiring her handiwork more closely. "Are you nervous?"

She gave a slight nod. "Yes, a bit. With Serendipity opening next fall, Lucia and I want people to walk away with a sense of what the boutique hotel and restaurant will be like. The tastes and comforts they can look forward to, whether dining in the restaurant, staying as a guest, or both. We want to give them a sample of the quality they can expect."

Liam took her hands, warming her feelings for him further with the gentleness in his touch. "I'm sure the food is going to knock their socks off. Knowing what a stickler you are, how could it be anything less than perfect?"

"You think I expect too much."

"No, I think you expect a lot because you have high standards. There's nothing wrong with that, sweetheart." He reached up and wove his fingers through her hair.

"I've got pretty high standards too. You and I might not always agree over the issues, but that doesn't mean I don't respect you for the way you stand your ground. In fact, I'm starting to realize I kind of get a kick out of it."

"Oh yeah?"

"Oh, yeah." He angled his head down, covered her mouth with his, surprising her at how comfortable he seemed to be getting with this kissing her thing.

Cat let the heat flow through her, melted into the deliciousness of his lips moving over hers, the little shivers beginning to tremble along her skin as he moved his hands up and down her back.

He dipped his tongue into her mouth, and she heard herself moan, then he did. She wished they weren't standing in the middle of the solarium because her body felt all loose and warm and a bit slutty, but her mind knew anyone could walk in at any moment.

On the peripheral, she heard something clicking and pulled back from the heat of their kiss.

Glancing around, she saw Eliana and Damien standing just inside the doorway of the solarium.

Amusement danced in her sister's eyes. "A little afternoon delight? Well, don't let us interrupt. I just came in to check on the setup for this evening's tastings, and Damien's been getting some photos for his feature."

Caterina backed away from Liam, ran her palms down her sweater, the sides of her skirt. Liam stuffed his hands into the pockets of his jeans, nodded toward Damien and El.

"Oh," Eliana said, clasping Damien's wrist and pulling him over to where Cat and Liam stood.

"Damien, this is Liam. He's the contractor for Serendipity." El looked at Liam with a beaming smile, appearing to be in an especially good mood and, if Caterina wasn't mistaken, enjoying the company of their newest guest.

"Damien's a photojournalist," Eliana told Liam. "He's doing a feature on holiday traditions in Loudoun County, and he's including the tour. He's staying here through the weekend, and hopefully, will use some photos from around the guesthouse and winery. It would be good exposure for us."

Damien reached out and shook Liam's hand. "Nice to meet you. Eliana has told me a little bit about the plans for Serendipity. Great name by the way. It sounds like it's going to be quite a place. I hope I get a chance to see it when it's completed."

"Thanks. Same here. I don't think I've ever met a photojournalist; sounds like an interesting job." Liam studied Damien a moment. "You look familiar. Have we met someplace before?"

Damien looked thoughtful, then shook his head. "No...don't think so. I'm on the road a lot, but it's possible our paths crossed somewhere."

"This table looks gorgeous!" Eliana exclaimed, drawing everyone's eyes to the centerpiece. "I can't wait to see everything when it's all done." She turned to Damien. "You need to come back in here when we get back from lunch to get some pictures, before the guests arrive tonight and the tables are cluttered with dirty dishes."

Caterina studied her sister a moment. When she'd gone up to her room for the evening last night, Eliana and Damien had been in the library, sharing a bottle of wine and a cheese platter. Cat hadn't thought too much of it, a light flirtation they'd both seemed to be enjoying. Harmless.

And here they were, together again, by chance or divine, she didn't know, and going to lunch. That was a lot of together time packed into two days when they'd just met. El wasn't one to fall hard and fast for men, but neither had Lucia been, and look what had happened when Antonio walked into her life. And although El had always been more carefree and flirtatious than the rest of them, something in the way she looked at Damien made Cat's antennae hum.

Should she be concerned that her sister might be falling for someone they knew nothing about? Damien seemed like a nice guy, and Caterina understood why El would be attracted to him physically, but did something about him attract Eliana in some way other men didn't? If so, she and her sisters might need to find time to get to know the man a little better.

Damien would be checking out Sunday morning. He and El would no doubt go their separate ways. She was probably spinning her mental wheels worrying about something that would resolve itself in a few more days.

Looking at Damien, Caterina said, "I wouldn't mind getting copies of any good shots you might get of the table setups. Even if you don't plan to use them, I can put them in my idea book."

She angled her head as a thought occurred to her and frowned. "You didn't...umm, get a picture of me and Liam...when—" She darted a glance at Liam who, from the way his mouth had curled, guessed the drift of her question and found it amusing.

Damien chuckled. "I might have inadvertently caught you in a delicate moment when I snapped some shots of the room, but don't worry, I won't be featuring those in any articles."

"I should hope not," Eliana said, wiggling her brows for Cat's benefit. "Unless they come with an X rating."

Liam leaned toward Cat's ear. "If that was your sister's idea of an X-rated kiss, make sure you lock the doors if you ever take me back up to your bedroom, because I wouldn't even consider that a peck."

Caterina tingled in all the right places—or perhaps the wrong places, given that those tingles would go unsatisfied right now—and swallowed the groan inching up her throat.

She still had a lot to do to get ready for this evening. If she was going to dive into a pool of wanton lust, she wanted to do it right. Prepare for it. Take a long soak in the tub. Dab on an elusive scent. Put on some lacy underwear. Lather a rich moisturizer over every inch of skin his lips might explore—

With a jerk, she turned and strode toward the kitchen. "I've still got a dozen things to do before I start dealing with the food. Liam, get the rest of those tables set up. Antonio, maybe Damien wouldn't mind helping you with the bars; they're heavy. El, don't just stand there looking pretty; come into the kitchen so I can tell you about the tasting setups."

And with that, she took herself as far from temptation as she could without leaving the guest house.

Nine

"A party without cake is just a meeting."
Julia Child

The Bonavera sisters all wore dark red, sequined dresses that distinguished them as the evening's hostesses. Each dress was different, but Liam noticed one thing they had in common. They all looked as if they'd been custom-made to show off every dip, curve, and swell of the women who wore them—to perfection.

Even Marcella, whom he'd never seen in a dress before that night, looked ravishing. He'd had to do a double take when he realized it was her. He knew she and Caterina were twins, but their personalities were so dissimilar to him that it was easy to forget. Although their facial features were identical, he'd never noticed how alike they were in height and build. He'd never seen Marcella in anything but work clothes or wearing jeans and a sweater, usually with her nose in a book. Tonight, in a floor-length, form-hugging dress with no shoulders, she looked every bit the manslayer her sisters could be.

His eyes rested on Caterina. She wore a short dress that embraced her like an enamored lover, from her shoulders to a couple of inches above the knee. It had long, narrow sleeves with a somewhat modest V-neckline in front, but modesty gave way to pure seduction when she turned to reveal a plunging back that ended below her waist, displaying a glorious expanse of creamy white skin.

He wanted to get his hands on all that skin. Lick his way up her back, taste her neck, spin her around and covet those full lips with all the hidden heat he'd tapped into each time he'd kissed her.

"Daddy, will you reach me up, so I can get one of the high candy canes from the tree?"

Liam looked down at Riley. He hadn't planned to come to the open house, but she'd remembered that it was tonight, and after helping with the decorating last weekend, she'd just assumed they'd be going. He'd picked her up from daycare, and when they got home put one of her shows on for her to watch while he got a shower, just as he did every other night.

When he came back out, she was sitting on the couch watching her show, and he saw that she'd changed into one of her good dresses. She'd looked at him and frowned. When he asked about the frown, she'd said, "You're not planning to wear that tonight, are you?"

"What's wrong with it?"

"Daddy." She'd given him an exasperated look that he thought must be inherent to all females. "Miss Caterina said this was going to be a special night, and that's why we were decorating everything to be so beautiful. You have to wear your nice clothes. Like me." She stood up, as if he hadn't noticed the dress, and looked up at him with bright eyes filled with excitement for the evening she'd been anticipating.

He didn't tell her that he hadn't planned on them going. He hadn't had the heart to disappoint her. No, he did what any father at his daughter's mercy would do. He went to his room, took off his tee shirt and sweats, and changed into something he thought she'd approve of.

Liam lifted Riley up and set her on his hip. "Which one do you want?"

"That one." She pointed to a candy cane near the center of the tree. He took hold of her waist and held her in the air.

"Would you mind looking this way?" Liam glanced to his right to see Damien aiming a camera at him and Riley.

"Riley, do you want to be in a picture of you getting your candy cane?" Liam asked.

"Sure." Riley reached for it and, as she wrapped her fingers around the stem, looked at Damien and flashed her dimples. His daughter was a true ham.

"Got it. Thanks," Damien said. He let the camera dangle from the strap around his neck and approached them.

"Are you having fun, Riley?" he asked.

She scrunched her forehead. "How do you know my name?"

Liam wondered the same, but then Damien cleared up the mystery when he said, "I met your father this morning. I was talking with Antonio and Lucia a few minutes ago, and when she saw you and your dad, she said, 'Oh good. Liam came, and he brought Riley with him.'"

Damien smiled down at Riley. "I guessed you were Riley."

She grinned. "You're a good guesser. Did you know I got to be in charge of the candy canes? Miss Caterina said it was an important job 'cause we needed to make sure every little kid could reach them."

Damien looked the tree over. "It looks like you did an excellent job."

"Thanks. Miss Caterina said I did a great job too. My dad got some pictures when we did the decorating. He took them on his phone, not with a camera like you."

"Hey, Riley! Thanks for coming tonight." Caterina had come up behind them. Liam glanced around, and their eyes connected. She slid him a smile that made him want to nibble it right off her lips.

"I love your dress," Caterina said to his daughter. "You look just like a princess in it. Give me a spin, so I can see it twirl."

Riley put one hand on her head, then spun around like a ballerina. The skirt on her dress flared out, then flattened back down when she stopped. Liam wondered where she'd learned that move. Probably watching one of her shows.

"Nicely done," Caterina praised.

Riley beamed. "I like your dress too. It doesn't twirl like mine, but it's still pretty. I like how it sparkles. When I'm growed up, I can get some high shoes like yours. Daddy won't let me get some now 'cause he says they're only for adult ladies, and you have to take years of practice to learn to walk in them."

Oh Lord, Liam thought. He'd be happy if the day Riley wore a dress and shoes like Cat's never came. He didn't even want to contemplate his baby girl dressed in something that would require him to threaten every guy who looked at her to keep his hands in his pockets or risk losing them.

Caterina chuckled. "Your daddy's right about that, but don't worry, when you're old enough I can teach you how to walk in heels, so it doesn't take so long." She shot Liam an amused, if mocking, look. "I've had lots of practice."

"I'm going to move through the rooms and get some more pictures," Damien, who Liam had forgotten was still standing there, said. "Before I do, why don't I get one of the three of you by the tree."

Before he or Caterina could respond, Riley grabbed one of Liam's hands and one of Caterina's and stood proudly in front of the tree she'd helped decorate. She glanced up at each of them. "Smile, guys."

On her command, they looked toward the camera and smiled as the flash went off. Liam glanced at Caterina. He didn't think a picture of the three of them would make the cut in an exposé to highlight the season, but it occurred to him that someone seeing it might assume they were a family. No one who knew them, but to someone who didn't know better, he could see how it might depict something other than the spontaneous moment it had been.

THE LAST GROUP of the tour guests walked down the wide front porch steps and made their way along the sidewalk toward the winery's gravel parking lot.

Lucia closed the polished double doors that had been left open for the night and then turned and leaned her back against them. "Congratulations, sisters mine. Tonight couldn't have gone more splendidly!"

"I'll second that," Caterina agreed. "Everything looked beautiful, the tour guests all seemed to enjoy themselves, and everyone had nothing but good things to say. The night, most definitely, was a success! And I couldn't be happier to see it end. I'm exhausted!" She dropped into one of the armchairs that flanked the large stone fireplace in the library and slipped off her heels.

Marcella claimed a corner on one of the couches and did the same, massaging her feet. "I don't know how any of you can stand to wear these all the time. One night of torture in them, and my feet are going to need a week to recover."

"If you wore them more often," Eliana said, from where she already sat on the opposite end of the couch from Marcella, "you'd get used to them. Put your feet up here, little sister." She patted the couch beside her.

Marcella swung her legs up. Eliana slid over, lifted Marcella's feet onto her lap, and started massaging them.

Marcella groaned. "I love you. You're my favorite sister. I'll pay you a dollar a minute to keep doing that."

"I love you back, honey. Keep your dollars, though; this one's on the house. You wouldn't be able to afford my rates."

"I'm going to grab a bottle and some glasses from the solarium, so we can celebrate," Lucia said, pushing away from the front door. "And some food. I'm starving. I don't know about the rest of you, but I haven't had a bite since lunch."

Cat got up from her chair. "I'll help you. I think we were all so busy this evening that none of us got a chance to eat anything. I'll make up a couple of platters from the leftovers."

"Do you need us to do anything?" Eliana asked.

"No." Caterina left her shoes by the chair and followed Lucia, padding toward the solarium in bare feet. "You take care of gimpy, and we'll take care of getting us some sustenance."

Antonio walked out just as they were entering.

"We're going to have some wine and nibbles to celebrate," Lucia told him. "Do you want to join us?"

"Thanks for asking," he said, "but I think I'll call it a night and let the four of you have this time to yourselves. Enjoy your success. You earned it."

"To a successful night!" Caterina proposed a short while later as they sat around the library. Each held one of the winery's signature glasses, etched with the Bonavera name, underscored with a cluster of grapes and trailing vines. The glasses reflected the flickering flames of the three large, white pillar candles, set in the table's opulent centerpiece, another of Lucia's creations. Inside their bowls, one of the winery's rich, ruby-red cabernet sauvignons glowed, liquid rubies in the dancing light.

"A successful night," her sisters echoed. They tapped glasses, and a clear, delicate chime rang out in blessing.

The lights in the library and reception flickered on and off twice, then went out. The other candles set about the room lit by an invisible hand, and flames sprang to life in the fireplace, leaving the four sisters bathed in nothing but the glowing, soft light of several dozen candles and the gently crackling flames from in the large, stone fireplace.

Lucia looked around. "I guess Rosa thought a more romantic atmosphere would be nice to celebrate our success. And," she added with an affectionate tone, "wanted us to know she was here celebrating with us."

"It looks so pretty with just the candles and the fire. You have to give it to her," Eliana said. "Subtlety might not be one of her strong points, but she sets a nice scene." She raised her glass toward the ceiling. "Thanks, Rosa. This is much nicer with the lights off."

Cat took a sip of wine and held it in her mouth a moment. She had to agree with Eliana. Their aunt could be a bit of a pain at times, but she clearly had a romantic side.

CATERINA STARED AT the seven dresses spread out over her bed. None of them were saying, *Wear me, I'm the one that's going to knock Liam off his feet.*

She needed to go shopping in Eliana's closet. Of her three sisters, Eliana had the most extensive wardrobe and would be most likely to have something that fit with Cat's style. If El didn't have anything that spoke to her, she'd check with Luch. If neither of them had anything that said, *He'll be down for the count when he sees you in me,* she'd have to search deeper in her own closet for something that might.

She turned at the sound of a knock. Marcella stood in the doorway. "What are you doing?" her twin asked, looking at the growing mound on Cat's bed.

"Ugh! I can't find anything for my date with Liam tonight." She picked up a dress and dropped it again. "I think I wore this the day I met him." She picked up another. "I wore this the night I broke up with Mitch and quit at the restaurant. Depending on how our date goes, I don't want any reminders of either, in case I decide I want to try to seduce Liam over dessert." She let that one slip from her fingers to rejoin the pile.

"If you decide you want to seduce him, I doubt whatever you're wearing is going to make much of a difference. The two of you have been straining to get at each other for weeks."

"That's not true!"

"Yes, it is. Eliana and Lucia will back me up on it. *There are none so blind as those who will not see*', sister dear."

"This family's just full of helpful quotes lately," Cat said sarcastically.

"We like to be helpful." Marcella put her hands into the pockets of her cargo pants and strolled into the room. "You're welcome to wear something of mine," she said, extending her sisterly helpfulness, "but if you're going for seduction, you'll probably have more luck in El or Lucia's closets."

"Thanks for the offer. It's sweet, and I do appreciate it, but I think you're right. If I'm ever trying to go for that salt of the earth, bohemian, carefree, and don't care if I'm trendy or out-of-touch look, you'll be the first one I come to."

"Damn, it's so awesome to be needed."

Caterina laughed. "You are needed, honey, in many, many ways, just not for your wardrobe."

"Speaking of being needed, Luch, El, and I agreed that we'll take care of the breakfast setup tomorrow morning." Marcella crooked her lips. "So, if your date night goes well and ends up becoming a date-morning-after, no worries, we've got it covered."

"*Man!* Did I ever *score* in the sister department! But considering Riley, it's unlikely I'll be—" Liam's words from the day he'd asked her out drifted back to her: *And tell your sisters not to wait up for you. Riley's having a sleepover with her cousin, so I get to stay out past her bedtime.*

"Actually," she said, thinking it best to cover all bases, "Riley's supposed to be spending the night with her cousin, so I may be getting in much later than I would otherwise."

Cat walked over and wrapped her arms around her twin. "You guys are the best! I'll probably be waking up in my own bed tomorrow morning, but if I do get in really late, it'll be nice not to have to get up early to do the setup."

"We just want you to go out and have a good time, whatever you decide that is, without worrying about things here."

"None of you think it's a mistake...me going out with Liam?"

"Pffft. Rosa saw it right from the start, and it didn't take the rest of us long to figure it out either. There's something between the two of you, and although you've tried to play it down, it's been gnawing at you for the last couple of months. You need to figure out if it's a thing worth pursuing. Until you do, you're not going to be able to find your balance again, Cat."

After Marcella left her to her own musings, Caterina thought a lot about what she'd said. Cel was the most internal of all of them. She felt no need to be seen, be heard, or prove herself to anyone. She was very much her own person, and comfortable in it.

She tended to sit back, listen, and observe, chiming in if it was important to her or she had something relevant to add. She saw more than others, often more clearly, so although they all teased her for her more serious, sometimes reclusive ways, when Marcella offered an opinion or piece of advice, it merited consideration.

And, being twins, she and Caterina had always shared a heightened perception of the other's thoughts and feelings.

Marcella was right that she'd been off-balance, Cat reflected. Ever since the debacle with Mitch and quitting her job. And it wasn't just because she was in limbo until Serendipity opened and she had something concrete to focus her energies on again. Opening the restaurant would be a major accomplishment, her most cherished dream, but, she realized now, it couldn't be all there was.

During the early years of her career, she'd put other aspects of her life on hold. Had focused solely on learning everything she could about the industry, distinguishing herself as a chef, making her mark. It had been enough then. It wasn't now.

Of course, she would aim for the stars with Serendipity. She'd always been an overachiever, she admitted, but she saw nothing wrong in that. Why waste time doing something if you didn't do it to the best of your ability? One or two Michelin stars would suit her fine, but she couldn't cuddle up with accolades at the end of the day. Rave reviews wouldn't warm her bed on cold winter nights or hold her close when she needed to feel loved. If her dreams for Serendipity came true, what good would it be if she had no one to celebrate with, to share in the success?

She'd always have her sisters, true, and they always had, and always would support and cheer her on, but that was different. She wanted—no, she needed—more.

Cat walked out of her own room and went down the hall, to Eliana's bedroom. Was Liam the *more* she needed? The thought didn't repulse her as it might have five months ago. Rather, she realized, the possibility that he might be the something, or someone, missing in her life to make her dreams complete made her very glad she'd agreed to go out with him.

A flutter of butterflies took flight in her stomach. What if, after everything that happened between them, he turned out to be her Prince Charming—someone she could truly be happy with—but she'd botched it up?

No. She wouldn't hex the night before it started. Despite their past, he wanted to go out with her tonight. She wanted to go out with him. Something—attraction, curiosity...her dead aunt—had been corralling them toward each other for weeks.

She needed to get out of her own way, let whatever it was take her where she needed to go to find out if Liam was the *more* she wanted, or if he'd turn out to be just another mistake in judgment when it came to the men she'd gotten involved with.

"I CAN'T BELIEVE you picked this restaurant." Caterina glanced around at the intimate dining room. White tablecloths over longer, floor-length dark gold ones covered the tables. Crystal glassware sparkled at every setting, winking beneath a gathering of chandeliers that danced across the ceiling, as if in invitation to indulge oneself. Ivory china, rimmed with gold filigree borders, waited in understated elegance for the culinary delights, yet to be revealed, that would be set upon them to tempt curious palates. Everywhere she looked, her eyes soaked in the stage that had been set to seduce the diners' epicurean senses before a fork ever touched their lips.

She looked at Liam in wonderment over his choice.

"I hope it meets with your approval," he said, his eyes searching her face as if looking for confirmation that he'd chosen well. "Nothing against the Spaghetti Castle. In fact, Riley and I both love it, but I wasn't sure it would be the best place to take a chef on our first date. Someone told me if I wanted to impress, this would be the place."

"I'm impressed. Not only did you pick a wonderful restaurant, you managed to choose my favorite one outside of New York." It touched her that he'd wanted to please her, and that he'd gone to the effort of asking around for suggestions. "You can tell whoever gave you the recommendation they couldn't have suggested better if they knew me."

"They do know you. In fact, when I asked, all three of your sisters said, '*The Silver Phoenix*,' in unison, without having to think about it."

"They would know." She smiled lightly. As they waited to be shown to their table, she was filled with warm feelings that she wasn't sure how to express. She felt embarrassingly happy. "Thank you, Liam," she said. "It's...it's perfect."

His eyes glowed as he considered her, apparently pleased her sisters hadn't steered him wrong. She would have been just as happy...well, no, she wouldn't have been, but she wouldn't have complained, if he'd taken her to the Spaghetti Castle. If they got along well and enjoyed their time together, it wouldn't have mattered to her if they'd done it over pizza or prime rib. Not that she wasn't looking forward to the divine meal she was confident she'd be enjoying here, but it was the man who most intrigued her tonight.

"I am surprised you were able to get a reservation on such short notice," she said, knowing how difficult it was to get into this restaurant, particularly on weekends.

"I made it three weeks ago, but even so, they only had two openings left for tonight."

"Three weeks ago?" Cat gazed at him in confusion. "But you only asked me to dinner four days ago. Unless you were intending to bring someone else when you made the reservation, and they bailed on you."

"I wasn't intending to bring anyone else." He slid a hand around her waist as they waited to be seated and gave an affectionate squeeze, then left it there, resting on her hip. She didn't object. She liked the way it felt, comfortable, right somehow, as if it belonged there.

"So, you made a dinner reservation," Cat said, wagging a finger between them, "for you and me three weeks ago and didn't ask me until this week?"

"Yeah. I was working up to it."

"Did you think I'd say no?"

"The thought occurred to me. I decided to spend a couple of weeks charming you first to hedge my bets."

"Mr. Dougherty." A tall, young man in black trousers, a starched white shirt, and a black bow tie addressed Liam. He held two menus resting in the crook of his elbow with one hand and extended the other toward the dining room. "If you'll follow me, I'll show you to your table."

Liam slid his hand to the small of her back as they walked across the room, past other tables with diners conversing over culinary delights, to a beautifully dressed table for two toward the back of the restaurant.

Caterina shifted self-consciously in her chair a few minutes later as they waited for the waiter to return with their wine order. Liam sat with his chin resting on his joined hands, watching her intently, the corners of his mouth curled upward every few seconds, as if amused by some private joke.

She wasn't used to being scrutinized so openly. It made her wonder if he liked what he saw or, in such proximity, had zeroed in on one of her flaws. Her nose was too straight. Her face, perhaps a bit narrow. Her hair was at that in-between stage where she couldn't decide if she wanted to grow it out or lop it all off.

"I'm not sure what I want to order," he said. "Everything on the menu looks good, but I doubt any of it will be as appetizing as you look tonight."

She beamed at him, her doubts scattering like autumn leaves in the breeze. "That was a corny thing to say, Liam, but thank you. I'm not opposed to corny flattery, and if we're sharing honest

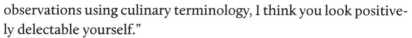

observations using culinary terminology, I think you look positively delectable yourself."

He chuckled, a rich reverberation that rolled over her and tickled her nerves. And he did look delectable. He'd almost knocked her off her feet when she'd walked into reception and seen him standing at the front desk talking to Lucia.

Dressed in a dark, charcoal-gray suit and a white dress shirt, with a black paisley tie, he could have walked right off the pages of a fashion magazine. None of the male models she and her girlfriends drooled over after they'd had a couple of glasses of wine had anything on Liam Dougherty dressed in a suit. Or anything for that matter, she conceded. He was hunky as hell in faded jeans and a tee shirt. This was just a different side of him. One that had surprised her because she wasn't used to it. She liked them both.

He's probably even more gorgeous wearing nothing at all.
Oh really? Did her dirty little mind have to go there?

She looked away to avert her slutty thoughts from becoming obvious. But damn, her curiosity was killing her, and was it so wrong for her mind to travel that path? She was a healthy, curious, horny woman.

"Should we decide what we want to order before the waiter returns with our wine?" Liam asked. He leaned forward slightly and lowered his voice. "I'm hoping I'll be able to convince you to come over to my place for an after-dinner drink since Riley won't be there. We could continue sharing observations then, in culinary terms if you like, about each other. Who knows where such talk might lead?"

His eyes held a suggestion of where he'd like it to lead. Maybe his mind had joined hers on the same road.

"I never pegged you for such a cornball," Cat said, grinning. "And I've never had a guy warn me about his plan to talk me into going home with him, in the hopes of getting lucky."

"When a man decides to pursue a woman, his next decision is when and how to get her alone someplace in the hope of getting lucky. We can't help ourselves. I'd tell you otherwise if I was a more selfish bastard who only wanted to get you out of that dress and have my way with you, but it would be a lie. I'd prefer to get you out of it and have my way with you honestly."

Their waiter returned with their wine. "Have you decided what you'd like to order?"

"We need a few more minutes. The lady distracted me from deciding."

"No rush," the waiter assured them. "Would you like me to bring rolls for the table while you're deciding?"

"That would be great," Caterina said. When he walked away, she smirked at Liam. "I *distracted* you?"

"You've been distracting me for about six months, sweetheart."

She shook her head but couldn't hide the smile his admission raised. She picked up her wine and held the glass over the table. "To honesty. I like knowing it's your preference. I don't know if it'll help you get me out of my dress tonight, but I do appreciate it."

"Does that mean I can stop wondering how to convince you to agree to the after-dinner drink and focus my thoughts on how I'm going to accomplish the other?"

Caterina picked up the burgundy, leather-bound menu and held it in front of her face. "I'll agree to an after-dinner drink," she said from behind creamy vanilla pages that were embossed in navy ink and full of tempting appetizers, soups, entrées, and desserts. "Beyond that, I'm not making any promises."

She settled on the petite filet of beef, rare, with parmesan-encrusted mashed potatoes, roasted asparagus bundles with dill butter sauce and cracked black pepper.

They conversed over their meals, sharing stories about themselves—what they liked to do in their spare time, what places they'd visited, those they never had but wanted to someday, why they'd chosen the careers they did. They talked easily, laughed easily, flirted easily, and often.

She'd settled on something else, she realized, after giving her order to their server. She would let the night play out. See where it led. Make no decisions until she needed to make them. And wherever it led, whatever she decided, it would be because that's what she wanted.

Ten

> *"Seize the moment. Remember all those women on the*
> *Titanic who waved off the dessert cart."*

Erma Bombeck

*L*iam swung into his driveway after driving home from the restaurant. The beams from the truck's headlights illuminated the front of a moderate-sized house with slate-blue Hardie-Plank shingle siding and buttercream trim. A small front porch, still big enough to accommodate the glider he and Riley often sat in on warm summer evenings to tell each other about their day, was centered beneath a large picture window.

Two comfortably worn wicker chairs, which his mom had given him when she and Dad moved to Florida several years ago, bookended a sturdy little table. He and Riley had made it together with leftover scrap wood that he'd salvaged from a project. He'd let her pick out the paint, the reason he had a bright purple table with lime-green legs decorating the front porch.

"It's homier than I imagined it would be," Caterina said a few minutes later, as they stood in the front room. Her eyes swept around the space, pausing a moment on the far corner, dominated by Riley's play kitchen, her desk and bookshelf, and the open-top, canvas storage boxes he'd picked up at a home store, so his daughter could keep some of her toys in the living room without the clutter taking over.

Caterina looked at him, a glint of humor in her eyes. "I guess I expected something...umm, more..."

"Single dad without a clue?"

"Yeah. A bit of that. Color me guilty of stereotyping," she admitted with a sheepish nod.

"My sister-in-law Becca is good at letting me know if things start to get too bachelor pad-ish here. I try to avoid leaving too many beer cans and dirty socks lying around for Riley's sake," he joked.

"It can't be easy. Being a single dad and raising a young daughter on your own."

Liam shrugged. "A wise woman once told me, 'Have to is a good master.' We do what we need to do. And as kids go, I'm lucky. Riley's pretty easygoing."

Caterina glanced away, then back, as if wondering whether to ask the questions he could see in her eyes. If they were going to have a relationship, and he hoped that was where they were headed, she had a right to know about his wife.

"It may be none of my business." She tucked a strand of hair behind her right ear. "But what happened to Riley's mother? I know she died. The day we baked cookies together, Riley told me she didn't have a mom, that she had to go to heaven."

She angled her head, her gaze steady, but sympathetic. "Was she ill, or..." A shadow fell over her face, as if she struggled with some emotion of her own. "Was she killed in an accident?"

Liam swallowed. The story never got any easier to tell. "She was hooked on OxyContin. OD'd when I was at work one day."

"Oh my God, Liam. I'm so sorry. That had to be horrible! Coming home to find the woman you loved—" She paused, seemed at a loss for words.

"I wasn't in love. I know that probably sounds cold," he said tonelessly and then decided to explain. "We'd been dating for about six months when Sylvie said she wanted to get married. I knew I wasn't in love, and I didn't really believe she was either. She started putting on the pressure though, said she hated living at her folks' house, that if I didn't marry her she'd leave town. I told her I wasn't ready. After fighting about it for several days, she let it drop. I figured she realized I wasn't going to give in and gave up on the idea. Things seemed okay for a while, but after a couple more months I started to think she was biding her time, maybe thought she could change my mind if she was patient. Little things she said and did. I knew that it wasn't going to happen, and my gut told me it was time to cut loose. We'd had some good times, but I wasn't in love. I realized staying together at that point would be unfair to both of us. Unfortunately, I'd waited too long. By the time I decided to end it, Sylvie was already six weeks pregnant."

Caterina observed him through somewhat narrowed eyes. It wasn't hard to guess her suspicion. He'd suspected the same thing. When he'd confronted Sylvie, she admitted that she'd stopped taking her birth control pills a couple of months earlier. He did the math. The timing coincided too closely with his refusal to get married when she'd first brought it up to be an accidental coincidence. He'd been furious, but it didn't diminish his responsibility. *You play, you pay*, his old man had said when he told his parents about the pregnancy.

"Riley was only two when Sylvie died. She was home alone with her when it happened. I didn't know about the pills. I never would have left Riley alone with her if I'd had any idea."

He swallowed back a wash of guilt. "When I got home, Riley was sitting on the floor next to Sylvie, playing with some dolls. I thought Sylvie had fainted or something. I rushed over and knelt beside them. Riley put a finger to her lips and shushed me. *Mommy's sleeping*, she said. I knew as soon as I touched her, though. Sylvie wasn't sleeping." Liam pushed a hand through his hair.

Caterina put a hand over her mouth. "Poor Riley. How did you—"

"I told her that her mommy had to go away to heaven. She was too young to understand what happened. She doesn't remember any of it now, not even her mom. Sylvie did what she had to when it came to Riley, but she wasn't what you'd call a doting mother. We argued constantly because she accused me of giving more attention to Riley than her. It was a ridiculous argument. Riley was two, for God sake!"

Liam felt the old frustration bubble in his gut. He hadn't been able to conquer all the anger over what had happened when he discovered the truth about the life his wife had been living on the side. A life he'd known nothing about until it was too late to intervene. He'd found the evidence of her affair with Mitch Gregory— phone messages, emails.

"I don't believe Sylvie intended to kill herself. She was too selfish to take her own life. I think she took the pills to scare me. Get my attention. But she overdid it, and, well...by the time I got home, I was too late to save her."

He sighed wearily. "Maybe if I'd tried a little harder to make things work, she'd still be alive. She might not have looked elsewhere for attention. Never would have gotten mixed up with—" Liam stopped short. He wasn't sure he should tell her about Sylvie's infidelity, or that his wife had been having an affair with Cat's old boyfriend. Caterina knew he didn't like Gregory, but Liam had never told her why.

"I promised you an after-dinner drink at the restaurant, and we're still standing here in our coats," he said, slipping his off and then reaching out for hers.

Caterina held his gaze, her rich, dark eyes penetrating. "It wasn't your fault," she said with unbridled conviction. "I don't know her story, but people make their own choices. From what you've told me, it doesn't sound like she made very good ones. But, good or bad, they *were* her choices. You can't own them."

"I understand all that but knowing something doesn't automatically make it easier to accept." The seriousness of the last few minutes had begun to cast a shadow over the evening. One he didn't want to linger under.

"This is getting a little heavy for a first date. Why don't we move on to something more pleasant?" He tossed their coats onto the corner of the couch. "I'll get us that drink, and then you can tell me more about your plans for the restaurant."

"What do you want to know about it?"

"I don't know. Tell me about the food."

"You want me to talk to you about food?"

Liam grinned. "Yeah. I don't know anyone else who talks about food the way you do. You make it sound very sensual. Sexy. You do things with your eyes and mouth when you talk about food."

"I do not," she said in protest.

"Oh, yes you do." He grabbed her hand and pulled her toward the kitchen. "It's very arousing."

Caterina gave a delicate snort, but when he glanced at her, he caught the hint of a smile tugging the corner of her lips.

When they got to the kitchen, he opened the bottle of wine he'd bought on his way home from work the day before. "It's not Bonavera's," he said, as he poured out two glasses, "but the clerk at the liquor store recommended it."

He handed her one of the glasses, and they tapped rims.

She took a sip. Nodded. "It's nice."

Liam drew a hand across his brow in mock relief. "Whew! You know, choosing a restaurant to take a chef to on your first date and a bottle of wine for a woman whose family owns a winery puts a lot of pressure on a guy when he's trying to romance her."

She smiled, a little off center, and he wanted to lean in and taste it. "So far you seem to be handling the pressure just fine."

"Yeah?" He grinned down at her. "Then I'll stick with my strategy."

He set his glass on the counter and reached for the JAM Wi-Fi speaker that Shawn and Becca had given him last Christmas. He turned on the power and waited for the Wi-Fi connection to come up.

"Play romantic love songs," he said.

"*Playing romantic love songs*," the JAM acknowledged.

He turned around. Caterina watched him with a raised brow. He walked toward her, and her brow inched higher. "The Way You Look Tonight" began streaming through the speaker, surrounding them.

Liam took her glass from her and set it on the counter next to his, held out a hand. "May I have this dance?" he asked, never taking his eyes off her stunning face. Her lips parted slightly as she laid a palm in his. He pulled her in, took her in his arms. And they danced.

With her head resting against his shoulder, the fresh, clean scent of her hair filling his senses, and her long, lean body moving against his like a wave gently lapping against a moonlit beach, they danced.

HE CONTINUED TO surprise her. In wonderful ways. If dancing in his kitchen didn't top the list of the most romantic things a man had ever asked her to do, Caterina couldn't think what could.

She liked the way his arms felt around her. Liked the way his hands drifted over her back, into her hair, stroked her cheek. Liked it a lot.

"How's this working?" he whispered against her ear.

Cat leaned her head back just enough to look at him. "How's what working?"

"My plan to seduce you."

"Why don't I show you?" She slid her hands up to his shoulders, lifted on her toes, and kissed him. Gently at first, and then, weaving her fingers into his hair, she angled her head and increased the pressure.

Liam opened his mouth and claimed her tongue. She tasted his hunger. Tasted her own. Could not deny the heat simmering between them or the desire it ignited in her. He took the kiss even deeper. Down a more intimate road. She went with him willingly, flames of want sizzling along her nerves.

Outside the snow continued to fall. The Bee Gees' "How Deep Is Your Love" began to play in the background. Liam spun her around. Cat felt her backside bump against the counter. Felt him move against her with an unmistakable rhythm. Her body picked up the tempo, welcoming every press, every slide, in an ancient dance.

"You're killing me," Liam said with a harsh groan. His hands roamed restlessly up and down her rib cage. "If you don't want this to go any further tonight, tell me to stop now, while I still have some self-control."

"And if I don't tell you to stop, what then?"

"It's likely we'll end up in my bed doing another kind of dance. One that involves a lot fewer clothes and a lot more physical contact."

Cat cradled his cheeks and gazed into his eyes. Aquamarine locked onto sable. She had no doubts about what she wanted. She may have just recently accepted it, but she'd known for weeks.

"Take me to bed, Liam. It's time for dessert."

He covered her mouth with a blistering kiss. When he came up for air, he took her hand and started to lead her across the floor. They passed the refrigerator and he paused, looked down at her.

A devilish gleam lit his eyes. "I've got some whipped cream in there. Should I grab it?"

She pulled her hand free from his, punched him in the shoulder, and walked out of the room. She heard him chuckling as his footsteps fell close behind hers.

"The door on the left, sweetheart," he said, when she'd gone about halfway across the living room. Cat turned, walked through the opening. She spotted a king-size bed on the opposite wall. Behind her, the door clicked shut.

A moment later, Liam's hands gently cupped her shoulders. He eased her around to face him. No turning back now, she thought. But she had no desire to.

LIAM LAY BESIDE Caterina, propped up on one elbow. He'd never experienced such intense, or satisfying, lovemaking. Looking down at her smiling face, he was inclined to believe she felt the same.

He drew a finger along her jawline. She was so damn beautiful. Her skin so silken, he didn't think he could ever tire of touching it.

Leaning down, he kissed her, softly, slowly, enjoying the shape and feel of her mouth, drawing a picture of it in his mind. "Stay the night," he whispered into it. "I don't have to pick Riley up until after lunch tomorrow. We can sleep in. I'll make you breakfast. I've got Fruity Pebbles and Sugar Pops. Or if you want something on the healthier side, Raisin Bran Crunch."

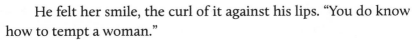

He felt her smile, the curl of it against his lips. "You do know how to tempt a woman."

"I try. Is that a yes?"

"No. As enjoyable as this night's been, I'm not prepared to turn it into the morning after. I didn't pack an overnight bag. I don't have a toothbrush. I'd like you to get to know the nice me a little better before you meet the morning me."

"Are you a grouch in the morning?"

"If I don't get enough sleep, usually. I need a couple of cups of coffee and to be left alone for about an hour. Are you?"

"No. I typically wake up in a pretty good mood and ready to go. I like my coffee out of habit, but I don't need it."

"I hate you."

He grinned, dropped another kiss on her lips. "I don't think so. I think you like me. A lot."

She chuckled. "You're right. I do like you a lot."

"Good, because I like you a lot too."

"Good. I'd still like you to take me home tonight. If we continue to like each other a lot after going out a few more times, we can plan a sleepover."

"I've got a feeling *plan* is the operative word for you."

"It's always important to have a plan. If you don't, there's no goal, nothing to measure against, no way to know if you're accomplishing anything or just meandering through life with no purpose."

"What about spontaneity, enjoying the moment, taking things as they come and seeing where they lead you?"

"You sound like my sister Eliana." Caterina rolled away from him and got out of the bed. "There's nothing wrong with enjoying the moment. I just happen to believe that if you plan ahead, the moment's not as likely to go wrong and disappoint you."

She picked up the dress he'd dropped on the floor after slipping it off her a couple of hours earlier. He watched her pull it over her head and shimmy it down that long, lean, gorgeous body, and was tempted to try and slide it right back off.

She looked around, spied her heels. Balancing on one foot, she slipped one on, then the other. Liam followed her every move. He got a kick out of her efficiency. Now that she'd decided it was time for him to take her home, the clock had started ticking.

Turning toward the bed, she put her hands on her hips and looked down at him. "As gorgeous as you are without them, I think you should put some clothes back on before you drive me back."

He pushed himself up to stand beside her. "I'd rather try to convince you to take yours back off and stay a while longer, but if there's one thing I've learned through our past dealings, it's that once you've made your mind up, it's almost impossible to change it."

He went into the closet, got out a pair of jeans and a sweatshirt, and dressed quickly. When they were in the living room a few minutes later, he glanced down at Caterina's feet.

"Are you going to be able to walk in those without slipping?" When he'd looked out the window a minute earlier, it appeared they'd already gotten an inch or two of snow.

"It might be tricky, but I'm well skilled at walking in heels. Even in wet or slippery conditions. I'll just hang onto you, in case."

Liam frowned. He'd enjoyed watching her walk around in heels on too many occasions to count, but he had no desire to see her land on her butt on his front sidewalk. "What size shoe do you wear?"

"Nine and a half. Why?"

He went over to the coat closet near the front door and pulled out a pair of snow boots. "Here, put these on. They're an eleven but should fit you well enough, and they'll be a hell of a lot safer than those." He dipped his glance toward her four-inch spikes.

Caterina took them without arguing, and after sliding out of her heels, slipped them on. "Thanks." She struck a pose, hand on cocked hip, knee bent. "How do they go with my dress?"

"Honey, in that dress, you could be wearing buckets for shoes and it wouldn't matter. No one would be looking at your feet."

He got their coats from the couch and held hers up for her to slip into. "Now put this on before I try to take it off you again and risk your ire for ruining your plan."

The snow was wet, and the walkway wasn't too slippery yet, as they made their way from the front door to the car. Liam held Caterina's arm, anyway. It gave him an excuse to touch her. He liked touching her.

After opening her door and waiting until she was settled in, he went around and got into the driver's side. When he backed out, he noticed a dark-colored Jeep parked on the street across from his house. It looked like the one he'd seen a few nights earlier when he and Riley returned from the holiday tour at the winery. None of his neighbors parked on the street overnight, so it must belong to someone visiting one of them.

From the corner of his vision, he saw Caterina wrap her arms around her middle. He reached down and turned on the seat heaters. She glanced over and smiled at him. The warmth of it flowed through him. He reached across the seat and took her hand, kept it in his.

He was very, very glad he'd decided not to hold her past relationship with Gregory against her any longer. It had been unfair to prejudge her because of it. It would be no different, he realized, than someone basing their opinion of him solely on Sylvie.

Gregory and Sylvie were a part of the past. One neither Liam or Caterina could change, but he wouldn't let it come between them any longer, not now that he realized how wrong he'd been about her.

SNOW CONTINUED TO fall, glistening in the truck's headlights as they drove back to the winery. The forecast called for snow showers off and on throughout the weekend. That would make the shop and restaurant owners in the surrounding small towns happy.

Snow this time of year always heightened people's Christmas spirit. Put them in the mood to decorate more, shop more, get into the season more, and spend more money than they did when Decembers stayed warm. There were statistics to back it up. The romance of it, Caterina supposed, and she had to admit, it had that effect on her.

"It looks like lights on in Serendipity," she said, cocking her head and squinting through the snowy darkness as they drove past the construction site toward her home. "I didn't know the electric was live yet."

Liam slowed the truck and looked backward, toward the building.

"Jesus Christ," he swore, his tone harsh as he threw the truck into reverse. "Those are flames!" He backed up past the entrance, then shifted the truck into drive and swung into the site.

"Oh, my God!" Cat breathed, horrified, as she now saw the pulsating glow through the windows of the side wing. She pulled her phone from her purse. "I'm calling the police."

Liam parked, just as her call was answered. He flung open the door, jumped out, and took off at a run. Caterina's heart pounded as she watched him sprint toward the front left side of the building, where the fire seemed to be located.

After giving the dispatcher the address, she slid out of the truck and hurried after Liam. "Call Lucia," she said into the phone's mic.

"Hey, Cat." Her sister's groggy voice came over the line a second later. "Where are you? It's, like one in the morning. Are you okay?"

"We're at Serendipity. There's a fire! I called the police! The fire department should be on the way, and—Liam!" She screamed his name. Fear slammed into her, and she began running toward the building. "Liam!" She shouted again as he disappeared through the front entrance.

What was he doing? He couldn't hope to put out the fire. There was no water supply on site. What was he thinking, putting himself in such danger?

Her cries went unanswered. Fear for his safety squeezed her heart. He should have come out. He should have come back out. Terrified that something had happened and he might be trapped, she went into the building after him.

The large central entrance had filled with smoke, but Caterina saw no evidence that the fire had spread to this area. It seemed to be contained to the wing that was to be Lucia and Antonio's private suite. She covered her nose and mouth with her coat sleeve and headed in that direction. The smoke stung her eyes, making it even more difficult to see.

Liam's clunky snow boots slowed her down, her feet sliding in them as they thudded against the floorboards. When she reached the doorway to the suite, she could barely see through the haze of smoke and flame. She swung her head from side to side and squinted. She saw Liam near the middle of the room, flames threatening all around him. He took off his coat and bent down. What the hell was he doing?

"Liam, get out of there! It's too dangerous!"

Sirens wailed in the distance, only minutes away. "For God's sake, Liam, we need to get back outside! Please! The fire trucks are on the way. I can hear sirens in the distance."

"There's someone in here! He's hurt. The fire department might not get here soon enough."

She started through the doorway. A blast of heat almost brought her to her knees, but she pushed forward. "Then I'll help you."

"No! Get back outside!" He hefted up a bulk and started to drag it toward the doorway. "Caterina, get the hell out of here. Now! I'm right behind you!"

She ran back through the building and outside, praying he followed close on her heels, as he said he would. The first fire truck barreled into view and onto the site. Red lights flashed, cutting the night like screaming harbingers of dread.

A car pulled in right after them, slamming to a stop with a skid on the snow-covered dirt, next to Liam's truck. Antonio and Lucia jumped out and raced toward her.

Caterina glanced back at the building. A wave of relief flooded over her when she saw that Liam had made it outside. His arms were looped around a man's chest as he walked backwards, pulling the body away from the building. When he'd gotten a safe enough distance back, he laid the man on the ground.

Liam removed the coat he'd wrapped around the man inside the building, bunched it up, and put it under the victim's head.

An ambulance, blue lights swirling, pulled in behind Antonio's car.

"What happened?" Lucia asked anxiously, her expression full of anguish.

"Liam was bringing me home, and we saw the flames. I called the police as soon as we realized it was a fire. Liam had already gotten out, and I saw him going inside while we were talking. I didn't know what he was doing, and I started to panic. I went in after him, to get him to come back outside. But someone was in there. He made me go back out, then he dragged the person from the building."

Two EMTs raced past Cat, Lucia, and Antonio. Liam stood as they approached him and the victim.

Cat's chest heaved, her breathing heavy with worry. "That's all I know."

Lucia put her arm around Cat's shoulder. They stood huddled together in the cold, dark night, snow continuing to fall around them, and watched as the first firemen aimed a hose at Serendipity and began drenching their dreams in a deluge of water.

"Do you have any idea who it is that Liam pulled out?" Antonio asked, his brows knitted together with concern. "Was it one of the crew?"

Caterina shook her head. She didn't know, but whoever it was, she thought, intentionally or unintentionally, he must be responsible for the fire.

Liam walked up to Cat. He took hold of her shoulders, his expression a mixture of concern and anger. "Are you all right?"

"I'm fine. But more importantly, what about you?"

Dark smudges and grime covered Liam's face. His sweatshirt and jeans had visible charring. She took his hands and looked at them. "Your hands! Liam, you've got burns all over them, and your wrists!" she said, horrified, as she pushed back the sleeves of his sweatshirt.

"They probably look worse than they are." He pulled them back, but his wince told her they hurt more than he let on. "I can't say the same for him." Liam glanced over toward the man the EMTs were lifting onto a stretcher.

"Is he going to be okay?" Lucia asked.

"He'll survive." Liam's jaw hardened. "I don't think his burns are life-threatening, but he'll probably have some extensive scarring as payback for what he tried to do."

Antonio followed the path of Liam's gaze. "Tried to do? You think it was arson? That he intentionally set the fire?"

"Yeah, I think he set it," Liam said with conviction, his expression taut, angry.

"Why?" Cat asked, grappling to make sense of such an act. "Who would want to do such a thing?"

"Your old boyfriend," Liam said in an acrid tone. "Mitch Gregory. That's who I pulled out of the building."

Caterina stared in shocked disbelief. Her stomach roiled, making her feel like she might throw up. She brought a hand to her mouth. This was her fault. If she'd never gotten involved with Mitch, Lucia's dreams wouldn't be going up in flames along with her own. All the work—Antonio's, Liam's, hers and Lucia's—turning to ashes as they stood impotently by.

And all because she hadn't wanted to believe she'd made another mistake when it came to her judgment about a man's character. Her sisters had tried to get her to see. But no. She'd dismissed their warnings because she hadn't wanted them to be true.

"Cat," Lucia said from beside her. "Oh, Cat."

Caterina closed her eyes. She couldn't bear to see the loss in all of theirs. A loss that wouldn't be there if not for her. She turned and started walking away, toward Antonio's car. She didn't think she could face Liam right now. Not after seeing the look on his face when he'd said, *Your old boyfriend. That's who I pulled out of the building.*

He might have saved Mitch's life, but Liam was furious right now. And if one of the reasons he hadn't liked her before was because he disapproved of her choice of boyfriends, he was probably furious with her too. And she couldn't blame him. She'd brought this on all of them.

"Where are you going?" She heard Liam calling after her.

She turned around. He'd followed her and was closing the distance between them. Her eyes felt hot, watery. She blinked back the tears she didn't want him to see. Tears wouldn't put out the fire, couldn't make up for what Mitch had done.

"Hey," he said and then pulled her against his chest. He wrapped his arms around her, held tight. "I hope you're not blaming yourself for any of this, because if you are it's really going to piss me off, and I'm already feeling punchy enough."

"He did this to get back at me." Cat swallowed. "He told me he'd make me pay for walking out on him and leaving him in the lurch with the restaurant. I never imagined he'd do something like this, go this far for revenge. It just proves what a bad judge of character I am. I never should have—"

"You're not responsible, Caterina," Liam said firmly. "And I'm not going to let you take responsibility for that bastard's actions. He did this!" He pointed toward the building, where the flames were quickly being extinguished.

There didn't appear to be much damage to the main part of the structure. A couple of windows were shattered, probably from the water pressure of the hose. Fortunately, she and Liam had discovered the fire before it had been able to spread beyond the left wing. She prayed when they could survey the damage it wouldn't be too extensive.

Cat looked down. Liam hooked a finger under her chin, lifted her head back up so she had to face him. "When I told you about Sylvie OD'ing, you told me I wasn't responsible. You said people make their own choices and that, good or bad, they're their choices, and we can't own them. Did you mean it?"

"Yes, but—"

"No. No buts, Caterina. You either believe it or you don't. Do you believe it?"

She swallowed. "Yes."

He ran a finger along her jaw. "Well, Gregory made the choice to set that fire. A bad choice. You can't own it. It was his, not yours."

"But if—"

Liam shook his head. "I don't want to hear it. You were right, Cat, and if I'm wrong to hold myself responsible for Sylvie's decisions, you're wrong to hold yourself responsible for Gregory's. No one died here tonight. We lost some time and materials. It could have been a lot worse."

Caterina nodded, tried to take some comfort from his words. She had meant it when she told him that his wife had been responsible for her own decisions. Mitch striking out against her and setting the fire wasn't much different from Sylvie trying to get back at Liam by taking the OxyContin. The only difference was, it had cost Sylvie her life. No one had died tonight. Liam was right about that. It could have been a lot worse. It might have been if she hadn't asked him to take her home, if he hadn't risked his own life to drag Mitch out of there.

Liam pulled her close again, held tight. "This isn't the end of Serendipity." He kissed the top of her head. "It's just a setback. Whatever we need to do to fix things, we'll fix."

The ambulance's engine turned on, and Cat and Liam both glanced over to see it back up. It turned around, then pulled out of the lot and onto the road to take Mitch to the hospital.

"Hey, you two," Antonio said, drawing their attention away from the departing vehicle. "I just talked to the firemen. They said the fire is under control, but we can't go into the building until after they get an inspector in there tomorrow and make sure it's safe, so there's no use hanging out here in the cold any longer."

"I agree," Lucia said from beside him. "I think we could all use something hot to drink. Let's go home. I'll make some tea and hot chocolate. El and Marcella were ready to race over here with us, but we told them there was no sense in all of us tramping around and probably getting in the way. They'll be anxious to know what's happening, and more importantly, that we're all okay."

She laid her hand on Liam's arm. "You come too. I doubt any of us are going to be able to sleep now, and I want to look at your hands in case you should go to the emergency room."

"The burns aren't that bad. I've had worse," Liam said, trying to shrug off her concern. "But I'll bring Caterina back and come in for a drink. I'd probably prefer something stronger than tea or cocoa, though."

"I've got a bottle of Old Pulteney, single malt, if you want to crack it open with me," Antonio offered. "I think I'm up for something a bit stiffer as well."

Liam gave him a thumbs-up. "That'll do."

Antonio and Lucia got into their car, Cat and Liam into his truck. As they pulled away, Caterina looked through her window, toward Serendipity.

It stood etched against the night. The lights of the fire trucks rolled across the façade, like red ripples over water. Behind it, she could barely make out the low, rolling crests of the Blue Ridge. And all around, big, soft white flakes of snow drifted down peacefully, in silent juxtaposition to the night's destruction.

Eleven

*"There are some things you learn best
in calm, and some in storm."*
William Carter, author

They gathered in the library—Caterina, Liam, Antonio, Lucia, Eliana, and Marcella. Antonio built a fire in the large fieldstone fireplace. Flames danced over the dry wood, chasing the night chill from the air.

Lucia made tea, hot chocolate and set out some biscuits and some fruit and cheese. They brought out wine, of course, and Antonio fetched his bottle of scotch for anyone wanting a taste of something stronger to warm their blood.

Eliana turned on the tree lights and Marcella lit the candles on the mantle and in the balsam fir centerpiece decorating the coffee table. There seemed to be an unspoken agreement that they needed to surround themselves with beauty and comfort after the ugliness they'd just experienced.

A soft glow embraced the room—embraced them—and issued in a calm that restored some balance to the night. How different the entrancing flames of the fireplace and candles, Caterina mused, with their soft light and welcoming warmth...how different from the wild, uncontrolled flames that Mitch lit to destroy, to punish her for refusing to overlook his infidelity and lies.

Lucia fussed over Liam, examining the burns. She'd taken several courses on dealing with medical emergencies in the event they ever had a situation at the guesthouse that required quick action. "You're lucky these are only first-degree burns," she said, turning his hands over. "I'll put some aloe on them, which should reduce some of the pain and swelling, and a light gauze wrap to help prevent any infection."

"I appreciate your concern, but you don't need to bother with that," Liam said, seemingly planning to tough it out. Just like a man, Cat thought.

"Yes, she does," she said from beside him, where they sat on one of the couches. "What if it were me who'd gotten the burns? Would you wave my sister off and tell her it wasn't necessary to tend to them?"

"That's different."

"Oh, really? And how is that?"

Liam looked around at the audience of expectant faces. He frowned. Cat raised a brow.

"It just is. I'm tougher than...In my line of work, I'm always getting...because you're a—"

Caterina cleared her throat.

"I, uh, don't think you want to go there, my friend," Antonio, being the only other male in the room and having experienced his fair share of similar conversations with Lucia and her sisters, advised.

Apparently recognizing concession as the wisest course of action, considering the odds, Liam let Lucia administer to his hands without further objection. As she did, he answered what questions he could about the fire.

191

"I only wanted to see if I could tell whether it was contained to the end suite. Caterina was calling it in, and I had no intention of going inside when I knew it shouldn't take the fire department more than ten minutes to get there. When I tried to see through the windows, I thought I heard someone yelling for help, and I knew that if someone was trapped in there, they might not have ten minutes."

"How'd he get trapped?" Antonio asked.

"I don't know, but he didn't seem able to stand up. Maybe he fell and broke something, or maybe he got trapped somehow and the smoke overwhelmed him. There was a lot of stuff in that area that he could have tripped over—sanders, ladders, toolboxes. Once he set the fire, he probably wanted to get out and away from the site as quick as he could. He could have easily fallen over something in his hurry."

Antonio gave his scotch a swirl. "I guess we'll have to wait to find out what happened until after the fire inspector and police put together their reports."

"I'm glad you were able to get him out, Liam, but what he did was stupid," Marcella said. "I wouldn't have expected him to go this far, but when Cat refused to let him intimidate her, I guess he decided to take his threats to the next level."

Liam turned and looked at Caterina. "You didn't say that he'd been trying to intimidate you, or that he'd made threats."

"He's a bully, Liam," Cat said. "It's how he tries to manipulate people." She didn't feel much like getting into her relationship with Mitch, but Liam had just pulled the guy out of a burning building. He had a right to some of the backstory. "You know I used to be the chef at Caulfield's, in Ashburn, until a few months ago. Mitch is the owner."

"Yeah, I know," Liam said.

"And you know we dated, but it didn't end well. He didn't like that I was the one to break things off, and he blames me because the restaurant lost business after I left. He lost some waitstaff, too, and thinks I convinced them to quit. I didn't, but he doesn't believe that. He came here a couple of times threatening to get even with me for all the problems he thinks I caused. The first time was last fall, not long after I walked out on him and the restaurant. He'd been drinking, and he showed up in a foul mood, threatening to get even with me. He woke everyone up with his yelling. It got ugly. He and Antonio almost came to blows."

Liam glanced at Antonio.

"He was way out of line," Antonio said. "Marcella almost got a punch in, if I recall correctly."

Caterina looked at her twin and grinned. "I know she wanted to, but I just wanted him to leave before things escalated any further." She drew in a breath and continued. "The second time was the night of the holiday open house, when you found us outside arguing. He tried calling me several times, but I never answered, so he'd leave threatening messages. But I didn't take them seriously."

"You never said anything about him harassing you with phone calls," Marcella said.

Cat shrugged. "I thought if I ignored him he'd get tired of calling and eventually fade away. They were always the same thing, how he'd make me pay for what I did. I thought he was just blowing hot air, blaming me for his own shortcomings. I know I realized too late that he's bad news, but I wouldn't have guessed he'd go so far. I probably shouldn't have taken his threats so dismissively."

"Bad news is an understatement," Liam said. "What he did is criminal." He studied her face a moment, searching her eyes. "And just to reinforce what I said earlier, you're not to blame for his actions. None of this is your fault."

"I know," Caterina said, "but we've still got to deal with the fallout from my relationship with him."

"Well, there's nothing we can do about any of it now." Lucia gathered her hair and started twisting it into a loose braid. "I'm going to get that aloe and some bandages to take care of our patient, and I suggest we not stress over it anymore tonight."

"I agree," Eliana seconded. "It seems we have more questions than answers, and we could talk about it all night without getting any closer to knowing what really happened."

Liam looked around the room. "Since you all look like you're in your pajamas, maybe you should go back to bed, try to get some sleep."

"Yeah," Marcella said with a hint of sarcasm, "like that's going to happen."

Eliana reached for one of the open wine bottles and poured herself a glass. "Maybe," she said, "since all of us, except you and Cat, are in our pajamas, we should have a pajama party."

"A what?" Liam frowned.

"A pajama party," Cat repeated, and his frown grew.

"Don't be so quick to scowl at the idea, Liam." All eyes turned to Antonio, and he chuckled. "I'm just saying. Lucia and I used to—"

Lucia elbowed Antonio in the ribs, and he laughed. "What's wrong, sweetheart?"

Cat rolled her eyes. "Okay, let's not go there. We all know about your pajama parties, or have you forgotten, mine and Lucia's rooms share a common wall?"

"Unfortunately for some of us," El chimed in, "given our current relationship status, we're not lucky enough to enjoy *those* kind of pajama parties right now. I was thinking more of a hang out, drink some wine, and eat junk until the morning, to take our minds off things. Like we used to when we'd come home from college. Except that Antonio and Liam are here, so we won't be able to talk about all the hunky guys we'd like to get to know better."

"You mean listen to you talk about them," Marcella corrected.

Eliana grinned. "Details."

Marcella shook her head, a smile on her lips at their sisterly banter. "Whatever. I'll hang out if the rest of you want to. It'll be better than lying in bed staring at the ceiling until the sun comes up."

Cat glanced at Liam. "What do you want to do? You're welcome to stay, and, with the snow, it might be better to wait until morning to drive back."

He rubbed the back of his neck. "I feel like I should go, try to grab a few hours of sleep even though I'm still keyed up. The snow's not a problem with the truck, and there's not that much."

She nodded. "It's your choice."

He stood up. "You should try to get some rest too. Even if you don't sleep, go up and lie down, try to relax."

"Party pooper," Eliana said, but her tone was teasing, and Liam grinned at the comment. He glanced her way. "Maybe next time."

Caterina walked him to the door. She wished he would have decided to stay, but she wouldn't try to persuade him to change his mind. He'd gone into a burning building tonight and saved a man he could barely tolerate. He'd done what any decent person would try to do, but that didn't mean his feelings weren't conflicted about it right now. Maybe he needed to be alone to deal with his own emotions without everyone else's clouding things.

"I'll give you a call tomorrow." He leaned forward and brushed a light kiss across her lips.

Cat gave a nod, swallowed. "Okay. I hope you can get some rest."

He reached for the door handle and pulled. The lights blinked off and on. Liam pulled on the handle again.

"What the—" He frowned down at Caterina.

She sighed and then glanced up toward the ceiling. "It's been a long night, Rosa. He wants to go home."

The lights flickered again. Liam tried the door again, to no avail.

"I think our aunt has other ideas," Lucia said.

"Can't you do anything about her?" Liam asked, facing Cat.

"Not if she's decided she doesn't want you to leave."

He gave a snort. "It was hard enough to believe your family has a ghost. Now I've got to deal with her being temperamental?"

Caterina sighed. "I know. I'm sorry."

Antonio walked over and put a hand on Liam's shoulder. "Looks like you'll be staying the rest of the night, buddy. Should I pour you another glass of scotch?"

Liam's shoulders slumped. "What the hell. Make it a double."

"I'M ACTUALLY HAVING trouble keeping my eyes open," Marcella said about an hour later. "I think I'm going to head up to bed."

"I didn't want to be the first to drop, but I'm feeling sleepy as well," Lucia said and looked at Antonio. "I'm going up too. You coming?"

"Maybe I should stay down here and keep Liam company, since Rosa's hijacked him."

Liam glanced over from where he sat on the couch, with his head leaning against Caterina's. "Don't stay up on my account. Tomorrow's probably going to be a rough day. Anyone who can grab some shut-eye should do it."

"Well, I hate to jump on the train to dreamland, especially since I suggested an all-nighter," Eliana said, "but a warm bed and soft pillow sounds very inviting right now."

"You should all go up," Cat insisted. "I'll see to Liam."

Eliana looked at her sister and wiggled her brows.

"Will you just go to bed?" Cat said with a snort, shaking her head, but Liam heard the amusement in her tone.

After Antonio and Cat's sisters had all taken themselves off to their respective beds, Liam slipped an arm around Caterina and pulled her against his side. She leaned her head back, looked up at him, and smiled lightly, welcoming, he thought, the comfort of his embrace after a long, disturbing night.

There were shadows under her eyes. More, he mused, would be shading her thoughts with worry about Serendipity. Still more would be darkening her spirit with guilt because of her association with Gregory. There was much he didn't know about her, much still to discover, but he'd discovered one thing. She bled on the inside, where no one who didn't know her well enough could see. Where no one would be able to detect that the confident, always-had-her-act-together woman she presented to the world could be vulnerable.

"Sorry about all the teasing. If you hang around here enough, you get used to it." She dropped her gaze, rested her head on his shoulder. It surprised him how much he liked having it there. How right she felt leaning against him, warm and trusting.

"It doesn't bother me. Remember, I've got two brothers. We rib the hell out of each other but don't let anyone else try."

She nodded. "Yeah, I get that."

"What I'm more interested in right now," he said, hoping to lift some of the shadows from her mind, "is how you're planning to *see* to me."

"What do you mean?"

"You told your sisters '*I'll see to Liam.*' So, how are you intending to see to me?"

"Well, you can choose. We have two open guest rooms this weekend, so you're welcome to try to get some sleep in one of those, or you can bunk with me."

"I'm probably not going to get any sleep if I share a room with you," Liam said, glad she'd chosen to detour down the very road he hoped she'd go.

"You're probably right."

"Right. Because you're probably going to keep me up the rest of the night demanding I satisfy your unquenchable need for my manly body."

"No. Because I've been told I snore like a bear."

"Say it isn't so."

"Sorry, you've been warned."

He sighed. "That does shoot a hole in the fantasy."

She shrugged. "I believe in honesty too."

"Okay, you know what, I'll muscle through."

"A manly man would."

He bent his head and kissed her. "Let's go to bed," he whispered against her lips.

"Let's."

CATERINA WOKE SLOWLY, cocooned in a blanket of warm skin. She felt dreamy. She felt sublime. She felt...safe. Her eyes drifted open to find Liam watching her.

"Good morning, beautiful lady." He smiled, a little crooked, and a lot sexy. Cat's heart swelled. Not because he'd called her beautiful. It was the way he'd said it. It was the warmth in the words behind the smile. It was the steadfastness of his gaze. The emotion she glimpsed in the blue-green depths of his sea-glass eyes, eyes that told her he cared about her, maybe even as much as she'd come to care about him.

"Good morning." She stretched her arms back, over her head, to try to release some of her morning grogginess, then let them fall back at her sides. "How long have you been awake?"

"About an hour."

"What have you been doing for the last hour?"

"Watching you sleep."

Caterina snorted. "That must have been riveting."

"More than you might imagine. I also copped a few feels while I waited for you to wake up. You seemed to enjoy it."

She had trouble not smiling.

"You especially seemed to like it when I did this." He cupped a breast, brushed his thumb over her nipple.

Cat's breath hitched in her throat. Lord, don't stop, she thought, arching against his palm.

"If you insist," he said in response to her nonverbal plea, and lowered his head to capture a trembling bud between gifted lips. His tongue and mouth teased, while his thumb and fingers tugged and rolled the other in delicious torture.

He'd tapped into a vein of desire she'd never known ran so deep. And he'd done it in under a minute. He either had an excess of talent, or she was excessively horny. Maybe a bit of both, she thought.

After another minute, she couldn't think, not clearly. Urged on by her own desire, she yielded to the feelings, the sensations, the magic of Liam's touch.

He drove her up. Took her higher. Higher. She moaned, and he caught it in his mouth, gave it back to her when she raked her nails down his back. She was hot and wet and needy, and when she grasped his hips, he answered the call.

Liam slid into her with a rumbling groan of pleasure that sounded as if it had been born in the depths of his very soul. He held himself still a moment as it echoed over her. Then he began to move, and Cat lost all sense of control. She gave herself up to all he offered. Surrendered to him. And in doing so, took him hostage.

"WHAT TIME IS it?" Caterina asked, when she finally roused herself from the beautiful cloud she'd been floating on in the aftermath of their early morning lovemaking.

199

Liam lifted his head and looked at the clock on the night-stand. "Six fifteen." He rolled onto his back and then pulled her on top of him, wrapping her in his arms. "Do you need to get up soon, or can we be lazy?"

"Normally I'd be down in the kitchen by now getting breakfast together for guests. My sisters are covering things today, though." She turned her head, so she could see his face. "The three of them decided I should take the morning off."

"Lucky me," he said.

"I think that was their intention."

Liam laughed. "I really like your sisters."

As he got ready to leave a short while later, Cat glanced at his hands and gasped.

"Oh my God, Liam, your hands. I forgot about the burns... when we were making love, I forgot—"

He hushed her by putting a finger over her mouth. "They're fine. That stuff Lucia put on them helped a lot. They don't even hurt anymore."

She took them in hers, turned them over. "They're blistered. You're just saying that to make me feel better."

"Cat, they're fine, seriously. And I wanted to make love to you. I would have been upset if you stopped me because of a few minor burns on my hands."

She frowned. "Well, I'm not going to let you make me so mind-less in the future that I forget things I shouldn't forget."

"Yeah, well, good luck with that." He grinned. "I plan to try and make you mindless every opportunity I get."

A short while later, after he'd finished gathering his things, Cat went downstairs with him to see him off.

"I'm going to ask my sister-in-law if I can pick Riley up later this afternoon. I want to go over to the site this morning to see if I can get in there and assess the damage on my own."

"I want to go with you."

He rested his hands on her shoulders, waited for her to look at him. "Let me check things out first. I promise I'll give you a full report. There's nothing you can do over there, and even though I think the damage was mostly contained to that one section, seeing it will probably only upset you."

"I still—"

"Hey, Liam, I'm glad I caught you before you left." Antonio, who had entered the reception area from the solarium, approached them. "Have you talked to the fire inspector yet to see when he'll be coming to the site this morning?"

"No. I was going to call from the truck. I want to get in there as soon as I can to see what we're dealing with."

"Okay. Let me know what you find out, and I'll meet you there." Antonio glanced between Liam and Cat. The corners of his mouth twitched. "By the way, there're warm muffins and sconces in the kitchen if either of you need some sustenance after, umm, well...if you need to refuel for any reason."

Cat draped an arm around Liam's shoulder. "Do you need to refuel for any reason, Liam?"

"I do, but I don't think a muffin will do it. I'll stop on the way home for a couple of bacon, egg, and cheese bagels and some hash browns."

He brushed his lips over hers and then opened the door. "I'll call you later. And listen to me about the site, okay?"

Rather than risk an argument, she nodded, and waited until he'd jogged down the porch steps before closing the door.

"I'm going to find my sisters. And to refuel," she said to Antonio and hooked her arm through his, pulling him along with her as she walked across reception. "Oh, and just so you know," she said, "it's scones, darling, not sconces."

"Really?" Antonio furrowed his brow. "I wondered why someone would name a pastry after a light fixture."

THE LAST SEVERAL weeks had been so hectic, Cat had spent almost no time trying to find out more about Rosa. She'd intended to, and it was unlike her not to follow through on her intentions. She'd told her sisters that she'd spearhead the research effort, and if she said she'd do it, then she should do what she said she would.

Feeling guilty for dropping the ball, she decided to spend some time that morning in her room, emptying out the old trunks. It would also give her something to keep her mind off the fire and what was happening over at Serendipity.

After she finished getting something to eat, she took a cup of coffee up to her room and, settling in, started going through the first of the two trunks. It contained an assortment of boxes and bags, some belonging to her aunt and uncle, and some to Rosa's parents.

There didn't seem to be any logic to what had been packed inside. Old newspapers, a box of receipts, some old photographs, and letters from her grandfather to their uncle Gino were stored away with a wooden jewelry box and miscellaneous knickknacks.

She suspected that at some point someone had decided to consolidate it all into the trunk to save on space. Some of it might have been kept for sentimental value, like the photos and her *nonno's* letters. Some of it might just have been put in there to go through at another time, and then forgotten.

Reaching into the very bottom of the trunk, Cat pulled out a long box that looked like it had been covered with flowered wallpaper and tied together with a pale blue ribbon. She set the box on the floor and ran her hand over the top of it.

The paper felt thick. It had a vintage look. The background was creamy with a golden hue. Caterina wasn't sure if that was due to age, or if that was just the color. The pale pink and powdery blue roses decorating the paper in a baroque floral pattern suggested it had belonged to a woman, most likely Rosa or her mother.

Cat looped her fingers around the ends of the ribbon and loosened the bow. She had to untie an extra knot, which took a bit of doing as it had been doubled and tied tight, but she managed to get it undone without having to get a nail file or some other tool to work it free.

After removing the ribbon, she lifted the lid off the box. Inside were several small books, like journals, most with leather covers, some with carved designs. A few had thick, paper jackets with a pretty garden print or some idyllic scene. All of them were tied shut with either leather cords or ribbon that had been incorporated into the cover for that purpose.

She picked up a soft, buttery-yellow leather one, and loosened the cords. Opening the front cover, she started reading.

> *Dear Diary,*
>
> *I'm going away for a while. To Italy. My best friend Claire invited me to come for a visit. She used to live here in Virginia, but her family moved there over ten years ago. I've only seen her a couple of times since she moved, when she came back to see her grandparents, but we write every month.*
>
> *I don't know exactly how long I'll be there, perhaps a month, or possibly more. I just don't know. Claire said I could stay as long as I need to. She's been trying to convince me to come visit for several years, and I kept saying I would, but you know how that goes. She has an apartment of her own now, and she said she has an extra bedroom, so it won't be a problem.*
>
> *I told David and my parents I wanted to go because I missed Claire, and that with David and*

*me getting married this fall, I might never get anoth-
er opportunity to go to Italy to visit her. David's not
happy about it, and my parents are a little concerned
about me going off on my own to another country
for several weeks, but I'm twenty-eight. Certainly, old
enough to look after myself!*

*I don't just want to go. I must go. I need to put
some space between David and me. I'm so confused
about my feelings for him. What if marrying him is a
mistake? The closer we get to the wedding, the more
doubtful I become. I thought I knew him, but after
we got engaged he seemed different somehow. Little
things. And maybe I'm just imagining the change in
him, but it makes me uncomfortable.*

*Claire's the only one who knows. I told her how
confused I was in one of my letters, that I just wished
I could get away for a while to sort out my feelings.
That's when she told me I should come for a visit.
I've spent the last few days making all the necessary
arrangements, and I'll be leaving next Monday.*

*I hope I'm able to find some answers while I'm
there.*

*Yours, Rosa
June 28, 1982*

Cat held her breath, pulled out another journal. She untied it
hurriedly, flipped it open, ran her finger down the entry until she
got to the signature. She checked two more, doing the same thing.

"Oh my God," she said excitedly, "these are her diaries. I've
just found Rosa's diaries!"

She got up from the floor where she'd been sitting in front of
the trunk and gathered an armful of the books. She couldn't wait
to show her sisters what she'd discovered. If they were going to

find a clue into their aunt's psyche, any reason she might still be hanging around the family home, chances were they'd find it in one of these.

When she got downstairs, Lucia was talking to a young couple who'd checked in Friday afternoon. They'd said they were celebrating their anniversary and were on a getaway weekend—their first time away together since their son had been born two years ago. El was in the solarium, setting up for the noontime tasting, and there was no sign of Marcella.

Cat ended up sending them all a text that she'd found something of Rosa's she wanted to show them and asked what time everyone could meet that afternoon.

The earliest they'd all be available at the same time wasn't until five, and Eliana only had an hour because she'd be doing a tasting at six. After the tasting, she was going out for a late dinner with Damien. The two of them had spent a lot of time together that week. They certainly seemed to have hit it off. Cat wondered if they'd keep in touch with Damien checking out today, or if their week-long romance would fizzle out the way most of her sister's relationships did after the second or third date.

With a little over four hours to kill before she could show her sisters the diaries, Cat took them back up to her room. She was tempted to go over to the site, but Liam was probably right. She should wait until he and Antonio could determine how much time and money it would cost to repair the damage first. It would still upset her when she saw it, but knowing they had a plan to fix it would help her focus on moving forward.

She also felt the edges of a headache. Going to the site and getting upset might make it worse. With the fire, and almost no sleep last night, it was a wonder she didn't have a full-blown migraine. She rolled her shoulders, felt the tension knotted there and in the back of her neck.

She didn't want to lose tonight to a migraine. As susceptible as she was to them, she decided to take some preventative measures.

Going into the bathroom, she took a couple of pills, then went back into her room. She lay down on the bed and closed her eyes. Twenty or thirty minutes should do the trick. Just long enough to let the pills take effect and hopefully prevent it from getting any worse.

She hovered on the fringe of wakefulness. Gentle fingers caressed her temples. Caterina sighed softly and then fell into a deep, dreamless sleep.

Twelve

"Tis an ill cook that cannot lick his own fingers."
William Shakespeare, *Romeo and Juliet*

he next few weeks sped by in a blur—filled with special events at the winery, the plethora of parties December dependably brought, and the usual hectic holiday whirlwind that typically escorted one from Thanksgiving into the New Year—in what seemed the blink of an eye.

January had dawned bright and white, under a six-inch blanket of snow. They'd gotten a few more inches last night, and if the weather reports were correct, it wouldn't be letting up soon. The wind blustered over the Blue Ridge, whistling and moaning a wintery tune that carried over the rows of now-dormant vines that had, in time, yielded the fruit that helped Bonavera Winery produce their award-winning wines.

After Cat had told her sisters about finding Rosa's diaries, they'd all agreed it would be better to wait until they got through the holidays, when the mid-January lull set in, and read them together. It would give them something to look forward to, and the holidays were such a busy time at the winery that they didn't need to heap any more on their already overflowing plates.

Caterina stood at her bedroom window, gazing out over the vineyard. Everything looked so fresh and clean. She didn't like the cold, but she could appreciate the pristine loveliness of the scene below. Snow carpeted the fields, draped heavily over thick, green pines, and etched the face of the foothills that marched in the distance, grounding all she knew.

She couldn't believe it was a new year. So much had happened over the last one. So much had happened just in the last month!

After the fire, Liam's crew had removed the damaged section of the left wing, taking the area down to the foundation. For now, it remained that way, with plywood and tarps temporarily covering the opening where it joined to the rest of the building.

Liam wanted to wait until the weather turned to continue work on that area, but once it did, they'd be able to frame and seal the new wing in quickly. Until then, work progressed on the rest of the project.

Caterina had so many ideas for the restaurant. She'd decided to call it Serendipitous. The boutique hotel would still be Serendipity, but she thought the restaurant should have a separate name, one that went hand in hand with the rest of the complex. And she hoped, no matter how people found out about them, whether through Eliana's marketing plan, word of mouth, or because they'd stumbled upon Serendipity by happy chance, as their name implied, that they would consider it a wonderful discovery. One they would add to their list of places to return to again and again. Caterina intended to do whatever she could to ensure it, with a creative menu, superior service, and a dining experience that made customers feel pampered. A meal at Serendipitous would indulge the senses and make love to the palate.

As chef and owner, she would have the freedom to flex her culinary muscle, do things she hadn't been able to do when she

worked for someone else. Never again for someone who didn't value what she could offer, as a chef...or a woman.

But she wouldn't dwell there. Mitch had been charged with
arson and was serving time for his crime. He was lucky to be alive,
thanks to Liam, but he'd been seriously burned and would require
several skin grafts. Caterina was sorry for his injuries. She didn't
like to think of anyone suffering that much pain, but he'd brought
it on himself.

Surprisingly, Eliana and Damien were still an item. Cat wondered if El had finally met her match. From what Cat observed, her
commitment-averse sister seemed more interested in the guy with
each passing week. Not that Cat objected. Damien seemed like a
nice guy. He treated El well, and he was certainly easy on the eyes.

She'd noticed that he didn't like talking about himself, was
adept at redirecting the conversation if asked a personal question, but that was no reason not to like him. Some people were just
more private than others. She, of all people, understood that.

Cat's relationship with Liam had taken a sharp turn as well.
One that both surprised and thrilled her. She never would have
imagined she could ever fall for him, but it warmed her heart
whenever she thought of him and how close they'd become. The
Liam she'd gotten to know over the last two months was so different from the man she'd thought he was. Although she'd put up a
valiant fight, she'd always been attracted to him. In the beginning,
it was purely physical, something she had no control over.

Her body still went into *I want to jump that man* mode whenever she saw him, but the attraction went so much deeper now.
Once they'd put their differences aside, she discovered he was a
good man. That was especially obvious when she observed him
with his daughter. Cat knew it had to be difficult raising a young
daughter on his own, no matter what a great kid Riley was.

Without a partner to consult on child-rearing situations,
being a single parent would be a challenge for anyone. Unless you

had a live-in nanny or family living close by that could help, you didn't get to take a break from the responsibility. You were it. Most of the time, she imagined, you had to go with your gut, make a decision, and hope you weren't screwing the kid up for life.

Her cell rang, and she walked over to the nightstand and picked it up. She smiled when she saw Liam's name on the screen.

"Hey," she said. "What's up?"

"My electrician isn't going to make it today. He's got a for-ty-five-minute drive, and the roads out his way haven't been cleared. He said he could try to make it over this afternoon if the plows come through, but I told him to forget it. I contacted the crew and told them I was calling the day."

"Okay. So, there won't be anyone at the site today?"

"No. I know you're already upset that we've lost a few weeks because of the fire, but one more day isn't going to make that big of a difference."

"No, you're right. I don't want anyone trying to get here if the roads are bad. They may not have gotten them plowed out here either. We don't have any guests right now, so I haven't been downstairs yet to see if the roads are snowed in here."

Cat wrapped her free hand around her waist and then sat down on the bed. She'd planned to stop by the site that morning to see how far along they were, since she hadn't been over in almost two weeks. Then, she'd thought she'd go to the new design center that had opened near the mall. She had been wanting to check it out to see if she might get any new inspiration for Serendipity's dining room, but there was a good chance she'd be stuck at the winery.

"Can I watch a show, Daddy?" Cat heard Riley's voice in the background.

"Give me a sec, honey. I'm on a work call," Liam answered her.

A work call? Cat's heart sighed. She shouldn't let the comment bother her. Yes, they'd hired him to build Serendipity, so technically this was a work call, but she'd stopped thinking of herself as just his client weeks ago.

Did Liam not want Riley to know he was on the phone with her? He had kept it all business. Hadn't asked how she was, what she was up to...if she missed him.

Maybe he told his daughter that because he didn't want her to know there was anything going on between them. Liam had never asked Cat to do anything that included Riley. He'd brought his daughter to the tree-trimming party, yes, and the open house tour, but those were group things. And Cat hadn't seen Riley since.

"I have to go," Liam said. "Riley's daycare is closed today, so I need to scramble up some breakfast for the two of us."

"Okay," Cat said, feeling deflated when she realized he had nothing else to say. "Well, thanks for letting me know."

"Sure thing. I'll talk to you later." And then he disconnected, off to do whatever he and Riley did in their private world—a world she increasingly wondered if he had purposely excluded her from.

Had Liam made a conscious choice to keep Riley and her apart because he didn't want his daughter to know he and Caterina were—what? Dating? In a relationship? Lovers?

Was he afraid they might form a bond he'd rather they didn't, in case things went sour? The thought drained more wind from her already-punctured mood. She adored the child. She adored the child's father. But if she wasn't just looking for a problem where none existed, and it turned out Liam wanted to keep that part of his life separate from her, it might just break her heart.

I'm in love with him. No horns blared. No bells rang. No gasp raced past her lips. It was a quiet truth. One she'd known in her heart for some time. She'd just never said the words so clearly to herself. So, there it was. She loved Liam.

She closed her eyes where she stood. She wanted love. She wanted children, a family. She wanted it with Liam. And Riley was a big part of it. She hadn't realized the importance of the whole

package until that moment. Now that she had, she didn't want to settle for anything less. What she didn't know was if Liam wanted the same thing.

"HI, MISS CATERINA!"

Cat looked down into the dancing eyes and smiling face of Liam's daughter and gaped in surprise.

"Riley! What are you...?" She blinked up at Liam, who stood behind his daughter with an amused grin deepening the creases at the corners of his gorgeous mouth.

"Do you have a snowsuit? Mine's purple. It's my favorite color. Do you like it?" Riley spread her arms to reveal a thick purple jacket over purple snow bibs. A pink wool hat, with a purple pom-pom the size of a grapefruit, bounced around on top like a vivacious cheerleader. It was pulled down over her hair and tied below her chin. Pink snow boots with white fur cuffs completed the ensemble.

"I do like it! It's very you."

"Daddy said we could build a snowman, and maybe a fort too. He said you and me could be a team, 'cause he'd probably still slaughter us with snowballs, 'cause we're girls."

"Oh, he did, did he?" Caterina spared Liam an arched brow. "Is that a challenge, mister?"

He shrugged, poked his tongue along the inside of his cheek. "Just telling it like it is, sweetheart."

Riley giggled. "Are you Daddy's sweetheart?" She looked from Cat to Liam, and back to Cat again, with a smile so hopeful it grabbed Caterina's heart and squeezed. It also set off a warning sign in her head that blinked: *Caution! Danger! Any answer you give could potentially cause harm, including, but not limited to, misunderstanding, anger, loss of boyfriend, and a broken heart.*

"It's just a term," Liam said, quick to jump in, saving Cat from stuttering out a response neither of them would feel comfortable with. "You know how I call Aunt Becca sweetheart sometimes, and Grams, because they're girls, and most girls are sweet. Miss Caterina's a girl, and she's our friend, and sometimes she's even sweet."

Liam flashed Cat a teasing grin. She didn't see the humor in it. Did he really think of her as just a friend? Or was he covering because he didn't want his daughter building her hopes too high when it seemed likely, from the way she'd looked between them with that innocent sparkle in her eyes, that Riley already seemed to be forming an attachment to Caterina?

"Sometimes?" Cat decided to roll with it, for Riley's sake. Now wasn't the time to ask Liam to clarify his feelings for her. She would though. And soon. He'd stolen her heart. Riley had too. She wanted more than friendship. She wanted forever. If that was an impossible dream, she'd rather wake up to the reality now, deal with it, and move forward.

She wouldn't make the same mistakes she'd made with Mitch, or any of the other men she'd believed, and trusted, and been wrong about. Her bad. She'd made the choice to overlook, make excuses, and convince herself all was right with her world, even when the threads of doubt had tiptoed around her brain whispering, *Are you sure, Caterina?*

No, she wouldn't make the same mistake this time. Because this time, she'd truly, impossibly—damn her if it was already too late—fallen in love with the man. And this time, her heart would be at too much risk if she handed it over completely to a man who wouldn't cherish it.

"LIAM! STOP!"

His laughter rolled over Caterina as she struggled beneath him. She pushed. She kicked. She balled up her fist, swung wildly, and finally managed to land a hit.

"Ouch! Jesus!" He pulled up with a jerk, rubbed his nose. "Not the face, sweetheart."

"Oh, what's the matter, dish it out but can't take it? Worried I'll mess up your pretty boy looks?"

"No, damn it. That hurt."

"Then you shouldn't have tackled me and shoved snow down my coat."

"You started it. So, I get to finish it." Liam picked up a palm full of snow and washed her face with it. Cat sputtered.

"You...you!" She couldn't think of a good enough word. And it was hard to sound mad when she was laughing between her screams. She tried to reciprocate, clutching up a handful of snow, but he caught her arm and held it down.

"Give," he said. Amusement sparkled in his eyes like sunbeams on a crystal blue sea. "Admit it. I win. Pledge your allegiance to the new master of Snow Kingdom."

He jerked suddenly when a snowball hit him square in the chest. He swung his head, narrowed his eyes, then threw his head back and roared.

Riley let out a peal of laughter. He stood up slowly, never taking his eyes from the girl. "I see the snow princess has stolen out from behind the castle walls to try and rescue her queen."

He began stalking her. Riley squealed in delight as he gave chase. "Queen Precious, help me." She screamed. "King Evil Ice is after me."

Cat scrambled up and reentered the fray. After exchanging several volleys, Liam decided to end the game by seizing a laughing Riley and tossing her up in the air, before catching her again and setting her on his hip.

"I've got you now, princess. And I think I'm going to lock you in my ice tower, so no handsome princes will ever be able to take you away from me."

Riley giggled, then planted a sloppy kiss on his cheek. A sweet stab of longing pierced Caterina's heart. Let me have this, she wished. *Just let me have this.*

"I THINK I can separate an egg." Liam looked at Cat as if he'd done it a couple of million times and it was no more difficult than blinking, which took no thought or concentration whatsoever.

Cat frowned at him. "Okay, we need three egg whites." She took the two small glass bowls she'd gotten out for separating the eggs and slid them across the kitchen island toward him.

"Not a speck of yolk," she said firmly, which earned her an exaggerated eye roll.

"What do I get to do?" Riley asked, standing beside Cat in a white chef apron that Caterina had rolled several times at the waist, so the girl wouldn't trip on it. She looked so adorable, and so excited to be able to help, Caterina felt hard-pressed not to pick her up and hug the stuffing out of her.

"Since you were such a good measurer when we baked cookies, you can help me measure the corn syrup and salt into the mixing bowl."

"Okay." Riley gazed up at Cat with adoring eyes. "I like coming to your house, Miss Caterina."

"Well, I like it when you come over. Now, let's measure the corn syrup first."

Liam watched them from across the island, with an unreadable expression.

"We need two cups," Caterina told Riley, her mind conjuring all the possible things he might be thinking, just to make herself crazy.

She showed Riley the mark to fill to on the quart glass measuring bowl. Next, they needed a quarter teaspoon of salt. "You can use your finger to level it out, Riley. When you're baking, the measurements need to be precise, or your recipe won't come out perfect."

"What's precise?"

"Exact," Cat said. "You know, just right."

"Oh. What if you make a mistake, and it don't come out perfect?"

Cat thought a moment. She knew what she'd do if something in her kitchen was anything less than perfect. She'd toss it out and start over. Her standards were extremely high, as they should be and as her customers deserved, but she wasn't going to tell a four-year-old she had to throw out her first bowl of homemade marshmallow fluff because she'd accidentally put in a half teaspoon of salt instead of a quarter.

"Sometimes it won't, but it might still taste okay, so you can eat it, anyway. But the next time you make it, maybe you're extra careful when you measure, and it comes out better. And then you start to get the hang of it, and every time you make the same recipe you get better at it, until you get so good at it, you make it perfect almost every time."

"That's just like tying shoes, Daddy," Riley said, glancing over at Liam with a look of pride at her analogy.

"Yep," Liam said, "just like it. The more you do it, the better you get."

"Till you can do magic, like Miss Caterina."

Liam looked at Cat, held her gaze. "Yeah. Just like."

His eyes glowed with a warmth that fed her dream and fueled her hopes. She didn't want to misinterpret the easy mood they'd been enjoying since coming inside to make hot chocolate and homemade marshmallow fluff for something more than it was. Like love. The kind she felt for him.

"Are you done separating those eggs?" she asked. Better to focus on the task at hand than to ponder his affections right now, she thought.

His eyes held hers for another heartbeat before he picked up the bowl of egg whites and handed it across the island to her.

Cat started to pour them into the mixing bowl, then stopped. "Liam! There's some yolk in here!"

"Not that much. No more than a few drops."

"No more than a few drops! Ugh!" She walked over to the sideboard, pulled out the under-the-counter trash bin, and dumped the fouled egg whites.

"Why'd you do that? It was only a few drops!"

"We're whipping the whites. They need to get stiff, Liam. They're not going to get stiff if they're fouled." She pulled three more eggs from the carton and expertly separated the whites from the yolks, poured them into the mixing bowl. "You said you knew how to separate them. I trusted you."

Liam shook his head. "Lord save me from perfectionists."

"It's not about being a perfectionist, Liam." Caterina stuck her nose in the air. "Some things you can let slide. Egg whites is not one of them!"

A short while later the three of them sat around the large square coffee table in the library enjoying hot chocolate with fresh marshmallow cream and a sampling of Caterina's homemade pastries.

Their wet coats, hats, gloves, and boots lined the hearth. A fire crackled in the large fieldstone fireplace, its cheerful flames licking over the logs, lending a toasty warmth to the room that seemed to wrap around them and fill Cat with a deep contentment she hadn't felt in years.

Riley sat between them on the couch, as happy, it seemed, as a bee that had found a forgotten glass of sweet cola on the veranda in summer. Occasionally, she would look up at Cat and Liam and smile, or ask a question, or tell a story about one of her friends from preschool.

Liam stretched his arm along the back of the couch between them, draped it behind Cat and let his hand dangle on her shoulder. Every few minutes he'd run a finger along the side of her neck, or trace her ear, or wrap a strand of her hair around it. Small gestures, light touches, intimate in their simplicity. And she hoped she wasn't blowing them all out of proportion.

Was he even aware of doing it?

"We should get going, Riley," Liam said a short while after they'd finished their chocolate.

"Do we have to, Daddy?"

"Afraid so, kiddo. I've got to make some work calls, and then I need to rustle us up some dinner, and you need to get a bath." He stood up and reached for her hand. "Tell Miss Caterina goodbye."

"Bye," Riley said, then surprised Cat by throwing her arms around her in a hug.

"Bye, Riley." Cat gave her a light squeeze. "Thanks for helping me defeat King Evil Ice and save Snow Kingdom today."

Riley looked up, her small mouth wiggling with a grin. She leaned forward and whispered into Cat's ear. Cat's eyes shot up to Liam, and he frowned.

"What did you whisper to Miss Caterina, Riley?"

Riley stood up and took his hand. "It's a secret, so I can't tell. And neither can she. But don't worry, Daddy, it's a good secret."

A couple of minutes later, Cat pressed her cheek against one of the front windows. She watched Liam pull out of the parking lot. The glass pane felt cool against her skin. The late afternoon sun cast shadows across the front lawn where their footprints zigzagged through the snow.

Through uneven, lump coal eyes that hovered precariously over a stub of a carrot nose, a snowman with a too-fat middle and a too-small head surveyed the battle scene of the make-believe kingdom Riley had invented.

Cat smiled lightly at a young girl's imagination and the secret she'd shared that still whispered in her head. *"Maybe you can be my new mommy and live at my house. Then we wouldn't have to say bye. But don't tell Daddy I asked. I'm not s'posed to ask people for stuff unless he says it's okay first."*

What would Liam think if he knew what his daughter had said to her? Would it bring them closer? Or would it open a chasm too wide to ever cross again?

LIAM BRAIDED RILEY'S wet hair after her bath that evening.

"Can I watch one show before bedtime, Daddy?" She stood in front of him in her Wonder Woman pajamas, giving him the pleading look she'd mastered when she knew she was pushing the boundaries and was trying to work on his sympathies.

"No, pumpkin. It's already past eight."

"Just a short one?"

"Nice try, but you have to get up early tomorrow, and you had a big day today."

"I liked playing outside and making the marshmallow stuff. That was fun. And Miss Caterina's really nice. I like her a lot."

"I kind of like her a lot too."

Riley cocked her head. "Do you think she's pretty?"

"Yeah, I do."

"Do you think she's prettier than your friend with the red hair? The one when we had pizza?"

Liam thought a moment. "Oh, her. Yeah, I think Miss Caterina's way prettier than that."

Riley nodded. "Me too."

"Just remember, Riley—"

"I know. Pretty on the outside's nice, but pretty on the inside's nicer."

He put the brush on the coffee table and stood up. "That's right. And now, time for you to get to bed."

After reading Riley a story and tucking her in, Liam went back out to the living room and settled down on the couch with a beer.

He hoped he hadn't made a mistake.

Dropping in on Caterina with his daughter had been a spur-of-the-moment thing. He hadn't seen her for several days, and as he sat in his living room that morning while his daughter played with her dolls, he realized he missed her.

It hadn't taken more than a mention that they could drive to the Bonaveras' to see Caterina, for Riley to be all in. "*If she isn't cooking, maybe we can build a snowman,*" she'd suggested hopefully.

"*Maybe we can,*" he'd agreed, amused at the thought of Caterina building a snowman. Of course, it would have to be perfect—its hat, scarf, and other accessories precisely coordinated. She would want to plan out how they put it together before they got started, so everyone knew exactly what needed to be done, what the end product should look like. He'd been surprised when she didn't try to redo their somewhat sad-looking snowman, but he suspected she'd wanted to.

Funny how Riley had immediately associated Cat with being in the kitchen, involved in some culinary activity, when he'd thrown out going over to see her. And interesting she hadn't asked why, when he'd never included Cat in any of their plans before, that they'd spent most of the day with her.

Had he intended today to be a test drive? Something he'd been leading up to without consciously thinking about it? Riley was the most important thing in his life. By taking her with him to see

Caterina, he'd risked the possibility that his daughter might form an attachment.

She already talked about Cat as if she was their new best friend. She talked about wanting to be a chef when she grew up, like Miss Caterina. She was going to wear pretty clothes when she got big, like Miss Caterina. And Miss Caterina was going to teach her how to walk in high heels...she said so.

Cat *was* nice to Riley. She seemed to genuinely like and enjoy spending time with his daughter. Accepting his daughter had to be the number one criterion for any woman he had a serious relationship with. It was nonnegotiable.

He wanted more than a relationship with Caterina, though, more than an occasional night out when he could get a sitter, or Riley had a sleepover at his brother's house. The truth was, he'd fallen for her. Hard. Why deny it? He loved her. He wasn't sure when it had happened, although he suspected he'd been stumbling in that direction for a while.

Did he want to marry her?

Liam stretched his arms behind his head, rolled his neck. Did she want to marry him? She enjoyed their relationship, he felt sure of that. And she liked his kid. But did she love him? Would she want to build a life with him, help him raise Riley, maybe have another kid or two together?

He rubbed a hand over his jaw. She'd better, because he intended to take a page from her book. Come up with a plan, and make it happen. And once he set his mind to something, he could be as damn stubborn about getting what he wanted as she could.

Thirteen

"Everything you see I owe to spaghetti."
Sophia Loren, actress

*G*athering for a meal, Cat thought, as she glanced around the table at the faces of the people she held most dear, was, at its most basic, an expression of love. It was a celebration of the senses, of coming together at the end of the day—to laugh, to share, to comfort, to take time out to connect with those who mattered most in life.

When she prepared food, she wasn't just mixing things together, tossing in a few herbs, a dash of salt, a splash of balsamic—she was sharing a part of herself. She'd graduated from a premier culinary school, had mastered technique, won numerous competitions against chefs with years more experience, and worked in one of New York's top restaurants. Anyone could learn technique, how to cook, but what she had was rare. With her, cooking was an art. It was her gift. She knew. When she cooked, she did so not from her head, but from her heart. And she did it with passion.

She sunk into the warmth of the evening, content. The conversation flowed around her as freely as the cabernet, mingling with laughter and the affectionate teasing so common in close-knit families like theirs.

"I remember meeting Rosa at your *nonni*, Rodrigo and Sophia's, shortly before she and your uncle Gino left to come to the States." Vincenzo DeLuca, Antonio's grandfather, lifted a piece of baked eggplant with tomato and mozzarella onto his plate, just one of the assortment of antipasto Caterina had made to celebrate his visit.

Vincenzo had traveled from Cortona, Italy, and arrived that morning for a three-week stay, his second trip to the States in less than a year. Antonio said that Lucia and her sisters had bewitched the old man with all their spoiling, because little could tempt him to leave his beloved homeland.

"*Una bella donna.*" He added two arancini, filled with minced veal, onion, tomato purée, and fresh thyme leaves; a piece of olive crostini, and some insalata caprese.

"Yes, Rosa was a *very beautiful woman*," he repeated in English as he picked up one of the arancini and took a bite. He closed his eyes, kissed his fingers to his lips. "*Delizioso!*"

He looked at Caterina with eyes so blue they would put a summer sky to shame and put a hand over his heart. "If I were ten years younger, I would marry you."

Caterina's smile came quickly. "It's clear where Antonio gets his charm."

"I hope I'm a little subtler than that," Antonio said with a teasing grin for his *nonno*, "but I can't fault his appreciation of the meal, Cat. Everything is exquisite."

"Ummm, it is." Eliana dabbed her napkin to the corner of her lips. "You should come more often, Vincenzo. In addition to the fact that we all adore you, we get to eat things Cat doesn't usually make just for us."

Cat gave El a meaningful glance. "If you're complaining about the meals I so selflessly prepare for this family on an almost daily basis, my dear sister, you *could* learn to cook."

El was quick to respond. "Oh, I'm not complaining. Just saying this is all so good, it's nice to get to try some of the delightful creations you can make, things that we don't usually get to sample." She gave Cat a beaming smile.

Cat shook her head. "Suck-up. I already told you I'd bring meals over from Serendipity for you and Marcella after we open. I'd feel guilty if I didn't, knowing you'd be living on boxed cereal or takeout, and Cel would probably end up in the hospital from malnutrition because she'd be too tired to make something for herself after working herself to the point of exhaustion in the fields during harvest."

"Thank you, thank you," Eliana said with a sigh. "You're my favorite sister."

"You told me I was your favorite sister yesterday when you and Damien got back with a pizza from your outing, and you asked me to select the perfect red to have with it," Marcella reminded El.

"And yesterday you were," Eliana said without a trace of guile.

Lucia laughed. "As you can see, Vincenzo, little has changed since your last visit."

"No. You are all as delightful as I remember."

"What do you remember about our aunt Rosa?" Marcella asked, returning to his earlier comment. "Did she ever mention anything about the man she was engaged to before she met our uncle?"

Vincenzo shook his head. "No. I never knew she'd been engaged to someone else until years later, after your *nonno* and *nonna* came here to settle the estate. Rodrigo told me the story—that Rosa's ex-fiancé had been the one to commit the murders."

"That's right. There was a witness, a friend of Rosa's who'd driven her home after the two of them had gone into town together. Rosa had forgotten her purse on the floor of the car. Her friend saw it as she was driving away and turned around to return it. When she got to the front door, she saw Rosa and Uncle Gino lying on the floor, dead, and her ex-fiancé standing over them. Apparently, Rosa walked in on the murder, so he killed her too. Whether he intended to kill them both, he never confessed. Aunt Rosa's friend escaped before he saw her and went straight to the police to tell them what she'd witnessed. According to the newspaper articles I found, it was an open-and-shut case," Caterina confirmed.

"We found some of her diaries in one of the old trunks that were stored in the attic," she said. "We haven't had a chance to go through them yet because everything's been so crazy the last few months, although I've glimpsed a couple of entries. We're hoping we might find something in them that will help us understand why she's still here."

Cat picked up her fork, swirled the last bite of spaghetti puttanesca around it. Antonio had told her it was his *nonno's* favorite. She'd nailed the sauce. The rich, intense flavors of anchovy, Kalamata olives, and capers, perfectly blended with garlic and onion, seduced the mouth, each bite promising more pleasure. The dish was appropriately named, Cat mused, being a derivation of *puttana*, the Italian word for whore.

"We were planning on getting together tonight to start reading them," Cat said, referring to the diaries, "before we found out you were coming for a visit."

"And I have ruined your plans."

"Oh no, not at all. The diaries aren't going anywhere, and you know we're delighted you've come. We're all secretly in love with you, Vincenzo, don't you know?" Cat gave him an affectionate smile, accompanied by a flirtatious wink she knew the elderly man would get a kick out of. "Rosa can wait."

The lights in the solarium where they were enjoying their meal blinked off and on twice.

Lucia glanced around the table and then up toward the ceiling. "She didn't mean you're not important, Rosa. We're not going to forget about you."

The lights flickered again.

"I don't see why you can't get started this evening," Vincenzo suggested. "And if none of you object, I'd like to join you. I've been curious about the woman ever since the morning she appeared at my bedside during my last visit."

"I'm in," Antonio said, slinging an arm around the back of Lucia's chair and giving her shoulder a squeeze. "You?"

Lucia nodded. "Why not? It's still early, and none of us made any other plans for tonight."

"If that's the case, I'll get a couple more bottles of wine." Marcella pushed her chair back, stood up to go get them.

"Pick out something to go with dessert while you're at it," Caterina suggested.

"Okay, what is it?"

"Tiramisu." Cat looked at Vincenzo. "Antonio told me it was your favorite."

Marcella nodded. "The 2015 Viognier. Not too sweet, with nice aromas of peach and honeysuckle."

"She doesn't even have to think about it," Eliana said as their sister walked out of the solarium. "How does she just know so quickly?"

"Her gift," Caterina mused. "Plus, she's got a catalog in her head of every drop she's ever produced, and I guarantee she remembers the characteristics of every one of those drops better than she can remember the names of the guys she's gone out with over the last few years. And there weren't that many to try to remember. If I can find a sommelier who's half as good as she is for the restaurant, I'll be ecstatic."

She picked up her wineglass, finished off the red she'd had with dinner. "Since I made the meal, the rest of you get to clean up. While you're doing that, I'll get some of the diaries. Should we reconvene in the library?"

"I thought we were having dessert first," Antonio was quick to say before Cat could leave the table.

"Don't worry, handsome, we'll have it in the library. None of us would want to deny that sweet tooth of yours."

Her soon-to-be brother-in-law flashed one of his killer smiles, and for one brief moment, Caterina almost felt sorry for Lucia. The man was heartbreakingly handsome. But then she remembered that her sister didn't have a jealous bone in her body, and even if she did, Antonio was so gaga over Luch, Cat wondered if he even noticed all the women who salivated as he passed them by.

"LISTEN TO THIS," Eliana said from where she sat sideways in one of the library's club chairs, her legs draped over one of the arms, swinging back and forth, in perpetual motion.

> *Dear Diary,*
>
> *I've fallen hopelessly in love. It is the last thing I would have dreamed would happen when I decided to come to Italy. I can still barely believe it. I thought I knew what love was, but I've never felt anything like this before. His name is Gino, and he wants to marry me.*

"Oh my God," El said, gushing, "isn't that romantic?" She held the open diary against her chest with a faraway look worthy of a Disney princess.

"Yeah, romantic," Marcella mimed, with noticeably less wistfulness and none of the dreamy quality their dependably imaginative sister had put into it.

Amused by each of them because they were both so true to form, Caterina grinned. "That's the first entry anyone's found where she mentions Uncle Gino. What does it say next?"

"Okay." Eliana held the book up and began reading again.

> *I should be thrilled, and I am. Truly I am, except for one problem. My engagement to David. Of course, I intend to end it. In addition to the doubts and concerns that led me to come here in the first place, I realize now I couldn't have been in love with him. What I felt for David doesn't begin to compare to the love in my heart for Gino.*
>
> *I fear what Father will say. He and David are close, even if Mother never warmed up to him, the way she does most people. Perhaps if I'd tried to find out more about her reservations, I wouldn't be in this situation. But then, if I'd broken up with David sooner, I might never have come to Italy. And I never would have met Gino. So maybe I had to travel that road to get here.*
>
> *I've often wondered about why things happen the way they do. How much of it is fate versus choice, and if we make a choice that veers us off our intended path, does fate intercede to give us another chance, to make another choice? A better choice?*
>
> *When I'm with Gino, it seems so right. I can't help believing we were meant to be together, that destiny brought me to Italy, so we would meet, and I would see the truth of it in my heart.*

Lucia looked at Antonio, who returned her gaze, and smiled. "Any of that stir a sense of déjà vu for you?"

"I do recall a similar conversation several months ago that included another bottle of Viognier, some lovely meats and cheese, and some incredibly sexy, lace lingerie." He grinned wickedly.

Lucia slapped his shoulder. "Focus on the conversation, sweetheart," she said, but gave him a peck on the cheek and elicited a chuckle from him by adding, "We can revisit the setting later."

Marcella leaned forward, cut a small slice from the remainder of tiramisu on the coffee table, and put it on a plate. "You had a conversation that related to Rosa's diary entry?" She scooched back onto the couch. "We didn't even know about them until a few weeks ago."

"Destiny, child." Vincenzo, who sat next to her, patted her knee. "They're talking about destiny. Your *nonno* and I knew, when they were both born on the same day as us, that it was a sign they were meant to merge our families. Antonio fought me on it. I had to trick him into even coming to meet Lucia."

Vincenzo wagged a finger at his grandson. "But we were right. All anyone need do is look at the two of them to know they were meant for each other. Stubbornness can't trump fate, not when it's given the chance."

As Rosa had written in her diary, Caterina wondered, did destiny really play a part in our lives? Lead us to different forks along the way that would in turn change its course based on which ones we chose?

She'd made bad choices in the past. She had regrets, but she'd made some good choices too. Like deciding to move back to Virginia and help her sisters try to hold on to the winery. She'd believed at the time that it would derail her plans to open her own restaurant, but it hadn't. Now, she'd be opening one sooner than she ever could have if she'd stayed in New York. She'd most likely still be a sous chef. At a highly regarded restaurant, yes; but realistically, she admitted, she might never have been able to raise the capital to realize her dream. Or, if she did manage it, to distinguish herself enough to survive in New York's highly competitive restaurant market.

She wouldn't have Serendipity. Without Serendipity, she never would have met Liam. Odd, she mused. For as long as she could remember, opening a restaurant had been all she wanted. Oh, she still wanted it, badly, but she'd realized over the last several weeks that she wanted something else even more.

Had destiny brought her to one of those forks that, depending on which road she took, would change the course of her life? And, she mused, the thought occurring to her for the first time, was Rosa's interference in their lives an attempt to guide her to the right path?

Cat pondered the possibility. If that were the case, what could have happened in their aunt's life that it would matter so much to her?

LIAM SAT IN the Bonaveras' library, waiting for Antonio to join him. Lucia had decided that since they had to rebuild her and Antonio's private quarters at Serendipity, she wanted to make some minor changes.

The cold snap that had kept them from redoing the build-out in January was, thankfully, behind them. February had issued in warmer than normal temps. They'd finally been able to make some progress, but if they were reworking the suite's design, he needed to know what the changes would entail before moving forward.

He glanced up from the new drawing he'd been perusing when he heard voices. Eliana and Damien walked out of the solarium and crossed the lobby toward the front doors.

"Hey, Liam," she said, making a detour into the library. "You remember Damien?"

Damien greeted him, and Liam stood, shook hands with the man. "How's it going?"

"Damien and I were just heading out to get some lunch." She glanced around at the empty reception desk, then faced him again. "Are you waiting for someone? Do they know you're here? I could run up and sound the alarms if you want me to."

"I've got a meeting with Antonio—and here he is now." Liam nodded in the direction of the hallway that Antonio had just rounded and was now making his way across the lobby.

"Okay, great. We'll leave you two to it." Eliana took Damien's hand and headed toward the lobby. She reached up and ruffled Antonio's hair as they passed him on their way to the front door. "How goes it, handsome?"

"No complaints, beautiful." Antonio nodded a hello to Damien. "How do you keep up with her?"

"I was a long-distance runner in college. Not that it totally prepared me for the whirlwind, but it helps."

"You're both lucky I've got such a wonderful sense of humor." El tugged Damien's hand. "Come on, Flash, I need food."

After they walked out, Antonio joined Liam in the library. He sat on the couch next to him, so they could review the drawing. "Thanks for coming over. I know you've been busy playing catch-up at the site."

"No problem. Burke and Shawn are both helping out this week, so we should be able to make up for some of the time we lost to all the snow last month."

Liam hitched his head toward the front doors where Eliana and Damien had just departed. "What's the story with this Damien?" He knew he'd seen him somewhere before the day they'd been setting up for the holiday tour, but he couldn't place where. In a restaurant, some store, the gas station. It could have been anywhere, but he just knew he'd crossed paths with the guy.

Although he'd always seemed friendly enough, something about Damien made Liam wary. "Is Eliana dating him now?"

"That's the word on the street," Antonio said. "Lucia told me she thinks this guy may be different."

"Why's that?"

"Apparently most men don't make it past the third date with Eliana, but she's been seeing Damien for about two months now, with no sign of lacing up her running shoes. Lucia and her sisters aren't sure what to make of it, but they're all hoping she's finally met Mr. Right."

Liam didn't want to raise a red flag when he'd only talked to the guy a couple of times and had little to base his discomfort on. Maybe it was because he sometimes got the sense Damien was watching him. But the man was a photojournalist. He told stories through the pictures of people and scenes he observed. He probably studied everyone and everything more intently than most people.

Just because he'd caught Damien observing him didn't make the guy suspicious. Most likely it was a habit, one of those behaviors that was indigenous to certain professions—like with cops, or psychologists, or writers. They were always studying people, analyzing their behavior, trying to figure out their motivations—students of the human condition.

"So, the biggest change to the original plan is that Lucia wants to shift the bathroom from the corner here, to the opposite side of the bedroom," Antonio said when Liam didn't comment further, and leaned forward over the drawing. "She decided she wanted to keep this corner open and add a window on the front and another on the side, so the room would get the morning light. I suggested if we were going to do that we could put French doors on the side that led out to a small, private porch."

Liam buried any lingering questions he had about Damien. "I'll bet she loved that," he said. "She'll have another area to decorate."

"She did," Antonio confirmed. "She's already picking out furniture for it."

They spent the next half hour going over other changes before wrapping up their meeting. As Liam was about to return to the site, Lucia came out of the solarium. He stopped to chat for a minute.

"If you don't have plans tomorrow evening, why don't you and Riley come for dinner?" she said. "Antonio's grandfather is visiting, and Cat's going to make a special meal in his honor. She loves to spoil him. We all do," she admitted. The look in her eyes softened, and it was clear her affection for the man ran deep. "Anyway, it would be great if you could come. I'm sure Vincenzo would love to meet you and Riley. He's always asking Cat if he's going to get to meet the man who stole her heart to see if he approves."

"Who says I've stolen her heart?" Liam asked, although the notion pleased him immensely since she'd stolen his.

Lucia looked at him as if to say, *Really, as if it isn't obvious to everyone?*

He chuckled. "That was a question, not a complaint. And if you don't think Cat would mind two more for dinner, I know Riley would love it."

"She's not going to mind. You know she adores Riley, and," she said, meeting his eyes with all seriousness, "in case you have any doubts, she feels the same about her father."

Had Caterina confided her feelings for him to her sisters, Liam wondered. He loved her. He'd accepted the truth of it. He'd never said the words to her, and she'd never said them to him. But that didn't mean she didn't feel them...and if she did—

"She's in the kitchen. Why don't you stop in and let her know I invited you? I'm sure she'll be happy to see you."

"I think I will," he said. Although he hadn't come here with the intention of seeing her, he saw no reason to pass up on the opportunity. "Thanks."

"You bet." The corners of Lucia's mouth curled up, and she gave a single nod. A stamp of approval, it seemed. If he'd gotten past Caterina's sisters, the battle to make her his was half won.

"TOUCH ANYTHING IN this kitchen and risk losing a hand," Cat said without turning around from the counter to see who had come into the kitchen. She continued mincing the fresh parsley she needed for her signature version of Chesapeake crab ravioli, just one of the several dishes she planned for tomorrow night's buffet.

Regathering the herbs into a new pile, she rocked her knife over them. She was going all out to make everything special, with some traditional Italian fare she knew Vincenzo would enjoy, but also adding in a couple of surprises that would showcase some local treasures, like the blue crab.

Vincenzo loved to eat. He was a man who appreciated food, celebrated it, and understood the power it had to comfort, to create memories, and to be the very fabric that united families and friends. And she was a chef.

What better a guest could she want to sit at her table?

"Does that go for the cook?"

Saliva began to pool at the sound of the voice that belonged to the man who'd captured her heart. She was like one of Pavlov's dogs. He took hold of her waist, eased her around, brought them hip-to-hip, face-to-face—and she melted—Valrhona chocolate, liquifying into molten desire in a double boiler. She reached behind her, set the knife on the cutting board, found a more interesting use for her hands.

"You can touch the cook. It's not usually permitted, but she's willing to make an exception in this case."

"Ummm." He bent his head, nibbled her lips as if he were savoring a delicate sliver of fresh Parmigiano-Reggiano. A shiver raced up her leg. "Lucky me," he said, and she felt him grin against her mouth.

"You are, because the cook likes you."

"Yeah?" He angled his head back, regarded her, his gorgeous blue-green eyes holding her captive. "How much?"

Something about the way he looked at her made Caterina hesitate. What would he do if she told him she loved him? Would he stay? Would he run? Would he stumble over a response about how he liked her a lot but didn't want to hurt her? Or, would he say he loved her too? Was she willing to risk telling him to find out?

I love you. The words formed in her head, as clear as the crystal wineglasses hanging over the kitchen island. They flirted with her lips, where they were less confident about revealing themselves.

"A lot, Dougherty. I like you a lot," she settled on. "More than I ever would have believed I could the first couple of months we knew each other."

He stood there, continued to study her, as if trying to look past her eyes and see into her thoughts, as if debating something in his own, and her heart raced. Her mind spun through a dozen possibilities, good and bad, in a brief span of seconds that felt like hours, before he reacted.

"So," he said, "Lucia told me you were making a special dinner tomorrow night for Antonio's grandfather. She invited me and Riley. You okay with that?"

Caterina blinked. "What? I mean, yes! I'd love it if you and Riley came!"

"Are you sure? You seem taken aback by the invitation."

"Yes, I'm sure! I was just...you jumped topics. I wasn't expecting it. I'd love if you joined us, though. You know how much I like Riley, and I know Vincenzo will just adore her!"

"Do you think Vincenzo will adore me too?" He nipped her bottom lip and then gave her a wicked grin. *Temptation. Yes, he was.*

"I hope so. I put a lot of value in his opinion, and it would be a shame if he doesn't and we have to send you home before dessert. I'm making a hazelnut torte, and vanilla ice cream with rum-macerated cherries. Simple, but sinfully good."

"Then maybe I should satisfy my taste for sweets and a little sin now, so I don't risk missing out."

He covered her lips with a steamy kiss that obliterated whatever witty response she might have given. Her body, however, provided a ready answer. *Help yourself,* it encouraged, twining one of her legs around the back of his, sliding her hands up his broad back, holding tight.

The oven chimed, relaying that it had reached the preheat temperature she'd set it to before Liam's arrival, for the hazelnut torte she was making in advance of tomorrow. But the warmth flooding her blood had nothing to do with the 350 degrees coming from behind its glass doors.

Liam pulled back, hunger coloring his eyes a deeper shade of teal—a hunger she understood because it gnawed within her too. A hunger in her body, and a hunger in her heart—to be held, cherished, understood—to be loved.

"I better get out of here. We're trying to make some headway this week, and it's not going to happen if I don't turn around and walk out of here within the next minute or two."

Caterina dragged in a breath of head-clearing air. "Yeah. Me too. I need to run out to pick up a few more things for tomorrow night, but I still need to put the ravioli together and bake my torte first."

He let go of her and stepped away, his expression intense as he walked backwards toward the door. It had her holding her breath again. Something was in his look that she hadn't seen there two months ago, but that she'd caught flickers of over the last several weeks.

Liam stopped at the doorway. "What time should Riley and I get here tomorrow?"

"I was planning dinner for seven, but there's no problem doing six, so you don't have to keep Riley out too late on a weeknight. Would six work for you?"

He nodded. "I'll make it work." He cocked his head. What was going on in that head of his? she wondered.

"This might not be the best way to tell you this." He hooked his thumbs through his belt loops. "But I thought I'd put it out there, let you chew it over, see how you feel about it so there's no misunderstanding about what's going on between us."

Cat's stomach clenched. Here it came. He liked her but wasn't looking for a commitment...didn't want her getting too serious... to hurt her...confuse her...mislead her—

"When I asked how much you liked me, Caterina, I was angling for a different response. It was probably unfair, since I was hoping you'd say what I wanted to hear, and things would be out in the open. Rather than play that game, I'm going to come clean, then I'm going to leave. You can think it over with no pressure to answer right now, and if you're not on the same page, we can take it up later."

He locked eyes with her. "I'm in love with you. I didn't plan on it, but it happened. So, I guess we need to figure out what happens next."

Her mouth dropped open. Liam spun around and walked out the door.

IT TOOK ALMOST a full minute before the weight of his words really sunk in, another three or four before she could do anything but stand rooted against the kitchen counter in disbelief. He'd stunned her with his proclamation.

When the initial shock ebbed, and she finally regained control of her body, she dashed out of the kitchen, ran through the solarium, across reception to the front doors, and flung them open just in time to see Liam's truck crunching its way down the gravel driveway.

"Chew it over!" she yelled. She stomped her foot as he turned left and headed up the road toward Serendipity. She gave one door a good slam, then the other. Twirling around, Caterina growled, low and long.

"Men!" Frustration fueling her, she turned back to the double doors, threw one open again, and shouted, "It would have been nice if you'd thrown in a little *romance* with that declaration, Dougherty!"

Sighing, Cat pushed the door shut, then turned and leaned her back against it. Liam loved her. She'd known he cared for her, known the day he'd brought Riley over for the three of them to spend time together, that their relationship had shifted. He wouldn't have risked the chance his daughter might start forming a bond with her if he didn't consider their relationship serious. But love—he wouldn't throw something like that out lightly. Not Liam. He wasn't someone who showed emotions openly, or easily. He liked to flirt with her, but he wasn't a romantic like Antonio, with his suave charm and poetic language.

A profession of love...no, it would not have been easy for him. The reality of what Liam actually saying those words to her meant sunk deeper. This was the big leagues. This was serious. This was—

"Are you okay, Cat?"

Caterina looked up. Lucia had come into reception. She stood by the front desk, watching Cat.

"You look like you're in shock," Luch observed. She angled her head, and then her eyes went wide. "Oh no." She hurried toward her. "Mitch wasn't here, was he? He's supposed to be in jail. He didn't get—"

"No." Cat shook her head. "He's not out, and he wasn't here." She put an arm around her sister, leaned into her a moment. Her sisters had been her anchor after she'd broken up with Mitch, and he'd come to the winery and threatened her, as well as after the fire when she'd struggled against a sense of guilt.

"You worry too much," she said softly, appreciating how lucky she was to have such a supportive family. "I'm fine, just...processing."

Lucia studied her face with eyes so like her own, and Cat thought she could have been looking into a mirror at them.

"Want to talk about it?" her sister asked.

Cat caught her bottom lip between her teeth, let out a shaky breath. "Liam's in love with me."

Lucia chuckled. "Tell me something I don't already know."

"You know?"

"Of course, I know. Everyone knows."

"Did he say something to you or Antonio?"

Lucia arched a brow. "Liam? We *are* talking about Liam."

"Yeah. Right. But how did you know when I didn't?"

"Because I have eyes. Because we all have eyes. And because it's often easier to see things from the outside looking in, than from the inside looking out. When you're on the outside, you're not looking through all the emotional filters. You're not putting your heart at risk by allowing yourself to see what's right in front of you."

"Somebody could have told me," Cat said.

"When did you finally figure it out?"

"He told me. Just now. Well, a few minutes ago. In the kitchen. He just blurted it out, without giving me a chance to respond, and then he took off. It was...surreal."

Caterina frowned. "He dropped it on me and told me to chew it over. No prelude. No wine, no flowers. The man was about as romantic as the whole salmon I've got on ice in the refrigerator to go with tomorrow's dinner."

Lucia laughed. "I'm dying for the details. El and Marcella will want them too. It's almost noon. Why don't I see if they can join us for some lunch? We'll order a pizza to keep it simple, open a bottle of wine, and raise a glass to you and Liam."

"He didn't propose, Luch. He just said he loved me."

"I know." Lucia wrapped an arm around Cat's shoulder, gave her a squeeze. "Are you happy about that? That he told you he loves you?"

At the core of everything, Liam loved her. Did it matter that she was wearing a chef's apron and holding a sudoku to mince parsley, instead of sitting in a candlelit restaurant wearing a scrimp of red velvet he wouldn't have been able to take his eyes off, her fingers flirting with the stem of a champagne flute?

And there was no doubt in her mind she loved him right back. A smile twitched in her heart, filled it up. Crept over her lips.

Caterina looked at her sister and nodded. "Yes. I'm happy."

"Okay, then a little sisterly celebration is definitely in order. We don't get to do it often enough, and what better reason than one of us finding our true love?"

Lucia was a romantic, like Eliana, even if El's romances never lasted beyond the first bloom. Caterina could easily envision sharing a life with Liam and Riley. Truthfully, she realized, she wanted it more than anything, even Serendipity, which had been the only thing she'd wanted for herself for too long.

As she'd told Lucia, though, Liam had only said he loved her. He hadn't proposed. He hadn't said he wanted to spend the rest of his life with her.

She'd chew on that. And chew. And chew. And chew, until she got tired of chewing on it and gave *him* something to chew on.

"If you want to order the pizza," Lucia said from beside her, "I'll round up our sisters."

"Okay," Cat said. She headed back to the kitchen where she'd left her phone. She'd order the pizza, then she needed to put the hazelnut torte for tomorrow night's dinner into the oven.

Fourteen

*"There's no spectacle on earth more appealing than
that of a beautiful woman in the act of
cooking dinner for someone she loves."*

Thomas Wolfe

Liam unbuckled Riley's car seat and lifted her out of his truck.
A dark, navy-blue Jeep pulled into the parking lot beside
them. The driver opened the door and got out.

"Hey, how's it going?" Damien asked, locking the Jeep with
a key fob and coming around to the back side, where Liam stood
with Riley.

"Can't complain," Liam said. "Do you remember my daughter Riley?"

"I do." Damien smiled broadly at her, his eyes crinkling around
the corners. "And how are you, Riley? I see you've gotten even prettier than the night we met."

She giggled. "I'm just fine, thank you." She spared a quick look
at Liam as if wanting him to take note she'd used her manners. "Are
you having dinner with us? Miss Caterina is making a special one,

and we got to come. I can't wait. She knows how to do magic with food and stuff."

Damien chuckled. "I am having dinner with you. Miss Eliana invited me, but she didn't tell me it would involve magic. You don't think we need to worry about turning into frogs if we eat the food, do you?"

"No." Riley's mouth wiggled. "Miss Caterina only does good magic with food, to make it more delicious. I got to make cookies with her. She showed me how."

"She showed you how to do magic?"

Riley's smile broadened. "Kinda. And I showed her how to strut like Peter Peacock."

"That's a story I'd like to hear. Maybe you can tell me about it at dinner."

"Sure."

Damien glanced at Liam. "Should we head inside? I've got a feeling this is going to prove to be an interesting evening."

"It always is when you get all four Bonavera sisters together," he agreed.

Liam expected the evening to prove interesting for other reasons as well. He hadn't spoken to Caterina since showing her his hand yesterday, but he hadn't been able to think of much else since. He thought she loved him too. He never would have risked her deciding to end things with him if he didn't. He hoped she'd had enough time to get comfortable with the fact they were in it, and should consider taking the next step. For him that meant marriage, or a permanent commitment.

Surprisingly, the thought of spending the rest of his life with her didn't even make him flinch. In fact, he'd never felt surer about wanting something in his life. He felt none of the angst, or opposed the idea in any way, as he had when Sylvie had tried to pressure him into marriage before he'd found out she was pregnant with his child.

His only concern was whether, although Caterina seemed to enjoy spending time with Riley, she would be willing to take on the role of mother, as well as wife. He told himself she would and hoped he was right, because if he wasn't, he'd have to walk away from the only woman he'd ever truly been in love with.

When they entered the house a couple of minutes later, they heard laughter coming from the solarium, and headed in that direction. A large circular table had been placed near the kitchen entrance, already set for dinner. In what he'd come to recognize as characteristic for the Bonaveras, gathering around food was something they celebrated, whether they were hosting an event, like the holiday open house, or getting together with family and a few close friends, as they were tonight.

A white tablecloth served as the landscape on which real china, not like the paper plates he and Riley usually ate off at home, and crystal glasses reflected the flickering light of a half dozen fat, white candles of varying heights that had been arranged into a simple but elegant centerpiece. A couple of bottles of red wine stood next to a silver ice bucket that nestled a bottle of white.

Caterina's sisters, Antonio, and an older man, who Liam guessed was Antonio's grandfather, were all gathered around the table, laughing at something their elder guest was saying.

"Oh, look who's here," Eliana said, spotting the three of them. She waved them over. "Come join the party!"

Lucia, the quintessential hostess, got up quickly and welcomed them with hugs. "Help yourselves to a glass of wine, gentlemen," she said with a gracious smile, before leaning down toward his daughter.

"Riley, we're all so glad you could come. We made a pitcher of ice-cold lemonade just for you. Would you like a glass?"

"Yes, please," Riley said. She looked around the table. "Is Miss Caterina here yet?"

"She's in the kitchen, putting the finishing touches on dinner," Lucia explained. "She should be done soon, and I know she's looking forward to seeing you and your dad." She looked up at Liam and smiled, a hint of amusement dancing in her eyes when she did.

After Antonio introduced them all to Vincenzo, Liam glanced toward the kitchen door. He'd assumed when he hadn't seen Caterina, that's where she was. He considered excusing himself for a couple of minutes to go in and say hello, face her privately first, to gauge her mood where he was concerned. See if he could figure out how she felt about his declaration.

"Maybe I'll go in and see if Caterina needs any help," he said.

"I wouldn't," Marcella warned. "Not when she's putting the final touches on things. She'll let us know when she wants help bringing out the plates, but going in there now would be like standing in front of a trigger-happy firing squad. Not pretty."

"Are you saying all those things one hears about temperamental chefs are true?" Liam asked, remembering how she'd pitched his egg whites simply because they'd had a minuscule drop of yolk in them.

"Oh, they're true," Eliana confirmed, "and none is more of a perfectionist, or tyrant in the kitchen, than our dear sister."

"Miss Caterina!" Riley exclaimed, her face lighting up as she looked across the room.

Everyone's gaze shifted to the kitchen doorway, where Cat stood with a smirk pinching her mouth, making it clear she'd overheard their comments.

Riley ran to greet her, and the smirk turned upward, lifting into a warm smile. Cat leaned down, gave his daughter a hug, and Liam's heart flipped over.

"Hi, sweetheart." Cat held Riley at arm's length. "I see you're wearing your favorite color."

Riley pulled the purple knit sweater she had on away from her waist and looked down. "It gots a unicorn on it," she said. "Uncle Shawn and Aunt Becca gived it to me."

"It's super awesome. I wonder if it comes in my size?"

"I'll ask Aunt Becca. Then we could match."

Caterina patted her shoulder and then regarded the rest of them. "The temperamental tyrant has finished preparing the meal. I left the strychnine out of the main course, but there's always the crème fresh I was going to make to top dessert. And now, if any of my ungrateful sisters would like to help me bring the food out to the buffet, our guests might be able to eat."

Amidst a slew of teasing remarks and a few assurances of unflagging sisterly love, Lucia, Eliana, and Marcella filed past Cat and into the kitchen. Liam walked over and took Riley's hand to take her back to the table.

He angled his eyes to Cat's, meeting them straight on. He found the answer he wanted in the warmth glowing from the deep, sable depths that regarded him. She glanced away, a soft smile caressing her lips. He wanted to yank her into his arms and cover them with his own. He'd sip the words out from her later, when he could get her alone, but her expression told him what he needed to know. Caterina loved him.

He licked his lips, bit back a smile, and she laughed lightly, shook her head.

"Go sit down," she said, as Marcella walked past them carrying a large platter with a whole, roasted salmon, stuffed with wild rice. "Dinner is about to be served."

THERE WERE FEW things Caterina treasured more than feeding the people she loved, unless it was watching them enjoy the food she'd made for them. She looked around the table at the faces of the people gathered together there. Her sisters, each so special to her; Antonio, whom she'd already come to love and think of like a brother; Vincenzo, who'd stolen all their hearts on his first visit earlier that year, and whose past was so entwined with her own grandfather's, their histories were inseparable—they were all her people, her family.

She shifted her gaze to Liam, to Riley. She hadn't thought she had any available love left to divvy out after Mitch. She'd been wrong. She had buckets and buckets of it, all spilling over, that she wanted to drown them in if they'd let her.

"This ravioli is unbelievable," Damien, who'd joined them at Eliana's request, said. "If this is any kind of sampling of the food you'll be making when you open your restaurant, the place will be so busy, people will need to reserve weeks in advance just to get a table."

"Wouldn't that be lovely," Caterina said. "And thank you, I'm glad you're enjoying it."

Damien was the wild card at the table. He'd shown up in their lives out of the blue, it seemed, when he was working on a piece to capture holiday celebrations of Loudon County through his photographs. He'd told them the photos would be used in marketing campaigns leading up to the holidays the following year, to attract more tourism, and thus boost the local economy during that critical, make-or-break final quarter of the year.

He was a bit of an enigma, and Caterina didn't quite know what to make of him yet, but if it turned out Eliana was falling in love with Damien, well...she and her sisters might need to invite him over for a friendly get-to-know-you-and-your-intentions dinner one night and forget to mention it to Eliana. If El didn't like it, she'd get over it because in her heart, she'd know they'd done it out of love.

Vincenzo dabbed the corners of his mouth with his napkin. "I would say you have outdone yourself, Caterina, but I have never eaten anything you've prepared that wasn't *delizioso*."

"You talk nice," Riley said, looking at Vincenzo.

"Ah, so you like the way I talk, piccolo?" His eyes warmed as he regarded her.

Riley nodded. "Umm hmm. I don't know what all your words mean, but they sound pretty."

"You have a fine ear, little one. Maybe one day you would like to learn Italian, then you would be able to understand the words."

Riley looked at Liam. "Can you teach me, Daddy?"

"I don't know how to speak it, pumpkin, but if you really want to learn, we can pick up a beginner's book, and I can try to help you."

"I can help you too," Cat offered. "My Italian's rusty since we don't get a chance to speak it much anymore, but I'm sure it would come back quickly."

"Maybe me and Daddy can come over this weekend, like we did when we made the ice castle, and you could tell me some words then."

"We could do that if your dad hasn't already made other plans," Cat said, not wanting to put Liam on the spot but delighted with the possibility of spending another day with the two of them if he was open to the idea.

"I'm sorry, Riley, but we won't be able to do that. This is your weekend to go to your grandparents, remember?"

Riley looked down at her plate. "I don't want to go."

"Honey, your grandparents are looking forward to seeing you. They'd be sad if they didn't get to see you," Liam said, angling his head to look at her.

"No, they won't," Riley insisted. "I say *horrible* things, and then Grandma cries and goes to her room, and Grandpa tells me not to talk about you and Miss Caterina because that's not nice."

Caterina's mouth dropped, and she shot Liam a quick glance. He stared at Riley. Cat saw the muscle in his cheek twitch, and she could tell he was trying hard not to get angry.

"What horrible things did you say to your grandmother?" Liam asked, keeping his tone gentle.

Riley knitted her brow. "She showed me some pictures of my mommy last time, and I told her I didn't remember her. Grandma said that was a horrible thing to say." She looked at Liam. "She told Grandpa it was all your fault and you were an awful father. And I got mad and told them my daddy was not awful."

"And then what happened?" Liam asked, seemingly having forgotten everyone else at the table.

"Then Grandma cried more and went to her room. And we didn't go get ice cream like they said we would 'cause—"

"Because why, sweetheart?" Liam brushed the hair away from Riley's forehead and then rested his hand on her shoulder. A gentle encouragement.

"'Cause I don't remember Mommy." Riley glanced up at her father, looking apprehensive, as if she thought he might be upset at her for forgetting too. "I'm sorry I forgetted her."

Liam pulled her toward him, against his side, and rested his chin on top of her head. "It's okay, honey. You don't have to apologize; it's not your fault. You were too little when your mom went to heaven to be able to remember her."

Caterina became aware of the others around the table. Everyone had gone somber. When she looked at Damien, she was struck by his reaction. He stared at Riley, a hand over his mouth. He closed his eyes a moment and shook his head. When he opened them again, the seriousness in his expression made her think Riley's story weighed heavy on him. Had it stirred unpleasant memories of something from his past?

Damien glanced her way, and their eyes connected for a moment. He looked away, cleared his throat, and then picked up his wineglass and took a sip. She got the distinct impression something was up with him, and she also got the sense he didn't want anyone to know. Was it simply a matter of him not being comfortable with his emotions, or was there more to it?

Liam straightened and looked down at Riley. "You and I can talk more about this when we get home," he said, glancing around the table a moment as if he'd just remembered he and Riley weren't alone. "But I want you to know you didn't do anything wrong, pumpkin. Okay?"

Riley nodded. "Okay."

He winked at her. "Let's just enjoy our visit right now. You did a great job eating your dinner, so you can have some dessert. I heard that Miss Caterina made something really good."

"I did," Cat said. "Would you like to help me bring it out, Riley?"

"Yes!" she said. Her eyes lit up, and the troubled mood that had descended upon her when Liam reminded her she was supposed to go to her grandparents that weekend disintegrated, like fog burning off under a high, warming sun.

Cat stood up and held out her hand. "Then come with me, sweetie. There's a final step to finish one of the desserts that you can do if you want to."

Riley scooted out of her chair and took Cat's hand. As they passed by Liam, his eyes slid up to meet hers. "Thank you," he mouthed.

No, Caterina thought. Thank you, for loving and trusting me enough to share this wonderful child.

"NOW WE'RE GOING to taste some reds." Caterina gathered the wineglasses from her group, who were positioned around the tasting bar. The guesthouse was booked for the weekend, and many of the guests had signed up for the four o'clock tasting when they'd checked in. It was a pleasant and convenient way to spend their first evening without having to get back in their cars after they'd already driven for several hours.

They had all three tasting stations open. A reservation had been made earlier in the week for a group of eight, to celebrate a coworker's birthday. Eliana had taken them, and unsurprisingly, her station was the most raucous. Caterina and Marcella each had mixed groups, a combination of walk-ins and people staying at the winery.

Cat took new glasses from under the bar and set one in front of each of her guests.

"I noticed you put out bigger glasses for the red wine," a young woman who'd said her name was Deborah, observed. "A lot of restaurants do that too. Is there a reason?"

"There is." Caterina uncorked a bottle of cab franc. "A good rule of thumb is, the bigger the wine, the bigger the bowl. For reds to show their best qualities, they need to have room for their bouquet to develop. A bigger bowl also allows for room to swirl the wine."

"Is that really necessary?" a fortyish-looking man sporting a close-trimmed beard and a Nat's cap, asked.

"If you don't, the wine police aren't going to come haul you off," Cat joked. "But there are a couple of good reasons to do it. When you swirl your glass, it allows oxygen into the wine to open it up. That will round it out and give it a softer nature. It also releases a wine's aroma, so you can smell more of it, and since we taste with our noses first, you'll enjoy it more."

She started to pour the first red. "We're going to taste three different reds. This is our 2014 cabernet franc. It's a medium-bodied red. It does very well in Virginia's climate, and some experts consider cabernet franc to be one of Virginia's best red wines. I'll let you be the judge."

Cat set the bottle down on the station sideboard. "Take a sip. Then take a taste of your fourth appetizer, which is a rosemary cracker with goat cheese and a dab of blackberry preserves, and, as we did with the whites, be aware of how the food affects the taste of the wine when you take your second sip."

After her swirling spiel, Cat noticed all eight of her charges gave their glasses a couple of twirls. A few held the glass to their noses and scented the wine's aroma before tasting it.

As they were tasting and talking amongst one another, she heard her phone buzz on the shelf below the sideboard and glanced down at it. Liam's name and number showed on the screen. She knew he planned to take Riley to her grandparents after he picked her up from preschool, so she hadn't expected to hear from him. She let the call go to voicemail.

"Go ahead and rinse out," she said, when she saw everyone in her group was ready to move on. "Our second red is a petit verdot, cabernet sauvignon blend. It's a fuller-bodied wine." She explained the wine's properties. "Because petit verdot has a big flavor, you want to serve it with big flavor foods that the wine won't overwhelm. We've paired it with Manchego cheese, toasted walnuts, and cranberries, on the same rosemary crackers as the last sampling."

Cat picked up her phone. "While you're tasting it, I need to return a quick call. I won't be more than a minute, and then I'll answer any questions you might have."

She stepped away from the tasting station and called Liam back.

"Hey, sorry I couldn't take your call," she said when he answered. "I'm working one of the tasting stations. My group just started on their second red, so I've got a minute or two."

"No problem. I dropped Riley off at her grandparents and am on my way back. Any chance you can join me for dinner? I could swing by the winery and pick you up."

"No can do. We've got a full house, and El needs me to work another station at six. Did everything go okay with Riley?"

"I'll tell you about it when I see you."

Caterina glanced at her station. They were still sipping and tasting and looked like they were enjoying themselves as they shared their impressions. One of the couples had mentioned that they were going out to dinner after the tasting and had asked if anyone wanted to join them. Two of the other three couples accepted the invitation, and they were already, it seemed, becoming new friends.

"I'm going to have to get back to my group in a minute. I told Eliana I'd help out if she needed me tomorrow, but I should be free after six if you want to get together."

"Okay, let's plan on dinner, then. If you don't have anything going on Sunday morning, we can go back to my place, and you can stay the night."

The prospect of having Liam to herself all night sounded delightful. "I'd like that," she said, "but why don't I meet you at a restaurant closer to you? That way, you won't have to wait around if I get pulled into something in the afternoon."

Cat glanced at her station again. "Sorry, Liam, but I need to go. I'll call you tonight, and we can pick a place."

After disconnecting, she returned to her group, but her thoughts lingered on Liam. He hadn't wanted to talk about Riley, and something in his tone when she'd asked made her wonder if something had happened to upset him when he dropped his daughter off at her grandparents.

CATERINA ROUNDED THE corner into reception on her way out to meet Liam, and saw Lucia and Marcella sitting close together on one of the library couches, leafing through what looked to be several eight-by-ten photos.

"What are you two up to?"

"You might want to look at these," Marcella said, "see if you know what they're about."

Cat walked into the library. "I've only got a few minutes, but what's up?"

"I found these pictures when I was restocking the closet in the room Damien stayed in when he was working on that holiday piece," Lucia said. She held up a large manila envelope. "This fell off the closet shelf and landed on my head. I'm surprised I didn't see it up there before this. I always check the rooms after guests leave to make sure they didn't leave anything behind, but it's flat, and it could have gotten pushed to the side of the shelf where I might not have noticed it. The pictures were inside."

Lucia handed Cat the small stack. "It's weird that it would have just spontaneously fallen on your head after a couple of months."

"I don't think it was spontaneous," Marcella said. "I think it was Rosa's doing."

Caterina looked at the top picture. A shot of her, Liam, and Riley standing in front of the tree they'd decorated for the open house. She remembered the three of them posing for it when Riley was hanging candy canes.

She shuffled it to the back of the stack and looked at the next one. Caterina angled her head and narrowed her eyes, squinting to take in all the details. The picture—one of Liam carrying Riley, who appeared to be asleep—was taken at night. The backdrop was hard to make out in the low light, but she recognized his front porch in the shadows.

Cat furrowed her brow. Why would Damien have a photo of Liam outside his house? From the angle it was taken, it had probably been shot from across the street. What would Damien have been doing in Liam's neighborhood, taking pictures in the dark?

She looked at the next shot. It had captured Liam and Riley walking through a parking lot. There was a low-profile building behind them, and on the side of the building, a fenced-in area that contained several plastic playhouses, some small picnic tables, and other items that led Cat to believe it must be Riley's preschool.

Still another photo showed Liam sitting in a booth at some restaurant with a redhead. In the background she could see Riley standing next to a fountain with a fish spouting water from its mouth.

She went through the rest of the stack, becoming more confused as she did. There were a few more of her, Riley, and Liam, together and alone at the open house, but most of the pictures wouldn't have had anything to do with the assignment Damien had been working on.

When she reached the last two shots, she felt her heart rate slow. One showed Liam and her walking out of his house together. It was the night they'd first made love. She had Liam's boots on. It was the night Mitch had tried to burn down Serendipity. The final one must have been shot through the front window of Liam's living room. It showed her and Liam in a passionate kiss.

"Okay," she said, "this is freaking me out. Why would Damien have these pictures? They have nothing to do with a photo exposé on the holidays in Loudoun County, or whatever the hell he said he was doing."

She pulled several of them out and waved them in the air. "These are all of Liam in random places. His house, some restaurant, Riley's school. And these," she tossed the two that had been at the bottom of the stack onto the coffee table. "What are these supposed to be? Was Damien following us around for kicks? Is the guy a voyeur or something? I mean, seriously, this is just creepy!"

"I don't know what it means," Lucia said, looking concerned. "I agree it's very strange, though. And worse, I'm sure Eliana has no clue about any of this. If it turns out he's got some kinky habit, it's going to devastate her. She told me just this morning she thought she was falling in love with the guy."

"Oh, that's great!" Marcella leaned back and crossed her arms. "She finally meets someone she doesn't think will fall apart if she risks a serious relationship with them and it doesn't work out, and he might turn out to be a Peeping Tom—or something worse."

"What do you mean, someone she thinks won't fall apart if they have a serious relationship and it doesn't work out?" Lucia asked.

Marcella shook her head. "Nothing. I...It's not my story to tell. Something that happened a long time ago. I promised El I'd never say anything."

Lucia sighed. "We can talk about that later." She gave Marcella a look that said, *and we will talk about it.* "But right now, we need to figure out what to do about this. Do we show Eliana these pictures and see if she knows anything about them? Do we confront Damien? I mean, obviously, something's not right here, and our sister could get caught in the cross fire."

"Where's El now?" Caterina asked.

"Damien picked her up about an hour ago," Marcella said. "I ran into them as they were leaving. Eliana said she'd be home late, but I didn't ask where they were going."

Cat glanced at her watch. "Look, I've got to run or I'm going to be late. There's nothing we can do right now, and I told Liam I'd stay the night, so I won't be back until tomorrow. Let's check in tomorrow afternoon after we've had a chance to mull over the possibilities and think about the best course of action where El's concerned. Until then, I vote we keep these to ourselves for the time being and not say anything to her."

"Okay," Lucia agreed and glanced at Marcella. "You good with that?"

"Yeah. Maybe one of us will be able to come up with a reasonable explanation, although I can't imagine what that could be."

"Would either of you mind if I tell Antonio?" Lucia asked.

"Fine by me. He might know something we don't." Cat gave the rest of the pictures back to Lucia. "Maybe you should put those somewhere El won't stumble upon them before we get a chance to talk to her."

"Will do," Lucia said. "And in the meantime, 1 think I'll do some research to see what 1 can dig up on Damien Roth."

Fifteen

"The truth is not for all men,
but only for those who seek it."

Ayn Rand

A blustery, February wind whipped the hair around her face as Caterina hurried across the winery's gravel parking lot toward her Jeep. She held the collar of her navy-blue, wool peacoat together with one gloved hand, to block the chill. Her mind swirled with a dozen questions but supplied no satisfying answers.

A shiver raked through her as she pulled out of the parking lot. She reached down and turned the seat heater on full blast. Spring couldn't get here soon enough. She wasn't a skier, and although she'd always treasure the memory of playing in the snow with Liam and Riley, she wasn't a fan of the white stuff. If everyone she loved didn't live here, she could move to California or southern Florida and never look back.

Ahead of her in the distance, the sky burned gold and orange to the west, splashing through a jigsaw of dark, marbled clouds, as the sun slipped behind the rolling silhouette of the Blue Ridge. She never got tired of sunsets. They were as diverse as the people she knew, some so vibrant, the sky could barely contain them, others, a soft whisper of powdered-blue and pastel-pink promise of fair days to come.

Although the dark rumpled clouds hanging over the mountains provided a dramatic contrast to the fiery color of that evening's sky, their looming drama seemed more a portent of unsettled rather than calm days ahead.

It made her think of the pictures Lucia had found. Were they just pictures that meant nothing? Or was there more to them? Something that could cast a shadow over the lives of the people she loved? If it weren't for the ones of Liam taken at various places other than the winery, they wouldn't have seemed odd. But like Lucia and Marcella, Cat could think of no reason Damien would have them.

Should she tell Liam about them before she and her sisters had a chance to ask Eliana or Damien about them? What purpose would it serve at this point, she wondered, as she merged onto the Harry Byrd Highway and headed toward Round Hill where she and Liam were meeting for dinner.

A short while later when Cat got to the restaurant, she saw Liam's truck parked near the front entrance. She pulled into the empty space beside it. Liam lived in Round Hill and had picked the restaurant. It was a casual Italian eatery that she hadn't tried before but, based on the reviews she'd read after he'd told her where to meet him, looked promising.

When she walked inside, she spotted Liam at a table next to a large stone fireplace at the back of the cozy dining area. He glanced up from the menu he'd been studying, looked toward the front entrance, and watched her cross the room.

"Hey, sorry I'm a little late," she said when she reached the table. "Marcella and Lucia stopped me on my way out to show me something, and I got caught up."

"No big deal. I think the servers have another three hours or so left in their shift before they start itching to get out of here."

"Yes, well, I think it's important to be prompt."

He grinned. "There's a revelation."

She hung her coat over the back of her chair and sat down across from him. "It's good to see you smile, even if it is at my expense," she said and glanced around the room. "This place is charming, and it's so cold, I would have come just to sit by this fabulous fire. It feels wonderful."

"Glad you approve. Riley and I come here when we're going a little more upscale. Even though it's casual, she insists we wear nicer clothes because, in her words, *they have tablecloths and nice plates, and the people bring you your food, and everything.* I think it's really because she likes to play dress up."

Caterina smiled lightly. "What girl doesn't?"

She could easily picture his daughter, in her animated way, saying something just like that. Cat smoothed her napkin over her lap, then regarded him. "Speaking of Riley, how did things go when you dropped her off yesterday? When we talked last night, you said you'd tell me about it when we got together. Everything okay?"

Liam shrugged, his frown telling her everything wasn't.

"Riley didn't want to go. She cried on the drive there, and if I wasn't worried they'd make things even worse than they are, I would have said screw it and told her grandparents she wasn't coming." He picked up his fork and started twirling it through his fingers, almost absently. "I felt like an ogre leaving her, but if I tried to explain my reasons, it would only have upset her more. And she's too young to understand, anyway."

Their server, a tall redhead with clear blue eyes and a runner's build, stopped by their table. "Are you ready to order?" he asked. Caterina hadn't considered the menu yet. She was about to ask for a few more minutes when Liam suggested a caramelized onion pizza.

"That sounds perfect." She handed her menu to their server.

When they were alone again, she resumed their conversation. "From what you said before we were interrupted, I sense there's more going on with Riley's grandparents than being upset she's not able to remember her mother." She reached across the table and took Liam's hand. "I'm not trying to pry, but I care about you both, and I can tell it upsets you. If you want to talk about it, I've got two ears willing to listen."

He stared at their joined hands a moment before meeting her eyes and then said, "I got a letter a while back notifying me that Sylvie's parents wanted to file for custody of Riley."

"What?" Caterina stared at him, her mouth parted in stunned shock. "That's absurd!" she said with a snort when she got over her disbelief. "You're a wonderful father. No judge would ever rule to take Riley from you."

"My lawyer said the same thing. Not without just cause."

"There is none!" she asserted, incensed on his behalf. "Don't they know how devastating that would be to Riley? My God, if they love her, why would they even contemplate putting her through such a thing?"

Liam shook his head, as if he'd asked himself the same thing a hundred times. "I don't think they've honestly considered what's best for Riley. Sylvie was their only child, and in their eyes, especially her mother's, their little girl could do no wrong. Whatever happened, whatever trouble she got into growing up, it was always somebody else's fault. Sylvie was self-absorbed, and if she didn't get her way, she'd pull some kind of stunt for attention. Which is what I think she was trying to do when she OD'd...but they blamed me for her death. Still do.

"I'm convinced that, in their own convoluted way of thinking, getting custody of Riley would be like getting a piece of Sylvie back. It would also be a way to punish me for making their daughter so miserable she ended up taking her own life."

"Which you know you're not responsible for, agreed?"

"Yeah. I've thought a lot about what you said, about not being able to own someone else's choices. You were right. It helps to keep things in perspective. It might not change my guilt in their eyes, but at least I've been able to start letting go of some of it."

"I'm so sorry you've been dealing with this, Liam. Have they actually filed papers?"

"I don't think so. Or if they have, no one's notified me yet. My lawyer responded to the initial letter from their attorney, informing them we'd fight any attempt to change custody. We never heard back after that. It's been several months, so maybe their attorney advised them they didn't have a case. That doesn't mean they won't still try. The last thing I want is for Riley to be thrust into the middle of a custody battle. The only thing that would come of that would be more strained relations, with my daughter suffering the most from the fallout."

"You're a better person than I am," Caterina said. "I'd probably refuse to let them see her after what they threatened."

"I considered it, believe me, but if they did decide not to pursue their plans, denying them any visitation with their granddaughter would probably just set them off again. I don't know the law on these things, but if I refused to let them see her, they might be able to get legal visitation rights that go beyond her once a month weekend visits. You never know how a judge might rule, and I don't want to risk finding out. Besides, despite what happened the last time she was there, she's enjoyed her visits with them in the past. They are her grandparents, and although they might despise me, I believe they do love her."

"If they do, they'll think of what's best for her, and that's being with her father. And they need to stop making her feel like she's bad and wrong because she can't remember her mother, who died when she was two years old, for God's sake. If they keep up with that kind of crap, they'll destroy any chance of having a good relationship with her when she's older and can decide for herself if she wants to see them."

"I appreciate your vehemence on my account," he said, giving her hand a squeeze.

"It's just..." Cat breathed a sigh of frustration. "Riley's such an amazing kid. Anyone who sees the two of you together would know what a great parent you are and how much Riley loves you. Her grandparents must be so unwilling to accept that their daughter could have been responsible for her own death that they're unable to take an honest look beyond their own skewed beliefs to see what a good father, and person, you are."

"Whatever the case, my daughter shouldn't be the one paying for it. I called her grandmother before taking her this weekend to tell her that Riley told me about what happened the last time she was there, and that she didn't want to come this time because of it. I also told her that I didn't care if she and her husband liked me or not, but if they wanted a relationship with their granddaughter, they better stop making her feel bad for something she neither understood nor had control over, or they were going to turn her against them."

"How'd that go over?"

He shrugged. "They didn't respond, but I'm sure they didn't like it. I don't really care; I had to say something. Riley's four, for Christ's sake. I probably should have left it at that, but I also told them that if I found out they made her feel bad about herself again, they wouldn't like the consequences. I'm not going to let her suffer because of their bitterness toward me."

"No, I think you were right to call them. They need to know what they did to hurt Riley. If they care about her, hopefully they'll realize they were wrong and it won't happen again."

"I guess I'll find out when I pick her up tomorrow." Liam rubbed the back of his neck. "This conversation's starting to weigh me down. Let's talk about something else."

Their pizza arrived a few minutes later, and they turned to lighter topics, but Liam's revelation about Riley's grandparents lingered in the shadow of her thoughts, scrabbling around for attention, like an itch she couldn't quite reach to scratch.

LIAM STIRRED. HE'D dozed off again after their early morning lovemaking, but he was awake now and likely to stay that way. Caterina lay in his arms, warm, all soft curves and satin skin. She felt right there. Righter than anyone ever had. He loved her. Plain and simple. It had taken him a while to take off the blinders and see her for who she really was, a while longer to build a bridge between them, but he was a builder, he was good at building things.

The conversation they'd had at dinner the night before disturbed his thoughts, a restless review that scrolled through his mind like an old movie reel. Had Sylvie's parents given up on their idea to try to take Riley away from him? If they thought they had a chance, his gut told him they'd pursue it. It wouldn't matter what Riley wanted. They'd find a way to justify whatever they did, despite their granddaughter's feelings.

So, had their lawyer advised them that they'd be wasting their time and money? Or had something else happened to change their minds?

Caterina shifted against him, lifted her head, and regarded him through eyes not quite awake.

"A nickel for your thoughts," she murmured sleepily.

"I thought it was a penny."

"Inflation. Everything costs more these days." She scooted up higher and laid her head on the pillow next to him. "So, what has you looking so serious before the sun has even had a chance to poke through the shutters?"

Liam stroked her arm, her skin a satin expanse under his work-hardened hands.

"Just wondering how Riley's doing. I can't forget the image of her wiping her tears away with her coat sleeve, looking at me like I was betraying her or something by not letting her stay home this weekend." He leaned his head back, stared at the ceiling. "Christ, I hope I didn't make a mistake letting them see her after what happened last time. For all I know, they could still be planning to try to get custody, and I wouldn't put it past them to ply Riley for information they could use against me."

Caterina slid an arm around his waist. "You did what you thought was best for everyone in the moment. I don't have to be a parent to understand how hard it is to know if you're making the right decisions for your child. Even if it is the right one, that doesn't mean everyone's going to be happy about it. And—" She shifted again and propped herself up on one elbow, looked down at him. "As far as Riley's grandparents are concerned, the only thing they'd be able to learn by asking her questions is that she thinks you're a great dad and that she loves you. I doubt any judge would hold that against you."

"You're probably right. I can't imagine what grounds they'd use if they tried to do anything. I've got a steady income, a home, she's well provided for, and she's a happy kid. I don't have a criminal record, I'm not out partying all the time or parading a stream of new lovers in and out of her life constantly, and I'm her *father*! That's got to carry a lot of weight. So, short of them pulling some incriminating pictures out of thin air, since there's nothing in my life worth chronicling that they could use against me, they can't have anything."

"I agree. I know it doesn't take away the worry or the concern about how their behavior impacts Riley, but with no evidence to show why they should—"

"What's wrong?" Liam asked, when Caterina stopped short and her eyes widened as if she'd suddenly remembered something important.

"I...nothing," she said, hesitating. "I lost my train of thought. I'm just upset, that's all. You're a good father. You shouldn't have to go through this."

Liam squinted. Caterina averted her eyes. Odd, but he got the feeling whatever made her *lose her train of thought*, as she'd said, wasn't something she wanted him to know about.

"And that's it?" he probed.

"What do you mean?"

He shrugged. "I get the sense there's something else bothering you besides me worrying about Riley."

"No." She swallowed. "Isn't that enough?"

It might be, if she didn't look so evasive, and his gut didn't tell him there was more. So what didn't she want him to know?

"Hey," she said, rolling over and getting up off the bed. "Why don't I make us something to eat before I have to leave? You hungry?" She started pulling on her clothes.

Quick change of subject. And convenient, since she obviously had no intention of telling him what was really on her mind.

"Yeah, sounds good." He'd let it go for now, but she was keeping something from him. Something, he sensed, that wouldn't make him happy when he found out about it.

"Great. I'll just go poke around your kitchen to see what I can turn into breakfast."

She turned, then hurried toward the door as if pursued by a demon. Liam frowned. He didn't want to doubt her, but her behavior troubled him, and after everything he'd gone through with Sylvie, he needed to be able to trust her.

CATERINA WHISKED SOME cream into the eggs she'd already cracked into a bowl. Liam didn't have much in the way of herbs or fresh vegetables, but she'd found some sliced American cheese she could use to make omelets and a package of frozen turkey sausage to cook up on the side.

She flicked her wrist without thinking about it. Her mind was consumed, roiling over what she should do. She'd already decided not to tell Liam about the pictures before finding out why Damien took them. Her sister was falling in love with the man. What if the pictures didn't mean anything? Were harmless?

If she told Liam now, he might jump to conclusions and confront Damien before anyone had a chance to explain. But if Damien didn't have a satisfactory explanation, what then? Had he taken the pictures for reasons none of them knew about? Reasons that could hurt Liam? The possibility they might be related to Riley's grandparents trying to get custody turned Cat's stomach. But why would Damien be involved in such a thing? He was a professional photographer, yes, but she wouldn't have thought he'd hire himself out for that kind of side work.

Did Damien know Sylvie's parents? Was he a friend of the family—a relative maybe? Had they asked him to try to get incriminating pictures of Liam as a personal favor? That would be a colossal coincidence. He just happened to be staying at the winery's guesthouse while covering the holiday tour, and Liam just happened to be the contractor for Serendipity...and her lover? Unless, of course, it wasn't a coincidence that he'd stayed with them.

Caterina shook her head. None of this made sense. She liked Damien. He seemed like a good guy. There had to be some other explanation.

She hated to think what it would do to Eliana if they discovered Damien had chosen to stay at the winery for reasons in addition to his story. Her sister avoided commitment, running from it faster than a gazelle being pursued by a cheetah. But El had discovered something in Damien that she'd been willing to walk out on that limb.

God, she hoped Damien had a good explanation. Because if he didn't, if by some chance it turned out the suspicion that crept into her head earlier that morning when Liam had commented about *pulling incriminating pictures out of thin air* played out, then it meant they'd invited Damien into their midst with open arms, and he'd betrayed them all. It also meant it could break her sister's heart.

"WHY DON'T YOU and Riley come by the winery after you pick her up this afternoon? Maybe we can play a game, and I'll make an early dinner." Cat threw out the suggestion as she got ready to leave a couple of hours later.

Liam and Riley were in the habit of going out for an early dinner when she came back from weekends with her grandparents. But since Caterina was his daughter's newest hero, she'd probably turn cartwheels at the idea. "I'll leave it up to Riley," Liam said. "If she says yes, why don't we order out, though? That way you won't have to cook, and no one has to do dishes."

Cat set her purse down on the edge of the entryway table to put her coat on. Liam held it up, and when she turned around, he slipped it on.

When she spun back to face him, she accidentally knocked the purse off the table. Some of the contents spilled out and scattered across the floor.

"One of the problems with having long arms." She looked at Liam and rolled her eyes in a self-mocking gesture. "They can turn even the most graceful among us into klutzes."

She got on her knees and started picking things up, stuffing them into her purse. No doubt, she'd dump it all back out when she got home and organize it in whatever system she'd designed for it. He knew she had one, but probably didn't want to take the time to do it now since she knew he had to leave soon to go get Riley.

Liam just shook his head and grinned, then stooped down to help gather things up.

He snagged a tube of lipstick that had rolled onto the tile entry, then picked up a small plastic bag. He held it up and tilted his head. His breathing slowed. Icy fingers snatched him from the moment, hurled him into another shadowy place.

Riley sat on the floor, playing with her dolls. She looked up at him and put a finger to her lips. "Shhh. Mommy's sleeping." He looked from his young daughter to the woman lying next to her. Her eyes were closed, her cheeks ashen, and her mouth hung open as if in shock over whatever reality came to collect her.

He dropped to his knees, knew terror when his trembling hand touched the cold, dry skin of her face. Dead skin. His mind reeled. On the coffee table was a plastic zip-bag holding several small pills, a spoon. They rested on top of a saucer from the china pattern with the gold flower border that her parents had given them as a wedding gift. Riley continued to play beside him. She combed one of the doll's hair, held it up for him to see, and smiled. How long had she been sitting there waiting for her mother to awaken?

Outside, the wind called to him. Liam. Liam.

"Liam!"

Liam shuddered. His breath wheezed out in a gush. He looked up. Caterina stood above him, staring at him, her purse hanging open on her arm.

"Liam, are you okay?" She reached down and touched his shoulder.

He brushed her hand away, stood up slowly, clutching the baggie he'd picked up off the floor. He'd picked up a similar bag of pills once, seen the powder residue on the saucer where his dead wife had crushed them, next to where his two-year-old daughter had been playing when he found them. He felt the same fear he had then, and the same guilt. What if Riley had found that bag before he'd gotten home?

"Liam," Caterina repeated. "What's wrong with you?"

He held out the plastic sandwich bag, dangled it in the air. "Is this what you were trying to keep from me?" His words bit across the short distance between them. He couldn't believe this. He should never have gotten so involved with another woman before knowing, without a doubt, that he wasn't putting Riley at risk.

Cat glanced at the plastic bag. "What are you talking about? And why are you so upset?"

Liam jerked his head to the side, looked away from her. "Jesus!" He balled his fists, fought the urge to hit something.

"Talk to me," she said. "I don't understand what's—"

"You don't understand!" He clenched his back teeth. "That makes two of us, sweetheart. I should have trusted my first instincts. I knew you'd be a mistake. Told myself a dozen times, but did I listen?"

Giving in to his frustration, he turned and punched the doorframe. "Damn it! And now Riley's..." He closed his eyes and dropped his head, stood there a moment before acknowledging her again. She was the kind of woman men wrote love poems to. Witty. Beautiful. The object of his heart's desire, and an illusion. He couldn't bear to look at her standing there, looking so confused when he held the evidence of her secret in front of her. Clearly, she didn't think he'd find out about her little habit, but he had, and it changed everything.

"Get out, Caterina," he said tonelessly.

"But—"

"I said go, before I do something I'll regret."

She put her hands on her hips and narrowed her eyes. "Oh, just like that. You flip out, tell me to go, and I'm supposed to leave without any explanation? I thought we were in a relationship, Liam. In good ones, people talk, they don't kick the other one out with no reason."

He rolled his jaw.

"I thought we'd moved beyond the point where you glare at me and do that thing with your jaw."

"I'm not in the mood."

"Look, I don't know what sprung out of nowhere to crawl up into your boxers and bite you, but I suggest we deal with it before you and Riley come over later."

Liam let out a derisive laugh. "You think I'll let you anywhere near my daughter now that I've discovered your secret? After what happened with Sylvie, the last thing Riley needs in her life is another drug addict to rip it apart."

Caterina's mouth dropped open and she gaped at him. "A drug addict?"

He waved the bag in the air again, and she glanced at it. After a moment, her eyes widened. "You think—"

He wasn't interested in a cover story. She'd been holding something from him, and when he'd tried to find out what, she hadn't wanted to talk. Funny, now that he'd found her stash she wanted to clear the air. Part of him wanted her to stay, to convince him he was wrong, but he held the proof in his hands.

"Caterina, I..." He pushed his fingers through his hair. He was a fool. It didn't matter how he felt about her. He had more important things to think about than himself.

He reached for the door handle, pulled it open. "Just leave. I'm done with this. And you can take these with you." Liam held the bag toward her. "Maybe it's good your old boyfriend's in jail. It looks like you're running low on these. If he can't keep supplying you like he did Sylvie, you might end up living a while longer."

He knew it was harsh, but he wasn't feeling very benevolent. Just the thought of the destruction Mitch Gregory had wreaked on so many people's lives made Liam's blood boil. That Caterina had fancied herself in love with the bastard at one time, well that, he couldn't deal with at the moment.

Cat hiked her purse strap over her shoulder. Liam saw her raise her chin and swallow. She took a step toward the door.

"I don't know what Mitch has to do with this or your wife's suicide. I thought we left those ghosts behind us. Apparently, I've either missed some pieces to the puzzle along the way, or there are a few things you haven't told me about that have shown up to haunt you."

She walked forward and stopped right in front of him. Got in his face. "Whatever the case, you're wrong. Wrong about whatever you *think* I've done, or did. You're wrong about me. I love you, Liam, but I won't be held accountable for your, or your dead wife's, mistakes. I hope you realize that, before it's too late for us to put things back together."

Without another word from either of them, she turned away from him and stepped through the doorway. She didn't look back. He watched her get into her car, start it up, and back out of his driveway. Then she drove away, taking his heart with her.

"I have a bone to pick with fate."
William Shakespeare

o, nothing," Cat said, looking at Lucia as they sat at the kitchen table a couple of hours later, sipping on hot chocolate and making do with a lunch of the leftover muffins from that morning's breakfast setup.

"Not unless Marcella found out anything. Antonio's just as clueless as we are. He's had more interaction with Damien than I have, but he said their conversations are usually about sports, or current events, or scotch. Apparently, they discovered they both have a specific fondness for what Antonio calls Speyside single malts from Dufftown. In particular, Glenfiddich and The Balvenie's. I admit I'm not up on my whiskeys, but he talks about them the way Marcella talks about the distinctiveness of a Bonavera wine, because of its terroir. So, they must have some distinguishing qualities that are characteristic of that region. Since I'm not a fan of scotch, and my attention span lasts about half of a second if the subject comes up, he enjoys talking to someone who shares his appreciation for it instead of yawning through the conversation."

"Hey," Marcella said, coming into the room. "Sorry I got held up. There were some people next door, on Jordan's property. They looked like they might be surveyors or something. I pulled over to the side of the road to see if I could figure out what they were doing, but I'm not sure."

"Maybe he's decided to finally unload it," Cat said. Their neighbor had inherited the house and property from his uncle, but it had been sitting empty ever since. Jordan's aunt and uncle had taken him in when his mom died, but Jordan's uncle was hard on him. A couple of years after he'd moved there, his aunt passed away, and Jordan's relationship with his uncle deteriorated.

Jordan never said, but their mother thought his uncle went too far in his discipline, especially if the man had been drinking. Jordan would show up at their house with scrapes and bruises, saying he'd tripped over something or telling some other story. Their mom would always insist he come in, let her take a look, give him something to drink, or invite him to dinner. Lucia knew him better than the rest of them because they'd been in the same grade in school, but if her sister knew anything, she never said. Maybe Jordan had wanted it that way.

"He's not selling," Lucia said. "I got an email from him a few weeks ago. He said he'd heard about Serendipity. He's thinking of leveling the existing house and rebuilding. He wanted to know if we were happy with our architect and builder. It sounded like he may be planning to move back to the area."

Marcella gnawed her bottom lip. "Jordan's moving back?" she asked, looking somewhat dazed, and, Cat thought, as if she'd suddenly forgotten how to breathe.

"Are you okay, Cel?" Lucia asked.

"I'm fine," Marcella said, sounding a touch defensive.

Cat and Lucia exchanged glances.

"Why didn't you tell anyone Jordan contacted you?" Marcella asked.

"I guess I...didn't realize it was...breaking news, and it slipped my mind." Lucia looked at Cat again and widened her eyes as if to ask, *Am I missing something here?*

"I didn't say it was breaking news. I just think you would have mentioned it. The property's been empty for years, and...I don't know. Forget it. I'm sorry if it sounded like I was jumping on you." Cel brushed her hand through the air as if to dispel the matter.

"We're supposed to be talking about Damien's pictures," she said. "Did either of you find out anything?"

"No," Cat told her. "We were hoping you might have."

Marcella shook her head. "I asked El if she'd seen any of the pictures Damien took. She said he gave her a couple of shots of the winery that he thought she could use in her marketing, but that was it."

"You don't think she suspected anything?" Lucia asked.

"No. She showed me the ones he'd given her and said she couldn't wait to see the holiday piece when it comes out next year. I think she just thought I was curious, same as she is."

"I don't know how we're supposed to find out why he took all those shots of Liam without asking him," Caterina said. She wasn't too happy with Liam right now for jumping to a false assumption and holding it against her instead of asking her what the pills she had in her purse were. He should trust her enough to believe in her. But she loved him. And she loved Eliana. And she didn't want to see either of them get hurt if Damien's intentions for taking the shots didn't turn out to be innocent.

"I don't see any other way," Lucia said. "I think we need to talk to Damien."

The kitchen door slapped shut, and the lights blinked off and on.

"And I think Rosa's trying to tell us something," Marcella said.

Cat frowned. "What would Rosa know about it?"

"I don't know," Lucia said, tapping the envelope with the questionable photos that lay on the table in front of them, "but this envelope was on that shelf without anyone seeing it since Damien checked out around two months ago. And it just happened to fall off and hit me on the head when I was restocking the closet? I don't think it was an accident, and I wouldn't be surprised if Rosa is responsible for it making its way out of his duffel bag, or wherever he had it, to begin with."

"Did you have something to do with those pictures, Aunt Rosa?" Marcella asked, looking around the room.

Rosa did her light trick, making them blink off and on twice.

Lucia sighed. "At least we've confirmed that. But how are we supposed to figure out why she wanted us to find them if all we have to go on is flickering lights?"

Cat didn't want her suspicion to be right. She didn't want to believe that Damien was involved in something that might hurt Liam. Had he taken other pictures that had already made it into the hands of Riley's grandparents? More damaging ones?

She bit her lip. She had no positive proof that the pictures had anything to do with that. He could have taken them for some other reason, but based on what Liam had told her, it was difficult not to be suspicious.

"Aunt Rosa," Cat said, closing her eyes a moment and trying to convince herself they weren't being ridiculous for trying to get answers from a ghost. "Do you know if Damien took the pictures with Liam in them for some reason not related to the photojournalist piece he said he was doing?"

They waited but nothing happened. Lucia and Marcella looked at Cat. She held her hand up to ward off their questions a moment.

"Do the pictures have anything to do with Riley?"

When they got no sign, Caterina felt her frustration grow. As much as she'd hoped to be wrong, it looked increasingly like her suspicion that Damien was somehow connected to Sylvie's family, and was trying to get them something incriminating to use against Liam, was correct.

"Okay, how about another question? Rosa, do we need to be afraid of Damien?" she asked, the thought popping into her head out of nowhere.

They all waited. Nothing.

Cat groaned in frustration. "Rosa, are you even still here with us?"

The lights flicked on and off.

"Okay, we'll take that as a yes." She exhaled slowly. She looked at her sisters. "Let's try something else," she said. "Can you just let us know, is Eliana safe with him?"

Cat felt relieved when the lights blinked in response. She wasn't sure what it meant that they were putting their faith in their dead aunt, but the woman did seem to know things.

"Another yes," Marcella said, all of them watching the lights intently for inklings from beyond.

At this rate, Cat thought, it could take them weeks to try to figure out what Rosa wanted them to know. If their aunt knew what she was talking about, or flickering about, Damien had taken those pictures. Caterina suspected for some purpose having to do with Riley, most likely to give to her grandparents. If their aunt was to be believed, they didn't need to worry about Eliana's safety with him but were still unsure if he posed a danger to anyone else.

"I wish Rosa could just appear and tell us what she knows," Cat said. "I guarantee Liam doesn't know anything about this, and...I'm worried Rosa might be wrong about Damien. Liam told me something disturbing, something I think the pictures are related to."

She hadn't planned to tell anyone about Riley's grandparents wanting to get custody. She didn't know if Liam would want her to. But these were her sisters. She could trust them. And they'd stumbled upon an envelope with a bunch of pictures of Liam in various places that Damien could only have taken if he'd trailed him there. That didn't sound harmless to her.

With Liam and Riley's interests foremost in her thoughts, she told Lucia and Marcella what Liam told her, and of her suspicions. She didn't tell them about the way they'd parted, or that Liam had said he was done with things. She'd interpreted *things* to mean *them*. But Liam loved her. He might be angry and confused right now, but he loved her. Her heart wasn't giving up on them yet.

"Wow." Marcella tapped her knuckles against her mouth. "Not a tough leap to make. What did Liam say when you told him about your suspicion?"

Cat propped her elbow on the table and leaned her head against her hand. "I didn't," she said with a sigh. "I didn't want to risk him confronting Damien before we found out more. And with El—"

"If it turns out that Damien's been deceiving all of us, there's no way she won't be hurt by this." Lucia caught the corner of her lip in her teeth, worried over it. "You don't think he's been carrying on a relationship with her just to gain more access to Liam, do you?"

"I don't know what to think," Cat said, although the same thought had crossed her mind. "Which is why we need to get to the bottom of this before it goes any further, and I can't think of how we do that other than, as you said, we confront Damien."

"Hey, Rosa," Cat said, frustrated by all the contradictions. "Can you do anything besides play with the lights? Like tell us what we're supposed to do with these pictures? Come on, Auntie, can you just give us a clue why you dropped them on Lucia's head, and what the hell you want us to do now?"

The envelope that had been sitting on the kitchen table whipped toward Caterina and fell into her lap, stunning her and her sisters. None of them said anything for several seconds, just sat there as if they'd been frozen in place, with gaping mouths.

"Umm," Marcella muttered, finally breaking the ice. "I'm guessing that means we're supposed to confront Damien with those if we want more answers."

They all raised their eyes to the ceiling, but nothing more happened. Apparently, their aunt thought she'd made herself clear.

Caterina leaned back and crossed her arms. "Okay. So, we go to the source." She picked up her mug of chocolate and took a sip, then looked at her sisters and said, "I wonder if Rosa was such a drama queen when she was alive."

"I HATE DOING this behind Eliana's back," Lucia said. "I know we agreed to talk to Damien first, but sneaking into her room while she's in the shower, so we can get his number from her phone's contact list? It just feels wrong."

Marcella continued scrolling until she found it, then quickly wrote it down on a piece of paper and stuffed it into the pocket of her jeans. "I don't like it either, but none of us had his number, and if we asked her for it, she'd want to know what was up."

"Got it," she said to Cat, who stood outside El's bathroom, listening at the door. "Let's get out of here before she catches us in the act."

"She's still in the shower," Cat said, grinning. "I can hear her singing, into the hand-held, I'm guessing, and probably doing some naked version of *Flashdance*."

"Thanks, I could have done without that image," Marcella quipped.

Lucia took Marcella's wrist in hand. "Come on, let's go find Antonio so he can make the call, and hope none of this comes back to haunt us."

"Not the best choice of words in this family," Cat said, following her sisters out of the room.

Antonio met them in the library a few minutes later. Marcella gave him the number and he placed the call, putting it on speaker so they could listen in.

"Hey, Damien, it's Antonio. I'm thinking of trying out that new whiskey bar you were telling me about one night this week and thought I'd see if you'd have any interest in joining me. Barrels, was it?"

"That's right," Damien said. "I've been trying to talk a couple of my buddies into going but haven't had much success. Most of them are beer drinkers who probably wouldn't appreciate it anyway. So yeah, I'd be interested. I can't do Monday or Tuesday, but I've got Wednesday evening open, if that works for you."

"Let me check with the boss," Antonio said. He held the phone behind his back. Caterina and her sisters watched him expectantly. "Wednesday okay?" he questioned in a whisper.

They all seemed to slump their shoulders in unison but gave a round of nods. Cat knew her sisters were just as anxious to get some answers, but they wanted to do it face-to-face, so they'd have to wait.

"Hey Lucia," Antonio said, raising his voice as if Luch was across the room. "Damien and I are thinking of meeting up Wednesday evening at a scotch bar he told me about. Does that conflict with anything I don't know about, love?"

Luch rolled her eyes but played along. "No, I haven't committed us to anything, *sweetheart*." She smiled at him. "Go ahead. It'll be nice for you to have a night out with the boys."

Antonio grinned, his eyes fixed on his soon-to-be wife. They were so in love it was palpable, Cat thought. She'd imagined she could have something similar with Liam. But whether he came around or not, she'd do whatever she could to reduce the chance that Riley's grandparents got ahold of anything to try and trump up their case. A picture might be worth a thousand words, but pictures could be manipulated to tell whatever story the photographer wanted to show. And unfortunately, as a photojournalist, Damien could probably portray things to appear any way he wanted them to.

"Sounds good," Antonio told Damien, drawing Cat from her musings. "Say, Wednesday around six-thirty."

After a few more exchanges, Antonio ended the call. "Well, that's done," he said. "Have any of you thought about what you're going to say to him?"

"We haven't gotten that far," Lucia said, "but I'm guessing when he walks into Barrels and sees all four of us waiting for him, without Eliana, he's probably going to wonder if we had you set him up, so we could give him the third-degree about his intentions."

"I know it's not looking good, but I really hope he has a good explanation for taking the pictures, and that they don't have anything to do with Liam's in-laws," Marcella said. "I haven't had a lot of interaction with him, but from what I have, I like Damien. He seems to treat El well, and she's gaga over him."

Lucia sighed. "I feel the same. And if he's not crazy about her, too, then he's a damn good actor. Or maybe he started out with one intention, but then fell in love with her."

"I guess we'll have to wait until Wednesday to find out." Caterina stretched her neck to the side and felt the pull. On top of worrying about the pictures, she felt completely disconnected from Liam. Was he still angry with her because of a false assumption? Had she been right to leave the ball in his court, and hope he loved her enough to seek the truth?

She didn't have answers for anything right now. Without answers she had no control over what would happen next. No control. No direction. And everything headed for a possible head-on crash with Liam.

"I'm going to open a bottle of viognier," Marcella said. "Anyone else in need of a drink?"

"We're opening a bottle?" Eliana asked, startling them all with her unexpected presence. She crossed the reception lobby and came into the library. "Count me in. Any occasion?"

They all stared at her, like a herd of deer suddenly caught in a spotlight.

"No, but since we're all here, it sounded like a good idea," Marcella said, regaining her wits first.

"A great idea," Eliana agreed. "I'll grab some glasses from the solarium." She gave smiles all around and said dreamily, "Yes, a great idea and the perfect way to wrap up a great weekend."

Cat watched her go off to get the glasses. She recognized the look she'd seen in her sister's eyes, and it only made what they were planning to do that much harder. Of all the men she'd dated, why'd Eliana pick this one to fall in love with?

LIAM RAKED A hand through his hair, pushed it off his forehead. It flopped back down again, almost to his eyes. He needed a cut, a low priority he usually put off until it got too long and started bugging him, as it did now.

He finished building the frame for the soaking tub that would be installed in one of the guest suites. Half of the rooms would have tubs, and this was the last one that needed a frame before they could be installed and plumbed. Then the wallboard could go up.

The tubs, and most of the sink vanities, were sitting in what would be the restaurant's dining room. Lucia had sourced antique cabinets, no two alike, to be repurposed as sink vanities. Every vanity would have a quartz or marble top, all of which would have to be measured on-site and custom made, because each one would be unique to that guest bath.

He'd let the stone people worry about that. All he had to do was install the bases once the wallboard went up. He had to give it to the Bonaveras, nothing would be cookie-cutter about Serendipity. When word began to spread, and with the right marketing, it would become a popular destination, he'd bet every nail and screw they'd put into it.

He gathered his tools and went downstairs to check on the progress in the left wing. He pulled his phone out of his back pocket and checked for messages. Frowning, he rubbed his thumb over the screen.

He hadn't seen or talked to Caterina in three days—not since he'd basically thrown her out of his house and told her they were done. She wasn't going to call him. If he wanted to salvage things with her, he'd have to make the next move.

He'd accused her of popping pills but realized now that it had been a knee-jerk reaction to finding that bag. She'd been trying to keep something from him—he hadn't changed his mind about that—but it wasn't the pills. Caterina wasn't doing drugs. He didn't know what they were, or why she had them, but they could have been anything. Just because they looked like the ones he'd found when Sylvie OD'd, didn't mean they were OxyContin. Instead of jumping to conclusions, and spending the last three days regretting it, he should have asked her. He'd reacted emotionally, let the past suck him in, mess with his head, instead of thinking clearly. Now he stood to lose her, and it was his own damn fault.

He stuffed the phone back into his pocket. His brother Shawn came in through the front door with Elliot. Liam had Shawn for the rest of the week while the hardwoods were being installed on one of his jobs.

"Hey, bro," Shawn said, "you ready to start dropping those tubs in so we can clear out the dining room and start building the partitions in there?"

"Yeah. I just finished the last tub frame. I've got something I need to take care of, though. You two go ahead and get started. Ask Roscoe to lend some muscle if you need help getting them upstairs."

"How long are you going to be?" Shawn asked.

"I'm not sure. Hopefully no more than an hour."

Before his brother could question him further, Liam grabbed his jacket off the floor by the front door and went outside to where he'd parked his truck on the hard, rutted ground.

He backed out from between Shawn and Elliot's trucks and bumped his way over the uneven dirt, up to the road. He needed to fix things with Caterina, and if she gave him any of that contrary mouth of hers, or told him she wasn't interested, he'd just have to find a way to kiss away her objections.

Seventeen

*"All you need is love, but a little chocolate
now and then doesn't hurt."*

Charles M. Schulz

I've been meaning to ask," Lucia said, late Wednesday morning when she and Caterina were clearing the breakfast setup. "Was it just me, or did you think Marcella's reaction the other day, when I told her Jordan sent me an email, seemed odd?"

Cat lifted a shoulder. "I don't know. She's always been touchy about Jordan. He was her first serious crush. I don't think she's ever gotten over him taking off, just when she approached an age that he might notice she wasn't a kid anymore."

"Seriously? Cel had a thing for him?"

"Are you kidding, Luch? She used to think they were going to get married someday. Of course, we were only eleven or twelve when I read that in her diary."

Lucia gave her a reprimanding frown. "You read her diary?"

"Hey, she left it on her nightstand for anyone to find. Besides, I was a kid. It's not like I'd do it today."

"Cel always has been too trusting. Did Jordan know?"

"I doubt it." Cat stacked several plates together. "He was your friend, and to him, I think Cel and I were just your kid sisters."

Lucia looked over toward the door and smiled. "Hey, Liam, how long have you been standing there? We never heard you come in."

"Just got here," Liam said from behind Caterina.

Her back was to the door, so she hadn't seen him yet, couldn't see his face to guess his mood. She set the stack of dishes she'd been holding down on the serving bar. He hadn't stopped by or called after she left his place Sunday morning. She'd begun to wonder if he would. She drew a steadying breath, then turned around to face him.

The wind had tousled his hair, a few longer strands brushed his eyebrows, blond streaks that only highlighted his gorgeous blue-green eyes. She'd missed those eyes. Missed him.

"Hey," he said, looking a little uncertain, she thought. "Can I talk to you?" He glanced at Lucia. "In private?"

"Oh..." Lucia brushed her hands against the sides of her skirt. "I was just going to go into the kitchen to, umm, to put these plates away." She grabbed the stack that Caterina had just set down and smiled.

Yeah, that's not obvious, Cat thought.

"It's okay, Luch." She touched her sister's elbow. "You don't need to go hide in the kitchen. Liam and I can go up to my room." She glanced at him, and he nodded.

So, he wanted to talk. And he hadn't balked at doing so in the privacy of her room. She took that as a good sign.

"Can I just get something out of the way first?" Liam asked a few minutes later after following Cat into her room and closing the door behind them.

She turned and looked up at him. "What?"

He caught her by the shoulders, pulled her toward him. "This."

Before Cat could catch her breath, he stole it with his kiss. And just like that, she fell into it, like an anchor drops into the sea, through murky depths in search of ground, to hold firm what might otherwise drift away. When he moaned, she dug in, clasped tight, kissed him back as if it might be their last. But in her heart, she already knew they had a lifetime of kisses ahead of them.

Liam pulled back, blew out a heavy breath, and then leaned his forehead against hers. "Okay, so I'll take that to mean you haven't written me off yet."

"And I'll take it to mean we're not done yet."

He tilted his head away, met her gaze. "I hope not."

Cat smiled lightly. "Me too."

"I'm sorry for being such an ass," he said, rubbing his hands up and down her arms. "I overreacted. It wasn't your fault, and you didn't deserve to be treated that way."

"You thought the pills you found were OxyContin, didn't you?"

"Yeah. They looked like the ones I found when Sylvie OD'd. When I saw them, I don't know…I freaked. I had a flashback of Sylvie lying there dead, and Riley—I remember thinking what if she'd found the pills before I got home, thought they were candy or something? She could have died too. I was so angry Sylvie put her at such risk. She was dead, and I was mad at her." He pushed his fingers through his hair, and it fell back over his forehead. "I'm sorry, Cat."

"You already apologized, so let's be done with that. I can only imagine how horrible it must have been for you to find Sylvie dead, and to think Riley could have ended up the same. I can even understand why you'd get angry, but I don't want to talk about that, not right now. I'd rather talk about why you jumped to the conclusion that I was taking the same pills, and what any of it had to do with Mitch." She took his hand and led him over to the bed, sat down and patted a spot next to her. "And just so you know, I get migraines. I have since I was a kid. The pills you found are a prescription for them. I always carry some with me, just in case."

"I should have trusted you and asked what they were, instead of jumping to conclusions. But I freaked when I saw them. They looked like the pills Sylvie had, and I couldn't think straight. It was like I was reliving those moments, and you got hit with the shrapnel." He glanced away. "Mitch Gregory gave Sylvie the pills."

"Mitch? But how did they even know each other?"

"I don't know when or how they met, but they hooked up."

"What? You mean they were sleeping together? While you were married?"

"Yep. I think she probably enjoyed the attention, and she might even have thought that I deserved it since she always accused me of not caring about anything she wanted." Liam sighed heavily, and Caterina's heart sighed with him. "We both made mistakes. Mine was marrying her when I knew I didn't love her."

"You thought you were doing the honorable thing."

"Honorable isn't worth shit when it's a lie. I could have agreed to support Riley, or raised her myself, and not have married her. Maybe if I'd stuck to my guns, she'd still be alive."

"Yeah, well, you already buried those self-incriminations, so don't go digging them back up again. It's zombie-guilt; it'll fester and eat away at you bit by bit if you resurrect it. You don't need that, and neither does Riley."

Liam looked at her and arched a brow. "Zombie-guilt? Did you just make that up?"

"Maybe. But it suits. My point is—"

"I know what your point is, and I'm working on it. I've gotten better at letting go of the guilt, but after what happened Sunday morning, I realized I haven't done as good a job of letting go of the anger, at Sylvie or Gregory, over the possibilities of what could have happened to Riley. I don't want it to sound like an excuse, because I acted like a jerk the other day, but it wasn't about you, Cat. It was about me."

Sylvie and Mitch. Her and Mitch. Fragmented comments rushed back to Caterina, flipped through her head like the pages of a book, with a plot twist she hadn't expected. But now, after knowing more of the story, it all made sense.

No wonder Liam didn't like Mitch. And if Mitch had been carrying on with Sylvie and giving her drugs, she could understand Liam's attitude toward her when they first met. It didn't make him right to have judged her because of them, it just made him human. *Lie with dogs...*, her mother used to say. That was often true enough, but not everyone ended up with fleas. Not if they walked away from the mongrel's den before they got infected.

Caterina reached for his hand. "I know that, and I get why you acted the way you did toward me at first, even though we'd never met. We both made assumptions and misjudged each other. It just goes to show how wrong we can be about people when we base our opinion of them on things we don't understand."

Liam rubbed his thumb over the skin on the back of her hand. "Yeah. You didn't turn out to be half as bad as I thought you were."

Cat punched him in the shoulder, and he grinned. "Are we okay here?" he asked, sliding his arm around her waist. "Because I'd like us to be okay."

"Yeah." She leaned into him. "We're good. I think we need to talk more about this to understand things better, but not right now."

Liam nodded. "Deal."

They sat on the edge of the bed. Caterina closed her eyes, content not to say anything more, just to be there with him in the moment, stitched back together. If they were like most couples, they'd have their share of misunderstandings and stupid arguments. But they'd find a way to mend the tears, restore the rips, and be all the stronger because the needle that bound them together was sewn with love. And Cat felt confident theirs could weather the storms.

Liam turned her toward him and held her gaze. "I love you, Caterina."

She smiled. "I know."

Cat also knew another storm might be brewing on the horizon. After she and her sisters met with Antonio and Damien later that evening, she'd know if her suspicions were correct, and if she'd made a mistake keeping them from Liam until after she could verify them.

"DOES ELIANA KNOW about this? Or that—" Damien looked around the booth, his eyes sweeping over all of them. "That you decided to ambush me under false pretenses?"

"Eliana doesn't know anything." Lucia spoke up first. "We didn't want to upset her if it turned out these were just random photos."

"They're not random, though, are they?" Cat asked, although she meant it more as a statement than a question.

Damien leaned an elbow on the table, covered his mouth with his hand. He looked down at the pictures lying on top of the manila envelope they'd found them in. He fisted his hand, tapped it against his mouth—a man considering his next move, Cat mused.

He left Cat's question hanging in the air for several seconds, either unwilling, or deciding how he wanted to answer it.

"They aren't random," he finally said, "but that's all I'm going to tell you here."

Caterina stared across the booth at him. All he'd tell them? That wasn't acceptable, not when there might be other pictures that could hurt Liam and Riley.

"We befriended you, trusted you, and more importantly, Eliana is under the impression her relationship with you has been genuine," Antonio said. "Whether we're right to do so is yet to be determined, but we wanted to give you a chance to explain what this is all about before telling her or Liam. We deserve some answers."

"Why don't we start with an easy one," Cat said, "like, who the hell are you, Damien? If that's even your real name."

He drummed his fingers on the table. He was cornered, on the defensive, and, Cat thought, it wasn't a position he was used to being in.

"You're right. You deserve some answers, but if I'm going to tell you what you want to know, Eliana has to be included."

"We don't want El to get hurt." Marcella, who'd done nothing but observe so far, spoke up.

"Whatever you might think about me, I don't want her hurt either." Damien picked up his glass and downed the rest of his scotch. "But I want to be the one she finds out things from. I owe her that much."

When they met up again about twenty-five minutes later at the winery, Eliana waited for them in the library. An open bottle of cabernet sauvignon sat on the coffee table. A fire burned in the large stone fireplace. Sam Smith crooned "Stay With Me" over the sound system.

Their sister looked over as they filed in through the door, her eyes widening in surprise when she saw Damien. She stood up from where she'd been sitting in one of the wing chairs, flipping through the latest edition of *Elle*.

"Hey," she said, all smiles, and as oblivious as a newborn fawn stumbling upon a hungry bobcat in the wood.

"Hey." Lucia, ever the caretaker, hurried forward and gave Eliana a hug. Nice, Cat thought. That's not going to make her wonder what's going on.

El smiled tentatively. "So, what's up?" She walked over and gave Damien a peck. "Hi. Did you just happen to get here when this crew came in, or are you in on why they called and told me to meet them in the library?" She grinned up at him expectantly. "Is this some kind of surprise?"

Cat worried her sister was about to be very surprised, but not in a good way. From the little she'd gathered from Damien's sparse comments, Eliana knew nothing about what he'd been doing behind their backs. And if his only interest in her had been to gain access to Liam, she'd be crushed.

Damien leaned down and gave El a quick kiss. Cat frowned. She'd never forgive him if he broke her sister's heart.

"Let's sit down," he said, and took Eliana's hand. He walked to the couch, took a seat, and El dropped down beside him. The rest of them followed suit, Cat and Marcella claiming the wing chairs, with Antonio and Lucia taking a place on the couch on the opposite side of the coffee table from Damien and Eliana.

El looked around, then frowned. "Okay, who died, found out they had a terminal illness, or discovered our image of Santa Claus, as we know him, is the result of a media blitz by Coca Cola to boost sales way back in the thirties?"

"Sorry, love," Damien said. "I'd like to think you'll still be joking around when you find out why we're all here, but I'm afraid that's wishful thinking on my part."

El put her hand on his arm. "What's this about, Damien?" Her expression turned serious, something Caterina rarely saw with Eliana. She was the most carefree of all of them, a roll with the punches go-getter, who rarely took no for an answer when she set her sights on something. But she was quick to move on to the next opportunity if it didn't work out.

The way her sister looked at Damien, Cat didn't think she'd have an easy time moving on after tonight.

"I haven't been forthcoming with you or your family about who I am or what I do." Damien looked away from El a moment, as if he were searching for the right words to explain—words that might help them understand, make him appear less culpable, be less hurtful.

Eliana shook her head, clearly confused, but held her tongue, waiting instead for him to explain.

Damien leaned forward and clasped his hands, resting his elbows on his knees as if he were bracing himself for whatever fall-out might come.

"I'm not a photojournalist."

"What?" Several voices questioned at once. Cat exchanged looks with her sisters. Eliana didn't take her eyes off Damien. She looked at him as if she'd dropped onto some strange movie set and was trying to figure out what was happening, and why she was there.

"I'm a private investigator."

"A what?" Eliana stared harder.

"Oh, Christ," Caterina said.

Lucia covered her mouth with her hands.

Antonio put his arm around his wife-to-be and pulled her closer.

Marcella leaned forward and snagged one of the glasses Eliana had set out before they got there, poured herself a glass of wine.

"I think I could use one of those too," Cat said, and her twin poured another glass.

Damien pushed a hand through his hair. "I was hired by a client to find out whatever I could about their son-in-law, Liam Dougherty. They told me they were concerned for their grand-daughter's well-being. That Liam was an unfit father, and they asked me to find proof they could use to get custody of her."

"That's a lie." Cat rushed to Liam's defense. "Liam's a wonderful father!"

Damien held up a hand. "Please let me finish. You want the truth; I'm trying to tell you." When he finished filling them in about five minutes later, Caterina wasn't sure what to believe.

"So, you never gave them any pictures?" Antonio asked.

Damien shook his head. "Like I said, my observations didn't back up their claims. I don't know how that envelope with the pictures I took ended up on the closet shelf in the room I stayed in. I had it in my duffel bag—but that's beside the point. After seeing Liam and Riley together, how they interacted, I couldn't in good conscience continue working the case."

"Did you tell them that?" Marcella asked.

"Yes." Damien leaned back with a sigh. "I told them I didn't observe anything to support their claims, just the opposite in fact, and that I thought trying to take Riley away from her father would be a mistake. They weren't happy about it. They insisted that they'd paid me good money to find something incriminating, and they wanted me to find something incriminating. I gave them back their retainer and suggested they treat themselves to an hour or two of therapy."

"Hah! You told them to go see a shrink?" Marcella asked with an appreciative grin.

Damien turned toward Eliana, who had been uncharacteristically quiet. He put a hand on her knee. She slapped it away.

"Eliana, I—"

"You used me," she said, not looking at him. "You lied to me and my family, and you used me...used all of us."

"I'm sorry. I never wanted to hurt any of you." He hung his head, and although she wanted to stay angry, Caterina couldn't help but soften toward him. He hadn't given Riley's grandparents any pictures. He'd quit the case and told them they were wrong about Liam. And, as she watched him, she got the feeling he'd just lost something he treasured and was helpless to do anything but watch it slip through his fingers.

El closed her eyes and drew in a breath. When she started to push up, Damien took hold of her wrist. She slanted him a cool glance. "Let go."

"Give me a few minutes in private, please," Damien said.

Eliana pulled on her hand, and he let go of it. She notched her chin up and firmed her jaw, but Caterina knew her sister well, and right now she drowned in a deep lake of hurt and betrayal.

"There's nothing you can say in private that will change anything," El said. "I don't want to see you again, Damien. I wish I could say it's been nice knowing you, but I really didn't know you at all, did I?"

With that Eliana turned away. Even the four-inch heels on her cherry-red stilettos, which at any other time would be clicking out a fast, lively pace, sounded hollow echoes of a broken heart.

He may have lied to all of them, Cat thought, but she could see one, indisputable truth burning in his eyes as he watched Eliana walk out of the room. He hadn't faked his feelings for her sister. Damien was in love with Eliana.

CATERINA TEXTED LIAM on Thursday morning to see if he could get away for an hour and come over to the winery, saying that she had something important she needed to talk to him about.

Now that they had the story about the photos and what they meant, she could tell him. She hoped he'd understand why she'd kept her suspicions from him until they could talk to Damien. Neither she nor Liam had lied to each other about anything, but they'd both kept things from each other. There'd be no secrets going forward.

When Liam arrived a couple of hours later, Caterina was in the kitchen working out a recipe for Serendipity's menu. The months had flown by since they'd hired Antonio, then Liam, and before they knew it, she and Lucia would be throwing open the front doors and welcoming guests to enjoy what had, not so long ago, all felt like a dream. In a few weeks, she'd start setting up meetings with suppliers, finalizing choices for linens, china, and a dozen other things. Things were about to kick into a higher gear.

No dream anymore, she thought with a smile. This was happening. She whisked a classic velouté sauce that simmered on the stove top with one hand and pumped the other in the air. "Go us," she said aloud.

"Someone's in a good mood."

Cat glanced over her shoulder. Liam stood just inside the doorway, a gleam in his eyes and a grin tugging at the mouth she loved covering her own.

She set the whisk down, turned the flame as low as it would go under the velouté, and faced him.

"Hey."

His grin widened. "Hey, back. You wanted to see me?"

"I always want to see you, Liam," she quipped. "You're so pretty to look at."

"What do you want from me?"

Cat slung a hand on her hip, watched as he crossed the room toward her. "I don't want anything. I do always want to see you, and you are pretty to look at, but you're right, I did summon you here for a reason."

He stopped in front of her, and she had to take a breath. How did he make all her most sensitive zones start tingling so easily, with just a glance?

"If you haven't eaten lunch yet, you can be my taste tester," she said, clearing her throat. "I'm trying out a chicken dish with velouté. I kept the sauce classic, but I want to experiment with the sides. You can give me your opinion which ones you like best with it."

"I have no idea what that word is with the chicken, but I'm thinking I'll probably enjoy whatever you want me to try a lot better than the ham sandwich I packed."

"Velouté, that's the sauce. Now sit down, and I'll get us each a plate. We can talk then."

He wrapped an arm around her waist and hauled her forward. "Dessert first."

"It's not the usual order," she said, rather enjoying his approach to a meal, "but if you insist."

"I do," he said.

Several kisses and tempting grinds against the kitchen counter later, Cat came up for air. She gave him a gentle push back. "Okay, let's sit down and eat before we melt into a puddle of lust, and someone has to clean up our liquid remains."

After she'd lifted lunch and they'd begun eating, Caterina said, "I've been keeping something from you for several days. I had my reasons, which I hope you'll understand, but you have a right to know, and I think it's time you do."

She dragged in a breath of resolve, let it out slowly.

Liam set his fork down and took her hand. "You look like you're about to start hyperventilating. Let me make it easier for you. I know about Damien."

Cat's mouth dropped. He reached out and lifted her chin.

"I know he's not a photojournalist, and that Sylvie's parents hired him to try to get the goods on me."

"But...but...how?"

"Damien paid me a surprise visit last night. He said he'd just come from here, and that there was something I should know that he'd rather I hear from him."

"You're kidding! He came to your house? He told you everything? About being a PI, about taking pictures of you and Riley?"

Liam nodded.

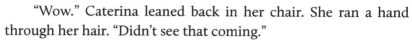

"Wow." Caterina leaned back in her chair. She ran a hand through her hair. "Didn't see that coming."

"You feel better now?"

"Yes," she said, "but you seem so, I don't know...calm. Were you angry with him? Did you hit him? Are you upset at me for not telling you sooner? What? Why are you so calm? Or is it all a façade, and you've got some big storm slowly building that's going to erupt in my face any minute?"

"Yes, I was upset when he started to tell me who he was and what he'd been hired to do. I'm still upset that Sylvie's parents would go so far, but the guy was doing what he does. He's a private investigator who was hired to do a job. He didn't know me, or Riley, or any of you. And to his credit, he walked away from the job when he discovered they didn't want the truth, they just wanted him to find something to hang me with. That took some integrity."

"He deceived us all, Liam. He broke El's heart."

"Yeah. I'm sorry about Eliana. I'm not defending him for what happened between them, but if you want my opinion, somewhere along the way, the interested suitor role he'd decided to play with your sister, so he could get information on me, stopped being an act. She got to him, and I don't think she's the only one who's hurting right now."

"Did he say something? About El?"

Liam shook his head. "No, but I've got eyes. I saw the way they were together. And Damien didn't look so hot last night. My guess is he's pretty broken up about your sister."

Caterina sighed. "I just feel so bad for her right now. She won't talk about it. She wants to just forget everything that happened—and him, like *he* never happened. But if you could see her...it's like someone hooked up a giant vacuum and sucked all the spirit out of her."

"She'll heal in time. People do."

"I know, but he left a mark. She won't trust so easily again."

"Do you think there's a chance she might forgive him, that they could work things out?" Liam asked.

"Sure, in a few centuries, maybe. Outside of that, no. He betrayed her trust. She won't forget it. She'll use what happened to build a wall around her heart, and I'm afraid it's going to take one very special man to ever be able to breach it."

Cat picked up a roll and began buttering it. "What about Riley, Liam? And her grandparents? Damien said he told them they were wrong about you, but that doesn't change what they tried to do."

"No, it doesn't. Riley's got her monthly sleepover weekend with her cousin, Spencer, this weekend. I called her grandparents to tell them we needed to have a talk about Riley, and that it would be in their best interests to meet with me. I'm going out to see them Saturday afternoon."

"Will you tell them you know they hired Damien to try to find something incriminating on you?"

"Yeah, and that if they don't back off I won't let Riley come for any more visits. Riley's my daughter, and my lawyer advised me that as her parent I have the right to make decisions about what is and isn't in her best interests. They can threaten to take me to court if they want, but again, my lawyer doesn't believe they'd be able to win a case. And," he said with a grin, "hiring Damien only hurt their cause. He told me from everything he observed, I was a model dad, and it was clear Riley was happy. What's that called, poetic justice?"

"Umm hmm. I love when that happens." Cat offered him half of her roll. "And if they back down, then what?"

Liam sighed. "I guess I'll leave it up to Riley if she wants to keep going for visits, and I'll see what happens. I don't want to confuse her by suddenly cutting them from her life when, for the most part, she's had a good relationship with them, and I know in their own warped way, they love her. But I'll be asking Riley about her visits, not grilling her or anything. You know, just, how was your visit, what did you do, that kind of thing. If I get even a hint that they're up to something or made her feel bad in any way like they did that other time, I'll take the decision out of her hands."

"You're a good father, Liam. And a good man. It must be so difficult to put your feelings about them aside and allow Riley to still have a relationship with them. I hope they can come to realize that someday."

He gave a light snort. "I won't hold my breath. I'll see how things go Saturday, and then pray whatever decision I make is the right one."

Caterina reached over and took his hand. "Just trust your gut. You'll make the right decision."

Eighteen

"Anyone can make you enjoy the first bite of a dish, but only a real chef can make you enjoy the last."

Francois Minot

I thought I must be a fool for letting Antonio convince me to stay three weeks this time. It's the longest I've ever been away from *mio amato* Cortona," Vincenzo said the following morning to Caterina and her sisters. "But it feels like I just got here yesterday. Now, we are saying *addio*, and already I miss each one of you."

They had all gathered in reception to send Antonio's *nonno* off with hugs, and to hold him to his promise to return every six months, as he'd said he would. They had known him for less than a year, but he'd carved out a place in each of their hearts. He was no longer Antonio's grandfather to them. He was family.

"Marcella," he said, motioning her to him with his hand. "*Prezioso bambino*, so quiet and thoughtful. Deep waters, as they say. Always working so hard, in your fields, with your wines. You are the busy, what do they call it here, *il castoro*."

"The beaver," Antonio put in with a roll of his eyes. "You've only got ten minutes to say your goodbyes if we're going to get you to the airport in time, *Nonno*."

Vincenzo wagged a finger at him. "You cannot rush the heart, Antonio. It speaks at its own pace."

"Yes, well tell it to speak a little faster if you want to make your flight."

"Ignore him, sweet one." Vincenzo wrapped an arm around Marcella's shoulder. "I see you watch the world, through wise eyes for one so young. You are full of gifts waiting to be unwrapped, to be shared, but you are content to let others' gifts outshine your own. Take some advice from an old man who has reached an age where one reflects more on their life, and the choices they might have made. Work a little less; things will still get done. You're an observer, so go ahead and watch the world, take it all in, but don't hold yourself so much apart from it. A man is coming who will claim your heart. Your destiny, my child. Share it with him, let him see you for who you are inside."

With that, he laid his palms against her cheeks and kissed her on the forehead.

"Are you guessing this," Marcella asked, "or do you know something I don't?"

Vincenzo smiled. "I have it on good authority. Your aunt paid me a visit this morning. The same as she did on the final day of my last visit. We had a little chat this time, though. She's seen the crossroads for each of you, and she wants to make sure you all choose the right path—the one to true love."

"Oh, brother," Antonio said. "Here we go with the destiny stuff."

Vincenzo scowled at him. "Hush, boy. Rodrigo and I were right about you and Lucia, or have you forgotten how fate brought the two of you together?"

"It wasn't fate, Grandfather, it was a holiday."

Marcella cleared her throat. "Getting back to me, can you give me a clue who this mystery person is? I'm not really into surprises."

Vincenzo patted her on the back. "Just keep your eyes open, little one."

He walked over to Eliana. "Ah, Eliana, I will miss your spark. So full of life you are, it bursts from you and showers over everyone around you like a refreshing rain. You are *contagioso*. Contagious."

"Sort of like the flu?" Eliana smiled lightly, the first Caterina had seen in days.

"Oh, no, nothing so terrible. *Contagioso*, like laughter, like joy." Vincenzo wrapped her in a hug and held on a moment. "Someone has hurt you lately, yes? There's a shadow draining your light. I have not seen it in your eyes these last few days." He held her back and looked at her.

"I'm fine," she said, giving him another limp smile, but everyone there knew she was far from fine.

Vincenzo hugged her again. "You are not fine. But your wounds will heal. You will not be sad for too long. A short while, yes. Some months to come. It will be up to you how long. The key, my child, is to listen to your heart. Trust it, and it will lead you where you are meant to go."

"Did you get that from Rosa too?" El asked, sounding more like a skeptic than a believer.

Vincenzo winked at her. "Believe, child."

"Grandfather." Antonio tapped his watch. "The time."

"You can drive a little faster to get me there," Vincenzo responded. "I have one more goodbye to say, and I will not leave before I say it."

He turned toward Caterina and held out his arms. She walked into them, weaving her own around his neck and holding on. "We're going to miss you so much, Vincenzo. You should try to plan your next visit to coincide with Serendipity's grand opening.

That should be in six or seven months, and you've already promised you'll be coming back around that time. I'll make you a meal that you won't soon forget."

"I wouldn't miss it, *bella donna*. But do you not remember, I'm coming for a week in May, when Antonio and Lucia get married."

Caterina stepped back. "Oh my God, how could I forget that? Maybe you should just come and spend the summer. We'd all love to have you stay longer than a few weeks. And it would give us plenty of time to spoil you good and proper."

Vincenzo chuckled. "That is very tempting, but I don't know if I could leave my Cortona for such a long time. I will have to think about it."

"Please do," Cat said.

"Grandfather."

"Yes, yes, I'm coming." Vincenzo flipped his hand toward Antonio. "Just one more minute."

"Goodbye, Vincenzo. You really should go before those back teeth Antonio's been grinding are worn down to the gums."

"He's an impatient one. Takes that after my long-departed wife, bless her soul. Now, as for you." He took her hands in his. "You're on the road you're meant to travel. There are some surprises in store for you and your Liam, but no hurdles you can't surmount together."

"That's good to know." Cat glanced around the room. "Glad to hear it, Rosa." She brought her eyes back to hold Vincenzo's. "Glad to hear it," she said again, and kissed him on both cheeks.

He winked at her. "Take good care of him, and little Riley too."

"I will," Cat promised.

"Okay, good, can we go now?" Antonio asked.

"Yes, we can go." Vincenzo made his way over to where Lucia stood serenely waiting by the front doors and looped his arm through hers. "Such an exasperating lad. Once I'm gone, maybe you can teach him some patience. I've tried for years, but like I said, just like his *nonna*, always in a hurry."

Lucia glanced back as she and Vincenzo stepped over the threshold onto the front porch and grinned at Antonio. "Coming, darling?"

"Maybe we could stop on our way to pick up some coffee from that little bakery you took me to the other day," Vincenzo said, rather loudly, to Lucia. "They make it good and strong, just the way I like it, and they have biscotti like the ones I get back home." Caterina wondered if the old man was intentionally trying to rile his grandson.

Lucia started laughing. Antonio snorted as he hustled after them. "Sure, we can stop for coffee, *Nonno*. No skin off my back if you miss your flight. Hell, you want to swing by Carpucci's and pick up one of those Italian subs you like, too, in the event you do make it to your gate on time? You can have it for lunch. I know how much you hate airplane food."

"Don't get smart with me, Antonio."

The door closed behind them, and Caterina faced her sisters.

"I sure am going to miss him," Marcella said.

Eliana wrapped her arms around her waist, hugged herself. "We all will."

"I've got an idea," Cat threw out. "There aren't any guests in residence, so why don't the three of us go out to lunch? We can go to Twining Vines."

"Sounds good to me," Marcella said, and glanced at Eliana. "You in?"

Eliana sighed. "I don't know. I'm not that hungry. Maybe the two of you—"

Cat walked over to Eliana and took her hand. "She's in," she stated, and started walking toward the hallway, pulling El with her. She remembered how she'd tried to sequester herself after her breakup with Mitch. Her sisters had rallied around her, forced her to go on living with her chin up. They'd have to do the same with El, keep her distracted long enough that her heart had a chance to begin mending.

"Now," she said, not willing to leave her sister alone to dwell on what she'd lost, "let's all go upstairs, put on something pretty, and go have some sister time."

"Fine," Eliana said.

Marcella trailed behind them. "Do I have anything pretty?"

"Don't worry about it," Caterina said with a light laugh. "I'll pick out something of mine for you."

"Wonderful, I hate having to think about what to wear. Just make sure it covers more than a quarter of my body, will you? I don't have the same comfort level you two do, dealing with men who think my eyes are located somewhere below my neck."

CATERINA WAS IN the kitchen plating food for a family dinner party that evening. It had been Lucia's idea to have one, and although no one said as much to Eliana, it would be a time for them to regroup, to point forward.

Liam was joining them. He was one of them now, hers in heart, and theirs because he was hers. Riley was spending the night at his brother Shawn's, for a sleepover with her cousin, Spencer, which she always enjoyed.

A smile played over Cat's lips. That meant she and Liam could have a sleepover of their own. Yes, they would have the entire night, long and lovely, to themselves. It seemed weeks since they'd last made love, and she craved the intimacy that physical connection gave them. She needed to love, to be loved by him, and to experience the pleasures of body and soul that only he could give her.

Vincenzo had said that Rosa told him Liam was her destiny. Cat didn't know how her aunt could know such a thing. The woman was dead, after all.

She frowned. A year ago, she hadn't believed in ghosts. She'd since discovered otherwise. What was destiny, really, she wondered. Something that's meant to be? If one is lucky enough to find love with someone, a love that makes them so happy, so content, just to be with that person, then surely there are certain people who are right for each other—that fit better together.

Like her and Liam. She knew she'd never felt this way about anyone before. So maybe he was her destiny. And if he wasn't, she didn't care. She was keeping him, anyway.

"Hey, sis, the gang's all here. Luch and El are trying to keep Antonio and Liam from filling up on appetizers. They sent me in here to see if I could help you get dinner out to the table while they've still got room for the main course. They're threatening to tape their mouths with duct tape." Marcella walked over and leaned against the counter.

Caterina chuckled. "Everything's ready. Let's start taking these plates out before they carry through on their threat. That stuff's a bitch to get off without taking some skin with it, and I'd like Liam's lips to remain intact for the private after-party I'm planning for the two of us."

"All the information I need, thank you." Cat's twin picked up the two platters she'd just finished arranging—one of winter vegetables roasted in olive oil and rosemary; the other, Belgian endive with pecans, cranberries, and warmed goat cheese salads—and headed back out to the solarium where they'd set a cozy table for six earlier that afternoon.

Cat finished slicing the rosemary and fennel-rubbed beef tenderloin she'd had resting on the stove top. She fanned the slices in two overlapping semicircles on the round, deep cobalt-blue and white marbled serving platter that had been their mother's, one that Caterina had always loved. Next to her mother's platter, she placed the shallow crystal bowl she'd filled with a cognac and mustard sauce she'd been experimenting with the week before and added some bright-green parsley for garnish. Then, she quickly washed her hands before joining everyone else in the solarium.

Liam's gaze warmed Cat all the way to her toes as she sat down next to him. Caribbean blue flames stole her breath away, because what she saw flickering in their depths confirmed her earlier musings. They belonged together.

Antonio, who sat to Caterina's left, cleared his throat. Reluctantly, she drew her eyes from Liam's, and looked at him. He held up a bottle of Bordeaux. "May I?" he asked with an amused smile.

Cat picked up her wineglass and held it toward him. "Yes, thank you. And don't give me that look, mister. I've got a long memory. In case you've forgotten, I'd be happy to remind you of your own lovesick self a few months ago."

"I was never lovesick," he objected. "That's purely a female trait." Which made Marcella almost spit out her own wine.

Lucia jabbed him with her elbow and he looked at her. "You were saying, Antonio?"

He fought a laugh. "I was saying what a lucky man I am to have found such a wonderful woman." Caterina marveled that, for a man so full of BS, he could manage to look so utterly charming.

"Oh, brother." Marcella lifted some vegetables onto her plate and then passed the platter to Eliana.

"Okay, changing subjects," Lucia said. "I was reading one of Rosa's diaries last night. It was dated just a few weeks before she and Uncle Gino were murdered. I don't know if her suspicion was correct, but she thought she might have been pregnant."

"Why did she think that?" Caterina asked.

"She'd begun feeling tired more easily and had been experiencing some nausea. She wrote that she and Gino had been trying to have a child, and she hoped what she'd been feeling meant their prayers were finally being answered."

Cat took a sip of wine. "Did you read any further entries to see if she was right?"

"Well, we know from going through them that she didn't write in her diaries consistently. Sometimes she'd go weeks without updating them, but there were two more entries after that one. The last was from the night before she died. She said she'd told Gino her girlfriend was picking her up the next day, and the two of them were going into town to have lunch together. She'd also made an appointment to see the doctor while she was in town, but she didn't tell him that part, because she said if she wasn't pregnant she didn't want him to be disappointed."

"So, we don't know, then," Marcella commented.

Lucia shook her head. "No, just that she thought she might be."

"That's so sad," Eliana said. "If she was. That's just so sad."

"I haven't had as much experience with her as the rest of you," Liam said, "but maybe that has something to do with why she's still hanging around."

Antonio nodded. "He might be right. Even if she found out she wasn't pregnant, it sounds like she and your uncle really wanted a child. Lucia, I think I remember you telling me she was in her early thirties when they were murdered. If they'd been trying for a while, and she'd been dreaming of having a baby for a long time, maybe she couldn't completely let go of her life here...like it was still unresolved or something."

"I guess that's possible." Lucia reached for a roll. "If so, I'm not sure what she's resolved by hanging around, though."

"Well," Marcella ventured, "she's got us."

They spent a few more minutes postulating Rosa's motives, but with nothing concrete to base anything on, the conversation soon moved on to other topics, with the noticeable exclusion of anything about Damien. No one was pretending he hadn't happened in their lives; they just didn't want to upset Eliana when her emotions were still so raw.

In the scheme of things, Liam hadn't suffered any major damage because of Damien. He was being very pragmatic about the entire thing as it related to him and Riley. If anything, Liam thought Damien's findings could only help his cause if Sylvie's parents ever decided to try for custody. Hopefully, when he met with them tomorrow afternoon, he could talk some sense into them.

Eliana, on the other hand, was an innocent victim. Damien may never have intended to hurt her, but hurt her he had. She would need time, and the fewer reminders she had about Damien, the better.

"Marcella, would you choose a wine to go with dessert?" Caterina asked, when she saw that the bottle she'd just picked up was empty. "Eliana, you can help me bring them out. It's chocolate mousse, with the homemade Baileys whipped cream you've been bugging me to make."

"At your service, favorite sister of mine," Eliana said, licking her lips, a glimpse of the El that Cat knew and loved poking through. "And to show my gratitude, I'll even help clean everything up later."

"Not necessary, Liam and Antonio are on cleanup duty."

"What?" the two men exclaimed in stereo.

Cat gave them both an arched brow.

"Um, okay, sure." Liam shrugged. "We can handle that, right, Antonio?"

Later that night, after they'd polished off dessert, two more bottles of wine, and everything had been cleared away and the kitchen restored to rights, Caterina and Liam sat in the library in front of a dwindling fire. The only other light in the room came from the candles flickering on the mantle and on the coffee table, casting a soft glow over everything.

Caterina rested her head on Liam's shoulder. "Thanks for helping clean up tonight."

"No problem. You worked your butt off all afternoon to make that amazing dinner."

"Yes, but I enjoy cooking, and I especially enjoy cooking for people I care about."

"Like me?" He tucked his chin, so he could look at her, and grinned.

God, he got her every time with that sexy, lopsided smile of his. She didn't want to sit down here in the library any longer. She wanted to wrap her arms around his warm, hunky body and make crazy, wonderful, sexy love to him.

"Liam, are you ready to go up to bed?"

"Are you?"

Cat licked her lips and nodded.

His grin widened, and a spark lit his eyes. "Thank God. I didn't know how much longer I was going to last down here before I hauled you up there and stripped you out of those clothes."

"Why didn't you just say something?"

"Like I said, you worked all afternoon. I thought you might want to sit and relax a while. I was trying to put my own selfish desires aside and be a gentleman."

"I appreciate that, but you can stop trying to be a gentleman now. I'd much rather you give your selfish desires free rein, so you can satisfy mine."

AS PARTICULAR AS she was about plans and schedules, everything having a time and a place, and Lord help whoever switched them up on her—Caterina made love to him with a passion and freedom that stole his breath. And he'd be perfectly content to lie under her luscious curves until he passed out from lack of air, as long as he knew her heart belonged to him.

And it did. Good thing, too, because it meant his plan stood a much higher chance of success.

"I've been thinking," Liam said, his hands enjoying the journey they were taking over the smooth mound of her hips, gliding down the silken skin to the valley that was her waist.

"You do that a lot."

"Yeah, well, we're lying here, and since I need some time to recover before I can satisfy those raging desires of yours again, it helps pass the time."

She smiled, and he felt it against his skin. "And what deep thoughts are helping you bridge that gap?"

Liam rolled her off his chest and turned onto his side, toward her. She had the face of a goddess, the body of one too. But it was the prickly control freak whom he'd watched strut around her kitchen island with his daughter; it was the woman who'd looked at him all those months ago, through vulnerable eyes, and asked what she'd ever done to make him dislike her so much—that he'd fallen in love with.

"Thoughts of you. Of us." He searched her eyes. Their warm brown depths reflected what he felt for her. "I want more than a night here and there with you, when I can find a sitter for Riley, or she has a sleepover at her cousin's. Riley's crazy about you. And Riley's dad's kind of crazy about you, too. And I was hoping you might be crazy enough about the two of us, that maybe the three of us could all be crazy about one another together."

Caterina stared at him. "What exactly are you suggesting, Liam?"

He wove his fingers through her hair. "I want us to be a family. You, me, Riley—it feels right. At least to me, and I hope to you, too. I don't just want today and tomorrow, maybe next year with you...I want the rest of your life."

"You sure about that? You do know that in my family that doesn't necessarily end when we die." She bit her lip. "Sorry, bad joke. You just caught me off guard. I mean, if I'd known we were going to have this conversation tonight, I would have planned it differently. You know, with candles, and a really good bottle of wine, and I'd have bought some special lingerie, and I'd have—"

"Caterina."

"What?"

"Do you love me?"

"Of course, I do. This has nothing to do with that."

"It has everything to do with that."

"Well, okay, maybe, but—"

"Cat."

"Yes?"

"Just say you'll marry me, and I'll let you have complete control working out the details for our wedding."

The corners of her lips curled impishly. "Promise?"

"I promise. Now, will you marry me?"

"Yes, since it was part of my plan to get you to ask me, Liam, I'll marry you."

He curled his fingers around the back of her head and kissed her. She would drive him crazy with all her lists and schedules, he had no doubt, but it didn't matter. He loved his daughter so much, and she brought him such joy. But he hadn't realized how much was missing from his life until Caterina sauntered into it in those ridiculous, spiky, Lord-how-he-loved-them, sexy heels of hers.

"I can feel you smiling against my lips, Liam. What are you smiling about?"

"I was just thinking about how far we've come from when we first met, and how you stormed into my life and stole my heart before I ever realized what was happening."

He felt her smile as well.

"I love you, Liam."

"I love you too."

The night moon rose silently over the Blue Ridge, glinting off the craggy crests like flecks of gold set in the ancient stone, and as it did, Destiny smiled—two more of her charges had found their way—but her work was never done. She turned her gaze toward two others, two who had been on their intended path but had gotten derailed.

It's time to get you back on track, Eliana, my dear.

The End

Enjoy the recipes from

Caterina

Spaghetti Puttanesca
Lyonnaise Potatoes
Marshmallow Whip

Spaghetti Puttanesca

In honor of Caterina's heritage and the country of my birth, this intensely flavored pasta will serve 4 to 6, depending on serving size. It's the perfect dish to enjoy with family and friends who appreciate the spicier side of things. Serve with a fresh tossed salad and warm, crusty bread with butter or herb-infused olive oil for dipping.

Ingredients

1/3 cup of extra virgin olive oil

2 Vidalia onions, diced

4 finely chopped garlic cloves

1/4 to 1/2 teaspoon of red pepper flakes (dependent on taste) *

6 Roma tomatoes, seeded and diced, or 3 cups of cherry tomatoes, halved

3 to 4 Tablespoons capers

6 oil packed anchovies, drained and chopped

1/3 cup of Kalamata olives, sliced

1/4 cup of fresh, flat-leaf parsley, chopped

12 oz. of good quality spaghetti

*Use fewer flakes if you want to reduce the heat, more if you prefer more heat. You can eliminate the red pepper flakes if you don't want any heat, but with only 1/4 tsp. it is not overly spicy.

The Process

Over medium heat, heat the olive oil in a large saucepan. Add the onions and cook for 4 to 5 minutes, until they become transparent. Stir in garlic and pepper flakes and cook for no more than 30 seconds to prevent garlic from becoming bitter.

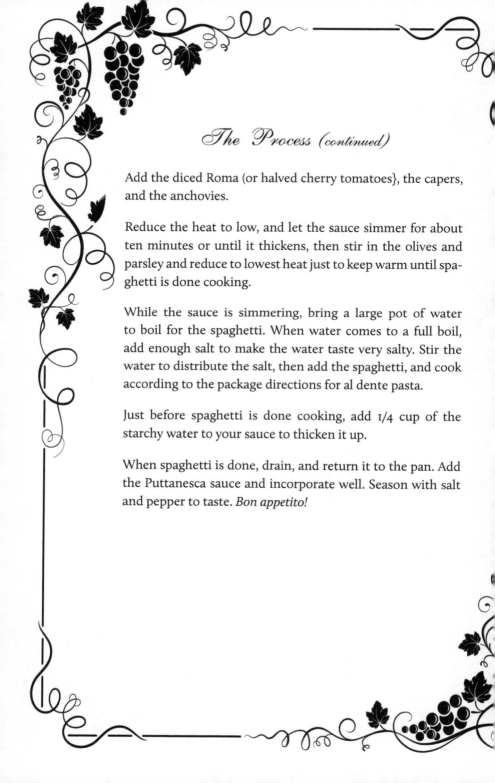

The Process (*continued*)

Add the diced Roma (or halved cherry tomatoes}, the capers, and the anchovies.

Reduce the heat to low, and let the sauce simmer for about ten minutes or until it thickens, then stir in the olives and parsley and reduce to lowest heat just to keep warm until spaghetti is done cooking.

While the sauce is simmering, bring a large pot of water to boil for the spaghetti. When water comes to a full boil, add enough salt to make the water taste very salty. Stir the water to distribute the salt, then add the spaghetti, and cook according to the package directions for al dente pasta.

Just before spaghetti is done cooking, add 1/4 cup of the starchy water to your sauce to thicken it up.

When spaghetti is done, drain, and return it to the pan. Add the Puttanesca sauce and incorporate well. Season with salt and pepper to taste. *Bon appetito!*

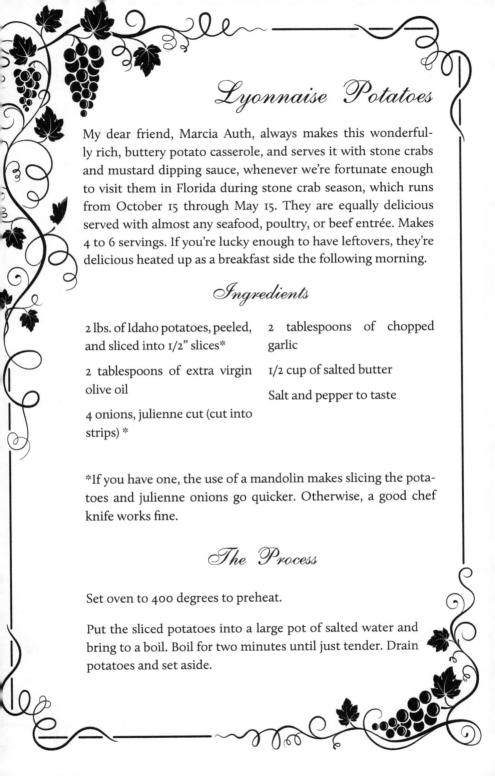

Lyonnaise Potatoes

My dear friend, Marcia Auth, always makes this wonderfully rich, buttery potato casserole, and serves it with stone crabs and mustard dipping sauce, whenever we're fortunate enough to visit them in Florida during stone crab season, which runs from October 15 through May 15. They are equally delicious served with almost any seafood, poultry, or beef entrée. Makes 4 to 6 servings. If you're lucky enough to have leftovers, they're delicious heated up as a breakfast side the following morning.

Ingredients

2 lbs. of Idaho potatoes, peeled, and sliced into 1/2" slices*

2 tablespoons of extra virgin olive oil

4 onions, julienne cut (cut into strips) *

2 tablespoons of chopped garlic

1/2 cup of salted butter

Salt and pepper to taste

*If you have one, the use of a mandolin makes slicing the potatoes and julienne onions go quicker. Otherwise, a good chef knife works fine.

The Process

Set oven to 400 degrees to preheat.

Put the sliced potatoes into a large pot of salted water and bring to a boil. Boil for two minutes until just tender. Drain potatoes and set aside.

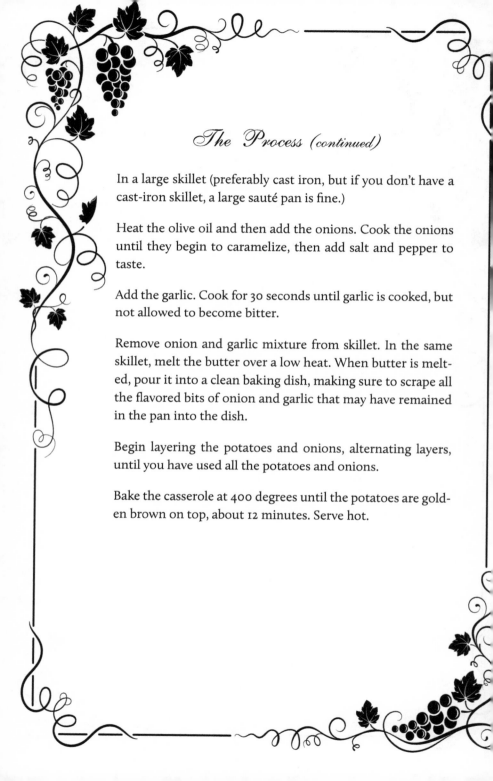

The Process *(continued)*

In a large skillet (preferably cast iron, but if you don't have a cast-iron skillet, a large sauté pan is fine.)

Heat the olive oil and then add the onions. Cook the onions until they begin to caramelize, then add salt and pepper to taste.

Add the garlic. Cook for 30 seconds until garlic is cooked, but not allowed to become bitter.

Remove onion and garlic mixture from skillet. In the same skillet, melt the butter over a low heat. When butter is melted, pour it into a clean baking dish, making sure to scrape all the flavored bits of onion and garlic that may have remained in the pan into the dish.

Begin layering the potatoes and onions, alternating layers, until you have used all the potatoes and onions.

Bake the casserole at 400 degrees until the potatoes are golden brown on top, about 12 minutes. Serve hot.

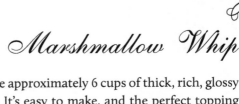

Marshmallow Whip

This recipe will make approximately 6 cups of thick, rich, glossy marshmallow whip. It's easy to make, and the perfect topping for a steaming cup of cocoa on a cold day. Recipe requires the use of a candy thermometer.

Ingredients*

3 egg whites that have been brought to room temperature

1/2 teaspoon of cream of tartar

1/3 cup of water

3/4 cup of sugar

3/4 cup of corn syrup

*Do not make any substitutions to this point!

1 teaspoon pure, high quality vanilla extract

The Process

Add egg whites and cream of tartar in the bowl of a stand mixer. Set aside.

Combine water, sugar, and corn syrup in a heavy-bottomed saucepan.

Over a very low heat, stir just until the sugar has dissolved.

Once sugar is dissolved, place a candy thermometer into saucepan, and increase heat to medium. Allow the mixture to come to a simmer on its own, without stirring so as to avoid crystals forming, until the candy thermometer reaches a temperature of 240 degrees Fahrenheit, or 120 Celsius.

The Process (continued)

When it reaches this temperature, remove the syrup from the heat at once.

On medium speed of your stand mixer, whip the egg whites and cream of tartar until soft peaks form. About 3 to 4 minutes.

Turn the mixer to low, and very slowly, add the hot syrup.

After all syrup is poured into egg whites, turn mixer to medium-high, and whip for 7 to 8 minutes until the mixture becomes thick.

Add the vanilla extract*, and whip to incorporate.

Allow mixture to cool completely.

Enjoy some now with cocoa, and store remaining whip in an air-tight container, at room temperature, for up to 5 weeks.

*For something different, add almond, coconut, or other extract, for a twist on your whip.

About the Author

Patricia Paris lives in the Chesapeake Bay area of Maryland, which provides much of the inspiration for her writing. When not writing, she spends her free time exploring the bay, battling the weeds that insist on invading her gardens, or experimenting with a new recipe in her kitchen. She is an unapologetic romantic, and loves to give her readers that happily ever after, every time.

CPSIA information can be obtained
at www.ICGtesting.com
Printed in the USA
FFHW021313181218
49912513-54525FF